continued . . .

D0052411

Who Left That Body in the Rain?

"Forming a triumvirate with Anne George and Margaret Maron, Sprinkle adds her powerful voice to the literature of mysteries featuring Southern women. . . . Highly recommended."
> —*Mystery Time*

"*Who Left That Body in the Rain?* charms, mystifies, and delights. As Southern as Sunday fried chicken and sweet tea. Patricia Sprinkle's Hopemore is as captivating—and as filled with big hearts and big heartaches—as Jan Karon's Mitford. Come for one visit and you'll always return."
> —Carolyn Hart, author of the Henrie O and Death on Demand mysteries

"Authentic and convincing."
> —Tamar Myers, author of *Grape Expectations*

"An heirloom quilt. Each piece of patchwork is unique and with its own history, yet they are deftly stitched together with threads of family love and loyalty, simmering passion, deception and wickedness, but always with optimism imbued with down-home Southern traditions. A novel to be savored while sitting on a creaky swing on the front porch, a pitcher of lemonade nearby, a dog slumbering in the sunlight."
> —Joan Hess, author of *The Goodbye Body*

Thoroughly Southern Mysteries

WHO INVITED THE DEAD MAN?
WHO LEFT THAT BODY IN THE RAIN?
WHO LET THAT KILLER IN THE HOUSE?
WHEN WILL THE DEAD LADY SING?
WHO KILLED THE QUEEN OF CLUBS?

DID YOU DECLARE THE CORPSE?

‹ A THOROUGHLY SOUTHERN MYSTERY ›

Patricia Sprinkle

A SIGNET BOOK

SIGNET
Published by New American Library, a division of
Penguin Group (USA) Inc., 375 Hudson Street,
New York, New York 10014, USA
Penguin Group (Canada), 90 Eglinton Avenue East, Suite 700, Toronto,
Ontario M4P 2Y3, Canada (a division of Pearson Penguin Canada Inc.)
Penguin Books Ltd., 80 Strand, London WC2R 0RL, England
Penguin Ireland, 25 St. Stephen's Green, Dublin 2,
Ireland (a division of Penguin Books Ltd.)
Penguin Group (Australia), 250 Camberwell Road, Camberwell, Victoria 3124,
Australia (a division of Pearson Australia Group Pty. Ltd.)
Penguin Books India Pvt. Ltd., 11 Community Centre, Panchsheel Park,
New Delhi - 110 017, India
Penguin Group (NZ), cnr Airborne and Rosedale Roads, Albany,
Auckland 1310, New Zealand (a division of Pearson New Zealand Ltd.)
Penguin Books (South Africa) (Pty.) Ltd., 24 Sturdee Avenue,
Rosebank, Johannesburg 2196, South Africa

Penguin Books Ltd., Registered Offices:
80 Strand, London WC2R 0RL, England

First published by Signet, an imprint of New American Library,
a division of Penguin Group (USA) Inc.

First Printing, February 2006
10 9 8 7 6 5 4 3 2 1

For Babs and Dave Rose,
for I was a stranger
and you took me in.

ACKNOWLEDGMENTS

I spent the fall, winter and early spring of 1966–67 in the village of Braemar, Scotland, to see if I had the discipline and any talent to write. The village took me into its heart and so entered my own heart that I have returned several times. The idea for this book has grown with each visit, and was finalized during a visit in the spring of 2003.

The village of Auchnagar in this book is not Braemar, and all persons in the book are fictitious. Only the cheerful goodwill and tolerant kindness toward strangers are the same.

History recounted in the book comes primarily from the 1978 edition of a series of histories written by Scottish historian John Prebble: *The Highland Clearances, Glencoe*, and *Culloden* (published by Penguin Books). The poem which Mac shouts into the mist at Glen Coe is a personal translation of the first stanza of Hermann Hesse's "Im Nebel."

I want to particularly thank the Kilgour/Ewan families, who treat me like a cousin and who all pitched in enthusiastically to help create this book. Thanks to Martin for consultation on certain legal aspects of this case; to Davie, John and Lisa for a fantastic ceilidh at Eddie's eightieth birthday party; to Liz for putting up with me on a tour of the western Highlands that formed the basis for Mac's tour here; to Julie and Eddie for chuckles, information, and countless cups of tea; to Davie for patiently answering frantic e-mails on such varied subjects as the price of wooden coffins and whether a touring piper would be permitted to play spontaneously at various sites, and to Julie, Eddie, Davie, Eileen, Lisa and even little Calum for sitting down and coming up with a name for Auchnagar. Finally, thanks to their patriarch, the former Dave Rose, a wise and humorous Scot who first gave me copies of John Prebble's histories of Scotland. Where I have failed to capture Scotland well, it is certainly not their fault! Davie, an accomplished piper, appears briefly as himself in the book.

Thanks also to the Morgan family—Cathie, John, and Mary—who graciously house me on each visit and treat me like family, and who agreed I could base Heather Glen on their Mayfield Guest House.

American piper Dave Love helped keep me straight on what an American piper would be likely to wear abroad, and Sulena Long shared her expertise after taking several American-based bus tours in the United Kingdom. I appreciate you both.

Dorothy Cowling and Marcia, real librarians in Calgary, asked to have their names in this book, but the characters do not resemble either of them in the least—eh?

Finally, I owe an enormous debt to my editor, Ellen Edwards, who helped me make this a far better story; to my agent, Nancy Yost, for wisdom on the bad days and chuckles on the good ones; and to Bob, my husband, encourager, and friend.

CAST OF CHARACTERS

MacLaren Yarbrough: Georgia magistrate and co-owner of Yarbrough Feed, Seed and Nursery

Joe Riddley Yarbrough: MacLaren's husband, co-owner of Yarbrough Feed, Seed and Nursery

Travelers on Gilroy's Highland Tour

Joyce Underwood: tour guide

Watty: bus driver

Laura MacDonald: MacLaren's young traveling companion, also from Hopemore

Jim and Brandi Gordon: business tycoon and his wife from the North Georgia mountains

Ken and Sherry Boyd: Savannah restaurant owners, musicians, and Scottish enthusiasts

Marcia Inch and Dorothy Cowling: Calgary librarians with Scottish heritage

Residents of Auchnagar, Scotland

Gavin and Kitty MacGorrie: Laird of Auchnagar and his American wife

Norwood Hardin: Kitty's brother and perpetual guest

Eileen Lamont: proprietress of Heather Glen guest house

Roddy Lamont: Eileen's grown son

Alex Carmichael: owner of village art gallery

Father Ewan: village priest

Ian Geddys: village joiner

Barbara Geddys: postmistress, Ian's sister

Morag MacBeth: child who cares for Barbara's animals

Sergeant Murray and Constable Roy: Auchnagar police

1

Roddy Lamont charged into the dining room of the Heather Glen guesthouse, interrupting our midday dinner. "Father? Father! Fit's to be done wi' the coffins in the narthex, then?" His petulant face was flushed and beads of perspiration dotted his forehead beneath a mop of ruddy curls. He must have run all the way up the hill.

We'd been in the village of Auchnagar for less than twenty-four hours, but I remembered enough of my morning lesson in broad Scots to know that "fit" meant "what."

Father Ewan, who ate his Friday midday dinner at Heather Glen on his housekeeper's day off, was a tall stocky man who enjoyed his food. He rose from the table with obvious reluctance. "Coffins? Whose are they?"

Roddy's shoulders rose in an eloquent shrug. "I just went in to mop the narthex, and the bl"—a quick look at his mother and he finished smoothly—"oomin' place is full of coffins. I was workin' in the back, y' ken, so I never saw them comin' in, but you shoulda told me if we're havin' a funeral—much less two." He pulled a blue handkerchief from his back pocket and wiped his face. His mother twisted her hands under her apron and glowed with pride at how seriously Roddy was finally taking a job, until he added in indignation, "I'm off to the bike rally at three, and this has put me behind."

Father Ewan looked with regret at his gooseberries topped with vanilla custard. He'd already said how fond he was of that dessert. But he laid down his napkin and gave those of us around the table a slight bow. "Excuse me, but

I'd better go see what this is about. I've had no notice of anyone dying hereabouts." He gave me a courteous nod. "If you're still interested, I can take you on that wee look 'round the chapel as soon as I sort this out, Mrs. MacLaren. Come along when you're done with your meal."

"It's Yarbrough," I corrected him. "MacLaren Yarbrough."

"And it's Judge Yarbrough," Laura MacDonald added—unnecessarily, I thought. Since the fact that I'm a magistrate back in Georgia mattered not one whit on a bus tour through the Scottish Highlands, I hadn't mentioned it before. It makes some folks so nervous to discover I'm a judge that I sometimes wonder what undisclosed crimes lurk in their pasts.

"We're going for a hill walk after dinner," Laura reminded me.

Since "a hill walk" in Scotland entails a strenuous climb up narrow mountain trails, I said firmly, "I'll skip the walk and visit the church."

"Well, come along when you're done, then." The priest was already heading for the door. "This shouldna take long—there's obviously been some kind of mistake. It'll soon be sorted."

I put down my napkin. "Why don't I come with you now? I can be looking at the grounds while you're occupied." That was a perfect excuse for me to skip the gooseberries, which lay in my bowl like pale green eyeballs. I'd been wondering how to get out of eating them.

I trotted after the two men as they strode out the back door and down the hill. Roddy was still full of grievance. "I saved cleanin' the narthex 'til the last, y' ken, so I could mop the flair and front steps, then leave them to dry while I came up for my dinner. I must have been Hooverin' at the back when Ian brought them in, but you'd think he'd have the sense to give me a shout. He shouldna just dump people like that and go away."

Seeing that I was panting from trying to keep up with Roddy's long legs, Father Ewan waved for him to stop opposite the schoolhouse halfway down the hill—or "brae"—and reached into the pocket of his black suit for a cell phone.

"Stop a wee whiley and let me give Ian a ring. Ian Geddys is our local joiner," he added to me as he punched in a number.

As he sidled away to talk, I asked Roddy, "What's a joiner?"

Roddy—who never stood if he could lean—propped himself against a house that abutted the sidewalk across from the school and gave me the look that folks from central Georgia, back in the States, would give somebody who asked, "What's a bird dog?"

"Y' dinna have joiners in America?" Clearly, he wondered how we managed to survive.

I shook my head.

He reached down the neck of his gray pullover and brought up a crumpled pack of cigarettes from his shirt pocket. The way the sweater sagged, that must be a frequent habit. He held the pack out to me, and when I refused, he took time to light up and exhale slowly. The way his brow was furrowed, he was trying to figure out how best to explain something obvious to an ignoramus. "He's a sort of builder, y' ken? He makes cupboards, lays carpet, puts up wallpaper—he joins things." He flapped one hand to conclude the explanation.

Father Ewan snapped his phone shut, stowed it in a pocket, and came back to us with a broad smile. "False alarm, lad. The coffins are stage props. Ian is out, but Barbara was home for her dinner, and she said the coffins are for that play the Americans are putting on tomorrow night." He nodded my way.

Guilt by association made me say quickly, "I don't know anything about coffins, and we aren't putting on the play. It's just being put on while we're here. Our tour guide wrote it."

"That must be the way of it, then." Roddy nodded with enlightenment. "The lass said to take them to the chapel, and that dunce Ian didn't ask what she meant by that." He squinted down at me through another cloud of smoke. "Folk not from here look at the sign that says St. Catherine's Chapel and think it's called 'the chapel'—never knowin' our lot's got the chapel and St. Catherine's is just St. Catherine's—not the chapel a-tall. Used to be Church of England, but nowadays it's just a meeting hall."

"I'm Presbyterian." I felt a continuing need to distance myself as far as possible from those "folk not from here" he was ridiculing.

"Och, then ye'll be wantin' the kirk, down by the manse woods." He pointed to a steeple off to our right, obviously glad to get all that cleared up for my benefit. Then he added to the priest, "Shall I shift them to one side, just, until Ian can fetch them? I've still got that flair to mop."

Roddy might not be good at working, but he was a master at complaint.

The priest hesitated, looking back up the brae toward Heather Glen. I suspected he was debating the possibility of returning for his gooseberries. Instead, he turned on his heel and said in the tone of one successfully resisting temptation, "That's the way, lad. I'll just give you a hand."

At the bottom of the hill, we turned left onto the walk that led to the small Roman Catholic church. I don't know when I've seen a prettier approach to a place of worship. The chapel itself was built of granite, like everything else in the village, but someone had rounded the outer edges of the stones just enough to replace severity with gentleness. A simple tower rose in the center and ended in a stone cross. A small rose window was set above arched front doors. Tall dark yews stood in an arc on the soft emerald lawn, arms reaching out to draw us down the walk, while welcoming masses of daffodils nodded on each side of the steps.

"Quite bonnie, aren't they?" Roddy nodded toward the daffodils as he reached for the giant ring that opened the dark wooden door. "Mum planted them a few years back, in memory of m' dad."

Father Ewan motioned for me to precede him up the stone steps. "Come along in. It won't take us but a minute to stack the boxes for Ian so Roddy can get on with his work."

When I followed them in, I shivered in the accumulated chill of three hundred winters. The small foyer (narthex, in church language) was unheated and the floor was stone—what I could see of it. One third was covered by a long table holding pamphlets and various offering boxes. The remaining space was almost filled by two wooden boxes, one long and one short, and there was no mistaking that shape.

The narthex was dim, lit only by sunlight that filtered into the sanctuary through dark stained-glass windows and found its way through the open double doors. I inhaled that scent of holiness that fills empty places of worship and tiptoed around the boxes toward the sanctuary while Roddy and the priest shoved one box over close to the table. Behind me, I heard them cross the narthex for the other, then heard Roddy exclaim, "Hold on! There's something in this one!"

"There can't be," Father Ewan protested. "Barbara said . . ."

Hinges creaked. Then Roddy exclaimed, "Who the devil is that?"

"I dinna ken," the priest replied soberly, "but whoever it is is very dead."

Father Ewan raised his voice and called to me—as if he hoped I hadn't heard what they'd been saying. "You'd best go on back up to Heather Glen. I'll show you around another time."

He obviously wanted to spare me the sight of whoever was in that coffin, but I had to pass it to get to the front door and Roddy was too slow in lowering the lid.

I saw enough.

What was it my husband had said just before I left home? Wanting him to come along, I'd reminded him, "You promised to go everywhere with me."

He'd replied, "I didn't *promise* I'd go everywhere with you, Little Bit. That was a threat, and it only applies around here. I figure you can't get into too much trouble in a country where you don't know a soul. Presumably you won't feel obligated to endanger your life trying to solve the problems of everybody in Scotland, and you aren't likely to be stumbling over dead bodies on a bus tour."

And now here I stood, in a chilly church in the heart of the eastern Highlands, with a member of our tour group lying dead at my feet.

$\approx 2 \approx$

Ten days before, I'd stared down at two suitcases lying on our guest-room bed ready for vacation. The trouble was, they weren't heading on the same vacation.

"You promised to go everywhere with me," I reminded my husband as he came in with a stack of clothes.

He didn't say a word.

Seeing that he only carried one pair of jeans and two polo shirts, I added, "You're gonna need more clothes than that for five days, and those shirts are blue. You packed green socks."

Joe Riddley shoved his clothes into the smaller bag with no concern whatsoever about wrinkles. "Fashion consultants will be left on shore. Where are my old sneakers?"

"Moldering in the back of your closet. But don't pretend you didn't hear what I said at first. And don't think I'll forget what I'm talking about if you don't answer me."

"Hope springs eternal." He headed back to our room.

I listened to make sure he was still rummaging in his closet, then fetched a small first-aid kit from a drawer and tucked it into his bag where he'd find it the first time he changed his shirt. I also sent up a quick prayer that they'd need nothing stronger than Band-Aids and antiseptic cream before the week was out.

In a minute he returned with another pair of jeans and two yellow shirts, scruffy sneakers tucked under one arm. Not for an instant did he hint that the extra jeans and shirts were my idea—just dumped them into his suitcase like he'd planned to add them all along.

"I didn't *promise* to go everywhere with you." Finally he gave the answer I would remember so clearly. "That was a threat, and it only applies around here. I figure you can't get into much trouble in a country where you don't know a soul. Presumably you won't feel obligated to endanger your life trying to solve the problems of everybody in Scotland, and you aren't likely to be stumbling over dead bodies on a bus tour. Besides, Laura's levelheaded, and she's promised to keep an eye on you."

If he had forgotten the night Laura MacDonald and I confronted two drug dealers with no weapons but my pocketbook and her knee,* I wasn't about to remind him.

"Don't forget," he added virtuously as he plopped filthy sneakers on top of clean clothes, "taking a vacation was your idea."

"*A* vacation." I headed to the dresser and started doublechecking to be sure everything was in my cosmetics bag. "Not two."

For months I'd been wanting to see more of the world than Hopemore, Georgia. I was tired of juggling work at Yarbrough Feed, Seed and Nursery with my responsibilities as a county magistrate, not to mention all the things Joe Riddley and I did at church and in the community. But I had envisioned a warm tropical island with us in new bathing suits, sipping exotic drinks beneath a thatched hut while wiggling our toes in a floor of sand. I'd planned to snorkel all morning and laze under a beach umbrella all afternoon with a stack of good books.

Instead, I was heading to Scotland, where the agency who'd arranged the tour claimed I'd need several layers to stay warm at the end of April. Instead of paddling in tepid water, I'd be following a tour guide up and down Scottish "hills"—which anybody with eyes in their head could see were mountains. And I'd be doing all that not with Joe Riddley, but with Laura MacDonald. Joe Riddley might be ornery as all get-out at times, but we'd been vacationing together for well over forty years and I saw no reason to change that.

Who Left That Body in the Rain?

Besides, while Laura's parents had been two of our dearest friends and I've known and loved Laura all her life, she was barely twenty-seven. I suspected we might have different definitions of the word "fun" on a vacation.

I shoved another pair of socks into my bag. "I never dreamed you wouldn't go with me. I've never been abroad without you, and that boat thing—"

"Don't you think we've covered that ground pretty thoroughly in the past few months?" His voice was gruff, and he turned his back to me. In the dresser mirror, I watched him slide something that looked like a jeweler's box from one pocket and slip it into my bag. He turned back to his case with a frown. "Have I forgotten something?"

"Underwear. If God hadn't created Eve, do you reckon Adam would have invented underwear?"

"If God hadn't created Eve, Adam wouldn't have needed underwear. He'd have obeyed God and run around happily naked." He left before I could come up with a good reply.

I picked up my well-thumbed travel brochure from the dresser and thought how smart the travel folks were to send everything via e-mail for us to download and print ourselves. Must save them enormous amounts of money. But as I crammed it into my pocketbook with all the other necessities for a transAtlantic flight, I glared at the perky "Explore Your Roots!" on the cover. All the roots I wanted right that minute were in Hopemore.

Don't get me wrong. I appreciated the fact that Joe Ridley had wanted to surprise me by giving me a two-week bus tour of Scotland that included four days in the village where Mama's family, the MacLarens, came from. I also knew he had an ulterior motive in sending me. Laura had told him about the trip, and she'd lost both her parents the previous year. She'd been working real hard since then, for she had inherited, along with her younger brother, three motor companies he had no inclination to help her run. Laura loved the companies and ran them smoothly and profitably, but she could use a break. When he'd told me about the trip, Joe Riddley had reminded me, "Remember how Skye and Gwen Ellen used to take the kids to Scotland every year or two? This will be Laura's first trip back alone. I think she'll like to have a friendly face along."

Before you get all soft and mushy about what a selfless fellow Joe Riddley is, though, you need to know that while I was on the far side of the Atlantic, he and our younger son, Walker, would be taking my two precious grandsons deep-sea fishing in the Gulf of Mexico.

"Cricket's sure to fall in," I warned for the fiftieth time as Joe Riddley came back with his rattiest boxer shorts. Every time I thought about that four-year-old loose on a boat in the middle of the Gulf, I felt desperate. I knew I ought to cancel my trip and go with them, even if I am prone to get seasick on a rowboat in a calm lake.

Joe Riddley didn't say a word, just started tucking underwear around his jeans, shirts, and socks with the same concentration Noah devoted to building the ark.

"You all are going to have to watch Crick every minute," I insisted. "You know how easily he burns. And how he climbs and wanders." Clear as day, I saw that small, brown-haired boy climbing a mast and pitching headfirst into the sea. My knees buckled. I'd have fallen headfirst myself if I hadn't collapsed onto the bed beside my case. "Ridd should be going, too." Ridd, Cricket's daddy, would keep a close eye on him. Too close for Cricket's liking.

"You know Ridd can't leave in the middle of a semester." Joe Riddley didn't miss a beat in the underwear-distribution business. "And unlike some people, he and Martha think a mere grandfather and uncle can take adequate care of their little fellow. Besides, Crick's almost five, swims like a fish, will wear a life jacket all the time, and has Tad to watch him." He zipped his case like a man who's had the last word.

I clutched the bedspread with both hands to keep from strangling him. "How can somebody who forgets long-sleeved shirts, his own toothbrush, and a razor remember to watch a child? Furthermore, let me point out that Tad's only eleven, with the attention span of a gnat. Less, if he takes along one of those video games he's always playing. Crick will drown before Tad notices he's gone. Besides, Tad's not a strong swimmer. He couldn't save anybody. And you men will be on the other side of the boat reeling in fish, paying no attention to those boys whatsoever. I'm not going to Scotland. I'm coming with you."

"It's a men-only trip."

When I didn't reply, he came over and took my chin in his hand. "It's gonna be fine, Little Bit. You still trust God to run the universe, don't you?" He worked my head up and down by the chin. "Well, why don't you trust God to take care of your grandsons, for a change?" He dropped my chin and turned away. "Dang it, much as I hate to admit it, you're right about one thing, though. I might need a long-sleeved shirt." He stalked out, calling as he went, "We're gonna take good care of those boys. You just ride through the hills of Scotland picturing Walker, their granddaddy, and their heavenly parent all keeping eagle eyes on them."

"And one of those might not get distracted by a fish." Still, I did feel a little better. Faith is a bit like a marriage license. Most of the time you take it for granted, but on wobbly days, it's good to call it to mind and lean back on the promises it stands for.

Joe Riddley came back with a red plaid T-shirt and added it to his case.

"You're gonna look like a rainbow," I warned.

"Fish will be jumping into the boat to take a gander at me. Probably a couple of mermaids, too." He stood erect and gave me a frown. "You got that international cell phone Walker lent you, so you can call every day and make sure things are okay here while I'm at sea?"

I pulled it out of my pocketbook and showed him. "I just have to figure out where to get a SIM card once we get to Glasgow." It still amazed me that something so small could bounce a message from Scotland to a satellite orbiting the earth, then send it accurately to Hopemore, Georgia. Walker assured me it would. He had even explained about buying a SIM card in Scotland so calls would be cheaper.

"Good. You finished packing? Laura's gonna to be here in less than an hour."

"I'm finished." I zipped my case while still sitting on the bed, for my knees were still too shaky to bear much weight. Pulling that zipper felt like closing the lid on two little boys' lives. Even God might get distracted by a really big fish.

I knew better than to mention the boys again, though, and I still had one more legitimate complaint. "You could at least drive me to Atlanta. You all don't leave 'til tomorrow."

"Laura's got a perfectly good Thunderbird and friends who'll let her park in their drive while you're gone. Besides, I've got a meeting at church tonight, and saying goodbye wouldn't be any easier in Atlanta than here." He reached out his long arms, pulled me up against him, and leaned down to rub his chin against the top of my head. "You know what your trouble is? You're already missing me, and you aren't even gone yet."

I leaned against him, smelling his dear, familiar warmth and feeling the strong, slow beat of his heart beneath my cheek. "I don't like going without you." I felt ready to bawl.

He spoke into my hair. "I'm beginning to regret it myself. Come on. We've got time for me to give you a little something to remember me by. And keep in mind, this is as close to danger as I want you to get in the next two weeks."

Laura arrived before I got my shoes on, my lipstick fixed, or my hair combed again. "Ready to go?" she asked from the stoop, too eager to leave to bother coming in.

Laura had inherited her daddy's big frame, deep voice, strong features, wide smile, prominent blue eyes, and sunny disposition. Her mother had wanted a cheerleader and beauty queen. She had gotten a plain, sweet child who captained champion soccer teams and grew up to get her MBA and take over the family businesses. Only recently had Laura forsaken mannish navy or gray slacks and blazers for bright colors, cut her thick, blond mane into a short, becoming style, and started wearing a little makeup. Today she looked almost pretty in tan jeans, a peach turtleneck, and a fringed jacket of chocolate-brown suede.

The way she eyed my disheveled hair and sock feet sent me dashing back to our room.

"I'm so embarrassed," I whispered to Joe Riddley, who was still tucking his shirt back in his pants. "Heaven knows what she's thinking."

"She thinks you're running late and pink with excitement. At that age, did you imagine that folks over sixty . . . ?"

"Hush!" I hissed. "She'll hear you!" I tugged my sweater down and put on my walking shoes. "I hope I don't die of heat prostration before we get there." The thermometer had been climbing all afternoon and was hovering around eighty. Even though we'd been warned that April in Scotland could be cold, there was no way it could be cold enough for a trench-coat liner. I zipped mine out and flung it on the bed as I hurried after Joe Riddley.

Laura covered the ground behind him with the bounce she used to have in her step heading into an important soccer game. I found my own spirits dancing a little jig. I hadn't been to Scotland in twenty years, and since then I'd researched where my own family had come from. When I finally stood in the village of Auchnagar, would I feel any sense of coming home?

As Laura popped the trunk, Joe Riddley told her, "Remember, now, I'm counting on you to keep Mac relatively sober and prevent her from haring off after kilted Highlanders. If you happen to find a fellow *you* like, though, bring him on back."

"Ben might object," I pointed out. Ben Bradshaw owned and managed the service department of MacDonald Motors, and had been squiring Laura for over a year. I sneaked a quick peek at her ring finger, but it was still bare. Drat Ben, what was he waiting for?

Joe Riddley slapped away Laura's offer to lift my suitcase with the familiarity of a man who had once changed her diapers. "Think I'm gettin' old and feeble? I can still arm wrestle you to the table, and don't you forget it."

"Stop squabbling, you two," I told them, tugging the neck of my sweater away from my neck, "and let's hit the road. I'm so hot, I'm fixin' to die." Getting into that car and slamming the door behind me was hard, though. My whole body felt like a magnet pulling toward Joe Riddley. But I resolutely clicked my seat belt to keep myself in and leaned out the window for one last peck. "You be good, now," I warned him.

"I'll be good or I'll be careful. You be both." He stepped

back so Laura could pull out. It took a while for my eyes to clear of tears, but Laura tactfully fiddled with the radio to find some good music and pretended she needed to concentrate on her driving to get through the traffic jam of downtown Hopemore, population thirteen thousand in the greater metropolitan area.

When we were finally on the two-lane leading to the interstate, I pulled out the list of people joining us in Atlanta. "There are only eight names, counting us. Do you reckon that's all that's coming? Looks like they'd have to have more than that to make a profit."

"Especially with hiring a bus." If there's one thing Laura and I both know, it's profit and loss. "Maybe another tour group will join us at the airport or over in Glasgow."

"Maybe so." I turned to another puzzling thing. "Did you notice that two of the women are named Brandi and Sherry? Could those possibly be their real names?"

"Sherry's is. She's a fiddler, married to Kenny Boyd, who is a piper. They come to all the Stone Mountain Highland games." As she passed a car, she gave her deep trademark chuckle. "I used to have the worst crush on Kenny when I was fourteen. I'd follow him around and save every gum wrapper he dropped. But if you tell him, I'll drop *you* off a mountaintop."

"So they are around your age?" I wondered if I'd be the only person over sixty on the trip.

Her reply didn't answer that question. "Oh, no, he's twelve years older, and Sherry's older than that. I just didn't figure the difference would matter, once he looked at me and fell in love." We laughed together at the dreams girls can dream, then she filled me in on what she knew. "Sherry's aunt owns a restaurant down in Savannah, but I heard she retired to Florida several years ago and lets Sherry and Kenny run it now. They still come to all the Stone Mountain games, but they hang out mostly with other musicians. I don't think I've spoken more than two words to them in ten years. Kenny and Daddy were buddies, though, and he wrote a real sweet note when Daddy died. He's the one who sent me the brochure for this trip, too."

She swung around a tractor and back into her lane just

about the time I expected an approaching lumber truck to meet us head-on and send us further than Scotland.

Just as abruptly, she changed the subject. "Are you looking forward to the trip, Mac?"

"Yes, I am. I haven't been to Scotland since Joe Riddley and I went with a church group twenty years ago. I'll enjoy seeing the tourist sites again, but mostly I'm looking forward to seeing Auchnagar, where Mama's people came from. We didn't go there before, and I hadn't even traced our genealogy. Now I know that Andrew MacLaren was born there in 1725 and married there in 1744. He and his wife arrived in the Carolinas in 1746 and got to Georgia in 1750, so I presume he left because of the Battle of Culloden. You go back to Flora MacDonald who came over after Culloden, too—right?"

"Right. But another branch of the family came over during the Highland Clearances and those MacDonalds married the other MacDonalds, so I have ancestors in both groups. Makes for an interesting family tree."

"Explains a lot about you, too. But remind me again. What were the clearances?" I knew she'd know. Skye Mac-Donald raised his children on Scottish history, music, and fairy tales.

"A period when landowners decided to raise sheep, so they kicked tenant farmers off the land. It was pretty brutal. That's why a lot of Scots emigrated to Canada and America. Kenny can tell you more about them. He's big into Scottish history. That's mostly what he and Daddy had in common, except Kenny gets real fiery about it—or used to. I don't know what he's like now that he's an old married man." She chuckled again and we rode a few miles in silence. She broke it to suggest, "You might still have relatives in Auchnagar. We found cousins on Skye several years ago. I'm having tea with them Friday afternoon, while we're there."

"Can you believe that by Friday we'll be having tea on the Isle of Skye?" I gave a happy little bounce in my seat. Every mile we drove seemed to make Scotland more real and Hopemore less so. "And in one week and two days, I'll actually see Auchnagar."

Laura set her cruise control and settled more comfortably

in her seat. "I just hope there's something to do there besides look up your relations. Otherwise, four days in one small village may seem pretty deadly."

Neither of us suspected at the time just how deadly it would be.

❧ 3 ❧

As soon as I saw Joyce Underwood, our tour guide, I thought of a brown mouse. Not because of her size—which was all-around medium—but because she had a long, pointy nose, mousy brown hair, and nervous brown eyes. She held herself warily, like she was watching to make sure you didn't reach out a paw to claw her, and looked like she would store all her nuts in a very private place.

With Laura's usual competence, we were first to arrive. We had been told to assemble at four-thirty at a motel near the airport where Joyce had spent the previous night, and that we'd leave our luggage there while we went to dinner in town.

Joyce met us in the lobby and greeted us by name. When she called me "Mrs. Yarbrough," I didn't bother to tell her it was Judge Yarbrough. "Just call me MacLaren," I said. After all, the woman looked thirty-five and I'm not in my dotage.

After we had stowed our bags, she said, "We've had a change in plans. Marcia Inch and Dorothy Cowling are coming from Calgary and their plane is a couple of hours late, so we're going to eat here and hope they arrive before we're done. The Gordons are driving down from the North Georgia mountains and should be here any minute. The Boyds are flying up from Savannah, but neglected to send me their arrival time. Why don't you wait over there?" We wandered over to the far end of the lobby and claimed uncomfortable vinyl chairs, where we sat experiencing the deflated feeling of folks who have hurried for nothing.

Joyce paced near the lobby doors for nearly an hour,

looking as anxious as a first-time babysitter. Finally a cab pulled in and two people climbed out. "This looks like Mr. and Mrs. Boyd now," she announced.

I didn't give her real high marks as a detective. The man climbing out wore plaid slacks with a dark green turtleneck and carried a bag labeled "Fragile—Bagpipes." The woman carried a violin case in one hand and a plaid cape over her arm. And before the cabbie had even gotten out and started unloading a trunk full of bags, Laura had risen and moseyed over near the door, where she hovered in uncharacteristic uncertainty. I figured she was wondering whether to go out to greet Kenny or wait until he came inside.

I hoped they didn't plan to play their instruments on the bus, but didn't want to think anything bad about them yet. That plaid Mrs. Boyd was carrying was the MacKenzie tartan, and my daddy's mama was a MacKenzie. We might be kin.

I revised that opinion as soon as she strode toward the door and left her husband to deal with the luggage. Women in my family carry our share of the load.

We didn't look anything alike, either. I am short with honey-brown hair, brown eyes, and the kind of figure Joe Riddley is sweet enough to call voluptuous. Sherry Boyd was taller than her husband and bypassed slender and thin to go straight for downright scrawny. She was also sallow-skinned, and had black hair and enormous eyes the color of semisweet chocolate. All the way across the lobby I could smell her musky perfume.

Totally ignoring Laura, she honed in on Joyce. "We're Kenny and Sherry Boyd," she said in a flat, nasal voice. She stuck out a hand decorated with gold rings on several fingers.

She could have been anything from thirty-five to forty-five, and was striking rather than pretty. She wore no makeup, was dressed in a black turtleneck and a long black skirt that touched her boots, and simply dragged her long straight hair back at her neck. Still, her plaid cape looked hand-loomed, her rings were certainly handmade, and her hair was pinned by an elaborate Celtic clip. I put her down as one of those arty people who don't care how they look so long as what they wear is unique and expensive.

"Was your plane late?" Having seen Joyce's anxiety for the past hour, I marveled she could sound so calm and friendly.

"No, we flew in last night," Sherry told her. "We had some shopping to do today."

I watched in admiration as Joyce pressed her lips together and took deep breaths. I've heard that's a good way to control your temper, but when I get mad, I always forget.

Laura made up her mind—or got up her courage—to go outside. "Hey, Kenny," she called.

The man turned with a look I sometimes see in the eyes of people hauled into my court for the first time—folks trying to hide embarrassment behind bravado. Or maybe I imagined it. The next instant, he had her in a bear hug. Flushed, she pulled away and bent to help with his mountain of luggage. He started gathering up the rest.

I eyed those bags and knew one thing: the Boyds had bought a whole set of new luggage for this trip. None of those cases had ever been slung in and out of baggage compartments. Kenny, however, looked like he might have been slung around a few times in life. His shoulders were slightly rounded, his face plump with heavy jowls. He was also short. Laura was nearly six feet, so he came approximately to her chin.

"She wasn't but fourteen when she had that crush on him," I reminded myself. "She didn't get tall for a couple more years. And maybe he was thin before he started eating his wife's cooking." Now his potbelly bulged over the belt of his tartan slacks. The only thing I could find remotely attractive about him was the red hair that waved away from his forehead and curled around his ears.

He was so engrossed in collecting luggage while talking to Laura that he staggered in without tipping the cabbie. The man glared after them, then left with a screech of burning rubber.

Kenny set down his bags and stuck out a hand to Joyce. "Sorry we're a bit late. We ran up to Phipps Plaza for a little while." "Phipps Plaza" is synonymous with "expensive stores" in Atlanta. Kenny seemed to presume his explanation would atone for keeping the rest of us waiting. "Honey, you remember Laura MacDonald." He pulled Laura toward his wife.

"Sure. Hello." Sherry gave Laura a hug that came straight from a Deepfreeze.

"That's MacLaren Yarbrough, who's come with me on the trip." Laura nodded in my direction. I waved from my chair. They'd be coming my way eventually, so there was no reason to make that trek across the wide lobby.

Kenny bounded over to shake my hand. "I like your checked britches," I told him. Mama always said if you can't find something nice to say about somebody, make up something.

"Tartan breeks," he corrected me. He lifted one leg and twirled it a little to show them off. He must have bought new loafers, too. Their shine was dazzling. "They're the Stewart hunting plaid," he added in an offhand way. "I'm a direct descendant of Robert the Bruce."

Thank goodness he'd chosen the Stewart hunting plaid, which is mostly green with navy, instead of their more flamboyant red tartan. But if you want my opinion (and even if you don't), neither checked britches nor tartan breeks look good on a chubby figure.

Laura joined Kenny and me, but Sherry had grabbed Joyce's elbow and pulled her into a corner next to a drooping ficus tree that the nursery owner in me wanted to give a long drink of water. Sherry spoke in a low, urgent voice, nodding toward Laura and me. Whatever she was saying, Joyce shook her head. Sherry pointed a finger at Joyce, used it to emphasize her words. Joyce stepped back like she was afraid of getting stabbed. Sherry followed. Joyce backed another step. Joyce reached the ficus and could go no farther. Finally she lifted one hand and shrugged. "I can check with our office," she said in a voice that carried all the way to us.

"You do that," Sherry told her. "That's what we were promised. Now what are we to do with this luggage until the flight?"

They were still carrying bags to the storage room when a

gray limousine pulled up to the motel and a uniformed chauffeur got out.

"The Gordons," Joyce breathed, more to herself than to us. She moved toward the door, as if to go outside to greet them, then must have changed her mind, for she went to the front window and stood concealed by the drape. We watched a tall, lanky man with a shock of thick white hair climb out on the far side and follow the chauffeur around back. Around sixty, he had a beak of a nose on a profile that could have been chiseled out of Stone Mountain granite.

Most folks would know at a glance that here was a man accustomed to giving orders and being obeyed. Joe Riddley has that same kind of presence. He just doesn't wear tailor-made suits and a gold pinky ring.

While the chauffeur lifted out four leather bags, butter-soft from much travel, the tall man made no effort to help except with instructions. When a violin case appeared, however, he reached for it and his ring glinted in the sun.

"What's with all the musical instruments?" I asked Joyce.

Joyce's attention was riveted on the limo's back door, so Laura answered. "It was in the last e-mail we got. We're attending a musical program on Skye with some local performers, and folks were invited to bring any instruments they play."

"I missed that part. I could have brought my comb and tissue paper."

Joyce still wasn't paying a speck of attention. Her eyes never left the limousine as the tall man opened the rear door nearest us. A black spike heel emerged, followed by long slender legs in black hose and a gorgeous plaid skirt in green and blue.

I couldn't have told you the difference between that plaid and the one Kenny was wearing, or the blue-and-green MacDonald tartan that decorated Laura's apartment, but Laura recognized it at once. "That's the Gordon plaid," she informed me.

I scarcely heard her. I was staring at a sleek combination of stunning figure and bright red hair that fell loosely to the shoulders of a hunter green velvet jacket, then curled at the ends. As the man moved aside, I saw that the woman had a face to match the rest—the kind of face that causes old men to launch ships, start wars, or desert their wives and children.

Joyce said a word I'd never have expected from those prim lips. Then she caught me looking at her, put on a tight, professional smile, and started toward the door.

I leaned over to Laura and asked softly, "What are those folks doing on a bus tour? Her outfit cost more than my entire wardrobe. And look at those diamonds!"

"I can't. I forgot my sunglasses."

The woman fluffed her hair, then headed for the lobby with a long, confident stride that made the curls bounce on her shoulders. She flung open the door and stood looking around, her lips curved in that smile models and movie stars cultivate, the kind that shows a lot more teeth than the rest of us have. It was unfair that somebody so beautiful should also have gorgeous eyes, but there they were, a light, clear gray under impossibly long lashes.

"Mrs. Gordon?" I'd known Joyce just long enough to know she was angry about something, but holding her temper on a short rein. "I'm Joyce Underwood, your tour guide."

"Call me Brandi. Everybody does. I'm so glad to meet you." Sounding as friendly as she was glamorous, she stuck out a hand. "Jimmy will be here in a minute. I'm really lookin' forward to this trip. We're gonna have so much fun!" Her voice was pure Georgia honey.

"We certainly are." Joyce looked like she was having trouble keeping her smile pinned to her face. "Let me introduce you to the rest of the group."

A wave of delicious perfume preceded her as Brandi came toward us. She gave me a smile that said she'd been waiting all day to meet me, and I felt real special—until I saw it was the same look she gave Laura, then Kenny and Sherry as they joined us. I wondered if it came natural or if she practiced it.

Brandi looked around again and bestowed approval on us all. "I'm so glad you all got here early too. Maybe we can get a bite of supper or something before we go to the plane."

"I asked you to be here by four-thirty." Joyce sounded like her jaw had frozen.

"Oh, really? I thought you said eight-thirty."

"That's when we have to be at the airport."

"Oh, dear!" Brandi gave everybody a look of contrition.
"I am *so* sorry. Jimmy told me it was four-thirty, but I erased
the e-mail and remembered eight-thirty. Well, here we are
now!"

"Yes, here we are now," Joyce repeated. "As soon as Jim
joins us, I'll make a few housekeeping announcements, then
we can eat."

Brandi called to her husband, who was following the
chauffeur and the bags. "Oh, Jimmy, you were right. Joyce
says we *were* supposed to be here by four-thirty."

"That's what I told you." He sounded more indulgent
than anything. "Sorry, Josie."

"It's Joyce," she said firmly.

He nodded. "Right. Joyce. Sorry." His voice was
brusque, almost dismissive.

I looked at Kenny and Sherry conferring to one side, at
Mr. Gordon turning to give his chauffeur some last instructions, at Brandi Gordon with her perfect smile, at Joyce who
seemed wound tighter than a woman ought to wind, and I
felt a surge of panic. I didn't want to fly all night across the
ocean and spend two weeks with these people. Whatever
had possessed me to go off and leave Joe Riddley this way?

I would ask myself that question several times before I
saw Atlanta again.

❧ 4 ❧

After a short welcoming speech, Joyce gave us each a green tote bag with "Gilroy's Highland Tours" in white letters. With the tote bags she handed out a final itinerary. "This has been revised based on questionnaire answers you sent back about places you particularly want to see." When Kenny and Sherry asked about a couple of places on the original list that were no longer there, she shrugged. "Nobody requested them."

"I didn't know we had to request places already on the itinerary," Sherry objected.

I hadn't either. I sure was glad Auchnagar hadn't been cut.

Joyce looked at her watch. "We can talk about that later. We need to go in to dinner right now. We're still waiting for two folks, so the motel has agreed to serve us here, in their private dining room."

Private dining room? Private dining closet was more like it. I felt we ought to take turns breathing. Laura was not shy about going first, so she scrunched along behind the chairs down to the far end. Jim and Brandi got ahead of me, so the three of us sat along the left side while Joyce, Kenny and Sherry edged in on the right. That left an empty seat on each side nearest the door. Until the others arrived, at least I'd be able to get out quick in case of fire.

That was the only sunny thought in an otherwise ghastly meal. I don't remember anybody appointing Kenny and Sherry to lecture us, but they immediately began a nonstop duet. He described the weather we could expect and places we simply must visit while she provided a counterpoint about why each place was better in winter, fall, or summer, and how much we would miss by going in spring.

Dinner had been advertised as "blackened chicken with green beans Chinoise." That translated into charred chicken breasts and almost-raw beans doused with soya sauce. To add insult to injury, the place didn't even serve sweet tea. In Georgia, that is a crime. If this dinner represented the quality we could expect for the next ten days, I wanted Joe Riddley's money back. Preferably in cash I could spend before he knew I had it.

When Sherry got caught up in a monologue about how much we were going to miss by not visiting Burns country in the south, I was delighted to see our last two group members finally arrive. I'd been picturing myself leaping across the table to strangle Sherry with her own hair.

I could have guessed that the newcomers were Canadian. Their sweaters were heavier than any I owned and the younger woman's face was red from heat, her bangs stuck to her forehead with sweat. She hovered behind her companion as they stepped through the doorway.

"It's good to finally be here, eh?" The older woman sank gratefully into the chair next to me, her voice soft and weary. "We—Dorothy and I"—she gestured to the tall girl behind her, who looked poised to take flight any moment—"had snow delays in Calgary, eh?" She gave us a rueful smile and pulled off her cardigan. "Hard to believe, as hot as it is down here."

She was tall and gaunt to the point of emaciation, her skin stretched taut over high, prominent cheekbones. Beneath thick black brows, her eyes burned like coals in a ravaged face surrounded by a soft, frizzy halo of grizzled hair. The gray hair, her frailty, and that sense of great weariness made her seem old, but when I looked closer I guessed she was closer to forty than fifty. However, her clothes sagged as if she'd taken them from a larger woman's closet, and as she turned to signal her companion to come on in and take a seat, I suspected I was looking at a woman who was terminally ill—maybe one who, like Laura, was making a pilgrimage.

"I'm Marcia Inch, by the way," she added, then nodded at her companion, "and this is Dorothy Cowling. We work together at the Calgary library. Dorothy works in reference and I am in charge of acquisitions."

With a bob of her head and a quick flash of the deepest dimples I'd ever seen, Dorothy sat down next to Sherry. Her sweater was so bulky and her long skirt so shapeless that it was hard to tell much about her figure, but she had pink cheeks, flawless skin, a round, pretty face, and a thick chestnut braid that hung down her back past her waist. We got a quick glimpse of pale gold eyes before she lowered her lashes.

They were barely seated when Sherry started up again on her litany of wonders we were doomed not to see, but Laura tapped her water glass with her knife. "Before you continue your interesting report, Sherry, could we go around the room and say who we are and where we are from? I'd like to know a little bit about why everybody came on this trip. Since I have the floor, I'm Laura MacDonald, from Hopemore, Georgia. For those of you who aren't properly educated, that's the county seat of Hope County, located midway between Augusta, Macon and nowhere. I came because I made several trips to Scotland as a child with my folks, but I want to see it again as a grown-up." She didn't mention her parents' deaths. Laura was not one to wear sorrow on her sleeve. She did add, "Plus, it's the first time off I've had in two years."

"That's awful," Brandi cooed. "What do you do?"

She gave a little shrug. "Work in an office."

Brandi's eyes widened and her lashes brushed her wispy bangs. "You must have a slave driver of a boss!"

"Sure do," Laura agreed cheerfully. "How about you folks?"

Brandi turned to Jim and took his arm, a signal for him to speak for them both. He had been shoveling in his dinner like burnt chicken and undercooked beans were his favorite foods, but he paused long enough to answer. "We live up in the North Georgia mountains, near Blue Ridge." His voice was husky, with an accent I couldn't place. "We came on this trip because Brandi has a hankering to see the Highlands by bus." He gave her a frosty smile. When she squeezed his arm, her diamonds caught the overhead light and sent rainbows dancing on the far wall.

How long would that marriage last once her figure sagged and her upkeep bills rose? Or once his health started to fail? From Joyce's expression, she was wondering the same thing.

"Do you play the fiddle?" Sherry inquired. I couldn't tell whether she was glad to meet a fellow fiddler or unhappy to have competition.

Jim nodded. "A bit." He picked up his fork again to return to his meal.

"He's marvelous," Brandi informed the rest of us. "Simply wonderful." She gave Jim's biceps another squeeze, her nails making it look like she'd drawn blood.

"Are you a Scot?" Marcia called down across me and Brandi. "You sound like my dad."

"No." He continued to eat like he found nothing to object to on his plate.

Brandi's teeth flashed nearly as bright as her diamonds as she smiled around the table.

"Jimmy owns Scotsman Distilleries, so he thinks he needs to talk like that. He's done it so long now, he's forgotten what he used to sound like."

The rest of us sat there like open-mouth flycatchers. Scotsman was an elite distillery up in the Georgia mountains that made limited quantities of very expensive single-malt scotch.

I gave myself a mental kick for not recognizing Jim. His craggy features had been pictured in several Georgia business magazines over the years, along with the kind of rags-to-riches story we in the USA love to claim as typically American. In Jim's case, a poor but ambitious young man had come down to Georgia from somewhere up north to work in a liquor distributing company in Albany. He had helped to build up the business, married the owner's daughter, and become CEO when his father-in-law died. Soon afterwards, he had sold that company and launched Scotsman Distilleries. Rumor was, he'd developed the recipe for his famous product as part of a basement hobby. None of the articles I'd read had mentioned whether his former wife had died or been traded in for this younger model.

And I should have recognized Brandi's tartan at once. A series of kilted Highlanders had worn that plaid on labels in my pantry for years, because Skye MacDonald and Joe Riddley had celebrated every conceivable occasion by giving each other scotch from Scotsman Distilleries.

I glanced down the table at Laura, but she was looking at her plate. Grief is bad about popping up at unexpected moments.

"I thought you looked familiar!" Sherry practically leaned across her plate trying to establish a connection. "We've bought our liquor from your old company for years and years, and my aunt was a friend of your former in-laws."

Jim didn't reply, clearly considering his dinner more interesting than that.

Joyce quickly turned to me. "What about you, Mrs. Yarbrough?"

I wished I could say something to make Laura smile again, but I wasn't feeling real humorous, between missing Joe Riddley, looking down at burnt chicken and raw beans, and thinking about dead friends. What I wanted to do was jump up and shout, "I came because my husband made me, dang it! He paid to send me away!"

What else could I say? Yarbrough Feed, Seed and Nursery might be important in Middle Georgia, but it was small potatoes compared to Scotsman Distilleries. I didn't want to inform folks I was a judge, either, and stuff a rag up everybody's chimney. Haven't you noticed how, when folks discover there's a judge or a preacher among them, they sit up straighter and act different?

When the silence grew long, I finally said, "Well, I've been married over forty years to one man, which ought to earn me some kind of medal, and we have two sons and four grandchildren. My husband sent me on this trip so he and our younger son can sneak away for a few days of deep-sea fishing without feeling guilty."

That got a little chuckle, as I'd hoped, and brought color back to Laura's cheeks. If folks presumed I was a housewife, that was their own stereotypes showing. "I'm especially looking forward to visiting Auchnagar," I added. "My mother's people came from there."

"So did my parents!" Marcia's smile was unexpected and sweet. "They emigrated to Canada soon after they married, eh? I came on this trip because my mother's sister keeps the guest house in Auchnagar where we'll be staying. Heather Glen, it's called. Dorothy and I will stay on a few days after the tour is over. Who were your people?"

"The MacLarens, but I don't know if there are any left. Most of the clan came from Perthshire, but our branch made its way up to Auchnagar a generation or so before they emigrated to the Carolinas."

I had the feeling that somebody around the table had given a start when I'd mentioned the MacLarens, but I didn't notice who it was.

"Did they come during the Highland Clearances?" Kenny asked.

"No, they came after Culloden," I told him.

"What were the Highland Clearances?" Dorothy asked Sherry in a soft voice.

It was Kenny who answered, and his words sizzled around the table. "One of the greatest, greediest betrayals of family that history has ever known. Women and children starved. Old people froze alongside the road. Men drowned because they were forced to make a living fishing when they had never handled a boat." He clutched his knife so hard I thought he'd bend it. "And for what? So a few rich men and women could get richer raising sheep than they had leasing their land out for family farms." He glared across at Jim and Brandi, but Brandi was checking her nail polish and Jim was still plying his fork with single-minded concentration.

Dorothy looked down at her plate, her cheeks flaming. "Sorry. I didn't know. Was that a long time ago?"

That time, Sherry answered. "They started around 1772 and lasted nearly a hundred years. Of course, they were a real boon to America and Canada, because that's when a lot of Scots came to both countries. That's why so many of us now go back to celebrate our ancestors."

"Don't whitewash it," Kenny said sharply. "Thousands of families were kicked out of their homes, sometimes into the snow." He glared over at Jim again, as if he had personally given the order. "Then the laird's men either knocked down the houses or burnt them, so the people couldn't come back."

"Sounds like General Sherman," I said, trying to lighten things up a bit.

"Just about," Laura agreed, "except these were their kinfolks they were burning out."

Kenny opened his mouth like he had more to say, but Joyce said quickly, "So tell us why you've come, Dorothy. Was it just to travel with Marcia, or are you Scottish, too?"

"Only partly, that I know of. My mother's people came from Tain, up near the Dornoch Firth." Her voice was little more than a whisper. "But I've always wanted to see Scotland, eh? So when Marcia said she was coming, I said I'd like to come along."

Marcia leaned forward and spoke in a confiding tone. "I have an ulterior motive for this trip, too. I'm hoping Dorothy falls in love with a Highland gentleman such as my nephew, who is a few years older than she. If they get married, they can keep me in style when I get old, eh?"

Dorothy turned bright pink and looked ready to dive under her plate. Fortunately for her, Kenny had a one-track mind. "When did your mother's people come over, Dorothy?"

"I haven't a clue. It was her great-great-grandmother, I think." Her face was almost as red as Brandi's nails and she was clearly distressed at being singled out for attention.

"You ought to find out about them," Kenny said earnestly. "You never know what you'll find. I discovered I'm descended from King Robert the Bruce, and we recently found out that one of Sherry's ancestors—John MacKenzie, who lived in Eilean Donan Castle back in the fourteenth century—actually gave refuge to Robert when he was being hunted by the English. Isn't that an amazing coincidence?"

I personally thought that was an amazing feat of boasting, but Brandi asked in a breathless voice, "You're descended from the *king*?"

Before Kenny could reply, Jim murmured to his wife, "A king who lived seven hundred years ago. By now, anybody could be his descendant." He shoved back his chair. "Would you excuse me? I need to make a few calls before we take off."

The rest of us on that side of the table sucked in our stomachs and pressed against the table edge to let him out. Joyce looked like she wondered if she ought to follow him, but I saw no need to cater to self-centered surliness. "How about you?" I asked her. "Where are you from and why did you come? Have you always been a tour guide?"

She seemed surprised at being treated like a regular person. "Actually, I'm a frustrated playwright." She gave an embarrassed little laugh. "I work to support my writing habit. In Auchnagar you will see a short play I was asked to write on the history of the village."

That cut off our water. We hadn't paid good money to attend amateur theatricals.

Everybody else seemed as blank as I was about what to say next until Laura finally said, "Have you seen a lot of the world?"

"Yes. I was a flight attendant for twelve years." She checked her watch. "Eat up, please. We won't have time for dessert, I'm afraid." She lowered her voice. "Not that you're missing much. I am really sorry we couldn't have had a better meal for your first day out, but they'll all be better from now on, I promise."

Before we left for the airport, I dragged my bag to one side and took out Joe Riddley's gift. It wasn't jewelry—it was several bills of a denomination that widened my eyes.

I hurried outside and gave him a call. "Buy yourself something pretty to remember the trip by," he told me. "I love you, Little Bit. Come back safely."

I went to the ladies' room and permitted myself one short weep. Then I fixed my face and headed back to the group. I was determined to have a good time on this trip, if it killed me.

Not that I ever expected that it almost would . . .

5

In the airport shuttle bus, Brandi confided, "Jimmy is on the board of an airline, so we've been upgraded to first class."

As soon as we stepped inside the airport, they were whisked away by a lacquered blonde in uniform and we didn't see them again until we boarded the plane. Then we got a real good view of them sipping complimentary drinks up front while the rest of us headed back to steerage. As Mama used to say, "There are some things money can't buy, but the more money you have, the fewer they are."

The rest of us went through security in a clump, with Joyce bringing up the rear, checking her notebook and counting heads at every bend to make sure nobody had strayed. We eventually began to complain, as people tend to do, wondering out loud why civilized, intelligent North Americans aren't rising up en masse to protest security processes that do little to deter terrorists, but harass and humiliate harmless citizens. Then Kenny pointed out, "When our ancestors came from Scotland, they were crammed seven hundred or more onto rickety ships designed to hold five hundred. They had too little food, sour water, and a real good chance of dying from cholera or dysentery before they landed. I guess we can put up with a little bit of standing in line."

"You are such a party pooper," Sherry said acidly.

But Laura said, "Kenny's right. We came on this trip to have a good time, so what difference does it make if we spend the next hour sitting in a waiting area or standing here? We might as well have fun starting now."

After that she, Dorothy, Marcia, and I had a real good chat while Sherry instructed Joyce on what we should have been told in order to get through security faster. Kenny read a dog-eared book entitled *The Highland Clearances* that looked like he'd read it several times before.

However, we were in that line a very long time.

By the time it was my turn to dump my carry-on and purse into bins and walk through the metal detector, I was in no mood to obey an officious guard who told me to remove my shoes and walk across that filthy floor in sock feet. I am not a terrorist, I am a judge. I'd worn those shoes through several airports and knew there was no metal in them, and I had no idea what foot diseases the last hundred people might have left behind. "Let's try the shoes and see if they beep," I suggested politely. "If they do, I'll take them off and go through again."

In thirty seconds flat I was being wanded up the body, down the body, under the arms, along the inside of my legs, and under the shoes, then I was patted all over. The woman who had been summoned to work me over kept murmuring, in a thick Eastern European accent, that she was sorry to be doing this. I was dying to ask if this didn't remind her of the worst days of Communism, but hated to get arrested and have to explain to my grandchildren why I hadn't gone to Scotland. I couldn't help snapping at the end, though, "This is enough to make radicals of us all." I got a small smile of what I am certain was agreement.

By the time we finally got on the plane, I was actually happy that Laura and I weren't sitting together, for I had an empty seat between me and the aisle and I sleep well on planes. When the lights dimmed I lifted the armrest, put my feet in the other seat, and snuggled down with a blanket and pillow, trusting somebody would wake me in Glasgow.

Only when I was about to drift off did I remember I was carrying a lot of cash, traveler's checks and a passport, and Joe Riddley wasn't there. Who would guard my pocketbook? Who'd nudge me if I snored? I swung my legs around and sat up, resigned to one heck of a long night.

I read a while, then—bored and stiff—got up and joined a circulating ring of folks hiking to stave off death from blood clots. Up at the thick curtain separating first class from us peons, I peeked through to see how the other one-half of one percent lives. Brandi was dozing and Jim had a spreadsheet on his laptop screen, in easy view. I work with spreadsheets every day, but I'd never seen one belonging to a multimillionaire, so I leaned forward to see if his was more interesting than mine. It wasn't. His columns were just labeled "patrons served" and "cost per serving" instead of "original order" and "stock on hand."

Back in steerage I waved at Laura, who was watching a movie, and pitied Dorothy and Marcia, who were in a long center row with three squirming children whose parents were dozing in the row ahead. After I'd made the U-turn at the back and headed up my own side of the plane, I found Kenny sprawled in an aisle seat glowering at a drink. Fumes surrounded him. Four small empty scotch bottles and a glass with a few melted cubes in the bottom sat on his tray table. Sherry slept against the window, wearing an eye mask. She had taken off her hair clip, and her hair slithered down her shoulders like black snakes. I tiptoed by with a little wave, but Kenny crooked a finger at me, so I stopped. I figured I could turn my head a little if I found it necessary to breathe.

"You friends with Laura?" His voice was a soft, hoarse croak.

"Yes. Her folks were some of my best friends."

"I liked old Skye. Knew him for years." He swirled the ice around in the bottom of his glass. "I guess Laura and her brother inherited the whole shebang, huh?"

I frowned. "You'll have to ask her about that."

"I guess." He pursed his plump red lips and blew air through them, staring morosely ahead of him. "Some folks have all the luck, don't they?" He was just sober enough to realize how that sounded, because he lifted one hand and wiggled it. "Oh, I don't mean Skye and Gwen Ellen dying. And Laura deserves the best. She was always a good kid."

"She still is," I assured him. "A real fine person."

"Yeah." He sank into either thought or a stupor.

I moseyed on and found Joyce working on a laptop with the screen turned away from the aisle. "We've got some busy bees on this tour," I greeted her. "You and Jim make me feel like a slacker. Are you writing another play?"

"No, just working on some line changes." She lowered the screen. "I'd made the laird seem weak in one scene. Are you looking forward to the trip?"

I allowed as how I was, and then—since she didn't seem to mind talking—I propped my backside on her armrest and asked, "How'd you come to write a play about Auchnagar?" What I really wanted to ask was, "Did you arrange this whole trip so you'd have an audience?"

She gave a deprecating little laugh that couldn't hide her pride. "It was a miracle, really. When I was preparing for this tour, I stayed a week in the village. Leaving the post office one morning, I literally ran into Mrs. MacGorrie—the laird's wife."

She paused, so I nodded, to keep her pump primed. "She's American," she went on, "but interested in Scottish history and ancient arts. She's turned an abandoned church into an arts center where they have demonstrations of ancient weaving and pottery-making and all sorts of lectures. So after I'd apologized for nearly running her down, I asked if there would be anything going on at the arts center you all might be interested in, and she offered to show me around. During the tour, we got to talking about what a good place the old sanctuary would be for plays, and I mentioned that I'm a writer. On a whim, I said I'd love to write a play about the history of the area. Next thing I knew, she was saying, 'See what you can do, and send it along. If I like it, we'll put it on.'"

"And she did like it"—from experience with one writer I know, I knew Joyce could go on for ages if I didn't cut her short—"so they're putting it on for us."

She nodded, her face bright. "And if it works, they'll perform it all summer."

"That's great! I'll let you get on with what you're doing, then."

I returned to my seat and fumbled in my carry-on bag for my book, but before I got it open, shouts erupted in the back of the plane.

Terrorists!

My first thought was echoed in screams and squeals as others struggled awake.

A bevy of flight attendants hurried toward the disturbance.

A few men rose halfway from their seats, ready to go if needed, but hoping their day for being heroes had not yet come. I honored them for being willing.

One of the flight attendants hurried back toward the front of the plane and a soothing voice spoke over the intercom. "There is no cause for alarm. Everything is under control. But please remain in your seats. The captain has illuminated the seat-belt sign."

She lied. Shouts and yells still came from the back of the plane.

However, just then one of the voices slurred, "Y'all git away, now. This is jist 'tween her 'n' me." That particular terrorist spoke like a drunk South Georgian. I'm used to those, so I slid toward the aisle and craned my neck to look without making my head too much of a target.

Kenny and Sherry stood in the aisle gripping one another by the forearms. I couldn't tell who was shaking whom, but in the dimness I saw her hair slinging back and forth like a dark string mop.

Two flight attendants sought to separate them, but Kenny elbowed them away. "Git y'r hands off me! We kin settle this if I kin just make her see reason."

"Shut up and sit down, you lush!" Sherry jerked one hand free and slapped him hard.

"I'm not puttin' up with any more!" His shove sent her staggering back several steps.

She rushed him, but her attack ended in a shriek as he grabbed her hair and yanked.

Again the flight attendants waded into the fray. Again the combatants shook them off.

I have settled a few domestic disputes in my time, so I

was fixing to head back there when I saw Joyce heading their way. "Stop!" she commanded.

"It's okay." Sherry stopped fighting and stood in the aisle panting. "Kenny just got a little out of hand. He's going to be fine, now, aren't you?" She glared at him.

Kenny glared back at her, breathing heavily. "I'll be fine if you'll agree to—"

"Don't you start that again," she warned, reaching for his arm.

He shoved her hard, and she fell across the armrest into her seat, where she swore at him as she struggled to get up.

When he raised a fist, I ignored the "Fasten Seat Belt" sign and went for real help.

Even first class had heard something going on back in steerage. Jim stood in the aisle peering through the curtain. "Please come," I told him. "Kenny is drunk and creating a scene." He shut his computer and followed me to the back.

"Hey, Ken." He grabbed Kenny by one shoulder. Kenny lunged like an angry bull, but Jim was bigger, and sober. He held Kenny without any trouble. "Calm down, now. Let's sit down and talk this over." He looked over the seats and spotted a vacant row in the middle a few rows back. He raised one eyebrow at a flight attendant. "Those seats available?"

She nodded, obviously relieved to have somebody else take charge.

"He doesn't need to leave. He's going to be fine!" Gasping for breath, Sherry fumbled in a pocket and retrieved her hair clip. In a smooth, practiced motion she secured her hair and arranged her face simultaneously. Once again she looked remote and in control. "He's terrified of flying," she explained, "so he tends to drink too much on flights. I can deal with him."

She stood and put out one hand to take Kenny's arm, but he swatted her away. "Don't you touch me, you—"

"Let him stay with me a while," Jim advised. "We'll be right back there."

Sherry obviously would have preferred to keep him at their seat, but after a short hesitation, she shrugged. "Whatever." She spoke to Kenny in what sounded like a warning.

"Just remember, honey, this is going to be a real good trip. Okay?"

For the life of me, I couldn't figure out why that should sound like a threat.

But Kenny, too, caught her warning tone. "Good trip?" he mumbled as he staggered behind Jim to the seats in the back. Before he sat, he turned and shot her a look of pure venom. "A real good trip to hell."

⇜ 6 ⇝

Nine days later, when the police sergeant would interview me about the body in the coffin and our group of travelers, he would ask, "Did anything unusual occur on this trip? Anything out of the ordinary?"

Unusual? Out of the ordinary?

"From the very first day," I would have to admit.

To begin with, nobody else met us at Prestwick Airport in Glasgow Wednesday morning. How could anybody be making money on this trip? I could tell that Laura was wondering, too.

When we reassembled after collecting our luggage and going through customs, nobody mentioned the fight. The way Kenny and Sherry acted, you'd have thought they'd slept soundly on the trip while the rest of us shared the same nightmare.

Joyce, however, looked strained and peaked, as colorless as the pale blue of her parka, which did nothing to enhance her brown hair and eyes. Still, she managed to stay pleasant while ushering us out into a cold drizzle where a short green bus waited, blazoned with "Gilroy's Highland Tours" in white and the name "Jeannie" in yellow script by the door. The driver gave Joyce a cheerful wave through the drizzle, looked the group over, then peered around for more of us.

"That's our bus?" I whispered to Laura.

"Will it *last* two weeks?" she whispered back. "Maybe I could sell them a new one and pay for my trip."

Seldom had I seen a shabbier vehicle. Did I say it was green? Actually, one fender was red, another black. Large dents decorated both the back bumper and the front, as if somebody had gotten angry and jerked the poor thing back and forth, hitting cars fore and aft.

Joyce gave it one dismayed look and strode over to speak to the driver. We didn't hear what she said, but we heard him cackle and exclaim, "Och, auld Jeannie here'll get us there and back nae bother. She's got a fine engine, has Jeannie." He smacked her side and turned as if he'd smack Joyce on the bottom, as well. She quickly turned toward Jim and Brandi—probably worrying that they'd quit the tour and go home. Jim directed a porter to stow their bags in the open luggage door with no more visible concern than if the bus had been a limousine.

The driver, who had the name "Watty" embroidered on his flat black cap in yellow script, was as shabby as his bus. His black wool pants sagged. His red shirt had faded to a dull rose. And under a scruffy black jacket he had on the most disreputable argyle sweater I'd ever seen. Joe Riddley would have looked like a fashion plate beside him. The man wasn't much taller than me, with lines like sunbeams radiating from button-black eyes and grizzled curls springing from the cap, which dripped water in four directions. "Mind yer step, mind yer step," he muttered as we deposited our bags and climbed up the high steps.

I stretched up and whispered to Laura, "Tip well. He looks like he can use it. But do we just tip at the end, or every time he stows our luggage?" Joe Riddley usually does our tipping.

"At the end, plus if he performs an extraordinary service."

"Looks to me like it's going to be an extraordinary service every time he heaves all those bags into the bus, as tottery as he is."

When he finished, he looked questioningly at Joyce. She gave him her plastic, practiced smile. "That's all," she said in her bright tour-guide voice. He shrugged and touched his cap.

When she got closer to Jim, though, her smile turned to another worried frown. "It's fine," he said shortly. He climbed aboard and slid into a seat near the front.

"Hey, it's warm in here!" Brandi bounded up after him. "And we can each have a seat and see out the window." She took the seat behind Jim.

Joyce climbed on last, consulted with the driver, and announced, "Since none of you had ancestors who came from Glasgow, we'll only stay here one night before heading north. I suggest you rest this morning. The bus will pick us up at two for a short tour of the city."

As we rode into town, my energy drained with the drizzle. I propped my head against the window and stared out at bleak trees against a charcoal sky. I nodded as pastures of sodden sheep gave way to slick wet streets of gray houses and Monday morning traffic. My watch showed that Joe Riddley still had hours to sleep. I wished I were lying beside him, reaching out a toe to touch his warm calf. I let out an involuntary yelp as we passed a large thermometer. "Two degrees?" I clutched my trench coat and knew I was going to regret having left the liner at home.

Dorothy laughed. "That's two Celsius, thirty-four Fahrenheit. Not too bad for early spring, eh? And aren't the colors marvelous? All those grays and browns! Whistler should have painted this." That morning, the pink in her cheeks looked more like delight than painful shyness.

"Look at that Scotch broom!" Brandi called, pointing to waterfalls of yellow flowers on bright green stalks beside the road. "We are really in Scotland!"

Nobody answered. My guess was that only Brandi and Dorothy were awake.

Glasgow in the rain is like any big city—slow and dreary. By the time we arrived at the hotel, I was so sleepy that I followed Laura to our room in a blur. I didn't bother to look for a nightgown, just stripped down to underwear and socks and fell into bed.

A big mistake.

The bed was so icy, I felt like warm ham in a frozen bun. I waited a few minutes for my body heat to thaw the sheets, but my corpuscles began to solidify instead. Finally I faced the inevitable, climbed out of bed, and rummaged in my suitcase for a flannel gown. I topped it with a sweater, climbed back into bed, and lay there mentally reviewing the clothes I'd brought. I concluded that to stay warm, I would need to wear so many layers I would roll through Scotland like a ball.

Why had I let packing in Georgia's heat lull me into ignoring the average daily temperatures listed in our trip materials? Why hadn't I remembered that "early spring" is a relative term, depending on your latitude? Even little Cricket knew enough to brag to his friends, "Me-Mama is going to Scotland and it's way up at the *top of the world!*"

I didn't get warm until about the time Joyce called to say the bus was ready to leave. That's why I elected, while others looked at Glasgow, to visit that great tourist attraction Marks and Spencer. I roved the department store filling bag after bag with sweaters, slacks, socks, a hat and gloves. While clerks rang up my purchases, I checked my watch to figure out where Joe Riddley and the boys might be. *They must be loading the car. Now they are heading west. They must have gotten to I-75 already.* Before I knew it, I had bought so many clothes, I had to buy a big new suitcase to put them in.

In the cab on my way back to the hotel, I tried to convert pounds into dollars to see how much I'd spent, but the figure soon reached an altitude that made it hard for me to breathe, so I gave up and concentrated on excuses I could give Joyce for exceeding our one-bag limit.

I found her standing on the sidewalk outside the hotel in too much of a dither to care.

Dorothy had disappeared.

"She went on the bus as far as the first stop, then left without saying a word. Nobody remembers even seeing her after we got off. We looked and looked, but never did find her." Joyce peered up and down the street, clutching her coat to her throat.

The wind was sharp and fierce, carrying that raw blend of dampness, diesel and industry that is Glasgow's peculiar odor. I shivered beside her, more than ready to go inside and find a cup of hot tea, but I hated to leave her standing there alone, worrying. "Sherry finally insisted that we go on without her. She said Dorothy is a grown woman and knows where we are staying, so she can find her way back to the hotel. But—"

But Dorothy didn't look like a woman with much experience in taking care of herself in strange cities. "What did Marcia say?"

"Marcia decided to stay here and rest this afternoon." Joyce peered up and down the street again. "I haven't bothered her yet." She took a few steps one way, then the other, balled her fists and shook them. "Drat! I don't know what to do. Do you think I ought to call the police?" Were her teeth chattering from fear, cold, or both?

"Not yet," I advised. "Come on inside and get something hot to drink. It's still light out, and surely she'll get a cab back to the hotel." I tried not to think about women abducted in broad daylight from city malls.

Joyce looked prepared to stand there all night if necessary. "I really want people to stick to the program. I'm not going to be able to manage this tour if people keep charging off on their own." Her voice was grim, and she glanced down at my new suitcase.

"Sorry," I apologized. "I simply had to have some warmer clothes. I'll stay right with you the rest of the way." I headed upstairs with my purchases. She remained on the sidewalk.

I tried out Walker's cell phone before tea, to see if Cricket's mother had heard from the men. "Haven't heard a word yet," Martha said cheerfully, "but they will have barely gotten to the Gulf by now. Don't you waste your trip worrying about them, Mac. They'll be fine."

"Are you trying to convince me, or yourself?"

She laughed. "Both. But let's make a deal. I'll worry and you have fun. You hear me?" I went down to tea thinking that the only thing better than raising two good sons is having both of them marry women you can love.

Laura had gone down before me and was waiting in the lobby.

"Sorry," I told her. "I was calling home. The store is fine, but there's no word from the sailors yet."

"MacDonald Motors is limping along tolerably well

without me, too. Downright humbling, isn't it, how well they can do without us?"

"And Ben?"

"Him, too." She tried to sound casual, but she was rosy and had a smile on her lips. "Let's eat."

Joyce, still watching for Dorothy, declined to join us. "Marcia is having dinner sent to her room," she told us. "Go on in and find yourselves a table."

The hotel was old but very comfortable, and the dining room was large, dark and elegant. If the food lived up to the decor, Joyce hadn't lied about our future meals being better than our first. Brandi, looking chic and expensive in a black sweater and slacks with her hair piled on her head, sat with Kenny and Sherry at a table for six. Since Sherry also wore black, the table looked ready for a funeral—an unfortunate thought with Dorothy still missing. I was glad to see a red jacket over the chair next to Brandi, where she must be saving Jim a seat.

I was about to head their way when Laura pointed out, "If we sit there, Dorothy and Joyce will have to sit together, and that could be awkward. Why don't we take that table for four near the window, where we can watch for Dorothy, too?" Laura has always been nicer than me. My strongest reason for agreeing with her was, I didn't think I could stand another Sherry-and-Kenny duet about Scotland that night.

"What did I miss this afternoon?" I asked when we'd been served a pot of tea and warm, thick scones with butter and blackcurrant jam.

"Not much. Joyce doesn't know a whole lot about Glasgow, but Watty and Kenny helped her out. Every time they stopped to breathe, Sherry told us about a place we'd rather have seen. Finally she and Brandi decided they'd prefer to shop than see more historic sites, so we went to a couple of stores. Joyce and I browsed while they bought everything in sight."

"Jim and Kenny must have loved that."

"They didn't go. Jim had a meeting all afternoon, and Kenny left us at four to go for a fitting with a tailor for a wool suit—"

"Which he'll get lots of wear out of in Savannah—"

She raised one eyebrow. "Who's talking? Aren't those new clothes I see?"

"Just a few things to make sure I survive long enough to get home. Besides, I figure if I have all these heavy woolens, it might inspire Joe Riddley to take me on a Baltic cruise."

"Dream on." She has, after all, known him all her life.

We sat nibbling scones and peering out into the gloom that was descending on the sidewalk. Nightfall, and Dorothy still not home.

With a worried sigh, I tried to concentrate on the menu. "Remind me what haggis is."

"Ground-up unmentionable animal parts mixed with coarse meal and onions, boiled in a sheep's stomach. It's delicious." She chuckled at my expression. "But not for the faint of heart. Try steak and kidney pie. That tastes like steak with gizzards, and I know you like gizzards."

The food lived up to its promise, but we didn't eat as much as we would have if we hadn't been worried about Dorothy. Every time the door to the dining room opened, we both looked up, hoping to see her. We were always disappointed.

After several strangers came and found tables, Jim arrived at the same time as our dessert. We were discussing the wisdom of advising Joyce to call the police when Kenny lifted his head and said, loud enough for the whole dining room to hear, "The truant finally returns."

Dorothy and Joyce stood at the door scanning the room. Joyce's mouth was a tight line but Dorothy had the rosy, happy look of somebody who has just had a wonderful time. Her golden eyes glowed, and when Joyce steered her toward the larger table, she crossed the room like she had a cushion of air beneath her practical soles.

I leaned across the table to ask Laura softly, "Does she have a boyfriend over here?"

Laura shrugged, not knowing any more than I did about our Canadian companions.

Kenny said in a loud, bossy voice, "You really shouldn't go wandering off like that."

Dorothy turned bright red and stumbled as she took her seat.

Sherry gave an elegant shrug. "I told you she could find her way back."

Brandi frowned at Dorothy. "But you really ought to have told Joyce where you were going. She's been very worried."

Jim went right on eating without looking up. As at dinner the night before, he ate like a man who feared this meal might be his last.

"Sorry." Dorothy didn't sound sorry at all. "There was somebody I needed to see. It didn't occur to me that you'd all be worried, eh?" She slid into a vacant chair, pink with embarrassment.

Once Dorothy was settled, Joyce joined our table and dropped into a chair with a huff of relief. Laura motioned our waitress over, and I poured Joyce a cup of tea. She closed her eyes as she savored several swallows, black and hot. Then she spoke with a little moue of disgust. "Herding cats. I should have stuck with being a flight attendant. At least after a flight, everybody leaves."

"Where was she?" I asked.

Joyce's shoulders rose in a shrug. "You heard her. She told me the same—there was somebody she had to see, and she forgot the time. And meanwhile, I stood out there over an hour getting all the grit in Glasgow under my contacts." She bent her head and one by one removed hard lenses, rinsed them in her water glass, and put them back in. Then she blinked a few times and gave us her prim smile. "At least that feels better."

Laura passed her hot scones and jam. "Is this your first tour?"

Joyce's lips twisted into a rueful smile. "Can you tell? It's my first and last." I was surprised and a bit chagrined. It had never occurred to me that we wouldn't have a seasoned, well-informed guide. She heaved a sigh that seemed to come from the soles of her feet. "It all sounded a lot easier than it is."

Laura chuckled. "Most things do. But hey, everybody speaks English, we're all grown-ups, and at least some of us have been to Scotland before. It's going to work out." After that she steered the conversation toward places they'd visited that afternoon. Having nothing to contribute, I listened, and watched.

Around Laura, Joyce relaxed like a woman who has found herself among her own people in a foreign land. Her face lost its uptight expression and her whole demeanor expanded. Even though at least ten years separated them, they were sisters in the casual way they held their bodies, handled silver at the table, and signaled waitresses. Both were obviously daughters of privilege, raised to take it for granted that the comforts of the world were theirs by right.

So what the heck was Joyce doing conducting a low-profit bus tour through the Scottish Highlands?

⟨7⟩

The rest of them went out on a pub crawl that night, but I'm not much for sitting around in bars. Besides, I was ready for my bed. However, between sending up prayer flares for my folks on the Gulf of Mexico and wondering about people on the tour, I didn't sleep much. I kept asking myself why Joyce was leading tours, why Jim and Brandi were on a bus tour rather than riding in a private limousine and staying in five-star hotels, why Kenny and Sherry had come on this tour when there were places they'd rather see at a different time of the year, and why Marcia had come at all when she was so obviously ill. As a group, we seemed several cups short of a gallon.

About the time I drifted off to sleep, Laura's alarm rang. "Just going for a run," she whispered. I dozed again, but never did really sleep. No wonder I felt a tad testy when we gathered at the bus—especially since Joyce had told us the night before to be there half an hour earlier than the schedule said. It didn't cheer me one whit that Laura and Joyce were pink-cheeked from their run. Brandi, Jim, Kenny, and Sherry were late, so the rest of us waited half an hour in the front hall when we could have been sleeping. Then Kenny showed up dressed out in kilt, matching tie, long green socks, white shirt, dark jacket, feathered bonnet, a sporran, and white spats. "Sorry to be late. I misplaced my spats."

From the look Sherry shot him, they'd had one royal spat that morning.

When Brandi and Jim sauntered down, I figured she was late because it took so long to look that good. She was stun-

ning in a green boiled-wool jacket and gray wool slacks—
slacks almost exactly like the new ones I wore, except hers
were five sizes smaller and six times more expensive. She
took one look at Kenny and exclaimed, "You look simply
darlin'! Stand over against that wall so I can take your picture. Now come over here, Sherry, and let me get one of the
two of you."

The rest of us surged out to the waiting bus with our bags.

When Kenny handed the driver their bags, he cocked one
bushy eyebrow at the bag labeled "Bagpipes." "Riddy for a
bit o' music, air ye, lad?"

"Och, aye," Kenny replied. "Thought I'd do a bit of playing on the way, like." In the few hours since we'd gotten to
Scotland, he'd developed an accent. I couldn't tell whether
it was unconscious, affected, or an honest attempt to speak
the language of our host country.

"That's right." The driver rasped one palm along a cheek
that would have been improved by a shave. "We can all do
with a bit o' music on the way north. Dulls the senses so ye
dinna ken ye're leavin' the English-speakin' wor-r-rld." He
hawked and spat out his contempt, but whether it was for the
Highlands or for an American bringing bagpipes to Scotland, I didn't know.

While they had this pleasant little exchange, the rest of us
stood with icy water dripping off our umbrellas and chill
seeping through the soles of our shoes. Still, I found my
blood tingling with excitement. It had finally sunk in. I was
in Scotland!

I joined Brandi in snapping pictures of our sodden fellow
travelers, the bus, even the driver. Brandi would have taken
more pictures if she hadn't noticed Sherry sharing Jim's umbrella as they stowed their violins in the luggage compart-
ment. She hurried to stand by her husband and take the arm
that held his umbrella. I got their picture like that. She looks
dry and friendly. He looks like an iceberg.

"She'll dee well to hang on for dear life," the driver muttered to me as he shuffled back and forth loading bags.

"I sure hope that man lives long enough to finish the
tour," I whispered to Marcia as we waited for him to get
around to our luggage. "He looks about a hundred and ten."

When he put my bags on I slipped him a little tip, mindful I now had two bags instead of one. "Buy yourself a cup of tea," I whispered. It always makes me mad and sad when society doesn't pay people enough for them to retire. I don't mind old people working if they want to, but this work was so arduous, I suspected that was not Watty's case.

He bobbed his head and pocketed the folded pound with a smile.

Kenny boarded last. Joyce took one look at the short sword at his side and the hilt of a knife poking up from his right sock and held out her hand. "No weapons. We'll put them below."

"A piper always wears a dirk and a ski-and-doo," he protested. At least, that's what I thought he said. Laura later informed me the short sword was a *sgian dubh*.

"If you don't turn them in, we don't stop at Loch Lomond."

He pouted, but handed her the weapons. "Be careful with the *sgian dubh*," he admonished. "It's very valuable. The cairngorm in the hilt alone is worth—"

Anybody could see that it might be valuable. The stone was as big as a robin's egg. "I'll stow them safely for you below," Watty offered. Kenny insisted on climbing off the bus and watching where he put them.

Marcia—who had taken the seat in front of me—turned around to say softly, "Now we know why we all had to get up half an hour early. Loch Lomond wasn't on our itinerary."

I nodded. "And from the expression on Joyce's face, she's planning to throw him in."

I scrunched up my toes in soggy shoes and added, "He won't get much wetter than I am already."

Watty, who was climbing back on, heard me and called back, "I doot this bit o' weather'll clair up before we're many miles away up the road."

"The weatherman promised," I called back, indignant. "He said clear skies to the north."

Laura leaned across the aisle to explain softly, "When a Scot says 'I doubt,' it means he doesn't doubt at all. He was agreeing with you. Now be nice."

When Kenny got back on, even though Sherry was sitting just behind the front door, he tromped down the aisle and paused, obviously hoping to sit with Laura. She had her coat beside her on her seat and didn't pick it up. "There's room for everybody to have a seat," she told him, but smiled to take away the sting. He slid into the seat behind her.

After the driver had shut the door, he stood in the aisle and made a little welcoming speech. "For those who cannae read, my name is Watty." We all chuckled along with him, but after that, I didn't understand enough words to make sense of what he said.

"Is he speaking English?" I asked softly.

"Aye," Kenny told me. "He's from Paisley, just outside of Glasgow. They have their own distinctive accent. You'll get used to it."

Maybe if I stayed in Scotland the rest of my life.

I had to admit, though, that Watty was entertaining as he described various attractions we passed. Some of the group were entertained because they could understand him and knew what they were looking at. The rest of us were charmed by the lilt of his voice. Sentences tended to slide down the scale and back up again at the end.

Everybody disembarked at Loch Lomond except Jim and Marcia. He claimed he had work to do, and she was nursing a cold. Watty offered me a hand to help me down. I would have expected his to be callused from all that driving, but it was as soft as my own. "I told ye it'd clair up. Are ye riddy to see some sights noo?" He smelled of cigarettes and chocolate.

"More than ready," I told him. "I've been in Scotland more than twenty-four hours, and all I've seen so far are a hotel and a department store."

"Och, we've a wee bit more to show you than that. Breathe deep. The air is sweet. And yon lake is lovely with the wind drawin' his fingers across her skin."

Not only a driver, but a poet.

The mist was too low for me to see whether the wind was rippling the water's skin or not, but I took breaths of the cold, damp air and smelled mingled fragrances of ever-greens, melted snow, and ancient soil. I stood for two or three minutes just enjoying breathing, wondering if each place has a distinctive smell and what Georgia smells like to people from far away.

Then the clear, fresh scent of Scotland was replaced by a universal one as Watty pulled a crumpled pack of cigarettes from his pocket, offered me one, and—when I refused—lit up. "Nasty habit, this. I'm givin' it up one of these days." He exhaled a ring that rose above his head and floated away. Then he gave me a wink. "Soon's I figure out how to dee that wi' chewin' gum." He moseyed off toward where Kenny was assembling his pipes.

Laura spoke into my ear, "Looks like you've beat Dorothy to it, and found yourself a Highland gentleman."

"He's not a Highland gentleman. He's from Glasgow."

"Still, I think I'd better call Joe Riddley and report."

"If I thought it would bring him running, I'd lend you my phone."

She gave me a sympathetic look. "Are you missing him a lot?"

Only about every five minutes—any time I saw something I wanted him to look at, or heard something he'd get a chuckle out of, or whenever I had to hoist those bags or calculate a price in British money—but I saw no point in putting a damper on her trip. "No, I'm storing up memories so I can bore him to death when I get home."

We strolled down to join Dorothy, Joyce, and Brandi, who all stood peering into the mist. Brandi exclaimed with delight each time an occasional parting showed islands in the middle of the loch.

Kenny settled the bag beneath his arm, stuck the mouthpiece between his lips, placed his fingers on the chanter and gave the bag a squeeze. A squawk soared across the water and into the mist. After the squawk, Kenny solemnly marched up and down the waterside while "Loch Lomond" reverberated among the hills.

I had gotten off the bus to enjoy the scenery and endure the music. I had no inkling that Kenny could play so well, or that his playing would touch something deep and plaintive within me. As the mournful notes rent the air, they created a vivid picture of lost love, sweet memories, and confidence that love survives beyond the grave. By the time the tune died into stillness, tears stung my eyes. "Is he really good," I asked Laura, "or is it just the setting?"

"He's good. He wins competitions all the time." I saw that her eyes were wet and pink, and she dabbed them with a tissue and turned away.

"Oh, honey! Is it your folks you're missing? Or Ben?"

She shook her head and spoke in a voice clogged with tears. "It's Kenny. We talked a while last night, and oh, Mac, he's so unhappy." Now what was I supposed to say to that?

Nothing, as it turned out. Laura must have felt she'd said too much, because she turned and strode off down to the waterside.

Meanwhile, Brandi was applauding. "That was pretty," she called. "What was it?"

"It's called 'Loch Lomond,'" Watty explained. "There's a legend that after the Battle of Culloden, the English chose some at random to be hung and sent ithers walkin' home, and this was written by a soldier who knew he'd be hung. He'd left his true love on these banks, y'ken? So he tells his comrade that by deein', he'll come home to her by the low road and arrive sooner than those who travel yon high road." He jerked one thumb to indicate the road we'd just traveled and began a hoarse rendition of the chorus: "O, ye'll tak the high r-r-road and I'll tak the low r-r-r-oad . . ."

Brandi's eyes widened in recognition. "I've heard that before. Play it again, Kenny." She tilted her head to listen as he played it again. Only Sherry seemed unaffected by his playing. She leaned against the bus, filing her nails.

"That was marvelous!" Brandi set gold bangles ringing as she waved at him. "Now play something cheerful." Kenny obliged.

The breeze was strong enough to penetrate my trench coat and sweater, and I was shivering all over, so when Kenny started a third tune, I decided to head back to the bus.

I found Jim busy at his laptop and Marcia working needlepoint. I slid in behind her and said, "No wonder the pipes are the national instrument of Scotland. What else could send music soaring so far among the hills and over the water?"

"They do sound fine," she agreed.

After a few minutes' silence, I asked, "Are you feeling any better?"

"A bit, perhaps." She produced a slight cough, then gave me a weak smile. "It's nothing for you to worry about, eh?" She returned to her needlework.

"What are you making?"

"Covers for my dining-room chairs. It helps steady my thoughts."

Another silence while I tried to think of something else to say. She didn't make it easy. "It's nice that Dorothy came with you on this trip."

She turned her work and started a row in the other direction. "Actually I only came to bring Dorothy. She's very shy, eh? And even though she's twenty-five, she still lives at home. Except for playing the flute, she's not shown interest in much of anything, but she lit up last summer when I first started talking about coming to Scotland. This spring, I was about to back out of the trip, but she asked if she could come with me, so I decided to come after all. I hope that seeing a bit of the world might inspire her to spread her wings and begin to live a bit."

Something she herself had said sent a spasm of pain across Marcia's face. Before I could reply, she had given a pained little "Oh!" and closed her eyes. Then she pressed her lips together and laid her head back against the seat as if life had become too heavy to bear.

"Are you all right?" I asked.

She nodded and murmured, "I will be in a few minutes."

If I'd been a nurse, perhaps I could have helped her. As it was, I looked out my window at the loch in the mist and felt utterly useless.

I also felt cold. The heat was dissipating from the bus, and my toes were already numb.

The others came back about two minutes before I froze to my seat.

We stopped for morning coffee in a small village, with time to visit a few shops. I invited Marcia to join me, but she claimed she didn't feel well enough. "Maybe tomorrow," she promised with another slight cough.

I didn't think she had a cold, though. I hadn't heard her sneeze once, and never saw her lift a tissue to her nose. Still, something was dreadfully wrong. Her eyes were huge in her face, her skin drawn so tightly over her bones it looked like it would crack any minute.

Finding myself alone with Dorothy briefly in a wool shop, I asked her privately, "Do you know if something's the matter with Marcia besides her cold? I mean, is she really ill and should we know it in case we need to get her to a doctor?"

Dorothy's eyes grew sad. "No, she's grieving. Her husband—a wonderful man, eh?—died right after Christmas, and it was a dreadful shock. He had cancer, but they never knew until three weeks before he died. Poor Marcia, they were very close, and she is wasting away with grief."

She reached out and stroked a plaid wool blanket. "Nice rug, isn't it?" the clerk asked.

Dorothy nodded with satisfaction. "This will be just the thing for my mum and dad."

I bought one for each of my daughters-in-law, as well, choosing Martha's because it was her family plaid and Cindy's because it would match her color scheme. Gradually, I am getting to know what they prefer.

When we got back to the bus, I stowed mine in my new suitcase, but Dorothy shook hers out and handed it to Marcia. "There. Wrap up in that and keep warm when you stay on the bus, eh?" I wished I'd thought of that.

Marcia thanked her and wrapped up in the blanket right away, then turned her head toward the window to avoid further conversation. As we headed north, I watched her reflection. She stared at the hills and sky with greedy eyes, like she could not get enough of looking.

৪ 8 ৬

After the murder, the Auchnagar police sergeant would ask me, "Do ye ken if the victim had any enemies among your group? Did you feel any tensions, like?"

"We had lots of tensions," I would admit, "but I didn't expect any of them to end in murder."

From Loch Lomond, we drove north to Glen Coe. Watty seemed to know a lot more about the region than Joyce did, so he kept up a running commentary. When we reached a stretch where mountains rose above bogs, hummocks, boulders and water that stretched to the mountain's very roots, he called with obvious pride, "R-r-rannoch Moor-r-r." A sweep of his arm sent the bus lurching over the center line toward an oncoming car. He righted it just in time.

" 'As waste as the sea: only the moorfowl and the pee-wees cryin' upon it,' " he called, " 'and far over to the east, a herd of deer, moving like dōts.' " When most of us immediately jumped up to look out the right windows, he cackled. "R-r-robert Louis Stevenson wr-r-rote that in *Kidnapped*. It hasna changed much, as ye can see. If you dinnae spot deer noo, ye'll see some soon enough. Next stop, Glen Coe."

As soon as we climbed down from the bus at Glen Coe, Dorothy set off alone down a narrow track like she was being drawn by an invisible beam, with the same spring in her step she'd had in Glasgow. Brandi said what the rest of us were thinking: "She looks like she's going to meet somebody."

Kenny wasn't watching Dorothy. He was too busy taking Laura's arm.

When he turned toward the glen, Sherry frowned at him and objected, "I want us to check out the shops."

"Go on. I'll be there after a while." He gave Laura what I could only call a fatuous smile, and pulled her closer to him. "I don't want Laura, here, wandering around alone and running into a Campbell."

Sherry glared at her husband. "There is nothing funny about a massacre." Her voice was sharp.

"Besides," Laura added, "I doubt there are any Campbells around." She removed Kenny's hand from her arm and stepped away from him.

I was just irritated enough with him and Sherry both to clap both palms to my cheeks and exclaim, "Oh, dear, I think my daddy's grandmother was a Campbell. Is that bad?"

Watty flapped one hand. "Dinna fash yerselves. The massacre's a matter of three hundred years and more. Go enjoy. Buy souvenirs. Improve the economy." He waved us all away like chickens and shuffled back to the bus.

Sherry began walking purposefully toward the shops, calling over one shoulder, "Come *on,* Kenny. I want to shop."

"Go." Laura gave him a little push. "I'm in no danger from Mac. Besides, my family came from Uist and Skye." Kenny took off after his wife, kilt rippling against his calves.

When he was gone, though, Laura frowned down at me. "You never mentioned you had a Campbell in your family."

"I don't. I just couldn't resist that, the way they were carrying on."

"It was none of your business." She turned on one heel and strode away.

Brandi hurried after her, exuding waves of exotic perfume. "Laura? Wait up. Would you show me around and tell me about the massacre? I don't know a thing about it, and Jimmy's staying on the bus."

I watched them go and felt a twinge of distress. I couldn't ever remember quarreling with Laura, and while what I had done wasn't nice, her response seemed out of proportion. I hoped she had better sense than to be renewing her old interest in Kenny Boyd.

Abandoned, I walked alone up the glen. Laura's voice came back to me in snatches carried by a brutal wind. ". . . sixteen ninety-two . . . wouldn't swear . . . invited to dinner . . . women and children. . . ."

I pulled my collar tight against my throat, shivering not just from cold. An odor of death and betrayal seemed to hover just beneath the thick gray clouds in the lowering sky. Snow capped the mountains, and shifting waves of mist made them look remote and menacing. I'd read the story before I left home, so as I walked, I tried to imagine the glen as it had been in 1692. I saw the old chief, looking a bit like Watty, first refusing to swear loyalty to the King of England, then changing his mind and setting off through February snow to Inverness, leaving his people behind. As I wandered farther and farther from the parking lot, I pictured the Campbells arriving in force, pretending to be friends and accepting the hospitality of the MacDonalds, whose homes would have been scattered all up and down the glen. I left the main path and followed a track uphill, trying to get a vantage point where I could see the whole sweep of the valley. But when I got to imagining the actual massacre, picturing the Campbells rising before dawn intending to wipe out every man, woman and child in the glen, I felt so weak, I had to lean against a nearby stone.

The valley certainly made a perfect trap. Cliffs rose three thousand feet on both sides, and the hills at the end were too rugged to be easily crossed. What panic there must have been! What terror! And what despair as women watched their children hacked down before the murderers turned on them. If there ever was a place imprinted with a day of destruction, this was it.

To add to the eeriness, the whole time I'd been walking a thick mist had drifted down from the hills, cold and clammy as death itself. Now, in an instant, the mist fell like a curtain to my feet and somewhere in the distance, pipes began to play. Mournful notes wailed from hill to hill. I could rationally tell myself there was a live piper—probably Kenny—

playing somewhere up the glen. It was easier to believe that the music was floating from beyond history to mourn the massacre at Glen Coe.

"This is spooky," I said aloud. Like my daddy used to say, "You have to talk to yourself occasionally, to be sure of getting some intelligent conversation." I hunched up in my coat and put out a hand, but I couldn't even see it at the end of my arm, much less the track that led down to the path I'd come in on. The boulder against which I leaned was all that was left of the world. As I peered through the whiteness for any familiar landmark and saw none, terror rose in me.

"You are in the middle of a national tourist attraction surrounded by other visitors," I reminded myself. At the moment, however, I was utterly alone and increasingly nervous. People did get lost and wander away from civilization, even in national tourist attractions.

I stood for several minutes hoping the mist would lift, but it merely got wetter and colder. To shore up my courage, I called out into the white nothingness a poem I once memorized in German and translated myself:

> *"Strange to wander in the mist,*
> *lonely is each bush and stone,*
> *each bough by its brothers missed,*
> *every one alone."*

"Mac?" Dorothy's voice floated down toward me. The way the mist distorted sound, I couldn't tell how far away she was.

"Here," I called back, trying to sound more confident than I felt. "Where are you?"

I heard her say, "That's someone from my tour. I'd better go. Will you come, too?"

A man's voice replied, "No, I'll stay. This will let up eventually."

"Keep talking, Mac," Dorothy called, "so I can find you."

For once I couldn't think of a thing to say. Finally I began to belt out "O Come, All Ye Faithful," the only song I could think of at the moment. I'd reached the second verse when

Dorothy loomed up right next to my rock, her face glowing like it had been in Glasgow.

"A bit disconcerting this, eh? But don't you just yearn to paint everything you see?"

"If I could see anything and I could paint, I might," I conceded, "but I'd prefer something a whole lot more cheerful. Who were you talking to?"

"Some chap I met," she said carelessly. "He's on a walking tour. Do you have any idea which way we go to get back?"

"Not really. I can scarcely see you, much less the path." I peered for a hint about which direction to take. That clammy whiteness was penetrating all my layers to the bone.

We both strained our eyes and saw nothing. We called, and heard nothing.

"Should we just start walking downhill and hope we find the path?" Dorothy wondered. "Or do you think we could get really lost? They wouldn't leave without us, would they?"

If I was her designated Captain Courageous, she had made a poor choice. I didn't feel brave at all. Still, I made a stab at reasonable thought. "Watty can't see to drive, and Joyce wouldn't dare desert us on the first day out. Since we know that one end of the glen is all mountains, we might as well start walking. We'll go downhill as far as we can, and turn left. If we start going uphill, we'll know we've gotten turned around, and head back." It sounded wise, but I knew we could wander up and down all day and never find our way out through the fog.

Still, having nothing better to do, we took hands and began to feel our way through the cold, clammy cloud. Single file, clutching each other as much for comfort as for safety, we stumbled blindly downhill until we found what was little more than a deer track, studded with rocks. It didn't look at all familiar, but we followed it down, grateful that it was lined on each side by clumps of heather that bounced us back like sponge rubber if we veered off the path.

About two lifetimes later a slight breeze swayed the mist enough for me to see an outcropping of rock below us that

looked familiar. "I think we're going right." I was so relieved, tears choked my voice.

"But let's don't let go one another's hands quite yet,"
Dorothy begged.

Looking for something to talk about, I asked, "Do you
paint?"

"I used to." She bit off the words as if she regretted them,
then rushed on like they had been the cork in her bottle. "I
started college as an art major, and I'd paint all day long
if—oh, sorry!" She fell, nearly taking me down with her. I
helped her to her feet and she dusted off her knees. "I've
torn my pants," she mourned. "Don't tell Marcia"—I
thought she meant about her pants, until she continued—
"but I'm only a librarian because my parents urged me to
take up something where I could earn my living, eh? If I
were independently wealthy, I'd paint all day."

"But eventually each of us has to do what we are called
to, not what our parents or anybody else wants us to do," I
told her bluntly. "If you've got talent, don't let it atrophy.
The world needs artists as much as it needs librarians." It's
real easy to give advice when you are both lost in a fog.

"But I don't know if I have the talent or courage . . ." I
couldn't tell if she was speaking to me or herself, and she
dwindled off into silence as we navigated a tricky part of the
path that went straight down into nothing.

Every second was a literal step of faith. When we reached
the bottom without turning an ankle or falling into some
abyss, we stopped, panting as if we'd been climbing up instead of going down. I dropped to a nearby boulder with a
silent prayer of thanks. Dorothy stood peering into the mist
and taking deep, joyful breaths. "Isn't this marvelous?" she
said in an awed whisper.

Suddenly, I heard a voice I ought to recognize, full of ir-
ritation and sounding like it was right beside us. "Don't
worry about the title. I told you, I've got it. Don't worry
about how. That's none of your business. Are you absolutely
sure about the other parcel?"

It took a minute to remember that voices carry in fog. It
took longer to figure out why the other person didn't answer.

Dorothy was quicker than me. "That sounds like Jim. He must be on his cell phone."

"The title is secure," Jim snapped. "It's my business how I did it. Your job is to smooth out the wrinkles on your end. Did you line up the lawyer in Inverness?"

After another pause, Jim's voice rose in a series of expletives that made me want to cover Dorothy's ears. He followed them with, "I told you Inverness. If you can't do it right, I'll do it myself."

I couldn't tell how far away he was, and didn't want him to think we were eavesdropping if we stumbled into him, so I raised my voice. "Dorothy, are you trying to inhale that mist?"

Jim's voice immediately grew lower and moved away.

Dorothy and I wandered for several more minutes before the mist finally began to lift and we spied the path up ahead. Dorothy turned to look back at the steep hills reappearing from behind the cloud and spread her arms wide like Julie Andrews in *The Sound of Music*. "Beautiful, wonderful mountains, I want to stay and paint you forever!"

I spread my arms and cried, "Blessed, ugly bus, I want to get on you and ride out of this place as soon as possible."

Dorothy laughed. "Come on, let's go look for souvenirs."

"No, I think I'll get on the bus." I hoped she couldn't see how I was trembling. I am old enough to realize that people do get lost forever, in fogs of various kinds. I wanted no souvenirs of that place.

Watty was dozing with his arms crossed on the wheel and his head on his arms. Marcia slept with her head on a pillow propped against a window. I read.

After a few minutes, Jim climbed onto the bus. Drops clung to his coat and hair and he brushed them from his sleeves. "Damned mist. I'd forgotten all about it."

I called softly, "Have you seen Scotland before?" Although that didn't seem quite the appropriate question, since he wasn't seeing much of it this time.

He barked a short laugh. "Once." Then he picked up his laptop and slid into his seat.

Something about that frozen syllable irked me into chattering. "We came about twenty years ago. We saw most of what we'll be seeing on this trip, but I hadn't researched our family then, so we didn't know to visit Auchnagar. I'm really looking forward to seeing it."

"Not much to see. Sheep, hills, boiled vegetables, more sheep."

That put the lid on my mayonnaise. He opened his laptop. I picked up my book.

9

Our second night we stayed in Fort William, at Gilroy's Hotel. I asked Watty, "Are this hotel and Gilroy's Tearoom, where we ate lunch, connected with Gilroy's Highland Tours?"

"Och, it's a common name, Gilroy," he told me with a shrug of one scruffy shoulder.

However, the hotel was clean and comfortable, and empty enough that Laura and I decided to pay extra and take separate rooms, because she usually liked to go to bed early, while I liked to read late. Then she crawled out of bed at ungodly hours to exercise.

That night, though, when I went up to bed, she and Kenny were sitting on a sofa by the fire discussing Highland Games they had attended in years past. Sherry went upstairs at the same time I did, leaving them to their reminiscences.

I dragged myself out of bed Friday still feeling like seven-thirty was the middle of the night. As I took my seat at breakfast, I shuddered at the volume of conversation around the table. Watty had found a gym in town that let nonmembers use it, so Joyce, Laura, and even Brandi had gone for a workout before breakfast. They had come back indecently wide awake, with Brandi boasting, "Joyce benchpressed two hundred pounds!"

The only weight I wanted to lift right then was blankets up to my chin. I leaned over and reminded Laura, "My life clock is set on Eastern Standard Time, so if I die over here, somebody owes me five more hours."

I staggered onto the bus figuring I could doze until our

first stop. I hadn't counted on the sun, the scenery, or the Scotophiles. By now we were really in the Highlands. To a chorus of "oohs" and "aahs" we rolled past a succession of pastures, lochs, and stark mountains sporting caps and streaks of snow, and through villages built of square gray stucco houses with dark slate roofs, looking like they had been rifled from a Monopoly game. Watty and Kenny pointed out special sites while Sherry informed us how much better they would look in summer, winter, or fall. Some of the places Watty named sounded so different from what was written in my guidebook, I concluded that to speak Gaelic you need a limber tongue and a sense of humor.

Brandi and Dorothy kept dashing from side to side to snap pictures. I took a few, but had just decided to doze and buy a coffee-table book when Brandi shouted, "Oh, look at those adorable calves!" I pointed my camera obediently at a field of shaggy Highland cattle with enormous horns, standing next to offspring that looked like brown wooly bears.

If I had been nominating candidates for Person I'd Most Like to Shoot Before We Leave Scotland, Brandi would have won first place that morning. She "adored" everything she saw with indiscriminate passion, until even Jim finally got enough and ordered her to shut up. She subsided for at least two minutes before exclaiming, "But, honey, look at those adorable lambs!"

I personally had already seen enough lambs to last me a lifetime, and was getting mighty tired of my companions. I gazed wistfully at a small stone house sitting in isolated splendor miles from everybody, and thought, *Those people could go for days without seeing another soul.*

I didn't realize I'd spoken aloud until Marcia turned in the seat ahead of me. "Do you know Yeats's poem 'The Lake Isle of Innisfree'?" When I shook my head, she quoted it softly. It was so lovely that I pulled out our itinerary and wrote the name on the back, so I could look for it at a bookstore. I especially liked the part about living all alone in a "bee-loud glade."

"That or one of those little stone houses would suit me fine," I told her.

"Crofts. They are called crofts." Kenny entered the conversation from across the aisle and back one seat. He had slid in behind Laura again that morning, but she had currently moved up to speak with Brandi about something.

As long as he was interrupting, I might as well ask him a question. "What's this see-lid thing?" I pointed to the word "ceilidh" on our schedule for that evening.

"It's 'cay-ley,'" he told me. "In Gaelic, 'dh' is silent, like 'gh' in our word 'night.' A ceilidh is a music program—which reminds me, I wonder if Joyce knows who's playing. I hope they aren't all amateurs." He got up and swayed forward to take the bench behind the one Laura had moved into, then called his question up to Joyce.

I didn't hear what Joyce said, but could tell from her tone that she spoke sharply. I couldn't blame her. Kenny had shown up in his kilt again, and twice had held us up by getting out to play when Watty had simply pulled over for a quick stop.

"I hadn't realized we'd signed up for the piper's tour," I muttered to Marcia when he was out of earshot. "I like the pipes, but am getting infernally tired of the piper."

"He's a pest," Marcia agreed.

Dorothy, behind me, leaned up to suggest softly, "If Joyce still has those knives she took from him, maybe we could find them and cut off his head."

Marcia asked across me, "Are you playing tonight?"

Dorothy nodded. "If they'll have me."

"She plays the flute," Marcia explained to me, "and they'll have her. She's good."

Watty pulled off the road. "Fifteen minutes to admire the Five Sisters of Kintail," he announced. Even Jim put away his computer and got off with the rest of us.

I don't know what I had expected to see, but it certainly involved women. Instead, the "sisters" were five mountains in a row. Watty came over to where I stood snapping their picture and jerked his head in Jim's direction. "Ye'd almaist think he was a r-r-real tour-r-rist."

With the wind mussing his hair and a drip of moisture forming at the tip of his nose, Jim did look less formidable. Less elegant, too, in tan corduroy pants and a worn brown leather jacket. Brandi, of course, was still gorgeous in a

short camel's-hair coat and peacock blue pants. When she
ran gracefully down to the shore and bent to pick up another
granite stone for a growing collection that was going to be
mighty heavy to carry home, Watty left me and drifted down
to chat with Jim. I couldn't hear Watty's words, but Jim's
reply was audible.

"Och, no. Just in a geography book, like. But they're nae
bad, are they?" Which, I was coming to realize, was high
praise in Scotland. Like Kenny's, Jim's accent was growing
richer the longer we were there. I wondered if musical people unconsciously picked up accents and, if so, how Jim
could maintain his Scottish accent in the north Georgia
mountains.

A short time later Watty announced, "We're comin' up on
Eilean Donan Castle noo. We're runnin' a bit late. Are ye
still wantin' to stop?"

"I certainly am," Sherry answered before Joyce could.
"This is my ancestral home."

"I'd better go in, too, to commune with the spirits of our
common ancestors," I joked softly to Marcia and Dorothy.
"My maternal grandmother was a MacKenzie—probably a
kitchen maid."

"You may be disappointed," Marcia warned. "I've read
that this castle isn't very old. It was blown up in 1719 and
not restored until the twentieth century. They didn't finish
rebuilding it until 1932, I believe. I'm going to stay on the
bus and rest a bit."

Once again, Jim accompanied Brandi. As we prepared to
leave the bus, Joyce requested, "Keep it to one hour, please.
We have a lot to see today."

Old or new, Eilean Donan was the castle depicted on the
cover of my guidebook, sitting on a small island out in a
loch, and was even prettier than its picture. Feeling a bit
proud and proprietary, I snapped a couple of pictures and
headed for the bridge. Even knowing that the castle wasn't
really old didn't diminish the fun of seeing how people may
have lived hundreds of years before and what was purported
to be a lock of Bonnie Prince Charlie's hair.

We all hurried as requested, except Kenny and Sherry. It
was nearly two hours before Joyce could drag them back to

the bus, and they arrived without their customary bags of souvenirs, both faces flushed. The way Sherry glared at Kenny's back as he climbed aboard, I was surprised he didn't burst into flame. He came back to sit behind Laura again and said with a little laugh as he dropped into his seat, "Had a bit of a dustup with the cashier in the shop. Took us a while to sort it out."

Before we stopped for our noon meal—at another Gilroy's Tearoom—Joyce announced in a strained voice, "To get to Dunvegan Castle and on to Portree by teatime, please eat quickly."

"But I want to stop in Kyle of Lochalsh," Sherry objected. "There's a jeweler there I particularly want to visit. And what does it matter when we get to Portree, so long as we're there for the ceilidh at eight? Or we could skip Dunvegan."

By then I'd had enough of Sherry and Kenny dictating our schedule. "Laura is meeting cousins in Portree for tea," I called, "and I particularly want to see Dunvegan. My guidebook says there are seals there, and I've never seen a live seal except in the zoo."

"Atta girl," Marcia said softly over her shoulder, and Dorothy leaned up to give me a pat. Laura, however, threw me a look I could not read, then turned to look out her window.

For those who don't know, Dunvegan is a large granite castle on the northwest corner of Skye, and sits squarely above the sea. It lies nearly fifty miles from Kyle of Lochalsh, where you cross from the mainland to the island, and the only way there is a tortuous, narrow road up along the Cullins, some of the most spectacular mountains in Scotland. Poor Watty was driving right into the sun, but none of the rest of us minded the drive, for the weather was superb, with huge puffy clouds that cast lavender and dark purple shadows on the gray hills.

"We could live here," I leaned up to suggest to Marcia. "I haven't seen a soul in miles."

She nodded, then her eyes brimmed with tears. "I've got

a bit of a headache," she said, getting to her feet. "I think I'll go lie down on the back bench."

Watty stopped occasionally to point out places of interest, but the wind was so strong that most of us stayed on the bus and looked out the window. Kenny invariably got off, marched up and down, and played the "Skye Boat Song." After his third rendition, Dorothy leaned up and asked me softly, "Do you suppose anybody has ever been murdered with a bagpipe?"

When we got to Dunvegan, Kenny climbed off the bus and held out a hand to Laura. "Come on, fair wench, let's go look for seals."

Sherry's glare was enough to daunt the stoutest of heart. Laura shook her head. "Thanks, but I'm sticking with Mac, here. She's the seal lady." I sure was relieved to see several frolicking near the shore. Seals aren't the sort of thing you can command at will.

Everybody but Joyce, Jim, and Brandi decided to look at seals before touring the castle. As usual, Kenny and Sherry led the way. Over one shoulder he lectured us on the life cycle and habits of seals while she punctuated his lecture with laments that these seals weren't as numerous or as active as those they'd seen on other visits.

I finally got so irritated by both Boyds' pontificating that I said, "I need to get out of the wind," and headed for protected, sun-warmed rocks. Laura and Dorothy joined me and we sat with our arms around our knees, delighted by what we agreed was an adequate number of reasonably active seals.

"Look at them pushing and shoving, like a bunch of kindergarten children!" Dorothy's laugh rang out over the water. She seemed a lot less shy since our time together in Glen Coe. "I was reading about Skye last night, and while this was the MacLeod castle, there were a lot of MacDonalds about. Just think, Laura, hundreds of years ago some of your ancestors may have sat on these very rocks looking at those seals' ancestors." She opened a sketchbook she'd bought that morning, and brought out a pencil. She looked real pretty that afternoon with the wind ruffling loose tendrils of hair around her face, her cheeks pink as her parka, and her gold eyes dancing at the seals' antics.

Laura gave a lazy chuckle. "Seals may have *been* my ancestors. The Scots believe in Selkies—seals who can take off their skins and become human. There's at least one folktale about a seal who married a fisherman and had seven children. Who's to say her husband and children weren't MacDonalds?"

"Tell us the story," I suggested. I knew she'd heard the story from her daddy. Skye MacDonald had loved Scottish fairy tales.

She stretched out her long legs. "Well, once upon a time a fisherman came upon a crowd of Selkies sunning without their pelts. Never had he seen anything so beautiful. Their skin was soft and pale, their eyes bright. And on a nearby rock lay a pile of soft seal pelts. The fisherman thought, 'If I could have just one of those, I'd be warm forever. If I could get several, I could sell them and buy enough food for the winter.' So he crept toward the pile of pelts. The Selkies saw him, though, and got there first. He could only grab one before they seized the rest and plunged back into the sea. As he was going back to his house, he heard someone weeping behind him. He turned and saw a beautiful naked woman following him with tears streaming down her cheeks. 'Oh, please, give me my pelt,' she begged. Instead, he took her home and married her. They had seven children, and he was very happy.'"

"I'll bet *he* was," I said sourly, "but I'll also bet the poor Selkie was sad."

"She was," Laura agreed. "Although she loved her children, she yearned to return to the sea. One day, when they were alone in the house, the youngest child asked her mother, 'Why do you weep so, Mother?' She replied, 'I am wishing I had a nice sealskin to make you a new winter coat.' The little girl said, 'I know where Daddy is hiding one. Up in the rafters of the room where we sleep. Sometimes he creeps up there when he thinks we are sleeping, pulls it down and strokes it. Then he thrusts it back up above the rafter.'"

"Poor man," Dorothy said softly. "He must have loved her very much."

"He also held her prisoner," I pointed out, shading my face from the sun.

"There is that," Laura agreed again, "but he probably knew what would happen, too, if she ever found it. When the Selkie retrieved her pelt, she kissed her child goodbye and ran toward the sea. The last sight the child had of her was as she turned on the shore, waved, and plunged beneath the waves. On lovely days, though, when the children went down to the beach, they would see a large seal riding the waves not too far out. It would lift a flipper while its eyes streamed tears—for seals cry salt tears, just as humans do, and she truly did miss her children." Her voice sounded a little choked up and her face was turned away. I suspected she was missing her daddy a whole lot right then.

"Well told!" I applauded. "And you're real normal for somebody with both intermarriage and seals in her ancestry."

Laura took a mock bow and barked like a seal.

"If you're going to tour the castle, it's time to begin," Joyce called down to us.

Laura got up and brushed the seat of her pants. "You all coming? They've got another lock of Bonnie Prince Charlie's hair, and a great dungeon."

"I've been here before and one castle a day is enough," I told her. "I'll stay here."

"And I'd like to draw a bit longer." Dorothy's pencil moved rapidly on her paper.

I sat enjoying the sun on my face and tried to ignore the stored winter's chill creeping up through my bottom. That was the afternoon I formulated the MacLaren Theory of Foreign Travel: *There is no law that says you have to learn something every single minute of your vacation.*

Watching how absorbed Dorothy was in drawing, I asked drowsily, "Were you off drawing in Glasgow when you disappeared?"

"No, I went to the St. Mungo Museum of Religious Life and Art. I've had a print of Salvador Dali's *Christ of St. John of the Cross* over my desk for years, and on our flight, I read in the airline magazine that the original was there. I couldn't come all this way and not see it, eh? It was simply magnificent!" Dorothy was never so animated as when she talked about art. She continued drawing and I basked in the sun. I don't know how long we sat there, but I was getting ready to abandon fresh air in favor of getting warm when we were startled by a shout. I sat up. Down the beach, Sherry and Kenny faced off near the water's edge.

Kenny waved his arms in the air while Sherry stood with hands on her hips. Both were yelling. The wind carried some of their words. ". . . crazy!" Kenny shouted.

Whatever Sherry replied ended, ". . . so help me . . . again . . . kill you!" She shook one long forefinger in his face.

He grabbed it and jerked upward.

She yelled with pain and yanked free. Then she whirled and stalked away.

He bent and picked up a stone.

"Hey!"

I don't think Kenny knew Dorothy and I were there until I yelled. Either the yell deflected his aim or he was a poor pitcher, because the stone hit the water to Sherry's right. She whirled at the splash. What happened next was too fast for me to be certain about, but I think her foot slipped and she fell in. I do know that Kenny threw back his head and laughed.

She screamed in shock and anger. No wonder. That sea must be full of melted snow. As she struggled to get up, Kenny ran toward her with one hand outstretched, as if to push her back.

"Hey!" I yelled again, scrabbling to my feet as fast as I could.

He looked around, then caught her hand and jerked her up, as if that had been his intent all along. When I got there, Sherry stood on the shore streaming water. Her hair was plastered to her back and she trembled like a paint-mixing machine.

"She slipped," Kenny told me.

She yanked her hand free of his. Her lips were blue. Her teeth chattered. Her hair hung in wet strings down her back, and the warm tartan cape she always wore clung to her in soaked, icy folds.

"We saw the whole thing," I warned. Since Kenny made no move to offer her his coat, I whipped off mine. "Here, let's get you back to the bus, and if we can find Watty, you can get some dry clothes."

She tugged off her cape and wrung it until water streamed between her fingers. Without a word she handed it to me and squeezed water from her hair. Finally she reached for my coat and wrapped it around her without an ounce of gratitude or grace. Hearing her teeth continue to chatter, I wished again I had brought that dratted liner.

"So help me, one day I'll kill you!" she hissed at Kenny before she turned and trudged toward the bus, leaving me to carry her sodden, briny cape.

Kenny set off along the water's edge, making himself scarce.

Dorothy watched him go with a troubled face. "Do you think he really meant to hit her with that rock?"

"Looked that way to me." I held the cape out so it wouldn't soak me too badly. "I'd better get back to the bus, too, or you'll have to carry me in one frozen cube."

I went so fast that I overtook Sherry halfway. When I came abreast, she flung short, angry sentences at me, willing to confide in anybody to get her grievance off her chest. "That fool maxed out a credit card. Embarrassed me to death when I tried to use it. Who knows what'll happen now? I warned him to use more than one. Did he listen? Of course not. He's not even sorry. I think he hopes—" She broke off, pulled my coat tighter, and squished along, polluting the fresh, clean air with huffs of fury and contempt.

On the bus, Marcia seemed to have recovered from her headache, for she was back in her seat working needlepoint while Watty dozed in the driver's seat. "I need my suitcase," Sherry snapped when he looked up drowsily to answer our knock. "I fell in the water."

He took one look at us both and swung down with more speed than I'd have suspected he had in him. As soon as he lifted the luggage door, Sherry snatched up a suitcase and set off for the castle at an angry lope. Watty looked at me, shivering in my sweater and holding the soaking cape. "Looks like you need something war-r-rm, as well."

I spoke through chattering teeth. "If you'll hand me that black suitcase, I bought some wool blankets this morning. One of them would feel real good right now." Since Martha was a nurse, I figured she wouldn't mind hers being used to save my life before I gave it to her.

Warmly wrapped, I climbed onto the bus, plopped Sherry's cape in her usual seat by the door, and willed my teeth to be still. Watty climbed aboard and started the engine. "Sit near the heater," he ordered. I maybe should have protested at the waste of gasoline, but I didn't. Instead, I slid into the seat behind him, since the heater worked better in front than in back. He reached for his thermos and poured strong black tea into the lid. "This'll warm you." I drank it greedily and gratefully. Who cared how long it was since that cup was washed?

When I gave it back to him, I tried to slip him another pound note, but he waved it away. "Och, no. You keep it. It was nothing."

"What happened?" Marcia called.

Encouraged by a sign of interest from her, I turned sideways in my seat and filled them both in.

"So you dinna see the castle?" Watty asked.

"No, but I saw it years ago, so I decided to stay by the water. I watched seals while Dorothy drew." I hugged myself to get warmer. The heater seemed slow, and in spite of the blanket and my sweater, goose bumps still ran up and down my spine.

"Drew?" Marcia's needle jabbed the fabric. "I never saw her pick up a pencil except to doodle until we got over here, eh? You don't think she's using that pad to hide behind, so she doesn't have to talk to people, do you?" She peered at me over glasses she wore for close work. "She's very shy, you know."

"She seems willing enough to talk the rest of the time," I said cautiously.

Marcia snipped her thread. "Well, I don't understand this drawing mania. It's very new." She started a new color and and expressed disapproval with every jab of her needle.

Without another word she continued to sew while Watty dozed and I tried to picture myself somewhere warm. All I could see was a boat on a sunny gulf with my husband and son standing on a deck with fishing poles while two little boys ran wild. Then I saw that boat starting to sink while Joe Riddley and the others waved goodbye. I could hardly breathe.

I forced air into my lungs and reminded myself I had chosen not to worry about them. In only—what, four days? I could give them a call. Until then, I'd have to steer my imagination in other directions. So I looked over toward the sea and tried to imagine how I would feel if I were a mother on the Scottish shore looking toward the new world that had swallowed my children.

I turned to Marcia and called back impulsively, "Can you imagine the courage it took to separate your family across an ocean, knowing you would most likely never see each other again? Our ancestors were braver souls than I am— both those who went and those who stayed."

She gave a queer little gulp and lifted her hands to cover her face. Next thing I knew, tears were dripping between her fingers while her shoulders heaved.

"Oh, honey, I'm sorry!" I could have kicked myself to yonder and back. How could I prattle on to a new widow about somebody going away and never coming back?

She shook her head and gasped, "This trip was a dreadful mistake. I just don't think I can endure it." When I started to join her, she waved me back. "I need to be alone, eh?"

The next half hour until the others returned were some of the longest minutes of my trip.

As Dorothy climbed aboard, I touched her arm. "I inadvertently said something to upset Marcia a lot," I said softly. "Could you go back and see if she's all right?"

"Of course."

Then I noticed her notebook and decided to be nosy. "May I see what you drew?"

She turned a faint pink, but opened her pad like an obedient child. The page was full of charming sketches of splashing seals, two children on the beach and, on a distant rock, a woman who looked remarkably like Laura, emerging from a seal's skin. "I'm no artist, but those look real good to me, honey," I told her.

Kenny, who had paused to talk with Watty, looked over her shoulder and agreed. "Hey, you're good!"

Dorothy threw me a distressed look. "They're just sketches." She grabbed the pad and hurried back to the seat I usually had, behind Marcia, where she sat clutching her drawings to her chest while she spoke softly. I couldn't tell if Marcia was listening. She had her head back again and her reddened eyelids resolutely closed.

Sherry was the last to return. She'd changed into a warm sweater and slacks and exchanged wet boots for sheepskin slippers lined with fleece. She handed over my damp coat with a curt, "Thanks," then turned to glare at Kenny, who was sitting behind Laura again. With a huff of disgust, she climbed over her wet cape and slumped against the window.

I decided to stay where I was for the ride to Portree. Since Sherry was just across the aisle, I had a good view of her the whole way. She glared at the narrow road ahead like she was daring the future to arrive.

10

Friday night, we stayed at another Gilroy's Hotel in Portree. Unlike American chains, where you can travel from city to city and find almost identical facilities, Gilroy's seemed to have bought up small local hotels and converted them, while retaining their own essential character. This one was cozy and charming, so small that the lobby and a large dining room occupied most of the downstairs, separated by broad double doors.

Before I dressed for the ceilidh, I had time to call our store. My son Ridd answered with good news. "We heard from Daddy and the boys. They're having a great time. Crick caught the biggest fish today, and Tad says he's learning to steer the boat. Neither boy wants to come back Sunday. Tad says he's ready to become a beach bum forever. Oh, and Daddy said when you called, to tell you all three sentinels are on duty, whatever that means."

I hung up and put on the gladdest rags I had with me—a long black velvet skirt and a frilly white blouse, topped by a warm wool stole in the MacLaren tartan, pinned with a cairngorm brooch. I'd bought the stole and brooch that very afternoon with some of Joe Riddley's gift money. I fluffed my hair, fixed my face, and headed down feeling real spiffy.

I almost retreated to my room again at the blended odors of hot wool and alcohol welling up to greet me. Like I said, I'm not much on sitting around in bars. The whole place smelled like a bar that evening, and every living soul remaining in the Highlands seemed to have driven to Portree

for the ceilidh. I hadn't realized this was such an event—
and wondered if our musicians did.

Before going into the dining room, I stepped outside for
a breath of air. In the parking lot I saw three other buses labeled "Gilroy's Highland Tours." All were big, shiny and
new. Poor Watty, I suspected they were putting him and
Jeannie the bus out to pasture together.

I pushed my way into the dining room. A number of musicians—including our four—were tuning up, filling the air
with the screeches of fiddles and pipes and the clatter of
drums. Once or twice I heard the piercing *tweet* of Dorothy's
flute rise over the din.

The room was so awash in Gaelic that I felt for the first
time that I was in a foreign country. I was glad to see Laura
at the far side of the room, watching for me. She waved and
I inched my way toward her. She, Joyce, and Brandi were at
a table for four. Joyce wore a gray sweater that made her
seem mousier than usual, but Laura looked pretty in a thick
red sweater and black ski pants, and Brandi, of course, out-
shone us all in her dark green velvet coat and Gordon tartan
skirt. An enormous cairngorm pendant hung between her
high little breasts, making my brooch seem piddly.

"Finally," Laura greeted me. "Want me to order you a
stout?"

"That's what I'm gonna be if I keep eating and drinking
like this." I slipped in between her and Joyce. "But I'll try
anything once. What's another calorie or two?" I'd have
changed my tune if I'd realized it came in pint mugs.

I scarcely noticed the four men at the next table until one
of them leaned toward us to ask, "Ye're the Americans,
then?" He was obviously most taken with Laura and Brandi,
but gallantly included us all in his grin. He was long and
lean, with gingery hair and a skimpy ginger beard. It was
impossible not to grin back at him, he seemed so delighted
to meet us.

A pudgy man who should never have worn an olive-
green pullover with that rosy face leaned in front of his companion to have a look at us. "Ye seem to be a few men short.
Shall we put our tables togither, then?"

"Och, let's wait to see if their lot can play." A third man

nodded toward the stage. "We don't want to be embarrassin' ourselves by associatin' wi' amateurs, noo, do we?" It took me a minute to recognize Watty nursing a pint. His cheeks were shaved, his hair was brushed into shining gray curls, and he wore a creamy Fair Isle sweater over pressed black slacks. He looked ten years younger and downright handsome.

"You clean up real good," I called over to him. "But I see you've chosen to sit with the home team."

"Chust 'til I see how your lot can play. These twa lads"—he nodded at Ginger Beard and Red Face—"drive for Gilroy's too"—they snickered, as if embarrassed to be found out—"and they contend that American musicians cannae keep up wi' Scottish ones. I don't want to embarrass myself by identifyin' too closely wi' ye until we see if they're right."

"Their piper was heistin' a chune out in the car park a leetle airlier," quavered the fourth man, who looked older than Moses. "He sounded fine."

"I've heard the piper, Dad." Watty dismissed Kenny with a wave. "It's t'others I'm worrit about." He winked at me.

"Ours play just fine," I informed him, without knowing whether they knew one note from another. "Can yours?"

Their whole table broke out into uproarious but goodnatured laughter. The pudgy man laughed so hard, he strangled on his drink and had to be pounded on the back. While the two older men performed that service, Ginger Beard leaned close and confided in a shout to be heard over the din, "Chust you wait to hear them. Davie Kilgour, the piper? He won a medal at the Braemar Royal Games a few years back, in front of the queen. He's come from Bridge o' Don for tonight's event. And the fiddler on the end? He's won more prizes than I can count."

Watty set down his empty mug and waved toward a passing waitress with a full tray of mugs. "O' course, ye cannae count very high."

"Och, aye, there is that." Ginger Beard took the mug he was handed and drained half of it in one draft.

The music started at a volume that discouraged conversation. Pipes and fiddles moved through several tunes without a break, and it looked to me like Jim and Dorothy were keeping up fine. As they played medley after medley, I could have sat there all night and listened. Ginger Beard helpfully called out the name of each tune for our benefit. Occasionally the music would stop, leaving our ears ringing. Then someone would climb onto the stage from the audience and give us an a capella solo. Most were in Gaelic and three sang the same song, but the audience didn't seem to mind. One man sang a very funny song in English about "Donald John," who went down from the fields to choose a wife to keep him warm but decided to buy an electric blanket instead. From the laughter, applause and stamping, I wondered if it was a song people knew and liked or if they were clapping because he'd made it up himself.

The musicians got at least as much pleasure out of performing as we did from listening. Kenny, of course, was in his element. Sherry was in the shadows, so I couldn't see her face, but Dorothy's was pink and glowing like it had been in Glasgow, and although Jim stayed near the back, his eyes were closed in what looked like pleasure as he sawed along.

Waitresses moved among the crowd distributing drinks. I nursed my stout, but didn't really like the taste, so I finally ordered a Coke with lots of ice. When I tried to pay, the waitress waved me away. "Och, it's on the house tonight." I thought that was darned nice of Gilroy's to provide for its guests that way. Must just be those staying in the hotel, though—waitresses were collecting from other guests, including the bus drivers.

Seemed to me like poor Watty kept getting stuck with most of their bills, too. The others managed to look the other way when each bill arrived. I hoped they weren't taking advantage of him, but decided Joe Riddley was right. I did not have to worry about the whole world. Watty was old enough to take care of his own business. Besides, I had worries of my own.

Drink was making Brandi friendlier than ever. Several times I practically had to lift her out of my lap. Joyce, on the other hand, was getting maudlin. "Life is a real bitch, you know that?" She spoke so low, only I could hear. "Some folks"—she nodded across me at Brandi—"get everything.

The rest of us get dregs. Dregs." She groped for a nearly empty mug, drained the last few drops, then realized that her own sat beside it, half full. She clenched her fingers around its handle so tightly, I hoped it wouldn't break and cut her. "There's no justice at all. Have you found that out yet, Mac? Justice is a myth. Some people get everything and the rest get nothing."

She lifted her mug and saluted me. "To equilibrium, and terrible consequences." She drained the mug in two swallows, then rose to unsteady feet. "'Scuse me. I need to puke." She threaded her way toward the lobby. I hoped she'd sober up a bit before she offended somebody in the group. People who are normally real inhibited have no business getting drunk in public. It's too embarrassing, for everybody.

When Joyce returned, her face was damp and pink but she looked relatively sober. The rest of the evening I caught her darting quick, uncertain looks my way, like she was wondering what confidences I'd pried out of her. I was too hot to care.

At one point, the host of the evening stepped forward. "We've got four fine musicians here all the way from America. What say we ask them to give us a chune while the rest of us have a wee dram?"

That was received with shouts, applause and stamping feet. Watty caught my eye and deliberately shifted his chair to put his back to us.

As the Scottish musicians filed off the stage and headed for the bar, the piper clapped Kenny on the arm in encouragement. Kenny stepped to the front of the stage and bowed. His accent, I noticed, was now pure South Georgia. "Well, folks, we aren't used to playin' together as a quartet, but my wife and I do play with each other from time to time"—he paused for guffaws to ripple through the audience, for the humor had gotten pretty raunchy by then, and almost anything was taken to have an off-color meaning— "so we'll be glad to oblige. Honey?" As she joined him, he said something to the drummer and started to beat out time with one foot.

Jim and Dorothy waited at the back like orphans who didn't get picked.

The way Kenny and Sherry played together, you'd never have guessed they ever fought. As the first notes sounded, people nodded in approval and Ginger Beard called to us, "'Lord Lovat's Lament.'" When the piece was done, the crowd clapped and called, "More! More!" They played a second piece, then an encore.

After that, one voice rang out, "Fiddles. Gie us chust the fiddles!" It was the award-winning fiddler, lifting his mug to Jim. I wondered if he wanted to show Jim up for some reason.

Sherry looked a question at Jim. He nodded and moved forward. Kenny stepped back with a frown. The two fiddlers conferred, then lifted their bows and began. I don't know what they played. If Ginger Beard told us, I missed it. I was too busy watching them, for there was chemistry between them that was magic.

Who would have thought a rich man would play so well? I had figured music was his hobby and that the others let him play with them to be kind. Instead, the music that Jim and Sherry sawed together set my feet tapping and made me want to spring up and dance. They played like they shared one instrument. They played like they had made music together since the birth of the world. They played—

"Aren't they fantastic?" Joyce asked me. "Better together than Sherry and Kenny, even."

I looked across at Brandi. If Sherry could have seen her, the heat from Brandi's eyes might have melted her bones, but Sherry played on in sweet oblivion. Her sallow cheeks were flushed and her eyes sparkled, while Brandi's talons tapped the table with tips like gore. She clawed at her lower lip with her upper teeth until all the lipstick was gone, and breathed in short, angry gasps.

When the fiddling finally stopped, the two musicians stepped forward and bowed, flushed and damp. The room shook with applause and stamping. Jim reached out one arm and drew Sherry to him in a big hug. Brandi sucked in a gasp of air and dilated her nostrils. The award-winning fiddler jumped onto the stage and caught the two other fiddlers in a generous hug. Then he waved the rest of the musicians back onstage for another set.

The old man at the next table who seemed, amazingly, to be Watty's daddy, quavered, "I havenae heerd fiddin' like that since Alasdair Geddys. Do ye mind Alasdair, Watty, or was he afore your time?"

"Och, aye, I mind him. You took me to Glasga to hear him when I was a lad."

The old man shook his head sadly. "We'd niver have made it through the war without Alasdair's fiddle."

Watty turned to explain to the younger men at their table, "Alasdair Geddys was one o' the finest fiddlers in the British Isles back then."

The red-faced driver lifted his mug and drained the last drops. "I've heard of him, right enough. Where was it he came from, then? Somewhere on t'other side, wasn't it?"

"Auchnagar. He came from Auchnagar." Joyce's American accent cut into their musical ones like a knife as she spoke loud enough for them to hear her. "His son and daughter still live there." She added, for those at our table, "I have a bit about him in my play."

Watty's father quavered, "I mind he had two sons, Watty. But the older—what happened to him? Pirates, was it?"

"I doot it was pirates, but nobody kent," Watty told him. "He disappeared soon after his dad was lost and nobody ever heard from him again."

"What happened to Alasdair, then?" Ginger Beard asked. "Did he dee in the war?"

"Pirates," the old man said firmly, nodding his head.

"Och, ye've got pirates on the brain. 'Twasn't pirates at all." Watty set his empty mug down with a thump and signaled for still another round.

How could men's bladders hold that much liquid? Mine was fast reaching its limit.

The old man insisted, "'Twas pirates, right enough. He went to Ireland to play, mind, and on the way over pirates got him."

"He got that drunk, he fell off the boat," Watty replied. "And puir lad, he couldna swim, so by the time they got turned aboot to try and recover him, he wasnae there."

"Och weel," said Red Face. "I doot Davy Jones is gettin' some fine music th' noo."

The skirl of pipes announced that the music was about to recommence. The musicians played while the rest of us drank, applauded, and dripped with sweat. I was a bit disgusted, though, to notice that the other drinkers at the next table still let Watty pick up most tabs, and that when he didn't, his daddy did. I wanted to shake some manners into the two young men.

Toward the end, Jim and Sherry played a trio with the award-winning fiddler and Dorothy was asked to accompany a singer with a particularly sweet voice. I could tell they were all having a fine old time. Finally the host stepped forward. "That's it for the night, folks. If the men will help shift the tables during the break, we'll hae a bit o' dancin' after."

I glanced at my watch. It was past midnight.

Across the room, the musicians climbed down from the stage. Kenny followed the Scottish pipers out. Dorothy made her way to us, glowing with happiness.

Ginger Beard gave her a private round of applause that turned Dorothy's face even pinker. "You were brilliant!" he told her. "Here, take my chair." He got up and shoved it toward her with a bow, waving away her protests. "Ye'll be deein' me a favor, keepin' it warm while I'm stretching my legs. Save me a dance when I get back, right enough?"

She nodded. As he sauntered across the room, she collapsed into the chair breathing hard and deep, like she had just come up from too long underwater. "It's hot up there, but wasn't that fantastic?" She turned to Joyce, fanning herself with one hand. "Thank you so much for setting this up, eh? When you said to bring our instruments, I never imagined it would be so—so—" She floundered.

"I didn't do anything." Joyce waved one hand toward Watty. "He found out the ceilidh was happening and that visiting musicians were welcome."

Dorothy leaned over and put her hand on Watty's. "Thank you so much. This has been wonderful."

Watty flushed happily. "Och, it chust happened. Now let's get some liquid inside you, so you'll be ready for the dancing." He caught the arm of a passing waitress. "A round for our visiting musicians."

"There's only me," Dorothy pointed out.

Sherry and Jim still hadn't come. I scanned the room, but they were nowhere to be seen. I turned to Brandi, and saw that the others were looking at her, too. When she noticed us, she scraped back her chair. "Excuse me. I have a headache."

Watty watched her stride across the room, chuckled, and saluted her back with his glass. "I doot ye'll be passin' it on to somebody else as soon as ye find her." He turned back to me. "May I have the pleasure of the first dance?"

I didn't really want to dance without Joe Riddley there, but seeing as how Watty had spruced himself up for the evening, I stayed long enough for one. To my surprise, the dances were group affairs—like square dances rather than foxtrots or waltzes. Also to my surprise, Watty was an excellent dancer. I enjoyed myself so much, I let him persuade me to stay for a second.

Laura danced the second dance with Ginger Beard in our set. Watty called it an eightsome reel. It certainly left me reeling. As we waited for our partners to fetch much-needed liquid refreshment afterwards, Laura leaned down to threaten, "I'm calling Joe Riddley as soon as I get back to my room. You're having far too much fun with that Highland gentleman."

I took the lemonade Watty brought with a grateful smile, but whispered to Laura, "You can use my cell phone if you like."

When Watty suggested a third dance, I might have stayed longer, but my bladder was threatening to burst. I decided to retire before I embarrassed myself.

When I got to the wide doors between the dining room and the lobby, Sherry swept past me with spots of red on her sallow cheeks.

As I climbed the stairs to my room, I heard Brandi's voice in the hall above me. "Just you remember, we have a deal. I've kept my side of the bargain so far, but if you welch on yours . . ."

Jim's reply fell like cubes of ice. "You betray me now, and I'll break your neck."

"Then you'd jolly well better . . ." A slammed door cut off the rest.

⇥ 11 ⇤

To say that things were a tad strained in our group the morning after the ceilidh would be like saying General Sherman paid a social call on Georgia. Joyce's job was no longer like herding cats. It was more like corralling coyotes.

Nobody had gotten enough sleep. Those of us who had gone to bed soon after the concert had been kept awake by thumping music, which didn't stop until four. I knew, because I'd sneaked a peek at the clock when Laura came to bed. Nobody got up that morning for an early run.

Those who had stayed at the dance must have drunk too much, as well, because they came to breakfast as prickly as a brood of porcupines. When my chair scraped the floor as I pulled it out to sit down, Kenny glared, Joyce grimaced, Dorothy shuddered and Laura held her head between her hands and growled, "Do you have to be so *noisy*?"

Jim and Brandi didn't show up at all.

Kenny ignored Sherry and latched on to Laura like a sandspur.

Sherry looked daggers at Kenny and Laura the entire meal.

The worry wrinkle between Joyce's eyes threatened to become permanent.

Watty wasn't his usual cheery self, either, and was dressed again in his disreputable sweater, baggy pants, and filthy cap. When I called, "Good morning!" he glowered.

As I slid into my seat on the bus, I murmured to Marcia, who sat behind me that morning, "The way Watty looks today reminds me of that old joke about 'I'd rather die like my grandfather, peacefully in his sleep, than screaming in terror like the folks who were riding with him.' You reckon he ought to be driving in his condition?"

"Nobody's compellin' ye to r-r-ride this bus." Watty flung a scarf I'd dropped into my lap and stomped back to the driver's seat.

"You have offended your Highland gentleman," Laura murmured, but her words were as lifeless as yesterday's seaweed at the high-tide line.

Brandi and Jim arrived just as Watty was telling us about our itinerary. "First we'll drive up the western side of the Trotternish Peninsula to Kilmuir Cemetery, where Flora MacDonald is buried, then we'll come down the eastern side of the peninsula and stop by Flodigarry Hotel, built on the site where Flora MacDonald and her husband used to live."

"Those sites were requested by Laura MacDonald," Joyce added—quite unnecessarily.

Brandi climbed the steps, turned her back on Sherry, and called, "Come on, Jimmy, there's plenty of seats in the back." She more dragged than led him down the aisle. He slid into a seat and immediately opened his laptop. Brandi took a seat on the other side.

Kenny sat behind Laura, making audible remarks about fiddles and flutes not being real Scottish instruments, merely adopted because they sound good as a backup to bagpipes.

Jim ignored him, but Watty finally snarled over his shoulder, "Pipe down, man."

I chuckled. "*Pipe* down?" I enjoy a good pun.

Goaded, Kenny glared like he'd like to hit me upside the head and opened his mouth to say something—probably rude. Laura said in an urgent voice, "Kenny, don't!" He subsided, then began a tirade about people who let amateurs play with professionals.

Marcia turned to address him in an icy voice. "Dorothy plays in a symphony orchestra and in a Scottish society band that wins competitions all over Canada." I turned around to give her an approving smile, but she had laid her head back and closed her eyes, as if exhausted by that effort.

"And nobody who knows a thing about music would call Jim an amateur," Dorothy said, her cheeks pink and her eyes snapping.

I turned, surprised that she'd show so much spirit.

Jim give her a slight bow with a frosty smile. "Much obliged."

Brandi called up to Laura, "Who was this Flora Mac-Donald, anyway?"

Kenny jumped in to answer. "She helped Bonnie Prince Charlie get safely to Skye after his defeat at Culloden, so he could catch a ship for France. She dressed him up as her maid and brought him with her through the English blockade. The prince got away safely, but Flora got caught eventually and was sent to the Tower of London for a year. Then she came back to Skye and married her sweetheart—who was also her cousin. They eventually emigrated to North Carolina to farm, and she became a heroine in both countries. Does that about cover it, shug?"

Laura didn't reply. She was staring out the window like he'd been talking about the heroine of some Mongolian revolution. Kenny shrugged and began to hum the "Skye Boat Song," breaking into words at the end: "Carry the lad who's born to be king, over the sea to Skye."

Sherry called down the aisle, "That's a bunch of crap and you know it. He wasn't a lad, he was a grown man. And he would have been a terrible king."

"You don't know that," Kenny objected.

"He was a terrible military leader. Thousands died unnecessarily because of the jerk, and Flora herself spent a year in jail. And how can you call her a hero in America? The MacDonalds supported the English during the American Revolution, which landed her husband in prison and got him banished to Nova Scotia. She went with him, then they returned to Skye. Heroine?" Sherry gave a rude snort. "The whole story is a bunch of romantic nonsense."

I didn't know much about Flora MacDonald, but Laura could trace her ancestry back to one of Flora's sons, so I didn't like to hear the family being trashed. "You have to admit Flora was brave," I insisted.

"And loyal to her country," Kenny added with that kind of pompous nationalism I find most irritating.

"Loyal to her family," Sherry corrected him. "Her stepfather didn't support the prince. He was an English official on the Isle of Uist. It's likely he persuaded Flora to help get the prince away so no more blood would be shed."

"Some say she was in love with the prince," I mentioned. "He was very handsome."

"Some say pigs can fly," Watty called sourly over one shoulder, "but I never saw one tak to the air. Let's just leave it that she was a brave lassie, and be done wi' it."

That punched a hole in everybody's bucket. We rode in silence until we reached Kilmuir Cemetery, which is dominated by the tall Flora MacDonald memorial. I'll admit I was impressed. None of the rest of us had ancestors worth huge granite monoliths, unless you believed Kenny's and Sherry's claims to noble blood.

Laura, however, barely looked at Flora's memorial at all. She mooched around reading gravestones apparently at random, then wandered off to one edge of the cemetery and stood gazing into the distance as if she were waiting for the rest of us to finish. Annoyed, I followed. "Granted, you've seen this before," I told her with the bluntness of one who used to babysit her when her folks were out of town, "but why bother to tell Joyce you'd like to see it again if you don't care?"

She looked down at me as if coming back from far away. "Sorry, what did you say?"

"I said the rest of us are getting a grand tour of your family burial ground, but if you aren't interested, I'm sure everybody would be willing to leave early and head to the mainland. What's the matter? You've been on another planet all morning. Too much to drink last night?"

She grimaced. "A bit. But that's not what's bothering me. I am really worried about Kenny. He says Sherry—" She stopped, and I suspected that she'd been about to blurt out something she was told in confidence. For several seconds she watched a plane fly high in the sky, then asked so abruptly that I knew we were changing the subject, "How did you know you wanted to marry Joe Riddley, Mac? Was there one minute when you said, 'I've got to do this, or I'll die'?"

I would have made a joke, but her expression changed my mind. "Our case wasn't typical. You know that. We met when we were four and six, and were enchanted with each other from the start. We grew up together, until he gradually seemed like the other half of me. There was one little period in college when I wavered a tad, but it didn't last long. He's the only man I ever really wanted."

"Daddy was all Mama ever wanted, too. She loved Daddy more than life." She peered off at the misty horizon, and we stood silently for a moment in honor of Gwen Ellen and Skye. Then she went on, desperation in her voice. "But other married people—I mean, look at Brandi and Jim, or Sherry and Kenny. They don't even seem to *like* each other."

"You can't make fine china out of common clay," I said bluntly. "No matter who you marry, you won't turn out like Sherry or Brandi. You're finer than that. You'll work and build a good marriage." It was time to stop pussyfooting around. "Is this about Ben?" I sure hoped so.

She turned slightly away and got real interested in rubbing a piece of lichen off a tombstone with one toe. "Yeah." She took a deep breath, flung back her head, and looked me straight in the eye. Then she announced, like she was Flora MacDonald accepting the job of disguising the prince, "I've been thinking it over, and I don't think Ben's the man for me." I got the feeling she was practicing on me what she planned to say to him when she got home. "One reason I came on this trip—the main one, in fact— was to see if I could live without him. Well, I can. I'm having a fine time without him, and apparently he's having a fine time without me. He hasn't called once since we got here."

"Have you called him since the first day?"

"Sure, every day, but we mostly talk about the business. I tell him a little about what I've been doing and he tells me what he's been doing, but he doesn't sound like he really misses me. Certainly not like he *needs* me. And I don't think I need him, either." She picked up a stone and hurled it over the distant wall. "I look at Marcia, consumed by grief, and I know I wouldn't be like that if Ben died. I'd be very sad, but I'd get up and go back to the office, keep on living. I wouldn't curl up and die." I knew she was still thinking of her mother when she said that.

I wished she were still small enough for me to put my arms around her shoulders and draw her close, like I used to when she was a tall, sweet little girl. All I could do now was take a deep breath and try to sound halfway coherent. "That's because you knew you were a whole person before you met Ben, honey. It took me forty years to learn that about myself. Remember when Joe Riddley got shot and we all thought he was going to die?"* She nodded. Her family had been real supportive of me in that time. "The second night in the hospital, around five in the morning, I was praying and crying and thinking, 'If he dies, God, just take me, too. I can't live without him.' Clear as anything, a voice in my head said, 'Nonsense. You don't *want* to live without him, but you will if you have to.' While I sat there watching the sun come up, something shifted inside me. I realized I am whole, with or without him. Since that day, I've known that I'm not married to Joe Riddley because I have to be, I'm married to him because I *want* to be—most days. The other days I stay married to him because I'm too busy to get a divorce right then."

She didn't crack a smile.

I sighed. Looked like I couldn't say a blessed thing that would help, so I finished up with, "Well, I haven't bought your wedding present yet, but you and Ben sure are mighty good together. You bring out the best in each other."

"I guess." Her face was so gloomy, you'd have thought we were discussing which fatal disease was likely to get her first.

"Honey," I urged, "if Ben ever gets up his courage to pop the question—"

Her mouth twisted. "He's already popped it. Several

*But Why Shoot the Magistrate?

times. But I've never been sure that what I feel for him will last forever."

That burst my blister. Here I'd been thinking terrible things about poor Ben, and all the time it was Laura—

"Folks in your generation worry far too much about feelings," I told her hotly. "Sure, feelings are important, but they come and go. The question is whether you care enough about somebody to stand up before God-and-these-witnesses and make promises you intend to do your dad-burned best to keep. Marriage is like the rest of life. It's not primarily about feelings, it's mostly about choices. Don't you forget it."

In a perfect world she'd have grabbed me in that rib-crushing hug she used to give me, and she'd have whispered, "Me-Mac, I love you. Will you dance at our wedding?"

In a fallen world, she shrugged. "I can't see tying myself for life to somebody I don't need and who doesn't need me." She turned and strode off toward the Flora MacDonald memorial, where Kenny was still investigating the MacDonald family history.

Poor Ben. Looked like he was history, too. But what raised my blood pressure was worrying that Laura would do something dumb with Kenny. She wouldn't be the first smart, strong person to take on a needy one because she confused ministry with marriage.

I stood there trying to decide whether to follow and nag some more—nagging being, by definition, telling somebody again to do what they didn't do when you told them the first time—or whether to pamper my chilly feet by returning to the bus.

What decided me was a scream.

It came from the parking lot, and ours was the only vehicle there, so I headed that way in the fastest trot a woman past sixty can muster. Sherry sat on the gravel beside the front tire, her hair disheveled and her cheek marked with four long red lines.

Brandi stood over her with one fist clenched. "You leave him alone, do you hear me? You had your moment of glory, but it's over." She brushed her hands like she had just finished chopping wood.

Sherry gave a hoarse, sarcastic laugh. "You think you'll keep him long? Ask him what happened to his first wife once he took over her daddy's business." She started to climb to her feet, but Brandi shoved her back down.

"He gave that old woman enough alimony to choke a horse. Now you leave him alone!" Her hands curved like talons.

Laura pushed past me and said in a voice of authority, "Hold up, there." Not for nothing had she been refereeing middle-school soccer games these past two years. As she stepped between them and held up her hands, I could almost hear a whistle blow.

Brandi stepped back. While Brandi was distracted, Sherry climbed to her feet and flew past Laura's arm. When Laura reached out to deflect her, Sherry grabbed a fistful of Laura's hair and jerked it hard. "You keep out of this. And keep your hands off my husband!" She jerked Laura's hair again.

While Laura tried to disentangle her hair, Brandi circled Laura and grabbed Sherry from behind. Sherry turned and raked Brandi's cheeks with her nails. Brandi tried to hold her off, and the two of them grappled and swayed like barroom brawlers. I grabbed Sherry and Laura managed to grab Brandi, but they squirmed like eels. We weren't having noticeable success in separating them until Watty waded in, admonishing, "Now, ladies. Now, ladies. We don't want to create a distur-r-r-bance."

That's when poor Joyce arrived. "What happened?"

Sherry and Brandi started a chorus of "She——" "She——"

"They had a little disagreement," Laura explained, panting and red in the face.

"Dear Lord." The way Joyce said it, it might have been a prayer. "Where are Jim and Kenny?"

"Jim decided to walk toward the Museum of Island Life," Watty told her. "I said we'd pick him up on the road."

"Here comes Kenny now," Laura announced. "Let's skip Flodigarry Hotel. I've been there before. Let's pick up the others and get on our way."

Sherry got on first. As Brandi climbed on ahead of me, she warned Sherry, "This isn't over. You can be sure of that." Her voice was soft, but menacing.

I couldn't see Sherry's face, but the stream of words that came from her mouth made Watty warn, "None of that kind of talk, now, or I'll be putting the both of ye off the bus."

⇛ 12 ⇚

We spent the next three days in the far north of Scotland, mostly pleasing Brandi. She had requested gardens, so we visited the Inverewe Gardens in Poolewe, where the Gulf Stream comes so close to the Scottish coast that palms and other tropical plants can grow, and I got an amazing photograph of a palm tree growing near a snow-topped mountain. We also visited the Lechmelm Gardens and the gardens of Dunrobin Castle just north of Dornoch Firth. The others complained a bit about "all this horticulture," but as a nursery owner, I was delighted to add gardens to my trip.

I was also pleased to discover that Brandi wasn't just a bubbleheaded bimbo with jealous tendencies. She was very knowledgeable about plants, and as we strolled together through the Dunrobin Castle gardens, she confided, "I'm looking for plants that might grow in North Georgia. Jimmy said that after this trip, I can design the garden the way I want to. We have thirty mountain acres, and I am itching to get to work on them."

"Will you hire somebody to help with design and planting?" It wasn't an idle question. Getting that commission could make up for Yarbrough's recent losses from the superstore.

"Oh, no, I'm a landscape designer myself. I'll hire somebody to do the planting, but I want to do the plan." She gave me her supermodel's smile. "That's how I met Jimmy, landscaping Scotsman Distilleries."

I tried to picture her driving a backhoe or digging with a shovel, but designer clothes kept spoiling the picture. More likely she'd stood decoratively on one side, giving orders and making sure her flaming hair could be seen from the boss's office window.

"If you need plants and help putting them in, let us give you a bid." I fished in my pocketbook for a Yarbrough Feed, Seed and Nursery card.

She raised one eyebrow. "Do you all work way up in the mountains?"

"Of course," I assured her. We certainly would if we got the job.

Between gardens, we rode through areas that Kenny informed us had been the most affected by the Highland Clearances. The rest of us rode in relative silence, trying to absorb a cataclysm that could empty land so completely that you'd never guess people used to inhabit most of it. The population was now clustered in small villages near the coast. I knew those villages must be the result of the clearances, but after two hundred years, they looked like they'd sat by the sea forever.

Brandi and I took photographs of view after view we'd never be able to identify later. Marcia stared out the window through the eyes of a haunted soul. Dorothy plied pencil to sketchbook, talking to nobody. Jim mostly worked, and treated Brandi coolly, like a distant acquaintance. Sherry discussed music with Jim when he'd let her and the rest of the time looked out the window or described places we ought to be seeing instead of where we were. Kenny attached himself to Laura like a thistle. She treated him with a gentleness that worried me.

Saturday night we stayed in another Gilroy Hotel, and Jim and Sherry brought down their violins and played by the fire. You might think that a musical evening would have relaxed us all, but it didn't. For one thing, Kenny sat on a couch with Laura and talked the whole time, showing her his *sgian dubh* and boasting about the bargain he'd gotten on it on eBay. "Look at that cairngorm!" he bragged, holding it up so I could see it, too. It truly was impressive, encased in an intricate design of metal that formed the hilt. But I wished he would hush.

Meanwhile, Brandi curled up on a sofa by the fire watching Sherry like a tigress. Sherry had put on lipstick, eye shadow, and blusher, and while she wasn't picture-book gorgeous, she was chic, stunning in her own way, and she and Jim were obviously having a great old time making music together.

Anybody could see that Brandi was not pleased, but it was Kenny who finally got enough. He got up, stalked over to Jim with a frown and announced, "I'll thank you to remember that Sherry is my wife."

Jim looked up as if Kenny were nothing but a gnat. "Och, aye," he said mildly.

Kenny stomped off with a cloud on his face. I later saw him and Laura talking earnestly in a booth in the bar. Dorothy and Joyce sat at another booth, but they didn't seem to talk much. I had the feeling that each was in her own private world, using the other as camouflage. I roamed from parlor to bar and back again, unable to settle and unwilling to go upstairs by myself.

Knowing what I do now, I wonder. Were we all picking up vibes that one of our group was cherishing well-laid plans for murder?

Sunday night found us at yet another Gilroy's, way up at John O'Groats. I came upon Jim and Joyce in the lobby before tea and overheard him accusing her of buying a Gilroy package deal. I could tell that beneath her calm façade she was anxious. "They did arrange the tour, yes. Are you dissatisfied?"

"I'm satisfied, Josie, so long as nobody else complains."

"It's Joyce," she reminded him.

"Sorry. Joyce." He went into the dining room.

She turned and gave a start when she saw me, then she gave me a crooked little smile. "Five days together and he still can't remember my name. Can you believe it?"

"Makes you wonder how he managed to accumulate all those millions," I agreed.

I set my clock for three a.m. that night, and called Joe Riddley right after he got home. He allowed as how they had all had a splendid time, had eaten enough fish to satisfy even

him for a while, and had managed to bring back both grandsons in one piece.

"You having fun?" he finally thought to ask.

"Sure am," I said. No point in telling him I missed him
like the dickens and was on a bus with several folks likely
to pull out somebody's hair before we were through. "Looks
like I won't be selecting Laura and Ben's wedding present
on the trip, though. She claims she came to see if she can
live without him, and she thinks she can. Says she can't
marry a man who doesn't need her."

"Of all the tomfoolery—"

"It's not utterly dumb," I disagreed. "You and I may not
fall apart when we're separated, but you do need me, and I
need you."

"Right now I need you to get off the phone so I can go
take a shower. I'm so covered with salt I could jump in a cattle pond and turn it into a second Dead Sea. Love you, Little Bit."

Like I told Laura, marriage is about choices. If I chose to
consider that a romantic way to end a conversation when we
hadn't spoken for a week, that's my business.

By Monday morning Sherry and Brandi were avoiding
each other to such an extent that when we stopped at noon
at a Gilroy's Tearoom and Sherry discovered she'd have to
sit with Brandi, she stomped back to the bus and said she
wasn't hungry. Watty spoke to the manager and another
table was magically set up over by the window. He fetched
Sherry and ate with her himself. She seemed to be eating a
lot for somebody who wasn't hungry. That was the first time
Watty had eaten in the same room with us. I wondered if he
ate alone usually because of company policy or because
they didn't pay him enough to afford Gilroy's prices.

He finished early and left. As soon as Sherry was alone,
Joyce carried her dessert and tea over to the table, but Sherry
looked up and said rudely, "Bug off."

Joyce came back to our table with a frustrated expression
on her face.

Joyce also made endless notes in a little notebook. I sure

hoped we weren't getting report cards when we got home. Conduct grades might be rather low.

Kenny stuck to Laura and took particular pleasure in baiting the rest of us.

For instance, as we wound our way along one narrow road amid fields of sheep, Brandi cooed, "Oh, look at the lambs. Aren't they adorable?"

Kenny snorted. "If you can overlook the fact that thousands of people were turned off this land so those adorable little lambs could graze."

When we stopped to admire a particularly stark and lonely vista, Marcia told me softly, "There are places up here where you can look for miles in every direction and never see another soul."

Kenny barked that laugh that was more rude than humorous. "That's because in one generation, between a third to a half of the people of Caithness, Sutherland, Ross, and Inverness counties were uprooted and dispersed."

"Leave it alone!" Laura said wearily. "Don't be a spoilsport."

I nearly applauded, I was so glad she was finally standing up to him, but Kenny shrugged and said humbly, "I'm simply stating facts, shug."

Dorothy turned on him as she had before, cheeks rosy and eyes snapping. "If we had wanted facts, we'd have stayed home and read books. I, for one, came to have a good time, and you are not helping one bit." She snatched his book from the seat beside him and carried it back to her seat. Opening it at random, she began to read.

In a few minutes, she gave a little gurgle. "Kenny didn't mention this part. Listen, everybody. 'The removal of the people from the interior had struck a hard blow at an old Highland custom—the distilling of whisky. To all respectable people this was uplifting news, for the practice had a terrible effect on the moral fiber of the mountaineers.' "*

Most of us chuckled. Laura brightened up enough to

*John Prebble, *The Highland Clearances* (Middlesex, England: Penguin Books, Ltd, 1978), p. 106.

admit, "Those may have been MacDonalds. I had a great-granddaddy who was a bootlegger in the north Georgia mountains."

Sherry turned around and called back, "If you'd lived here then, Jim, you'd have had some competition."

"Read the rest of the passage, Dorothy," Kenny commanded.

She found her place and continued, " 'To secure for the farmers a regular market for the grain they had been selling to illegal stills, Lord Stafford was proposing to build a distillery at Bora.' " She asked in a puzzled voice, "Does that mean that first he shut down the people's stills, then he built one of his own?"

"You got it," he snapped.

"But that's not fair."

Kenny laughed. "Do you think rich folks care about what's fair? All they want is their profits."

If he expected Jim to repent and give all his goods to the poor, he was in for a sad disappointment. Jim typed steadily like he was alone in his own office, ignoring us all.

Monday night, I shared a room with Joyce.

There was no Gilroy Hotel in Dornoch, so we stayed in a small hotel with a good view of the Dornoch Firth, which is famous for its swans. I went up to bed a bit early, planning to call home and then read awhile, but my cell phone wouldn't work inside, so I pulled my clothes back on and headed downstairs, where I found Joyce arguing with the desk clerk.

"Water has leaked through the ceiling and is all over my bed," she complained.

"I'm very sorry, madam, but we have no other room," the harried clerk told her. "We're absolutely full up tonight."

I would have been glad to share again with Laura, but she and Kenny had gone out, and I didn't like to move into her room without asking, so I offered, "I have two beds in my room. You can move in with me, if you like."

Joyce accepted, although I could tell she'd rather have a room of her own. I didn't blame her. If I had her job, I might go to my room every night and drink myself into oblivion—

or curl up with good murder mysteries and picture several of our group as victims. She moved her things, then went back downstairs. I read awhile and turned out my light around eleven.

I woke in darkness to quiet weeping, then a fierce whisper. "I can't quit now!"

She sounded so desperate, I couldn't pretend nothing was the matter, so I fumbled for the lamp beside my bed and clicked it on. "What's the matter, hon?"

Her bed was rumpled, the covers flung back, and she stood in a long flannel gown by the window. Beyond her, the moon was bright enough to glint off the nearby firth and off tears streaming down her cheeks. Not wanting to embarrass her, I flicked off the lamp, but threw back my covers. The room was chilly and I hadn't unpacked my robe, so I grabbed my bedspread and pulled it around me as I padded over in sock feet to stand beside her.

Her arm was chilly to my touch, so I fetched her own spread to tuck around her, and we stood like two squaws in a Western movie looking over steep slate roofs silvered by moonlight. They were lovely, with the sea just beyond. I wondered how many displaced Highlanders had yearned for the beauty they had left behind.

However, it was Joyce's aching heart I needed to be concerned about right then. "What's the matter?" I repeated.

Her tongue slid back and forth against her upper lip. Finally she heaved a big sigh and turned a tear-streaked face to mine. "The tour. It's awful, isn't it? I'm sorry I woke you up, but I couldn't sleep, thinking about it. Kenny keeps holding us up so he can play the pipes and picking on everybody else. Marcia feels rotten. Sherry is obnoxious and Brandi just as bad—"

"—And Jim never looks at a thing," I finished.

She tried an unsuccessful little laugh. "I'm not normally a quitter, Mac, but if it weren't for you, Dorothy, and Laura, I'd be tempted to jump ship and go home." Shadows rearranged her features, made her face look longer and stronger. With her hair disheveled, she could have been a wild mountain woman in a rage. Then her eyes filled again, looking like underwater sapphires as she blinked rapidly to hold back the tears. "You all must be having a terrible time!"

I went and fetched a tissue. "It's not that bad. Most of us ignore the squabbles. We're having a real good time, honest." Fortunately, "we" is a flexible pronoun.

She sighed. "I wish I could be more like you. You always seem so relaxed and cheerful, and have a good time no matter where you are."

I could think of several times in the past two years when I had not been relaxed or cheerful, and hadn't had a particularly good time. Locked in a deserted warehouse, for example, or circling my kitchen table while a madman tried to inoculate me. However, I never turn away a compliment when offered, so I just said, "Well, honey, I have been having a good time on this trip. You did a good job of picking the places we've seen."

Joyce turned away to blow her nose. "Bless your heart. You're so sweet." Her voice was muffled by the tissue.

"Were you raised down South?"

She stiffened.

"I've often noticed that folks who grew up in the South tend to talk Southern when they get tired or disheartened," I explained, "and you sounded real Southern just then."

She shrugged without turning around. "I went to high school up north and stayed there afterwards, but my folks were from Georgia."

"What part?" That question is as automatic for Southerners as swatting flies. Northerners generally ask what country somebody's ancestors came from. We're more concerned with which *county* somebody's folks come from, in case we may be related or have mutual friends. Southerners don't really trust strangers, but we're willing to accept you if we can establish as rapidly as possible that we have a legitimate reason to.

She hesitated. "The middle part."

That covers a lot of territory, but I didn't like to press her. "Are they still there?"

"No. Daddy died years ago and Mama—she died a little later." She blew her nose again. She probably had her reasons for being vague—like the fact that her teeth were still chattering in spite of the blanket.

"I've lost my parents, too, and you never get over that." We stood there for a minute or two looking out the window, then I said, "You know what I wish we had? A cup of hot tea. Shall I call down and order up some? Or would you rather get into bed and forget these dratted folks?"

"I can make tea." Our room was so small that one sideways step brought her to her suitcase. Before I could switch on the lamp again she had reached into a corner of her case and brought out one of those little electric converters and a coil that heats water in a cup. "Herbal okay with you?" She held up two bags. "So it won't keep us awake?"

I was so busy admiring a woman who had traveled for a week and still knew exactly where to put her hands on something in her suitcase, I was slow to answer. Seeing she was still waiting, I nodded, although I generally think herbal tea tastes like brewed grass.

Her hand hovered over her case, and she murmured in dismay, "I've just got one mug."

"I bought one this afternoon." I was already rummaging in my Gilroy's Highland Tours bag, where I was storing smaller souvenirs. "I'm taking it to our cook, but she won't care if I use it first. She'll like the swans. I've got some shortbread somewhere, too. I bought it for my older granddaughter, but it's silly to carry it around when I can get more later."

Joyce went to the bathroom to fill our mugs. I heard water running and figured she was also washing her face. Sure enough, she returned with her hair combed and her face clean, looking more like her usual brown-mouse self. Pity. I preferred the wild mountain woman.

Still, we had a good old time sitting on our beds sipping tea and munching shortbread in the middle of the night. "This is the most fun I've had on the whole trip," she confessed.

"It ranks right up there," I agreed. But I sure hoped I wouldn't have to go home and tell Joe Riddley that a slumber tea party was the highlight of my trip.

"Don't tell the others I got so moody," she begged. "I must be having PMS or something."

"Your secret is safe with me, honey. In your shoes, I'd be running down some hill screaming, if I wasn't hitting somebody with one of those big claymores."

She smiled, then grew serious. "Would you tell me something?" I nodded. "The other night at the ceilidh, when I had too much to drink, did I say anything—well, odd?"

I thought back. "Not that I can recall. Of course, I'd had a bit to drink, as well." When she still seemed anxious, I added, "You sounded pretty bitter, I think. I wondered if you'd been through a nasty divorce or something."

"Oh, yes. It was real nasty." She took a sip of tea and added, "He got almost everything—even all the furniture we'd bought together, because his lawyer listed it as 'used.' I got the junk we'd bought in thrift stores, because his lawyer listed it all as 'antiques.' "

"What about your lawyer?"

"He didn't do a blessed thing. But I don't like to talk about it." She stood and held out her hand. "You want some more tea?"

"No, I'm warmed and fed." I stretched and yawned. "It will be good to get to Auchnagar tomorrow, won't it? When do we arrive?"

"Sometime in the afternoon." She went to wash both our mugs, then brought them back and set them on the dresser. "Ready for bed?"

While she went to brush her teeth, I snuggled down into my bed and tried to get the sheets warm again. As I drifted off, I had a notion that something about our evening's chat had puzzled me, but I was too sleepy to remember what it was.

⇜ 13 ⇝

You don't need to know a thing about our two nights and a day in Inverness. We mostly saw sights and shopped—except for Jim, who left the hotel early Wednesday morning and didn't return until time for tea. Sherry, Kenny, and Brandi continued their merry game of "Let's see who can drive the others crazy first." It was hard to determine who was ahead.

Thursday morning, however, I woke up singing. I kept singing as I packed. By mid-afternoon we'd be in Auchnagar, where I could take solitary walks on the moor, prowl around the village, and maybe find traces of my long-lost relatives. Most of all, I looked forward to four days of not being confined on a bus with the rest of our obstreperous group.

I never anticipated looking down at one of them in a coffin the very next day.

Within an hour after we got underway, though, I'd have consigned several to a lesser but still painful fate. To begin with, when Brandi and Jim got on, Jim slid into the seat by the door, so she slid in behind Watty.

Sherry climbed on and told Jim (pleasantly, for her), "You've got my seat."

"I'd like to watch the road today." He sounded about as movable as Georgia's Stone Mountain.

All of us—including Sherry—could tell Brandi was waiting for her to make a scene. Instead, she shrugged. "Sure." She took the seat behind him and started talking about fiddling.

That did not please Miss Brandi, so she started talking about plants for their new garden. They were like two little girls playing tug-of-war over one doll. Jim didn't listen. He was leaning forward, hands clasped on the rail, staring down the road. I figured that his old bones, like mine, must be tired.

Brandi transferred her chatter to Watty, who practically put us in a ditch a couple of times answering her over his shoulder. Dorothy leaned up from behind me to whisper, "Think anybody would object if I stuck my scarf in Brandi's mouth and tied it tight?"

"Not me," I assured her. "I'm ready to rest, but I don't want to do it in a hospital."

Laura and Kenny had gone to the back bench that morning, where they carried on a soft conversation. However, what I could hear of it disturbed me. He was asking real personal questions about the motor companies' business, and I didn't like to hear Laura discussing her private affairs with a man she hadn't seen for ten years.

Marcia was morose and stared at the scenery through a film of tears. I saw her wipe several away. Even Joyce was jumpy and short with us all. I suspected she was worried about her play, and I wished I had the nerve to say, "Hey, honey, we aren't expecting Broadway. Relax and have fun."

It appeared to me like Dorothy and I were the only ones enjoying ourselves, which was a real shame, because we were traveling through some mighty pretty country.

Auchnagar lies in the heart of Scotland, in the Grampian region, among mountains called the Cairngorms. Maybe I'm prejudiced because of my ancestors, but now that I've seen the eastern Highlands, it is easy for me to see why the royal family still goes there for an annual vacation. Unlike the stark hills of the West, these big rounded mountains tumble over one another like fat brown puppies. Bright splashing streams, which Watty called "burns," somersault over boulders and plunge into silver rivers that slide through broad fields to the North Sea.

When Sherry lamented loudly, "It's such a pity we came in April. When the heather's in bloom, these hills are a glory of purple," I had finally had enough of her complaints. After all, the air still held a tinge of mauve, while unexpected patches of daffodils and yellow Scotch broom brightened the roadside and grew along what Watty called "drystane dikes"—walls of stones made without mortar—that outlined pastures filled with black-faced sheep and lambs.

"Next time," I called up to Sherry a mite tartly, "why don't you come at a time of year when you won't have to spend your trip ruining everybody else's?"

"Yon trees," Watty called loudly, waving toward thick stands of evergreens, "have all been planted in the last for-r-rty years to r-r-replace for-r-rests cut down in the last war-r-r."

I was ashamed to have fussed at Sherry so publicly that Watty felt a need to smooth over my gaffe. "Sorry," I called, but Sherry ignored me.

At Watty's direction, we all craned our necks for a quick view of Balmoral Castle, and fifteen minutes later were glad to disembark for lunch in Braemar. Marcia roused herself to walk with the rest of us, led by Watty, up through the village to view the outside of the house where Robert Louis Stevenson wrote *Kidnapped*. En route, Kenny pontificated about some ruins by the banks of Cluny burn. I didn't pay him much attention until he said, "It was Malcolm Canmore's hunting lodge—you know, the one who defeated Macbeth."

I climbed back on the bus reflecting that if we let them, almost anybody can teach us something. I hadn't realized until then that Macbeth was a historical person.

From Braemar, we wended our way through more mountains until Watty announced, "In chust a wee while we'll be in Auchnagar."

I leaned up in my seat and asked Marcia, "Excited about seeing your family?"

She gave me a wan smile. "A little nervous, really. There's only Eileen—my mother's sister—and her son, Roddy, and I've only seen her once and never met him." She raised her voice a notch and her dark eyes lit with a gentle twinkle. "Roddy's thirty, so I've earmarked him for Dorothy, eh?"

I looked over my shoulder and saw Dorothy looking out the window like she wasn't listening, but her cheeks were bright pink again.

"And you've only met your aunt once?" Encouraged by that rare shaft of light in the clouds that hovered over her, I wanted to broaden it if I could.

She nodded. "When I was nine, Mum brought me over to visit her parents, eh? But as far as I was concerned, it was a dreadful trip. I hated the food and the rain, and my grandparents were austere, dour folks who wouldn't spend money on what they called 'frivolities' like heated rooms or television. I was disgusted to have such backwards relatives, and didn't mind sharing that opinion." Her lips curved in a smile of rueful remembrance. "Eileen called me a 'wee holy terror,' eh? And I was, right enough. To make matters worse, I couldn't understand half of what they said, and it made me furious that Mum could. Before we left to go back to Canada, I announced to all my relations that I hated Scotland and would never return. Poor Mum was mortified, eh? After that, she came back on her own every few years, but she never brought me or my brothers." She gave a low chuckle. "Eileen and Dugald hadn't had children yet, and Mum always said they had Roddy the following year to show they could make a better job of him than she had of me." At last she laughed aloud.

I laughed with her, astonished at how that changed her whole appearance. She must have been lovely before her husband's death consumed her. I hurried to keep the conversation going. "So you haven't seen your aunt at all since then."

"No, but after Mum died last spring, I knew Eileen would want to know, so I wrote to tell her. She wrote back, giving an e-mail address and saying she and Dugald had bought this guest house several years ago and she's been running it alone since his death. We started e-mailing back and forth, and we've both revised our initial opinions of each other, eh?" She chuckled again. "She seems quite pleasant." Marcia hesitated, then added sadly, "Paul and I even talked about coming over to meet her last summer. He wanted to attend a history seminar on Skye. But Mum had been sick a long while, and I was so weary . . ." Her voice trailed off.

"Caring for a sick person can be exhausting," I agreed, sorry to see her losing the animation she'd just had.

She sighed, then words burst from her. "I wish we had come! But before we'd made firm plans, Eileen wrote that she had this group from the States coming to stay this April, and they'd offered her two places for the price of one." Her eyes filled with sudden tears. "I suggested that we postpone our trip until now, to celebrate our fifteenth anniversary. I never imagined it would be too late." Her lips trembled and she pressed her hand across her mouth to still them.

"I'm proud of you for deciding to come anyway and bring Dorothy," I told her briskly.

She shook her head. "Don't be proud of me. It was Eileen and Dorothy. Eileen insisted that I still make the trip, even without Paul, and Dorothy offered to pay Paul's share. But I wasn't ready. I should have realized that. It's been so hard, visiting all the places we looked forward to seeing together." Now it was her voice that trembled, and she turned away from me to look out the window.

I was glad to hear Watty call, "We're going over the pass noo." At that moment the sun came from behind clouds to beam us over, and we began to descend into a small cup of a glen surrounded by hills and split by a lively burn. In spite of Marcia's sadness, my spirits rose so high, I felt like a balloon was slowly wafting the bus downwards. When the village lay full before us, I gave a little bounce in my seat.

"Recognize your ancestral home, Mac?" Laura called from the back.

"No, but I'm glad to know my folks had the good sense to live here. Isn't it beautiful? It has such a *friendly* look."

"That's where the Laird of Auchnagar lives." Joyce pointed to a granite house nestled among trees. It was no castle, but it would have held four or five big Victorian houses like Joe Riddley and I had lived in for most of our married life.

As we neared the village, I couldn't look fast enough. Even Marcia wiped away her tears and got excited. She and I must have looked like herons exercising our necks.

It wasn't a big place. Maybe thirty gray houses with brightly colored window facings and doors straggled up- and downhill on short, narrow streets. Six or seven shops faced one another across the main street, including a mod-

ern chalet so raw it must be new. Ski paraphernalia filled its
window.

"Eileen wrote that a ski lift was put in last year," Marcia
told me, sounding as proud as if she were a native. "They
hope to attract tourists all year round, like Braemar and
Aviemore."

"That's the arts center where our play will be." Joyce
pointed to a small building on our right. Like every major
structure we'd seen, it was built of granite, with a square
tower and arched oak doors.

"Looks like a church." Maybe Kenny didn't mean to
sound skeptical, but he did.

"It used to be the Anglican church," Joyce agreed, "but
it's not used for worship now." I got the feeling she didn't
mind knowing something Kenny didn't. "There aren't many
Anglicans in Scotland, so Mrs. MacGorrie told me they only
used to meet in the summer, anyway, when tourists came.
She's the laird's wife," she added, just a shade too casually.

The main street crossed the small burn on an arched stone
bridge, then wended its way uphill past a war memorial, a
second clump of shops, and an ever-present Gilroy's Hotel.

"Why aren't we staying at Gilroy's?" Kenny asked.

"They're painting right now," Joyce explained. "They
recommended Heather Glen."

"Marcia's aunt runs it," Dorothy reminded Kenny.

"Oh, that's right. I'm sure it will be great." He subsided
with unusual courtesy.

"Look!" Dorothy exclaimed as we passed a small gray
shop marked with the familiar post-office sign. "That
woman looks like you, Jim!"

It didn't take an artist to see a similarity in the shock of
white hair and large hooked nose.

Jim looked, then laughed. "I had the same experience in
Israel last year. It's this schnozz." He caught his nose between his thumb and forefinger and wiggled it. "You'll find
hooked noses among Scots, Jews, Arabs, Germans—a lot of
people have them. Just goes to show we must have a common ancestor somewhere."

"But maybe your folks did come from Scotland," Marcia
suggested.

"Nope. My ancestors were all Prussian."

"Gordon's not a German name," Kenny objected.

Jim laughed again. Twice in one day set a record for the trip. His next words surprised us even more. "I legally changed my name. Do you think a Grünwald would have much credibility as a seller of Scotch whisky?"

"That's dishonest!" Kenny sounded as upset as if Jim had admitted to stealing a presidential election—not that anybody ever did. "It's hard enough to track genealogy without people changing their names."

Jim didn't bother to reply.

At the end of the shops the main street forked. Joyce was standing by the door now, as eager as the rest of us to get off the bus. "The left-hand fork, halfway up," she told Watty. "There's a meadow across the road where you can park."

"Och, aye." Watty downshifted, climbed the hill in low, and swung into a grassy vacant lot. Across the road stood a tall house with a third floor up under the roof, judging from the skylights. Before we could climb down from the bus, a tall thin woman ran out the back door of the house across the road, followed by a muscular young man in cords and a heavy sweater. She wore a gray tweed skirt and a thick blue sweater, and had Marcia's gray frizzy hair, long, lean grace, and eyes that looked like dabs of coal. But this woman's face was bright and cheerful, and she was already chattering when Watty opened the door. "You made it fine, then. Welcome to Heather Glen. And isn't the weather grand for your arrival?"

We all let Marcia go first. As soon as she climbed down, Eileen wrapped her in a hug so fierce I feared it might crush her ribs. "Janet's wee Marcia! I'm so glad you've arrived."

As the rest of us disembarked, she jerked a thumb toward the young man and said, "He'll get your bags." The young man had already headed without a word to where Watty was dragging out luggage. He was muscular and rather attractive, with auburn curls standing like a tonsure around a receding hairline. He greeted Watty with a wide grin that showed white strong teeth, and Watty said something that made him throw back his head and laugh. Then he picked up three of the largest bags. When Dorothy reached for hers, he said, "I'll get the rest in a minute. Dinnae strain yourself, lass," and winked at her.

Dorothy, of course, turned bright pink.

"Is that Roddy?" Marcia asked Eileen, watching him cross the road toward the back door.

"Och, no, that's Alex Carmichael, who's staying with me until his digs are ready. He offered to come up to help with your bags because Roddy's working down at the chapel this afternoon. Come along, then, and we'll get you settled. We'll have plenty of time to talk later." As the rest of us headed to pick up our smaller bags, she peered at each of the men. "Which of you is Jim Gordon?" When Jim raised his hand, she fished in her skirt pocket and brought out a slip of paper. "You've a message from the laird. He wants you to call. They're inviting you and your wife to dinner tonight."

﹩ 14 ﹩

Jim slid the paper into his pocket and went to fetch his fiddle. Sherry wore envy smeared like chocolate all over her face. Kenny scowled. I looked around to see how Joyce was taking the news that Jim was on dinner-party terms with the folks who were footing the bill for her play, but she was over by the bus watching Watty take out the bags.

I had thought the house rather severe, to tell the truth, built smack up against the road with only a narrow sidewalk between them. However, that turned out to be the back. Eileen led us through a high green double gate at the side, down a gravel drive, and around the corner to the front door. Now we could see that the house was lovely, its door and window facings painted dark green, with two bay windows upstairs and two down overlooking the hills.

"You can use the back door after this, if you like," Eileen told us, "but I always bring guests in the front at first. The view is so bonnie." We all turned obediently to admire it.

A long, narrow lawn of emerald grass ran downhill to a garden patch covered with straw. Beyond the garden was a small stream, then the broad shoulder of the first hill sloping gently to the summit. The lawn was dotted with shrubs, fruit trees, and bare patches that would surely be bright flower beds in a few weeks. Several feeders on low branches were attracting a bevy of birds that darted in and out, keeping a wary eye on us. I took deep breaths of fresh cold air, looked at hills that hadn't changed much since the first humans saw them, and wondered how my ancestors could have stood to leave that place.

"It's a grand day, isn't it?" Eileen sounded as proud as if she'd produced the weather.

"It sure is," we agreed.

"Why do you have such high fences?" Dorothy asked. "Surely you don't expect burglars."

Eileen tilted her head and gave a peal of laughter. "Och, no. They keep out the deer." She nodded toward the hills. "In the autumn, you can see dozens. Even now you can glimpse one now and then, and at night they roam the village. Be careful if you go walking in the dark."

A bell attached to the door jangled as we pushed it open, and somewhere inside we heard three muffled barks. "Dinna mind the dog," she reassured us. "He's all bark and no bite."

The wide entrance hall was warm enough but had a smell of cold, as if central heating was a recent investment. A rose-patterned carpet covered the floor and led up white enamel stairs. To the left of the hall was the dining room filled with small tables covered in brightly colored cloths. The kitchen must be behind that, given the serving hatch in the rear wall.

"The lounge is just there." Eileen nodded to the right. The room looked comfortable and cozy with flowered fabric on sofa and chairs and the rose carpet throughout. A fire burned in the grate, and I felt like I could spend hours in there with a book.

We trailed Eileen upstairs, past a small landing lit by a stained-glass window that flung jewels onto the floor, and emerged in an upstairs hall surrounded by seven doors. Eileen consulted a list, directed us to our rooms and handed out keys, one per person per room. Laura and I got one front corner room, Marcia and Dorothy the other. Ours was large and sunny with twin beds and one of the bay windows facing the hills, the same view I had just admired at the front door. The wallpaper was dotted with small blue cornflowers and the chenille bedspreads were a soft sky blue. "I may stay forever," I warned Eileen.

She laughed. "You're welcome to stay as long as you like."

Jim and Brandi were given one back corner room, Kenny and Sherry the other. Joyce got the small central room over the front hall. Two bathrooms flanked the stairwell.

"Our room is too small." Sherry stood in the door like a balky mule refusing to enter the barn. "And it's just got one bed."

Jim—who had complained about Gilroy's a few nights back—said nothing about the size or location of their room.

Eileen seemed unruffled by Sherry's complaint. "I've only the two rooms with twin beds down here," she informed Sherry, "but just you go on up the stairs and take whichever front room you like. The back ones are occupied by Alex and my son, Roddy, but they're out all day and most evenings, as well, so they won't be any bother for you."

Sherry lugged her tote up the stairs followed by Kenny, but was back down in half a second. "There are no windows in those rooms—just skylights."

"The roof slopes, you see." Not by the slightest inflection did Eileen indicate that Sherry ought to have expected that on the attic floor.

"We'll stay here," Sherry announced, returning to her former room, "but we'll need more towels. I have to wash my hair."

"I'll bring them up in just a wee whiley." Eileen turned to the rest of us, who were still milling around our doors. "Do any of you need anything? No? Then I'll go down and make you some tea."

As she left, Dorothy said to Marcia, "She doesn't speak Scottish."

Eileen turned on the steps with a twinkle in her eye. "Och, it's chust the Queen's English I was speakin' for you," she said broadly, "seein' as how ye're from abr-r-road. But if ye'd prefer, I can speak proper from now on." We shared a laugh, then she reverted to "the Queen's English" to inform us, "A wee cup of tea will be served in the lounge in fifteen minutes."

After the tea—which was served with a three-tiered plate of cookies, scones, and cold pancakes—I needed a walk. I'm not much on earnestly walking around and around a track for the sake of my health, but I love a ramble, and ever since Joe Riddley had told me about the trip, I had pictured myself walking through the heather.

Glen Coe did not count.

"The easiest walk is down through the village, along the burnside, up through the manse woods, and back around to the village center," Eileen told me.

"Will I be walking through heather?"

"Och, no, it's all fine road, that." I must have looked disappointed, because she added, "If it's heather you're wanting, go up to the top of the brae, here, and around by the reservoir. On the far side you'll find a track that circles back down to meet the road. You can't miss it."

Having ascertained that one got "to the top of the brae" by going uphill on the road that passed the guesthouse, I thanked her and set out.

Within ten minutes I had decided it was a good thing I'd taken my walk that afternoon. In another twenty-four hours I'd be too old to haul my body up and down Scottish hills. The climb was steeper than I had expected, and I was panting by the time I got to the reservoir.

Lying in a plateau of the hill, it was no bigger than a cattle pond back home, casually fenced with wire and apparently relying on gravity to supply the village faucets and on large rocks in feeder streams to purify the water that was shared by humans, deer, rabbits, and other creatures. I hoped the old rule I'd learned from my daddy sixty years before still applied:

"Go downstream five big rocks past where animals drink, and the water's clean." I couldn't help wondering, though, how much acid rain and airborne chemicals might be in that water now.

Several tracks led from the reservoir, and I wasn't sure which one Eileen had meant. All meandered through the heather in crooked patterns that I suspected had been laid out by grazing animals rather than human feet. I followed one at random, hoping it led to a road that I kept glimpsing now and then downhill to my right. Feeling adventurous, I tried leaving it at one point when the way looked shorter, but discovered that walking on heather is like walking on foam rubber. It bounces and gives underfoot, then throws you back up. After a few attempts for the sake of saying I'd done it, I stuck to the track worn by generations of animal feet.

I walked for more than an hour, scarcely noticing when

the track began to climb uphill again away from the road. I was too busy absorbing the scenery and the fact that I, MacLaren Yarbrough, was fortunate enough to be walking alone in the Scottish Highlands. Could anything compare with the beautiful freshness of those ancient hills, or the silence? The heather must have muffled noise, for when I stopped walking and stood absolutely still, I could well imagine I was the only creature alive on earth. The only sounds I could hear were sibilants—the splash of a stream rushing down the hillside and wind swishing in a belt of trees. Not one bird, beast, human or mechanical engine added its staccato counterpoint. I thudded my feet to make sure I hadn't lost my hearing and was startled to flush a bird. It flew away with an indignant squawk.

I stood still for so long that a tiny deer moved near me. It would scarcely have come up to my armpit and was a light golden brown, very dainty. Eileen would later tell me it was a roe deer. Only when it ambled away over the hill did I resume my walk. But as the path continued without coming anywhere near the road, I checked my watch a bit anxiously. The sun was poised on the top of a western mountain, and the sky was already beginning to fade in the east. As much as I was enjoying the hills, I preferred to spend the night in a warm bed.

Spying a smaller track heading off to the right, I plunged downhill. As I reached a large, flat boulder surrounded by bright yellow Scotch broom, I heard men's voices below me. There was a wide belt of trees down there, so at first I presumed they were foresters finishing their day's work. Gradually I realized that one of them was very angry. Reluctant to pass them while they were arguing, I crouched behind the broom and hoped they'd soon leave so I could get home before dark.

Then one raised his voice in a thick accent that sounded a whole lot like folks back home. "You cain't cut me out! Not after all I've done!"

The other's voice was clear and sharp. "Och, I'm offering you more than you deserve."

"I don't want your damned check. I want a share of the business."

"Don't be ridiculous. You're putting up nothing." That was no Scot. It was Jim Gordon, with the accent he'd cultivated for business purposes.

"I arranged the whole shebang," the Southerner objected.

"You arranged nothing. I contacted you, remember. You're being fairly paid for the little you've had to do."

He got a stream of profanity that described just how fair the other thought his pay was. "You cain't get away with this," he finally threatened. "We're partners, Jimmy, like it or not."

"I wouldn't be partners with you if you were the last man on earth. I ken what you did to your last partner, and you needn't think I don't. Bill Gray never stole that money. I had a man trace it for me, and I know how you did it. I don't frankly care, but if you try and threaten me, I'll see you in jail for the rest of your pitiful life. Take the check."

"You—" Another stream of profanity was followed by a thud.

"Norwood! What the dickens have you done?"

The woman's voice was both unexpected and a relief. I peered cautiously around my bush and down across the broad rock. Jim Gordon was climbing up from the ground, holding his stomach. A short stocky man with a head full of unruly gray curls was standing nearby panting like a small angry bull. The woman—taller than he and solid rather than stout—was coming out of the trees brandishing a walking stick in his direction.

"This has nothin' to do with you, Kitty," the Southerner called in a petulant tone.

"You fool," she stormed at him. "Jim, are you all right?"

"I'm fine." Jim dusted off his pants. "Just like always, Norwood got a little hot under the collar. He didn't hit me, he butted me with his head."

"He's trying to cut me out of the deal, shug," Norwood raged. "After all I've done."

"I'm not cutting you out," Jim repeated. "I'm offering you a check. A handsome one, I might add, considering how little you had to do."

"I want a share!" Norwood protested. "I deserve—"

"You better watch out for Norwood. He can be dangerous." Was she warning Jim, or threatening him?

"You don't go hunting rattlesnakes without a big stick, Kitty, and I've known you and Norwood long enough to know you've got rattlers on both sides of your family. I've got a stick."

"What kind of stick?"

"Never you mind. Norwood and I understand each other."

"How'd you know Norwood was over here? He's kept real quiet about that, back home."

"With good reason," Jim said bluntly, brushing off his pants, "but a friend saw him on a plane to Zurich, a while back."

"What friend?" She and Norwood asked it in unison.

When Jim didn't answer, she changed the subject. "You're comin' for dinner—you and your wife—aren't you?"

The way she stressed "wife" made the word downright immoral, but Jim's answer was mild. "Aye. I called and left a message with whoever answers your phone."

"And what's her name again—your wife's?"

"Brandi."

"What's she like?" The edge was still in her voice.

I took a better look at her. She was perhaps fifty, with wide bands of gray framing her face while the rest of her hair was still dark and cut short to cup her chin—the kind of haircut that looks simple but requires really good hair and a lot of money to achieve. She was practically but expensively dressed in dark slacks, walking shoes, and a tweed jacket. Her face was full of strength, as was the arm that had wielded the stick. Her expression was wary as she waited for Jim's answer.

He bent to pick up his cap. "Smart. In more ways than one. She ran a landscape-design business before we married. She's decorative, as well. And always cheerful."

"Which nobody could say about poor Irene." Her voice was flat.

"Nobody ever accused Irene of being cheerful," he agreed as he set his cap on his head.

"Don't you forget that Irene is my lifelong friend."

"I won't forget. But you remember that Brandi is my wife. We'll see you around eight." He loped off down through the trees.

The woman shook the other man's arm. "You utter fool. Hit, hit, hit—that's all you know. Jim could have killed you if he'd wanted to. He's terribly strong."

"He is not leaving me out of this deal," Norwood insisted, pulling away from her. "I set it up, persuaded Gavin—"

"I persuaded Gavin. You persuaded me."

"I deserve a share."

She gave a short snort of impatience. "I warned you fifteen years ago, greed is going to be the death of you. How many years have you known Jim Gordon—thirty? You ought to know by now that nobody crosses him and wins. Now come on."

"What are you doing up here, anyway?"

"I came looking for you. I figured you'd try something dumb as soon as I heard that Jim had called you, so I drove around until I saw your car beside the road. You weren't hard to find, with all that racket you were making." She looked up, and I ducked back behind my bush.

"You have defiled this place," she said, "and it's sacred to me. Up there on that rock is where I first met Gavin. We sat and talked for hours."

"After you'd climbed up there for the express purpose of running into him, accidentally on purpose. And having vetted him, your heart went pitty-pat and you decided, 'Having outlived a magnate, why not buy myself a little laird?'" Norwood's tone was rude.

"It was a sounder investment than most of yours. Come on, I have things to do before dinner." She turned and strode down the hill toward the trees, leaving him to follow.

I crept from my hiding place, but I wanted to give them time to drive away, and the big flat rock made a real good place to wait. Broom circled it on two sides, creating a natural break against the wind that roiled down from the hilltop and hiding it from the road. As I settled onto its broad surface, I had to agree that fighting did not belong in this place.

Tier after tier of mountains rose in the west, brown in the foreground and fading to blue and then purple against the now-salmon sky. A bird drifted in lazy spirals high overhead in a deepening darkness. Below me I heard rustles as small creatures settled in for the night.

While I waited, I wondered: What had that fight been about?

It didn't take rocket science to figure out that Jim had not come on this trip simply to please his wife. Brandi might have *ooh*ed and *ahh*ed her way around the Highlands, but she had little knowledge about or interest in Scottish hills or heritage. From what I'd overheard after the ceilidh and what she'd told me at Dunrobin Castle gardens, Jim must have promised she could landscape their garden if she'd provide a cover so he could come inconspicuously into Auchnagar to make a business deal. The deal involved the laird, through his wife, who was Jim's ex-wife's friend. A bit complicated, but still comprehensible.

She was a type of woman I knew well. Mama used to say, "Honey, some women may be steel magnolias, but that one is more like cast-iron honeysuckle: a sweet-smelling layer over a well-seasoned hardness, and common as all get-out." Kitty MacGorrie's accent was a thin Scottish veneer over pure Southern, so it must have been back home that Jim and his first wife knew her.

I also recognized Kitty's and Norwood's blunt rudeness for what it was. They talked to one another the same way my brother and I sometimes do, and there was a family likeness in their faces. He must be several years older than she, but women like Kitty don't yield to anybody.

What business could draw Jim to this place? An overseas distillery? I wasn't real clear on how scotch is made, but surely a distillery would require more water than Auchnagar's little burn could provide. And why come by stealth? If Scottish villages were anything like Georgia small towns, they would jump with joy at the promise of another employer. Why not drive up to the laird's in a limousine and stay in comfort at the laird's house while you completed the deal?

I shivered in a rising wind, and realized the pink in the

west was fast turning gray. The path down through the woods between me and the road was already inky black. Above me, the meandering track I'd arrived by was still visible, but daylight would not linger long enough for me to get home that way. I set off downhill at a stumbling trot that nearly pitched me head over heels. The fact that I reached the road without twisting an ankle was due more to my guardian angel than to skill.

I went marching along the narrow road at a brisk pace, hoping no deer were out roaming that night. I was real glad to see a flashlight approaching.

"Hello!" I called, trying to sound cheerful.

"MacLaren?" It was Dorothy, accompanied by a tall skinny companion who held the light. "This is Roddy, Eileen's son," she said when I got close enough to see them more clearly.

He shone the light up into his face and grinned. "Her charming, handsome son."

Starting from the bottom of the light and traveling upwards, he had a big Adam's apple, a weak chin, a wide mouth, a big nose, his mother's dark eyes, and a shock of greasy red curls. "Dorothy feared you'd got lost on the hill, but I told her we'd find you, right enough. Come along, noo. Tea's ready."

As I fell into step beside them, I was glad of their company, but Roddy didn't speak to me much. He was too busy showing Dorothy what a fascinating, charming fellow he was. In years of raising boys and sitting as a judge, I'd seen a number of grins like his and heard a lot of similar patter. They invariably went with a charming, shiftless, and spoiled-rotten rascal.

❧ 15 ❧

Roddy joined us in the dining room for tea and continued to exercise his charm on Dorothy. Instead of turning bright pink and going into her shell, she seemed to enjoy him. She laughed at his jokes and finally agreed to accompany him down to the hotel bar that evening "to sample the fascinatin' night life we have to offer in Auchnagar on a Thursday evening."

After tea, Eileen invited Marcia back to the kitchen for what she called "a wee natter." The others decided to go with Dorothy and Roddy down to the hotel bar, and when Marcia informed Roddy that Dorothy played the flute, he urged, "Bring it along. The place is dead quiet this time of the week." Sherry decided to take her fiddle, as well, but when Kenny asked them to wait while he got his bagpipes, Roddy informed him, "Pipes are no permitted in the bar except for dances and special occasions."

I elected to settle by the fire with a book to enjoy some peace and quiet. When I found myself nodding soon after nine, I went upstairs, chose the bed nearest the window, drew back the curtains, and climbed under the covers. The hills were black against a slightly lighter sky while thousands of stars dotted the sky like bright shards of hope. I didn't exactly feel the spirit of Andrew MacLaren hovering over me, but did have a deep sense of homecoming.

I was just falling asleep when I heard Jim and Brandi return from the laird's. I roused briefly when a herd of elephants trooped up the stairs just as the grandfather clock in the downstairs hall struck twelve. When I waked at half past two, I knew I had to cross the chilly hall to go to the toilet, and hoped the dog wouldn't bark an announcement of my journey to the household. In the dim light, I saw that Laura still wasn't in.

As I left our room, she and Kenny came tiptoing up the stairs. "Think about it," I heard him whisper. "I hope you'll say yes."

"Your bed's by the door," I called softly and hurried into the bathroom. When I got back to our room, she was in bed with the covers pulled over her face.

I woke at seven to the calls of many birds. I tiptoed to the window and watched Alex Carmichael fill several feeders, then rest his hands at his waist and survey the mountains while taking deep breaths, as if he couldn't get enough of the hills or the air. I got up, washed and dressed, but it was still more than an hour until breakfast. What was I supposed to do with myself until then? I headed downstairs figuring a short walk before breakfast wouldn't kill me. I might even earn virtue points, since our early joggers seemed to be sleeping in after their evening at the bar. But I sure wished I had a hot cup of coffee.

When I heard voices in the kitchen, I knocked. The dog barked. Roddy opened the door a crack, holding a golden Lab by its collar. He wore jeans and a sweater, but was still in sock feet. "Mornin'," he greeted me, with such a roguish grin that I found myself grinning back.

"Would it be possible to get a cup of coffee?"

"Och, aye," he said graciously. "Go into the dinin' room and I'll tell me mum. She's fixin' my breakfast just noo, but she'll bring one right out, nae bother."

My estimate of the night before was confirmed. Whoever married Roddy Lamont would be getting the kind of man who not only took it for granted a woman would cook his breakfast, but who presumed she wouldn't mind interrupting that process to bring somebody else a cup of coffee he could have easily carried himself.

However, when Eileen arrived with a steaming cup on a tray with milk and sugar, I merely said, "I appreciated your son and Dorothy coming to my rescue last night. You must be glad to have him around the house."

"Aye. He's a good lad, Roddy. Not settled yet, but a fine lad."

"Does he help you run the guesthouse?"

"Och, no. He works down at the ski lift as long as the snow lasts, and this spring he's working part-time cleaning our church until he finds something better." My guess was that jobs for young men in the village were few and far between. I also suspected that Roddy didn't stir his stumps to be at the front of the line when permanent jobs did come available.

"Is there any place to get a paper this early?" I asked.

"Aye. Down at the bottom of the hill, across the bridge, there's a wee paper shop. You can't miss it."

Given how easily I had missed the path the previous afternoon, I had reservations, but sure enough, I found the small green shop and its tiny proprietress, who stood in semidarkness with carefully waved hair and all sorts of papers and magazines set out before her on the counter. I left with not only a Scottish newspaper, but several bars of chocolate to stave off starvation between meals and postcards to send home to my grandchildren. They wouldn't care if the cards arrived after I did. Children always enjoy getting mail.

I paused on the stone bridge that spanned the stream and leaned on the parapet to watch the dark foaming water rush around huge boulders before plunging down the hill. As a child, I had loved standing on small bridges. How long had it been since I'd last stopped on one, or had nothing better to do than watch water run downhill? Feeling many years younger than I am, I snatched up two tall weeds from beyond the bridge and dropped them in. As soon as they landed, I dashed to the other side and peered over to see which would come out first.

"Fit ye deein'?" an indignant voice piped from the region of my elbow.

I turned to see china blue eyes staring up at me severely. They belonged to a small girl of perhaps seven, with a cascade of red-orange hair falling in waves from beneath a brown knit cap. She carried a navy blue bookbag slung over her shoulder by one strap.

"I beg your pardon?" I asked, uncertain what she had said and a lot more interested in looking down to see when my first weed appeared.

"Fit ye *deein*'?" Seeing that I still didn't understand, she propped one small hand on her hip, knit her eyebrows— which were so pale they were mere brushstrokes above her eyes—and gestured to the other side of the bridge with a bare hand reddened by cold. "Runnin' like a chicken from one side o' the bridge to t'other without lookin' to see if a car was a'comin'? You coulda been *killt*."

One car had gone up the village road in the quarter hour since I came down it, and its tires had crunched noisily on loose gravel. Still, I recognized the mother's voice in the child's, so I nodded. "I sure could have. I'm sorry. I was in a hurry to see which of my boats would come out first. Look! There's the first one now. It's really a weed," I added for clarification.

She flopped onto the parapet, which came to her armpits, and peered down. Together we watched the valiant victor bob downstream. When the loser still hadn't appeared a minute later, the child said with the shrug of experience, "I doot it's hung up on a rock."

I hated to see her leave, so I asked, "Do you live in the village?"

"Och, aye. Over there." She flapped her hand in the general direction of the hotel and whatever lay behind it. "D'ye come from America, then?" She seemed as willing to chat as I.

"Yes, but my ancestors came from Auchnagar. They were MacLarens."

She thought that over, then shook her head. "I nivver met them," she admitted, "but it's maybe that they lived too far-r-r out of town." She cocked her head and peered up at the blue sky. "Ye've got good weather for your visit."

After I'd agreed that yes, the weather was fine, she gave me a long look, then asked, "Are ye a good American or a filthy rich one?"

Startled, I replied, "A good one, I hope. Do you know many filthy rich ones?"

She picked up one foot and used it to scratch the calf of the other leg. "Just the laird's wifey. I simply cannae abide her. He only married her for the money, you know." Sounded to me like grownups had better watch their words around this child. "And that brother of hers is nae better, struttin' around like it was him is Laird of Auchnagar."

"What was that you said to me first?" I asked hastily, eager to change the subject. "You know, the 'fitchy deein'' bit."

She watched her toe scuffing gravel. "I dinna mean to be r-r-rude. I was just wonderin' fit ye were deein' scampering about like a lamb in a public r-r-road."

When I got back to my room, I was going to practice rolling my r's like that. For now, I laughed. "A lamb? Me?"

She threw back her head and joined in, showing two new front teeth. Then she grew solemn again. "Wi' all the tourists we get, and the laird's wifey drivin' like she owns the r-r-road, nivver lookin' to see if somebody's aboot, ye'd do well to look fit ye're deein' next time."

I thought that over. "So 'fit ye deein'' means 'what are you doing'?"

"Aye." She waited to see if I had any more brilliance to offer. When I didn't, she shrugged. "I must be awa up the road, then." She added casually, but with an air of importance, "I feed Barbara Geddys's dog, cats, and hens before school. She has far too much to do, bein' postmistress and all, so she likes me to help out a wee bittie. But Mum says I mustna be late for school again, or I'll nae be allowed to help Barbara a-tall." She heaved the sigh of one with the cares of the world on her shoulders. "School is such a bloomin' waste."

"Watch out for the laird's wifey," I teased.

She gave a hoot of derisive laughter. "She'll nae be oot o' her bed at this hour. But come ten o'clock she'll be barrelin' doon the r-r-road, headin' for the post office. Ye can set your watch by that. And if Barbara's been a bit slow puttin' out the mail? Och, what a to-do!" Again, I had the feeling she was quoting somebody else.

She propped herself against the bridge again, school forgotten. "Are ye on holiday?"

"Yes, a Gilroy's tour."

"Then I doot ye'll be staying wi' Eileen Lamont, since the hotel's being painted."

"All except our driver. I don't know where he's staying."

"Och, he's stayin' wi' Mum, as usual. He's nae bothered by a bit o' paint. Cheerio, then." She gave a little wave and trudged over the bridge, leaving me in startled silence.

"Perhaps her mother runs a bed and breakfast," I muttered as I headed up the brae. Many women did. But the way the child had said, "stayin' wi' Mum" sounded a lot more personal than renting a room. Did Watty have something going with the little girl's mother? If so, it didn't sound like they were particularly discreet.

When I spotted Eileen dusting the lounge, I mentioned, "I ran into a little girl on the bridge. Red hair, blue eyes, and no fear about telling me I should look when I cross the road."

"That'll have been Morag MacBeth. A right wee terror, that one. Skips school as often as she goes, and wastes her time drawin' animals when she bothers to show up a-tall. But och, what can ye expect? Her mother's aye busy with the hotel. It's no life for a child, growin' up in a back office. Are ye ready for your breakfast? I was just about to ring the gong."

Relieved, I headed upstairs to set down my parcels, accusing myself of having a dirty mind. Gilroy's must put its drivers up in their hotels, which confirmed the connection between the two I'd suspected all along.

I found Laura sitting on her bed tying her shoes. "Look who's up bright and early this morning," I greeted her. "You've slept two hours past your usual time. I've already been down to the village."

My impressive accomplishment went unnoticed. Laura merely glanced up from her shoelace and said, "It ought to be time for breakfast soon." Then she bent down like tying a shoe took all her concentration.

"Did you have fun last night down at the bar?" I didn't

think either of us wanted me asking about what had happened afterwards.

She shrugged. "Nothing special." She got up and went to brush her hair.

"Do you think Dorothy likes Roddy?"

"Maybe. She sat with him and the guy who carried our bags up—Alex something or other—but Roddy did most of the talking." In the mirror, I saw her peer at her own reflection, chewing her lower lip. When she reached up to her neck, I knew something was bothering her. All those years when Laura wore her hair long, she had a habit of sucking a strand when upset. Even now that the hair was gone, she still reached for it in distress.

Kenny's last words to her the night before came barreling out of the back of my thoughts, and I realized they'd been rattling around in there all morning. Had he offered to divorce Sherry if Laura would marry him? Was she distracted today because she was turning his proposal over in her mind? If so, that was news I could gladly postpone until after breakfast.

Laura didn't look like a woman about to accept a proposal, though. She looked like she was about to take an exam for which she wasn't fully prepared.

❧ 16 ❧

When we entered the dining room, Kenny and Sherry sat at a table for four in the middle of the room. He looked up like he hoped Laura would sit with them, but she didn't even look his way—just headed for a table for six in the bay window, where Joyce and Dorothy were already sipping tea. That table was definitely the most inviting, with sunshine streaming in, but Kenny frowned as if she'd made a poor choice.

Marcia helped bring in our oatmeal and said she was eating with Eileen in the kitchen.

Roddy joined us, however, and again made himself the life of the party talking about a motorbike rally he planned to attend that weekend with a friend, and a bike he hoped to buy. I listened with only half an ear.

By the time I'd worked my way through oatmeal followed by fried eggs, broiled tomatoes, broad slices of bacon, and toast with butter and jam, all washed down with tea, I was in danger of being unable to leave my seat. I nearly groaned aloud when Eileen came through to ask how many of us would be there for midday dinner. "Marcia, of course, and you, Dorothy?" she asked, holding up two fingers as a counting aid.

"No, I have other plans." Dorothy's voice was little more than a whisper. "But I'll be back for tea."

Sherry claimed Eileen's attention, asking about the village shops and ways to get to the next village, which was larger. Roddy leaned across the table so far I thought he'd get his Adam's apple in what was left of his fried egg. "And where might ye be goin'?"

Dorothy looked down at her plate. "Out and about, eh?"

"Don't you go helping Alex, noo," he warned. "I heard him last night, tellin' you all about how his helper's left and he's falling behind in his work, but who cares when a picture gets framed? Today, tomorrow—what's the difference? Come for a spin on my bike. Let me show you the greater Auchnagar environs." He spread his arms to encompass the world.

"Thanks, but not today." Dorothy threw Marcia an apologetic look, shoved back her chair, and fled.

Eileen stopped in the middle of offering to call a neighbor who might be driving to the next village, to ask if Sherry could have a ride. "Did you upset her?" she asked Roddy.

"Not me," he assured her, reaching for the jam. "It's Alex. Makin' up to her like mad, he is." He caught my eye and gave me a saucy wink.

"Did he not tell her about Shana in Aberdeen?" Eileen demanded.

"Not likely." He shoved back his chair and stomped out.

Eileen sighed and confided to all of us, "Och, and she's an awfu' lassie, jealous as they come. Always on to Alex about moving to the city where he can make more money, while poor Alex is fixin' up rooms above his wee shop, thinkin' Shana'll come round and move in with him when he's got it lookin' nice." She sighed again, then remembered why she'd come into the dining room. "But I was taking a count for dinner. Will the rest of you be here?"

"I'm going to walk up the brae and across the moor this morning," Laura told her, "but I'll be back by dinnertime. I'll leave at nine-thirty, if anybody cares to join me. Mac?"

"No, I walked up that way yesterday afternoon, just before tea." I watched Jim, who was sitting with Brandi at a table for two in the corner, but he didn't miss a chew. "I want to explore the village a bit this morning," I added, "see if I can find some MacLarens."

That got Jim's attention, for some reason. "Try the cemetery," he suggested, adding to Eileen, "I've got an appointment and don't know how long it will take. I'll get a bite somewhere." When Brandi looked from him to Sherry with speculation in her eye, he asked, "Why don't you go shopping with Sherry?"

"I'd rather go walking with Laura."

"Suit yourself." He seemed far more interested in his eggs.

Kenny leaned toward their table. "How was dinner in the exalted circle, Jim?"

It was Brandi who answered. "We had the best time. The laird's wife, Kitty, turned out to be an old friend of Jimmy's from Albany!" She looked around to make sure we were all duly impressed. "It was such fun for him to see her again. And her brother, Norwood, was a scream."

Sherry looked up, her eyes wary. I was reminded of a snake waiting to strike. "Not Norwood Hardin, the one whose company ruined all those people?"

"That was his name," Brandi agreed, "but I'm sure he never ruined anybody. He was charming. He told us all about your little play, Joyce. He's the star," she added for the rest of us.

Sherry ignored Brandi. "Did you know Norwood back in Albany, Jim?"

"Slightly." He gave no indication he was in cahoots with the man. No wonder Donald Trump could make it as a television star. Acting must be a way of life for tycoons.

Brandi widened those beautiful eyes. "But I don't think Norwood would ruin anybody. He was the cutest thing in the world!"

Sherry gave a disgusted snort. "Cute nothing. He and his partner, William Gray, owned an investment company that stole millions from their clients, including my aunt Rose. Gray was the one who got convicted, and he went to jail and died there—claiming he was innocent, of course. Cute little Norwood testified at Gray's trial that he was appalled at what his partner had done, and he'd had no idea what Gray was up to. But afterwards, did he care what happened to the people who were ruined, or give up a penny of his own fortune to help them? Ha! Aunt Rose lost every penny she had invested for retirement. She planned to live in a Palm Beach condo. Instead, she's in a mobile-home park near Brooksville on what we paid her for the restaurant. That's all she has left." Sherry buttered a piece of toast like she was slathering Norwood in hot tar. Jim chewed his eggs like Sherry was speaking a foreign language he did not understand.

Brandi gave a bored sigh. "Well, I thought Norwood was delightful. He acted out a couple of scenes from the play, Joyce, and they were hilarious. He kept us in stitches. I can't wait to see it, can you, Jimmy?"

Joyce, across from me, choked on her tea. While Laura was pounding her on the back, Kenny mused, "So Aunt Rose's former broker is now the laird's brother-in-law?" He sounded like he was trying to figure out how to parlay that into a dinner invitation of their own.

Joyce shuddered and pressed her hands to her temples. Poor thing, nobody wants to be told your historical drama is hysterical and the lead actor used it to keep folks in stitches. But when she stood, she told Eileen, "I think I'm starting a migraine, and the actors are driving out from Aberdeen for rehearsal at three, so I'm going back to bed. I won't want any dinner."

"Shall I bring you up a wee tray at half past twelve?"

"Please don't. The only thing that helps is to take a pill and lie perfectly still for hours. Can you all get along without me?"

We assured her we could and she hurried out the door. "I was afraid that woman was gonna break sometime," I murmured to Laura. "I hope she's okay in time for her play."

Eileen went to phone her neighbor and returned to inform Sherry she could have a ride to the next village between ten and eleven. Sherry left. Jim and Brandi got up and Brandi and Laura arranged to meet in the downstairs hall at nine-thirty. When they'd gone, I felt like a third wheel, so I left Kenny and Laura sitting at different tables, obviously waiting to be alone.

I wrote a few postcards before setting out for the village around nine-fifteen. As I started down the stairs, I heard Kenny shouting, but couldn't distinguish his words. When I rounded the landing, he came storming out the dining room door and hurried past me up the stairs, his face puce and his eyes pink with tears.

"Kenny!" Laura stood in the dining-room door holding the frame, her face pale. Her eyes, too, were pink and wet. When she saw me looking at her, she glared. "Don't ask, Mac. It's none of your business." She, too, strode up the stairs and I heard our door slam.

I headed for the village greatly disturbed. Laura hadn't been rude to me since she was fourteen. Not until I was well down the brae did I realize that Kenny hadn't said a word at breakfast about how he planned to spend the day.

The woman at the post-office counter was the woman Dorothy had thought looked like Jim. There was a slight resemblance: white hair, bushy eyebrows, and a certain look around the eyes, but if you travel at all, you know there are a finite number of faces in the world. I'm forever running into people who look like somebody I know. And as Jim had pointed out, it was their noses that looked the most alike.

She waited on me with courtesy but little warmth. As she handed me stamps and change, I saw that her hands and wrists were twisted with arthritis, and she wore no wedding ring on her poor swollen fingers. I hoped she could soon retire in a modicum of comfort.

"I met a little girl on the bridge today who said she feeds your hens and pets," I told her.

Her stark face brightened. "Wee Morag. Aye, she loves animals, but her mother cannae have them in the hotel, so she comes up and takes care of mine. She's a right wee dear, that one." Which differed slightly from the "wee terror" Eileen had described. "Are ye over from America, then?" She thawed enough to lean on her counter.

"Yes, hoping to find some trace of my ancestors in Auchnagar. I thought I might look in the cemetery, for a beginning."

"Aren't ye wi' Watty's tour? Ask Joyce, then. She stayed a week last spring readin' kirk records and gatherin' information. I'd think she knows what there is to know."

"She was researching a play," I told her. "She had accidentally run into the laird's wife—I think it was in your very doorway—and the laird's wife said if Joyce would write a play, perhaps she would put it on in the community center. It's going to be Saturday night." I stopped when I remembered the post office had a notice for the play in its window.

Her lips twisted in what I suppose was a smile of sorts. "Is that how Joyce tells the story?"

"How would you tell it?"

"That she researched the village, found out Mrs. Mac-Gorrie comes in here every morning at ten, and hung around to bump into her. She had to come twice—the laird's wifey was out of town the first day." Her chuckle was deep and infectious.

I chuckled, too. "I guess writers get desperate at times." I picked up my stamps and turned to go. "Until I can talk to Joyce, maybe I'll try the cemetery. Is it next to one of the churches?"

"Och, no. Cross the burn, turn right, and go three-quarters of a mile. Ye cannae miss it."

As I passed through the village, I saw Sherry in a pricey-looking wool shop, fingering a plaid cape like the one she had on. She rubbed the material between her fingers, then nodded and handed the clerk her charge card. If she didn't stop buying, we were going to have to tie a storage container to the back of our plane on the way home.

Barbara Geddys had failed to mention that there was only a narrow verge between the road and a barbed-wire fence, or to remind me to walk on the right to face oncoming traffic. Having nearly been struck by a car whizzing up from behind, I crossed the road and walked close to the fence, wondering how many cemetery occupants had arrived there after taking that very stroll.

The burial ground was marked by a tall monolith rising above a high stone wall that framed a square of land cut from surrounding fields. A small parking area sat in front of the cemetery and a simple wrought-iron gate was set in the center of the wall. Inside, the cemetery seemed small to hold all the people who had died for centuries, and the earliest grave I found was from 1845. This cemetery, then, must have been started during the dismal preoccupation with funerals of Victoria's reign. Where had villagers been buried before that?

The only MacLarens were a small family that had died out in 1935 with an apparently single woman named Margaret. Disappointed—and annoyed that Joyce hadn't supplied me with information she might have about MacLarens, since I'd said on my questionnaire I wanted to know about them in Auchnagar—I copied down the names and dates and wished my family had done its research in time to meet the last MacLaren.

I was bent over an adjoining plot, peering down at the flat stones in the grass and trying to make out the name, when I heard a whoosh behind me and something large and furry landed on my back. I sprawled across the grass with a yell, and felt hot breath on the back of my neck.

"Godfrey! No! Down!" Feet came running. I struggled to get out from under the heavy animal, which was now licking me like a favorite toy. I was making little headway when I suddenly felt myself freed in one strong jerk. I looked up to see a man in a kilt standing above me, holding what looked like a brown and tan rug by the collar. The rug lurched back at me, long tongue lolling, ready for another lick. "Godfrey! No! Down!"

It collapsed at his feet into a large English sheepdog, watching me hopefully.

I did not see what that Scotsman wore under his kilt. I was too flustered getting to my feet.

"I do beg your pardon!" Godfrey, encouraged by the man's friendly tone, started up, but his master shoved his haunches. "Down!" The dog fell to a crouch and stayed, his tongue lolling, ready to play at the slightest signal. "Did he frighten you? He has no manners whatsoever." The man's face was full of distress. "I'd have come sooner if I'd realized you were here." His accent was different from Watty's or those of the villagers, precise and easy to understand. "You were behind the monument, you see." He pointed.

I turned, and did see. The base of the monolith was between me and the gate.

"But, of course, he isn't supposed to be inside." The man

cast an anxious look toward the road and rubbed an ear in embarrassment. "We share the cemetery with the Catholics, you see, and Father Ewan is very strict about this being consecrated ground. Not that we Presbyterians don't respect graves," he muddled on with an expression that said he knew he was digging his own grave deeper the longer he talked, but felt compelled to try and make me understand, "but they take these things so much more seriously than we do. I mean, not more seriously, but they won't let dogs—" He came to a full stop.

"I'm a Presbyterian," I said, in case that might help.

It must have, for he brightened. "Godfrey, on the other hand, is a bundle of original sin. He sees any forbidden place as a challenge. As soon as I opened the door and he spied the open gate, he leaped out." He frowned down at the dog but when Godfrey sat up and gave him a happy smile, his owner's frown turned into a reluctant grin. "You old rogue." He bent and rubbed the big dog's head. "Just like a child spying an open biscuit tin."

"It's okay. I have a beagle back home." I held out a hand to let Godfrey sniff me. He rewarded me with a lick, and I scratched him behind one ear.

"I do beg your pardon," the man said. "I haven't introduced myself. I'm Gavin MacGorrie." He stuck out one hand and looked down at his other in bewilderment. "I had some flowers here somewhere."

"I think you dropped them near the gate." A clump of red lay beyond the monolith.

"Thank you. Stay, Godfrey!" he commanded, and went to retrieve his bouquet. The dog whined, but remained beside my feet.

So this was the Laird of Auchnagar. He looked nothing like I would have expected. I had pictured a man of commanding height and bearing, more like Jim Gordon, who would stride down the village street while everybody watched with pride. This man, who couldn't be more than forty, had thinning dark hair lightly touched with gray at the sideburns and eyes as brown as Godfrey's. He was of insignificant height and build, with a diffident air and a scholar's stoop. And his kilt looked as worn and comfortable as Joe Riddley's favorite pair of corduroys.

"It's the anniversary of my mother's death, you see," he explained as he returned with a bedraggled bouquet. "I always bring flowers. But I've ruined this lot, haven't I?" He looked down at them in dismay. "My wife arranged them so all I had to do was stick them in the vase, but look at them now. Kitty will kill me, Godfrey, and it's all your fault." He bent again to fondle the dog's head. Godfrey made little happy noises in his throat. Apparently he feared his mistress far less than his master did.

Remembering the woman I'd seen the night before, I calculated that the laird's wife was as tall and somewhat heavier than he, and must be at least ten years older. I had no doubt that she wore the pants in the family, in more ways than one.

"Let me see what I can do with the flowers," I offered. I arranged them as we walked together toward the monolith.

He went to his car for a plastic jug of water and filled a stone urn by the base of the stone, then took the flowers from me and stuck them in with little ceremony. "There you are, Mum." He stepped back and rubbed his hands together with a dry papery sound. "They look fine. I cannot thank you enough. Kitty takes this annual ritual very seriously." He leaned over and cupped one hand around his mouth to confide (although we weren't in earshot of a soul except Godfrey), "Far more seriously than Mum would, if she knew a thing about it." He seemed very pleasant, as lairds go. I hoped I wasn't supposed to curtsy or something.

He whistled and Godfrey came bounding from where he had obediently remained. "Will you accept a ride back to the village by way of an apology for Godfrey's lack of manners? And mine!" he exclaimed. "I never asked your name."

"I'm MacLaren Yarbrough. I was looking for ancestors' graves, but I only found modern stones here. Where are the older graves?"

He looked around the churchyard, puzzled. "You know, I have no idea. We have a family plot on the estate, but—" He looked distressed again, as well he might. Not to know where the peasants are buried would seem a serious breach of lordly responsibility.

"I'll ask in the village," I said, letting him off the hook. He looked relieved.

"Where are you from, Mrs. Yarbrough?" He was at least socially proficient. He had remembered my name and looked for my wedding ring before he spoke.

"Georgia."

"My wife is from Georgia!" He rubbed his hands together again in pleasure. "Have you ever been to Albany?"

"Several times. We live not too far from there."

He beamed. "Now, I insist. You must let me give a fellow Georgian a ride."

I looked at his ancient Land Rover and thought of all the hair and drool Godfrey had deposited over the years. "No, thank you, I'm enjoying my walk."

I was declining what might be my only lifetime offer to ride with nobility, but at least I could brag that a laird once made me a proposal and I turned him down.

"Well, I will certainly tell Kitty I met you. We have quite a contingent of Georgians in the village just now, did you know? They're on one of Gilroy's tours."

"I'm with them. I believe you already know one member of our group—Jim Gordon?" I wanted to see his reaction. Would he look furtive?

Not at all. "Oh, yes. Jim, Kitty, and her brother, Norwood, were friends back in Albany. He brought his wife to dinner last evening. Pleasant woman." He didn't sound the least bit attracted by Brandi's charms.

I grew bolder. "Jim said he has some business in Auchnagar." I have found that making a statement is often better than asking a question.

He beamed as if I'd brought up his favorite subject. "Oh, yes. He and I plan to build a first-class hotel just down the road." He gestured away from the village. "We hope to get it up and running in a year or so. Skiing is big business in this part of Scotland, but Jim also wants to build a golf course adjacent to the hotel, to attract summer visitors." He looked about him at the brown fields and bare hills. "It will spruce the place up a bit. At this time, we only have the one hotel, Gilroy's. And while it's clean and comfortable, it doesn't attract—"

He let that trail off. I suspected he'd been about to say "the best people" and then had remembered I was on a Gilroy's tour.

He whistled for Godfrey, who came bounding our way with delight. "I will probably see you again, for I believe Kitty has arranged a little get-together for your group tomorrow evening, following a dramatic performance written by one of your number." He cupped his hand again and confided, "My brother-in-law is highly pleased with the piece. He used to act in amateur theatricals, you know, and he's appearing in the play. He quite fancies himself as the laird." The droll look he gave me before he headed to his Land Rover left me smiling as he drove away.

I still had time before dinner to cruise the shops looking for a special souvenir for Joe Riddley and one for myself. I found a bookstore and hoped for a book on the MacLarens, but settled for a small book bound in Stewart tartan silk and titled *The Clans and Tartans of Scotland*. When I carried it over to the counter, the clerk asked, "Are you with Gilroy's tours, then?"

When I admitted I was, she asked, "Did your friend make the bus all right?"

Sherry must have been there, too. "I don't know. I thought she was getting a ride. She and Eileen were talking about somebody who might drive her."

"Och, that's all right, then. She was in here asking about taxicabs, but we dinna have any in Auchnagar. I hope she remembers to catch the late bus, or she'll need to stay the night."

"I'm sure she'll be back long before that," I assured her. "Thanks for asking."

The shop that eventually caught my eye had a window filled with oils and watercolors of Scottish scenes. Several small framed watercolors depicted scenes from Auchnagar, and would be perfect souvenirs. I could not only get them in my extra suitcase and enjoy them daily, but also leave one to each of my sons to remind them of their own heritage. Not that they'd care much about that while they were still middle-aged, but they eventually might. The less future you have, the more you value the past.

"Welcome!" called someone from the back room as the bell tinkled over the door. Alex Carmichael came through to the shop. When he saw who I was, his smile widened until his eyes almost disappeared. "One of Eileen's guests," he exclaimed. I heard a rustle from the other room, like a small mouse had scurried to its hole.

I explained about the watercolors, and he spent time helping me choose from several that were similar, pointing out details in each. We finally settled on a scene of the bridge I had just crossed and the mountain I could see from my window.

"You didn't paint these, did you?" I asked as he rang them up.

He laughed. "Och, no. I used to paint, right enough—even went to art school. I'd drive through Auchnagar on my way to and from home, and plan how I'd come up here after graduation to live and paint. Instead, I got a summer job in this gallery and discovered I preferred helping artists sell their work. It's very satisfying to match the right picture with the right customer. So I bought out the former owner, and here I am." He gave a judicious look at the two water-colors we had selected for my souvenirs. "I think ye'll be pleased with these."

"I'm sure I shall."

It was his chin that convinced me. It was strong and square—the kind of chin I've always associated with men and women of character. I found myself wondering whether strong chins and strong character were genetic traits that went hand in hand, or whether a child with a strong chin had to develop a strong character to survive the chin until he or she grew into it. Either way, this was a young man I instinctively trusted to give me a good deal, although the watercol-ors cost more than I had expected once we had converted pounds to dollars.

I rationalized that Joe Riddley wasn't the only one who could give me presents for my trip. I could afford to treat myself as well. But as I boldly handed over my charge card,

I did feel a little twinge of guilt. There I was, not two hours after criticizing Sherry for charging her way across Scotland, doing the same thing. Talk about looking at the splinter in somebody else's eye around the log in your own. . . .

But as long as I admitted I had a log in my eye, I might as well make it a big log, so while Alex wrote up the sale and wrapped the pictures, I browsed the shop again and selected unframed prints for each of my granddaughters, as well. I was carrying them back to the cash register when, through an open door to a back room, I recognized the dark head with a swinging braid bent over a table.

"Dorothy?" I called before I thought.

She whirled, and the blood rushed to her face like I'd caught her shoplifting.

"Dorothy's helping me out," Alex informed me. "My usual framer had a baby a couple of weeks ago, and I've gotten far behind."

"I did this in high school and college," Dorothy added, still standing there like she expected me to haul her off to jail any minute. "She's a judge," she added to the young man with a scared look in her eye.

I had no idea how she'd found out, but it didn't matter. "I don't have any jurisdiction in Scotland," I assured her, "and I won't be talking to immigration authorities anytime soon."

She gave me a relieved smile, but still looked so worried that I said to Alex, to boost Dorothy's morale, "Dorothy's an artist, as well. Did you know? She does terrific sketches."

The color had subsided in Dorothy's cheeks, but now it rose again.

"And paints as well," Alex agreed. "She mentioned that last evening, and we made a deal. I can't rightly pay her, since she doesn't have a work visa, but I've offered her a canvas and the use of some oils and brushes this afternoon. I've got a lovely deck on the back with a spectacular view. Dorothy can work out there, if she likes and it's not too cold." From Dorothy's expression, I doubted she'd have cared if it had been lashing snow.

I climbed the hill to dinner wondering if there was something in the air of Auchnagar that made people a little crazy. Here Jim was, planning to build a hotel with a golf course in partnership with his ex-wife's friend and her husband, although after what "wee Morag" had said about Kitty having the money in the family, I wasn't sure what the laird had to do with the deal. Laura was sitting up half the night with a married man. Sherry was buying heavy woolens to take back to South Georgia. And Dorothy was more than half smitten with and working illegally for a tall, good-looking giant who had a girl in Aberdeen. I'd thought the quarrels of the past had been bad, but three days in Auchnagar could be worse.

Looking back, I'm glad I had no inkling just then of how bad they were about to get.

⸙ 17 ⸙

Laura arrived at the dinner table looking more at peace and greeted me cordially enough, so I presumed we wouldn't mention our earlier encounter. As Eileen brought our soup, she asked, "Did you enjoy your walk up the brae, then, Laura?"

"Sure did," Laura replied. "I met a troop of Girl Guides and arranged to climb the big hill out the window, there, with them this afternoon. You want to come, Mac?"

"I guess so." Maybe I could come up with a good excuse before it was time to leave.

"Did you wear Brandi out this morning?" I asked. We were the only two diners in the room.

"She begged off at the last minute this morning, but I'll see if she's interested this afternoon. We should get a glorious view of the whole glen."

Brandi never came to dinner. Neither did Kenny or Joyce. Marcia carried in wide bowls of dark red oxtail soup just as Eileen ushered in a Catholic priest. "This is Father Ewan. On Fridays, his housekeeper goes away to her sister's and he takes his dinner with us."

The priest was a man of many interests, including the history of Auchnagar. When Laura mentioned that I'm a Presbyterian elder, he insisted that I let him show me his church. Why not? It was as good an excuse as any for not climbing a mountain.

I tell you this—as I later told Joe Riddley—to explain exactly why I ended up, less than an hour later, standing over a wooden coffin in the Catholic church, peering down at a body.

It took me a minute to realize that Father Ewan was speaking to me. "I said, I don't suppose you know who he is, do you?" He took my elbow to draw me away from the sight.

"I'm afraid I do. His name is Jim Gordon, and he's a friend of the laird's wife. His wife is with him on the trip. He played the fiddle." I didn't know why I added that. For Jim, maybe.

I felt a deep sadness that his plans for Auchnagar had come to this. He was just like that man in the Bible, who increased his barns only to be told, "This night your soul will be required of you." Poor Jim should have left work at home and enjoyed his last vacation.

Father Ewan pulled me toward the door. "You stand watch," he told Roddy. "I must call the police." Ignoring Roddy's lively protests, he asked me, "Are you all right? It is a shock—"

I settled for a nod. If I listed for him all the dead bodies I'd seen in the past two years, it might sound like bragging, and being well acquainted with death is nothing to brag about.

Outside, I clasped my hands tightly together to stop them from trembling and inhaled deep, crisp breaths to keep my dinner down. He pulled out his cell phone and asked, "Since you are acquainted with the deceased, would you wait with me until the police come?"

"Of course." If this had not been a natural death—and I suspected it was not—I'd have to tell what I knew eventually. Might as well get it over with. But what did I know? I needed to think carefully before I said anything rash. I sure didn't want to have to call Joe Riddley to say, "Sorry, hon, but I'll be late coming home. I'm a witness in a murder case."

It was too cold to be standing around outside. Especially since, as we'd left in haste and I'd thought we'd be inside most of the time, I had come away without my coat. The breeze that teased my hair had an edge to it, and the sunlight was as pale as skim milk and about as satisfying. I leaned up against one of the doors, which was sun-warmed at my back and out of the wind, and concentrated on keeping my teeth still. I noticed that the police station was just up the hill and across the street. Father Ewan could have run over in less time than it took to turn on his phone and dial the number. I suspected he had stayed out of kindness and concern for me.

"Constable Roy will be right down," he said, and meant it literally. A young police officer was already running from the station, putting on his cap as he ran. He slung one leg over his bike and coasted downhill to the chapel.

He looked more like a truant from middle school than a proper policeman. Straw-blond hair poked untidily from under his cap and his rosy face looked like his mother had given it a good scrub before he left home. His expression as he dismounted was so wary that I knew immediately he wasn't accustomed to dealing with sudden death. "Fit's gan' on?" he greeted Father Ewan. Thanks to Morag, I could translate easily. He'd asked, "What's going on?"

Father Ewan didn't waste time on introductions, but launched right into our noonday events, including a regretful footnote about the gooseberries covered with custard.

"And fit's she deein' here?" the bobby demanded.

I wasn't offended. I'd been asking myself the same thing ever since I saw Jim.

Father Ewan gave a careless flick of one hand. "Och, she was up at Lamont's and came down wi' me to tour the chapel."

The bobby's skeptical look said what he thought about people so dedicated to tourism, they accompanied a priest on his way to look at coffins.

"The trouble is inside, Neil," the priest reminded him gently.

The bobby steadied his bike on its kickstand and mounted the steps two at a time. "I'll chust have a wee look, then, shall I?"

We heard Roddy start up a complaint as soon as the church door opened. "Ye took yer sweet time gettin' here. I cannae stand aboot all the bloody afternoon. I've got a bus to catch. There's a bike rally I want to attend, to see about buying myself that new bike, and if I'm no there, the bloke'll be selling it to somebody else. I have to catch the three o'clock bus."

The door closed before we heard the bobby's reply.

"They were boys at school together," the priest murmured, "and twa of a kind. Always in some scrape or another, usually trying to get out of work. I'd never have believed Neil Roy would become a constable."

The unlikely constable came back out looking rather more worried than he had gone in. "I dinnae ken that bloke. Do you?"

"No, but she does." Father Ewan flapped one hand toward me, then stepped back and left the floor—or, in this case, the gravel path—to me. "He's in her group."

"Och, a tourist." From the relief in the bobby's voice, you'd have thought tourists could be expected to come to Auchnagar for the express purpose of dying.

I thought he'd ask me a few questions and take the answers down, but all he asked was, "Are ye with Gilroy's?" When I nodded, he said, "We'll need to talk to Watty, then. But first, I'd better gie the sergeant a ring. He'll take it from here." He made the call and spoke urgently, then hung up looking relieved and told the priest, "Sergeant Murray was chust finishin' his dinner. He'll be right doon. He'll call the doctor, as weel, although he cannae do much for yon body." He turned to me. "The sergeant told me to ask ye a few questions, then ye can go."

I felt suddenly dizzy. Maybe it was hearing somebody I'd eaten breakfast with a few hours ago referred to so casually as "yon body." I sat down on the top step and laid my head on my knees. "Give me a minute for my head to stop swimming."

"Nae bother." He settled himself comfortably beside me on the steps and lit a cigarette. "We'll just save the questions until the sergeant arrives." I got the feeling that fairly well summed up his whole approach to life. He looked like he could sit and smoke forever.

That gave me time to think what I wanted to say. I should tell the sergeant what I had overheard the afternoon before, but I hated to do that without finding out first how Norwood

Hardin had spent his morning. Words have power. Accusations stick. If Norwood were innocent, he'd still be remembered in Auchnagar as having once been a suspect in a murder case. And Jim had certainly riled several others on this trip.

I found myself thinking desperately, "Please let this be death from natural causes." That's the kind of prayer our souls groan out when we aren't thinking straight. Whatever was done was done. No amount of prayer would ever change that.

The young bobby must have been worrying about the trouble murder could cause him, too, for he asked, "Do ye think death could have been caused by a weak heart or something?"

"I doubt it." I shifted on my step, trying to ignore the achy cold seeping into my bones. "Can you think of a single reason why somebody with a weak heart would come to this church and lie down in an empty coffin to die?"

The look he and the priest exchanged said clearly that they could imagine American tourists doing practically anything, but they were too courteous to say so aloud. I think we were all relieved to see a police vehicle draw up in front of the church, followed by a black Ford. The bobby stood up. "Here's the sergeant and the doctor noo."

The police sergeant had straight dark hair, red cheeks, and a strong, square chin, and looked far better in his navy uniform than the stout man who climbed out of the Ford in a baggy three-piece suit and reached into the back seat for his medical bag. As they turned our way, though, I saw that the doctor sported a magnificent red-gold mustache that bristled above well-shaped lips.

They nodded at Father Ewan, looked curiously at me, and headed up the steps, followed by Constable Roy. In a few minutes the sergeant came out to ask me, "You knew the victim?"

"Yes. He and his wife are—were on my tour. We're staying up at Heather Glen."

He opened the door and called back into the narthex, "Ye'll need to fetch his wife, Neil. Just say there's been an accident. Dinnae let on that her husband has died."

"And where will I find her, then?"

"Check at Heather Glen. If she's no there, check the shops."

Constable Roy came out, picked up his bike, and tooled away.

"What about me?" Roddy called through the open door. "I'll have to scarf me dinner whole to make me bus. I've got a bike rally to attend."

"Nivver mind your bike rally, lad," the sergeant called back. "I'll need you to stay wi' the body until somebody comes to fetch it."

Is there any point in noting that Roddy did not take that news with grace?

The doctor came out and jingled his keys, ready to leave. "Ian's hanging paper in our spare bedroom. Shall I send him down to make a statement?"

"Och, dinnae bother. We know where to find him when we need him. I'll chust be taking her statement first." The bobby nodded toward me.

Given that they were both looking my way, I might as well ask: "Do you know the cause of death?"

"Aye." The doctor nodded, strode up the walk, climbed in his Ford, and drove away.

"Let's awa' up to the station, shall we?" the sergeant invited.

Father Ewan suggested that there was no point in taking the Land Rover that short trip up the hill, so the two of us walked. I was more than ready for a hot cup of coffee when we got there, but the pot behind the sergeant's desk had been made so long before, it was black and tarry. The only thing it had to recommend it was steam.

While Father Ewan and I clutched our mugs and inhaled the fumes, Sergeant Murray called for reinforcements. Police in every country do pretty much the same thing when there is a suspicious death, but it takes longer in small towns. In a city, experts would have begun to congregate at once. Sergeant Murray's reinforcements had to come from the nearest large town and were presently out on another incident. "It'll take them the best part of two hours to get here," he told Father Ewan in disgust. "Meanwhile, tell me what you know about this man."

Father Ewan deferred to me. "His name is Jim Gordon," I began. "He owns a distillery in America that makes Scotch whisky, but he says he's of German extraction. He is traveling with his wife, who was planning to climb the brae above Heather Glen this morning, but changed her mind at the last minute and didn't go."

"She did, did she?" He made a note.

"Jim has apparently known the laird's wife, Mrs. Mac-Gorrie, for some years, and the Gordons ate with the Mac-Gorries last evening. I think she'll be able to tell you more than I can."

All that time I was still mentally debating whether to tell him what I had overheard between Jim and Norwood. I am a sworn officer of the law, but not of the Scottish law. If I told what I'd heard, I'd have to admit I had been eavesdropping and might cause trouble for an innocent man. On the other hand, if Norwood had killed Jim—

I still hadn't reached a decision when we heard the squeal of tires outside the station.

A vehicle door slammed and the station shook as the door was flung against the wall. "Fa's dat I hear aboot a body in one of my coffins?" a man demanded truculently. "I dinnae ken what someone's trying to pull, but they were empty when I delivered them."

This had to be Ian Geddys, the joiner. Tall and muscular, with wispy hair of faded red and a pink, indignant face, he was somewhere in the neighborhood of forty-five and carried not a chip on his shoulder but a whole tree, grown over decades from who knew what roots of bitterness.

"Why did you deliver them?" Sergeant Murray asked mildly.

"I had an order." He reached into his pocket and brought out a crumpled letter.

Sergeant Murray donned the same kind of half-glasses I wear for reading and held the letter by one corner. When he'd perused it, he whistled. "That's odd." He laid it on the desk and motioned for me to come look at it. "Do you recognize this signature? Dinnae touch!"

I thought about telling him I was a judge and knew the drill, but decided not to complicate matters. I found myself suffering from an acute—and, Joe Riddley would say, unusual—case of "I don't want to get involved any more than I have to."

The letter bore no letterhead. It requested that two wooden coffins be built and delivered to "the chapel" on the morning of that day by noon. It stated they were for a theatrical production, and could be removed after the production "and disposed of as you will." It was signed in a heavy black scrawl: *James Gordon.*

I looked up in astonishment. "But—why on earth—?" I came to a halt.

Murray's eyebrows arched above his glasses. "Do you recognize the signature?"

"I've had no reason to see Jim's signature, but I can't think why he would have ordered coffins for the play. Joyce Underwood, who's in charge of the tour, wrote it and Mrs. MacGorrie is producing it. One of them would be more likely—"

"That old wifey, her finger in every pie in town," Ian muttered under his breath. He raised his voice. "But she dinnae order the coffins—or pay for them, either."

"Are they paid for, then?" the constable asked in surprise.

"Ye dinnae think I'd make them wi'out bein' paid?" His indignation swept the room. "And it was dollars he sent, enough dollars to make it worth my while."

"How many?" asked the sergeant.

"Nivver you mind how many. It was enough."

Father Ewan scratched one side of his nose. "Then maybe, for once in his life, Roddy was right. He guessed that whoever ordered them thought that 'the chapel' meant St. Catherine's where the play is to be performed, and you took them to the wrong place."

Ian's hot blue eyes glared at the priest, then turned on me like I was personally responsible for the error. "If the bloke meant St. Catherine's, why did he no say so?"

"You'll have to talk with our tour leader about that," I said firmly.

"And who's the bloke in the chapel noo?" he demanded of the sergeant.

The sergeant gave him a wry smile. "The bloke who ordered the coffins."

I could tell that the volcano of Ian's temper was likely to erupt again, so I said quickly, "I've told you what I know. May I leave now?"

Sergeant Murray considered, then nodded. "Aye. You run along and leave us to sort this out. But dinnae be leavin' the village for the time being. I may have more questions for you."

"I have one for you. How did Jim die?"

"A hard blow to the back of the head, looks like. We'll have to do an autopsy, of course."

I left the police station thinking I had one more question: I wanted to know how the laird's brother-in-law had spent his morning. If he had a good alibi, I needn't mention their quarrel.

And if you are remembering that Joe Riddley didn't want me involved with murder, I'll tell you what I told him: I wanted to talk with Norwood so I wouldn't *need* to be involved.

❦ 18 ❧

The wind cut through me like a knife as I hurried up the brae, so I clasped my arms around me, stuck my hands under my arms for warmth, and tried not to envision Jim's face floating just ahead of me.

I stood in Eileen's small back hall for a moment to thaw and listened wistfully to the chink of china and the low voices of her talking with Marcia. I wished I could join them, but there's a difference between being a family member and being a paying guest. As soon as I got my breath back, I would head down to the village tearoom for something hot to drink.

Before I could reach the staircase, Eileen opened the door. "MacLaren! Where on earth is your coat?" Without waiting for an answer, she took my arm and pulled me toward a huge green Aga—a stove with a heavy black top, like my grandmother used to have. Glad to see her filling the kettle, I stood as close to the Aga as I dared until I felt warm. To erase Jim's image, I forced myself to concentrate on the yellow kitchen with its dark green floor, crisp white curtains and tablecloth embroidered with bright daffodils, tulips, and iris, and large floral calendar.

Eileen and her cheerful kitchen must have been good medicine for Marcia, for she was bustling around setting out cups, saucers, and spoons like she felt at home in her aunt's kitchen, and when I stopped shaking, she motioned me to a chair at the table.

"Have you talked to the police?" I asked as I sat down.

Eileen nodded. "Aye. Constable Roy was up and said

there's been an accident in the village. He wanted to speak with Mrs. Gordon, but I haven't seen her since breakfast."

Marcia turned from putting cookies on a plate. "Do you know what happened?"

"Unfortunately, yes. Jim Gordon's been killed."

Marcia gasped. Eileen pressed one hand to her heart and murmured, "Dear God!"

I took a sip of strong black tea to steady my own nerves before explaining, "Father Ewan and Roddy found him in one of the coffins that were left in the chapel. He was apparently struck on the back of the head."

Marcia sank into the chair across from me and took a large gulp of tea. Eileen gave me a wary look. "They don't think Roddy had anything to do with it, do they?"

I don't know why that hadn't occurred to me. Roddy certainly had the best opportunity, and he had an aversion to work. If Jim had gone into the chapel for a tourist's visit and tracked dirt over a floor Roddy had already mopped, would Roddy's annoyance have escalated into a hard shove? People who get knocked down do sometimes die of head injuries, if they hit something like a stone floor. And what better defense than to come charging up to his mother's dining room yelling that somebody had dropped coffins off at the church?

When I heard a little moan, I realized I had waited too long to answer. Eileen was as white as her curtains, her eyes nearly as large as her cake plate.

"Nobody said a thing about Roddy," I assured her quickly.

"Then why hasn't he come home for his dinner?"

"Sergeant Murray asked him to guard the body." Seeing that she was about to ask another question, I added firmly, "I really don't know any more than I've told you."

Except that Norwood Hardin had quarreled with Jim and knocked him down, and I wasn't going to say a word about that until I could talk to Norwood. The best time and place for that would be very shortly, down at the theater sometime after three.

A glance at my watch startled me. It wasn't even two.

How could that be, when I'd spent half a day at the church and another half at the police station?

And only six hours before, Jim Gordon had been eating his breakfast in the next room.

Marcia saw me glance at the connecting door and seemed to read my thoughts. "We never know how long any of us has got, do we?" Her voice was thick with tears.

Neither Eileen nor I felt inclined to reply, so we all finished our tea in silence. Then I thanked them, excused myself, and headed upstairs for a rest. I felt, as Daddy used to say, like I'd been rode hard and put up wet.

The house seemed so vast and empty, I found myself tiptoeing up the stairs. Which is why I startled Joyce, who was creeping out her door like a silent mouse as I reached the upstairs landing. We both jumped.

She wore her blue parka and gloves and carried her Gilroy's tour bag.

"I'm sorry," I greeted her, "I didn't mean to scare you. But surely you aren't going out with that headache?" The shadows under her eyes were as blue as the parka, her cheeks were flushed, and her eyes themselves were like glittery brown beads. I feared she had a fever.

She pressed the fingers of her free hand to her temple. "We have a rehearsal at three, and I have a few props I need to take down, as well." She held up the bag. "I hope a little fresh air first will help." She passed me and hurried down several steps.

"Wait!" I called. She kept one foot poised over the next step down while I stood there like a mute, trying to figure out the best way to tell her one of her tour group was lying dead in a coffin intended for the performance. Not all the fresh air in Scotland was going to help poor Joyce's headache after she heard that—especially after she figured out her precious play was sure to be cancelled because of Jim's friendship with Kitty MacGorrie.

I wished somebody else would show up to tell her, but nobody did and Joyce was growing restless, so I decided to blurt out the easy part first. "There was a mistake. The coffins intended for your play were delivered to the Catholic church instead of to St. Catherine's."

She turned and her foot apparently slipped, for she nearly pitched headfirst down the stairs. I had a quick vision of Joyce in that other coffin before she caught the rail and demanded in a puzzled voice, "Coffins? What coffins? We don't need coffins."

"They were ordered for the play, delivered to 'the chapel.' But the joiner thought that meant the Catholic church just down the brae."

She shook her head. "But we don't need coffins." She took another slow step down, as bewildered as the rest of us.

I steeled myself for the next part. "Wait," I called a second time. "That's not all."

She stopped again, but from the way she leaned slightly forward, I knew she was eager to get away. I went down a few steps, too. This was not news I wanted to shout. "Jim Gordon was found dead in one of the coffins."

"Jim?" She collapsed onto a step as if somebody had stolen her muscles. Her voice was as blank as her face, and the flush in her cheeks drained, leaving her as white as a big china cat sitting on the sill of the stained-glass window. "Jim is dead?" She clutched the banister as if afraid she'd fall without support. "Are you sure?"

I nodded and tears filled her eyes. "But how? What happened?"

I was touched by her sympathy for a man who had not always made her job easier. "I don't really know, honey. The police think he was hit over the head, then put in one of those two coffins delivered to the chapel while Roddy was cleaning in another part of the church. They will probably want to talk to you, since you're in charge of the group, but—"

"Me?" She clung to the banister. "Why me? I don't know a thing." Her eyes were wide and her breath came in short gasps. "You are positive that Jim is *dead*?"

I nodded.

She let go of the banister and rubbed her face with both hands as if to clear cobwebs from her skin. "I can't believe this. Have they called his family?"

"They're looking for Brandi, I believe."

"We'll need to call his daughter, too. Brandi might never

get around to it." She stood and sighed. "They'll cancel the play, I guess." Her voice was low and tragic. "And I don't have a clue what I'm supposed to do with the rest of you now."

The clock in the downstairs hall chimed two.

Joyce turned at the sound and snatched up her bag. "I cannot deal with this right now. I just can't." She clattered down the rest of the stairs and I heard the front door bang behind her.

⊰ 19 ⊱

I tried to doze, but kept thinking of poor Jim, of Brandi, and of the trouble all this was going to cause for Joyce. I tried to read, but couldn't concentrate. I told myself to get out and look for ancestors, but couldn't bear to meet curious people who would surely know I'd been with the priest when the body was found. Things like that have a way of getting around a village.

Marcia and Eileen must have heard me pacing, because there was a discreet knock at my door. "MacLaren?" Marcia called softly. "Eileen asks if you'd like to come down to her room."

"I'd be delighted. My own company is real tedious right now."

Eileen's room was behind the lounge. It held a single bed, a chest, an oak desk in one corner for accounts, a soft carpet underfoot, and three armchairs drawn up to a cheerful fire. The golden Lab dozed near the flames. He lifted his head when we walked in, gave me a long, steady look through chocolate eyes, decided I was acceptable company, and thumped his tail three times on the rug. Then he laid his head on crossed paws and resumed his nap.

"Your dog is better behaved than the laird's," I told Eileen, who was sitting to the left of the fire embroidering another tablecloth.

"Godfrey is a real menace," she said fondly. "He'll lick you to death if you let him. Chancellor, now, he's so old, all he wants is a nap and his tea." She bent and patted the big golden head. "Still, he can make a right noise if somebody comes in. That's all I need."

Marcia resumed the chair where she'd left her needlepoint, and I sat between them feeling pretty useless with nothing to occupy my hands.

Eileen knotted her thread, snipped it off, and asked as she rethreaded her needle, "What do you think poor Mrs. Gordon will want to do now, MacLaren?"

"I have no idea, but I'm afraid we may all need to stay in the village until the police no longer have questions to ask. Will that throw out your schedule?"

"Och, no. I don't usually take guests this early. We open for the skiing season, then close down until the second week of May. I just opened this week to accommodate this group because they are painting down at Gilroy's. I always take their overflow when I can."

That seemed like a good opening to find out more about Watty's arrangements down there, and talking about Watty might take our minds off Jim. "Does Watty come this way often? He seems to know a lot of people in Auchnagar. Several have mentioned him by name."

"Och, aye, he's in and out. One of his buses comes almost every week." Eileen placidly plied her needle, creating a purple pansy.

I didn't think I'd heard her correctly. "His *buses*?" I pictured a fleet of ancient relics.

She laughed. "Don't judge the company by that old trap he uses. It's his favorite, because he started out with it and named it for his wife. Poor Jeanne—she only died a couple of years ago. They were very close." I was trying to adjust to the notion of a gruff old driver having enough sentiment to hang onto a broken-down bus because he'd named it for his wife when Eileen added, "He's done real well for himself, Watty has, between the bus tours, the hotels he took over from his dad, and the chain of tearooms he bought a few years ago."

"Watty?" Marcia and I were a unison chorus of disbelief.

"Aye. Don't let those wretched clothes and that tatty old bus fool you. He's got pounds and pounds in the bank, not to mention the properties."

"So why is he driving a bus?" I asked when I could speak again. When I thought about the tips I'd handed him from time to time, and how he always whispered, "Thank you, miss," I could have whopped him upside the head!

"He only drives when he makes his inspection tour," Eileen explained. "He likes to check things out once a year himself, to be sure they're keeping up to his standards. He dresses tatty and drives that old bus to see how new employees who don't know him will treat him. And he usually fills the bus with people who can't generally afford a holiday at all—pensioners, or union widows, people living on modest incomes. He's real strict, Watty is, that his places be clean, well run, and courteous to everybody, no matter how rich or poor."

Little things fell into place with a click. The snickers at the ceilidh when I asked the younger men at Watty's table if they drove for Gilroy's "too." The fact that they let him and his dad buy their drinks without protest. Maybe even the fact that all the drinks at our table were "on the house." The way he disappeared at every Gilroy's Tearoom and Hotel. The table that magically appeared after Sherry refused to sit with Brandi. Even the fact that our musicians were invited to join in the ceilidh, which was obviously an honor. All of that pointed to a smooth, powerful hand behind the scenes. I had taken it for granted that Joyce was working for a well-run agency, or that the presence of Jim on the tour got us better service. It never occurred to me that Watty—

"Does Joyce know, I wonder?" Marcia wondered.

"She must," I replied. "If Watty planned the tour, she must be working for him. But I wonder if she ever met him, or if they communicated like she did with us, by e-mail?"

Marcia chuckled. "In that case, maybe she's part of his inspection tour."

"Somehow I doubt Joyce will care whether she passes. After this trip, she already knows there are easier ways to support a writing habit. But speaking of habits, when Morag said Watty always stays with her mum when he's in Auchnagar . . ." I let the sentence dangle like the thread from Eileen's needle as she finished one flower and started another.

"Aye. They're very close." Eileen seemed to have no more problem with that than Morag had. "Watty's dad was from Auchnagar, you know. He left before the war, of course, and went down to Paisley. That's where he got started in the hotel business. But the old man used to bring Watty as a lad, and Watty keeps poppin' up quite often now, since his wife died."

It took a bit of adjustment, but perhaps I could picture Watty as the stepfather of little Morag. If that was what Watty had in mind . . .

I remembered our conversation at the ceilidh. "We met his dad on Skye, and he and Watty were talking about someone named Alasdair Geddys, who Joyce says also came from here. I suppose Watty's dad would have actually known him?" I tried to remember exactly what they'd said, but it was muddled. Or maybe I'd been a bit fuddled by that pint of stout.

"Och, all the men knew Alasdair," Eileen said comfortably. "He had a still up in the hills behind his place that was famous for miles around."

I stared. "A still? I thought they said he was a fiddler."

"Aye, but fiddlin' doesn't put food on the table, and although Alasdair inherited a good many acres, neither he nor his bairns ever took to farming. He grew grain and made whisky, using the good water in the burn runnin' through his land. Nowadays, Barbara grows a wee patch of vegetables each year and lets out the rest to the laird for sheep. The rent and her work at the post office keeps the roof over their head."

"Barbara down at the post office is Alasdair Geddys's daughter?" It hadn't occurred to me to connect that old woman with the famous fiddler, even though they had the same last name and Joyce had said his son and daughter still lived in Auchnagar. "She looks too old," I said before I thought.

"She's had a hard life, Barbara." Eileen finished with the purple thread and reached for yellow. "And she aged something terrible after her dad drowned and her older brother disappeared, leavin' her to take care of wee Ian. She wasnae but sixteen, poor lass."

"That's Ian, the joiner?" I was beginning to put it together.

"Aye. He's much younger, of course. There's nine years or more between them. Their mother died when Ian was born, so their dad raised the bairns, such raising as they got, but he worked the older two very hard. Barbara was four years behind me in school—"

"Surely not," I interrupted. "She must be years older than you."

"She's four years younger, right enough, and their brother, Hamish, was a year older than me. From the time Barbara was nine and he fourteen, he was workin' with his dad and she was doing all the cooking, washing and scrubbing that ever got done in that house. After Hamish disappeared, she had to find work to feed herself and wee Ian, as well."

"What do you mean, 'disappeared'?" Marcia asked. I was glad she did. I love a good mystery.

"He just didn't come home to dinner one night," Eileen explained, "and nobody ever heard from him again. The accepted explanation was that he'd gone on the hills that mornin' and gotten lost in a dreadful storm that blew up midday. He was aye a strange lad, Hamish—kept himself to himself, if you understand what I mean. And he was a great one for walkin' the hills alone. But that storm came up all of a sudden, with lashing snow and fierce winds, and the hills can be treacherous in a storm, even to those who know them well. We didn't have a mountain rescue team back then, but men from the village combed the hills for days after. They never found a sign of him." She made a French knot for the center of a flower, then went on. "Afterwards, there were some who said he was in such despair over his father's death, he could have done away with himself, but my mum aye thought he didn't want to be saddled with a sister and a bairn at twenty-one, and took advantage of the storm to disappear. Don't mention that to Barbara," she added quickly.

"Of course not." I didn't figure Barbara and I would ever be on personal terms, anyway. "But surely he wouldn't have left two children—"

"Och, Barbara was sixteen by then, and had left school.

But wee Ian was only seven, and the poor lad grieved for years over his brother and his dad."

"I thought he seemed to carry a chip on his shoulder," I remembered. "No wonder."

Eileen's sympathy was all for Ian's sister. "Barbara's aye taken care of Ian. She went to work the week after Hamish vanished, and she's aye worked since, even after the arthritis twisted her arms something terrible. That barn of a house takes every penny she makes, I'm sure, because Ian's not likely to help her much. He's close with his money, Ian is. He was a quarrelsome, selfish lad who grew into a quarrelsome, tight-fisted man. How did he take the news that somebody put a body in one of his coffins?"

"Not well," I admitted. "You'd have thought it was a personal insult."

I didn't mention that Roddy had taken the order to remain with the body with equally poor grace. Mothers never like to hear such news about their children.

The back-door bell jangled as someone came in, but Chancellor only flapped his tail. Eileen set down her embroidery. "That must be Roddy back."

He flung the door open with a crash and was half through his sentence before he got into the room. "I'm needin' my dinner. I'm fair famished."

Eileen rose. "I've kept it warm. What's happening down the village?"

"Nae much." Roddy shrugged out of his jacket and dropped it on the floor. "The police from down the way finally got here. They were settin' up when I left. But I've missed the bus, and if I dinnae get to that bike rally, somebody else'll be getting that motorbike I've got my eye on. Can I have the car and money for petrol?"

"I'm needing it. I've arranged to take Marcia out to visit your great-auntie this evening."

I excused myself and went upstairs. I've done my lifetime share of that sort of negotiating, and it never goes better with strangers around. Besides, the grandfather clock had just chimed three, so Norwood Hardin ought to be arriving to rehearse Joyce's play.

I tidied up a bit and put on my coat, gloves, and my new

wooly cap, then went back downstairs. On my way out, as a courtesy, I knocked lightly on the kitchen door and stuck my head in to say I'd be back in time for tea.

Roddy sat at the table, attacking a half-eaten plate of food with the desperation of the young male in a hurry. His cell phone rang while I was still speaking, and from the way he yanked it from his pocket and uttered a surly, "Hullo?" I surmised the discussion with his mother had not gone his way, that he was hoping a friend would bail him out, and he wanted his mother to feel his displeasure. Like I said, I've done my share of that kind of negotiation. I know the moves.

His face changed. Whoever was on the other end was not the person he had expected.

His eyebrows drew together in displeasure and he started to splutter. "But—but—but I—there can't be!" He sounded desperate.

Somebody on the other end was equally determined. I could hear the staccato voice from where I stood. Finally Robby gave a sullen, "Right, then, I'll be down in a jiff."

He shoved the phone in his pocket, then slammed the table with one palm and shouted for the whole village to hear, "They've found another bloomin' body in t' other coffin now, and I've got to go back doon the hill. At this rate, I'll nivver get oot o' town!"

❧ 20 ❧

"Who is it?" I don't know which of us asked it, but I know I was suddenly chilled in spite of the warmth of the Aga. My mind ran down the list of likely prospects in our group while we all looked the question at Roddy.

He was determinedly shoveling in the rest of his food before obeying orders. "Dinnae ken. The bobby didn't say." He spoke through a mouthful of boiled potatoes. He chewed angrily and flung down his fork. "Why does this have to happen to me?"

If I was to maintain the myth that I am a nice person, that was my exit cue.

At the foot of the brae, beside the church wall, several official vehicles were pulled up helter-skelter. I also saw a dusty Land Rover that looked like the laird's, and was delighted to see my recent acquaintance, Constable Roy, standing guard inside the gate while a crowd was plaguing him with questions. "Come on, laddie, at least tell us who it is," one man kept shouting.

Roddy brushed past me with no sign of recognition, spoke roughly to the constable, and was sent in the direction of the front door. I inched through the crowd until I was close enough to Constable Roy to ask, "Who is it this time? Surely not another member of our tour group?"

He stared over my right shoulder with a wooden expression and spoke in an equally wooden voice. "I cannae release any information to the public at this time."

"I'm not just the public," I reminded him. "I was in on the finding of the first body."

"Sorry, mum, but I cannae give out information at this time."

"But is it one of our group?"

"Sorry, mum." He looked staunchly ahead.

Miffed, I turned and headed down the brae toward the village. As a judge and a lifelong resident of Hopemore, I was used to getting more information from the police than other people did. Still, like I'd reminded Dorothy, I had no authority here.

I did have enough experience with small towns to know where news was most likely to be spread, so I headed for the post office. The place was full of women and a solitary man, chattering at the top of their lungs, and Barbara Geddys was harassed and irritable behind her counter. I heard her snap at a customer in the hush that fell when I entered.

One of the women fixed me with washed-out blue eyes and demanded, "Are ye the one that was wi' the priest when the first body was discovered?"

I gave her a friendly smile and the answer I'd worked on, coming down the brae. "People keep asking that. I guess we look alike. Do they know who the second victim is?"

A babble arose around me. I couldn't understand half of what was said, but what I gathered was that the new body was a man, the police hadn't said yet who he was, and every family in the village was taking a frantic poll of all their relations to be sure they were alive and well. I also heard that he'd been put in the chapel while Roddy was absent from his post long enough to walk up through the village to the paper shop for a pack of cigarettes.

What worried folks most was that nobody had seen a thing. How could anyone carry a body through the village without being seen? Or drive it to the chapel and wrestle it out of the car? People were beginning to murmur about a Phantom Murderer, which was not good. Panic breeds violence.

I left without buying stamps—which I didn't need, anyway—and headed across the bridge and along the road to St. Catherine's, steeling myself for my conversation with Norwood Hardin. I didn't relish confessing that I'd overheard his private quarrel, but it had to be done. I also wanted to talk with Joyce. She had gone down the hill and through the village after I came up. Had she seen anything or met anybody on her way?

When I came to the gray building that had once been a church and now was a community center, I was glad to find the front door unlocked. I crept quietly into what had once been a sanctuary, a high, dim space lit by tall arched windows with opaque glass and inadequate chandeliers. White paint and a stone floor contributed to the general atmosphere of unrelieved chilliness. I kept on my hat and gloves.

Given that the play was sure to be cancelled, I was surprised to see three people onstage, talking quietly among themselves. One of the men was short and square with a bristling dark beard. The other was taller, thinner, with fair hair and a sharp profile. The woman had a mane of hair that streamed down her back like melted caramel.

Joyce sat halfway back on a dark wood pew, her parka draped over the pew in front. As I slipped into the very back pew, the woman called out to Joyce, "We're ready with Culloden."

And as if nothing at all had happened to affect the play, Joyce called, "Right."

They weren't in costume, of course. All three wore corduroy jeans and heavy sweaters. But in spite of that, I found the scene compelling. It depicted not the battle, but the return of a son after the battle. The mother was frantically trying to make sure her son wasn't found by English supporters scouring the region. He was desperate to know what he should do, how he could live, if he couldn't set foot outside his own home. I couldn't help thinking of my ancestor Andrew MacLaren, and realized for the first time that for him and others who left Scotland after Culloden, emigration was only one in a series of wrenching experiences. They had wrestled with the decision of whether to heed Prince Charlie's call, had traveled miles from home, had fought in a devastating military defeat where brothers, sons, and comrades were hacked to death beside them, and had crept back to their own villages and towns in terror of being ambushed. But home was no longer safe. They were forced to dodge and hide while they tried to decide what to do next. I wondered if the long sea voyage came as something of a relief.

When the scene was over, I applauded heartily. The lines weren't great, but the actors clothed them in a poignancy that made me wonder how Andrew had made his own decision, and whom he'd had to leave behind. It is not names, deeds, and civil records that interest me about my ancestors. It is stories I can never know.

Speaking of stories I didn't know, where was Norwood? He was neither sitting with Joyce nor onstage with the other actors.

Hearing me clap, Joyce turned in surprise. "Hey, Mac-Laren. What do you think?" Her face was flushed with pride, pleasure, or both, and her hair was tousled—probably by the wind. She looked more like the wild woman I'd seen in the night than our mousy guide.

"Sounds real good, honey," I said hesitantly, not knowing whether she had forgotten that Jim was dead or had decided to ignore it for the duration of this rehearsal. I understand that writers can sometimes be self-centered, but this seemed to be carrying it a bit far.

While the actors talked among themselves onstage, apparently making revisions in what they'd just done, I left my place and went to join her.

As I took my seat, I steadied myself on the chair in front, which held her blue parka. "Careful," she warned. "It's sopping wet. I brought coffee for everybody, and managed to spill mine. I rinsed it out, but it's still stained."

"Aren't you freezing without it?"

"I'm too excited to finally be seeing the play to be cold." She was glowing with happiness and more relaxed, less tense than I'd ever seen her before except that night in Glasgow, eating with Laura. But the way her cheeks were flushed and her eyes glittered, I hoped she *was* simply worked up over the play, not coming down with something. She added in a low voice, "You probably think I'm cruel, making them go through this for nothing, but I had to see it, Mac. I just had to, before it all—dies, too." She clasped her hands between her knees and bowed her head as if in prayer, or pain.

"Have you heard there's been a second body found?" I asked softly.

She stiffened. "Another member of our group?"

"I don't know. They haven't released the name yet. But the body was found in the second coffin that was ordered for the play."

"Oh, my God." The way she moaned it, I knew it was a prayer, whether she did or not. She looked at me with a wild expression. "We didn't need coffins. I didn't order coffins. What's going on?"

"I don't know, honey. Maybe we'll hear something in a little while. But from what folks are saying in the post office, nobody saw a thing. You didn't meet anybody coming through the village, did you? Or see anybody around the Catholic church?"

"I met one old woman with a bicycle, but that's all I remember. I wasn't paying much attention, to tell the truth."

"Too bad. But I take it your headache is better and you got your props here on time?" Her tote bag sat beside her on the floor, collapsed and apparently empty.

She heaved a huge sigh, like she was trying to exhale the news I'd just brought. Then she nodded. "Yes to both. The books up on the table are actual histories written in that period. I found them in an old bookshop and thought they'd be a nice touch. Not that anybody will ever see them now."

"But they do add an authentic touch," I assured her.

She glanced up toward the stage, where the actors were beginning to block out new moves for the previous scene. "That last scene was good, wasn't it? Tell me honestly, the play does work, doesn't it?"

If we were talking real honestly, the play was a fantasy in her head at that point. It wasn't likely to reach Broadway, given the subject, and I doubted that the laird's wife would ever restage it after Joyce left town. Still, I didn't like to burst Joyce's balloon, so I said, "Sounded real good to me." I added, "Did you talk to the police yet about Jim?"

She chewed her lower lip and blinked away tears that had filled her eyes. "Not yet. First I wanted to walk a while, trying to get used to the idea that he's gone and to figure out what I ought to do about the group now." She rubbed one cheek with her palm. "But I never did."

"Which?"

"Either. I still can't believe Jim is gone, and I don't have a clue what to do."

"Call the agency back home," I suggested. "This can't be the first time they've had a death on a tour."

She gave me a strange, worried look. "Yeah, that's what I ought to do, I guess." She glanced up at the stage, and I suspected one reason she was focusing so hard on the play was not simply to see it performed at least once, but to postpone talking with her bosses and explaining the mess her first tour group was in.

"I think the police are likely to expect us to stay at least until they have interviewed all of us," I continued. "I asked Eileen if that would put her out, but she says she doesn't have any other guests coming for a couple of weeks."

Joyce's eyes widened. "A couple of weeks? We can't stay here that long. Who'd pay?"

I had no answer for that, so maybe it was time to bite the bullet and do what I came for. "Do you know where I could find Norwood Hardin? I heard he was going to be here."

I expected her to ask why I needed him, but she just screwed up her mouth like she'd eaten an unripe persimmon. "He's supposed to be. If you find him, tell him he is very late."

She had spoken into a gap in the conversation onstage. The short actor called down, "Are you talking about Norwood?"

"The one and only," Joyce said shortly.

"If we don't rehearse the sword scene, somebody is likely to get killed." The actor picked up a sword lying on the stage and swished it through the air. "The most likely candidate is me."

It occurred to me that they might not have heard of the coffins in the chapel yet, if they'd driven straight from Aberdeen to rehearsal. "Speaking of killed," I called, loud enough to be heard on stage, "have you heard that two men have died or been killed in the village this afternoon, and put in coffins over at the Catholic chapel—coffins the joiner says were ordered for this play and delivered there by mistake? And do any of you happen to know anything about the coffins?"

"I didn't order them," Joyce added quickly.

The three actors came to the edge of the stage to stare down at us. They shook their heads in unison, then exchanged puzzled looks. "We don't need coffins," the woman pointed out.

The shorter man demanded, "For real? Two men have been killed in Auchnagar? This afternoon?"

I couldn't tell which he found more unbelievable—that murder had been done twice that afternoon, or that murder had been done in Auchnagar.

"They appeared this afternoon." I corrected the story. "I haven't heard when they were killed, or even what happened to the second one. The first one was hit on the head."

"A friend of Mrs. MacGorrie's," Joyce added.

The shorter one swore. "We might as well pack up and go back to Aberdeen, then. There's no way this play is going on now."

The taller one demanded, "Did you know all this, Joyce, and let us go on rehearsing as if nothing had happened?"

Joyce didn't speak.

It was inexcusable, but I decided she didn't need another load on her shoulders right then. "I just came to tell her," I told them.

The woman shrugged. "We might as well pack up and head back." They started collecting scripts and jackets. "What's to be done with the props?" she called down to Joyce.

"Just leave them," Joyce said wearily. "I'll talk to Mrs. MacGorrie later."

I still needed to find Norwood Hardin, or to tell Sergeant Murray what I had overheard between him and Jim. The time was past for worrying about ruining his reputation—which was dubious, in any case. At least two people had been murdered, and I could well be giving Norwood the time he needed to skip the country.

I stopped by the chapel and worked my way through a crowd that seemed twice as large as before. "Hey, Constable

Roy," I greeted him again. Again he looked over my shoulder with that expression I suspected he'd seen on some television show, so I spoke to his chin. "I need to speak to Sergeant Murray on a matter of importance."

He shook his head. "He's interviewing somebody else just noo. If ye'd care to wait—"

The wind was rising again, and the day winding down. I'd rather wait in my warm room. So I fished in my pocketbook for a card and jotted down a note. "Remembered something. Will be at Heather Glen." I hoped Sergeant Murray wouldn't be inclined to ask how it happened to slip my mind that Norwood had threatened Jim.

Back at the guesthouse, Eileen put her head out the kitchen door as soon as the back-door bell jangled and the dog barked. "I thought you might be Roddy."

"He's not back yet?"

"No, and I cannae for the life of me think why they're keeping him so long. Do you ken who it was that died?" Worry had made her lapse into broad Scots.

"They haven't said yet." I could think of several reasons Roddy might be kept, but none of them was likely to comfort her. "Maybe Roddy saw or heard something."

"Och, he never pays attention to fit's gan on around him. He's aye got earphones in his ears and music playin'." She turned back to the kitchen, then thought to ask, "Are you wanting a cup of tea? Marcia and I've moved our base of operations to the kitchen, and she's just made her first oat bannock. They can be a comfort when you're anxious."

I followed her inside, where Marcia stood over a griddle, turning something with an uneasy expression. "Is it done?"

Eileen peered at it, but I had the feeling her attention was still on the back door. "Och aye, it's well enough. Slide it onto the plate, now." Marcia brought it to the table looking as proud as if she'd prepared a four-course dinner. "Now we'll cut it and have a wee taste," Eileen told us. "MacLaren, would you pour us out some tea?"

Pleased to be treated like family, I brought down cups and saucers from the cupboard and poured from the metal pot that seemed perpetually full. We were each given a quarter of the oatcake and pronounced it a success. We were sharing Marcia's second oatcake when the doorbell jangled and the dog bayed again.

Dorothy poked her head in, her cheeks pink, her eyes full of tears and her lashes spiky with them. "Have you heard what's happened in the village?" Without waiting for us to answer, she spilled it all. "Jim Gordon is dead and another man, as well. They found their bodies over in the Catholic chapel this afternoon. Can you believe it?" She stumbled toward one of Eileen's kitchen chairs, collapsed into it, laid her head on her arms, and burst into tears. Through her sobs, she cried, "And Jim made such beautiful music."

As an epitaph, it wasn't bad.

❧ 21 ❧

"You didn't happen to hear who the other man was, did you?" I asked when she'd quieted down a bit.

Dorothy nodded, and gulped like a child. "The laird's brother-in-law, the one Brandi said was so funny. Stabbed, they say." She wept again.

I felt a chill sweep up inside my clothes. The whole time I'd been looking for Norwood, he'd been dead in the second coffin?

Roddy stormed home a few minutes later, incensed. "They blistered me for leavin' the chapel long enough to get some smokes," he raged. "They cannae expect a man to stand watch over a corpse a whole afternoon without a single reek. How was I to know somebody would choose chust that very time to bring in another body? And now they say I cannae leave the village while they're investigating. I've got to call my mate and tell him I'm not comin' to the bloody rally." He glared at his mother, daring her to object to his choice of words.

She simply said, absently, "Aye, you'll have to do that," then asked the question that worried her. "They don't think you had anything to do with this, do they?"

"They havenae said it, but I wouldnae put it past them." He went to call. Eileen's hands trembled while she fetched two more cups and spoons and added water to the teapot.

Marcia turned to Dorothy with a sharp look. "What were you doing all day?"

"Working." Dorothy pulled off her coat and gloves and headed for the Aga, where she stood with her back to us while she held her hands over the stove top to warm them. "The gallery in the village needed someone to frame pictures, and I know how to do that, so I volunteered."

"You mean Alex Carmichael's place?" Eileen turned from pouring Roddy's tea and gave Marcia a worried frown.

A wave of pink rose up Dorothy's neck beneath her braid. "Yes. He's not paying me," she added, turning to give me a quick, anxious look. "He just gave me a canvas and let me paint on his deck this afternoon."

"I hope ye know that Alex has a steady girl over in Aberdeen," Roddy told her, returning from his call. "Crazy about her, he is." I hoped Roddy would never come live in the American West. He'd never be at home on the range— he was much too fond of the discouraging word.

Dorothy, however, just pulled her braid to hang over one shoulder and announced with dignity, "I'm not marrying the man, I'm working for him." She tugged the braid for emphasis as she spoke—and looked mighty attractive, I might add. Roddy seemed to think so, but I could tell his mother wanted to talk with him privately.

I pushed back my chair. "Dorothy, why don't we take our cups into the lounge while Eileen gets on with her preparations for tea?"

When we were comfortably settled before the fire, I asked, softly, "When you sat on Alex's deck painting this afternoon, you didn't happen to see anybody go into the Catholic church, did you?" I wasn't sure how many backyards and bushes might block the view between Alex's deck and the chapel door, but they weren't far apart, so it was worth a shot.

She started to shake her head, then hesitated. "I saw Roddy leave, while I was setting up my easel. But once I get to painting, I don't think at all. I just paint what I see and don't think about anything else. I painted today until my hands got numb, but I wouldn't have known I was cold if Alex hadn't come to ask if I was warm enough." In spite of what she'd told Roddy, her voice was soft and her dimples flashed when she said Alex's name.

"Are you sure you aren't in danger of confusing devotion to art and devotion to the art-gallery owner?" I teased softly.

She tossed her braid and it swung around to hang down her back. "Of course not. Alex is *old,* eh? Thirty-three his last birthday. But he's asked me to stay here and work for him a year, and he says I can paint when we aren't busy. He says he can't pay much, but I have some savings. Do you think I should?"

"How badly do you want to?"

"If I could have just one year to see if I'm any good, eh? And if people like my work— Oh, Mac, if I just could!" Dorothy got as pink when she was earnest as when embarrassed.

"Take it, if you want it and can afford it," I advised. "You'll never be younger or freer than you are now." It's so easy to give advice like that to other people's children.

I took a bath and washed my hair before tea, while the bathroom was free. Laura came up to the room while I was drying my hair. "How was your mountain climbing?" I asked.

"Hill walking," she corrected me, flushed and happy. "It was fine." She was still subdued, though, and she got more so when I filled her in on the two deaths.

"Poor Joyce," she exclaimed. "What do you do when a member of your tour dies?"

"It's doubly hard because they're sure to cancel her play." I chose my new heather gray slacks, but added a bright green sweater. Catching Laura's expression, I said, "Brandi's not going to expect us to wear mourning, and I'm certainly not mourning Norwood Hardin."

Nevertheless, Laura chose black slacks and a gray sweater. As she went to brush her hair, she commented, "I wouldn't have Joyce's job no matter how much you paid me. I wouldn't put it past Brandi to demand that the travel agency pay to return Jim's body to the States. Did you know that Sherry wanted them to refund part of her ticket price because you're on the tour?"

Putting on my shoes, I stopped with one leg in midair. "Why on earth should they?"

"Joyce said that the deal was, if somebody on the trip persuaded somebody else to come, they were to get a discount on their ticket. Since Kenny sent me information about the trip, they got a discount when I signed up. Once Sherry saw you were here, too, she wanted Joyce to refund more money for you. I tell you Mac, that woman—" She broke off and dragged a brush through her own hair instead of finishing the sentence.

"Did Joyce give her the refund?" I considered tying a colorful scarf around my neck, then decided to forego it. Not only did it look too jaunty for the way I felt, but there was still a killer loose in the village. I didn't want a handy scarf around my neck if he or she got ideas about adding me to the tally.

"No. Joyce told Sherry she'd check on it, but later she told her that if anybody got a refund because you came along, it would be me. That made Sherry furious, as you can imagine. She doesn't like me."

"She doesn't like you because you spend a lot of time with her husband." There, I'd brought up the forbidden subject.

Laura huffed. "Sherry's got him between such a rock and a hard place, he doesn't know which way to turn." I waited to see if she would name the rock or the hard place, but she merely asked, "Ready for tea?"

Laura, Dorothy, and I sat alone that night at the table by the window. Marcia was eating in the kitchen with Eileen, the Boyds didn't come at the gong, Brandi still hadn't returned, and Joyce chose to sit alone at the empty table in the far corner, in the seat where Jim Gordon had eaten breakfast that morning. I wondered if she'd chosen his seat deliberately, or because it had its back to the rest of us. She was trembling in spite of having on the heaviest sweater I'd seen her wear on the trip. I remembered that she'd had to walk all the way back from the theater without a parka, and wished I'd thought to take her down something to put on. When Laura noticed that Joyce was alone, she left Dorothy and me and went over to join her, but Joyce waved her away. "I'd prefer to be alone, if you don't mind."

"Is there anything we can do?"

"Not really. You would not believe what a mess this all

is, and I don't have a clue what I'm supposed to do now. But I don't think you can help. Thanks." She looked utterly drained. I wondered if she'd ever really gotten rid of her migraine, she was so pale.

Sherry came in late, looked around, and demanded, "Where's Kenny? I want to show him some china I bought in an antique shop. It's eighteenth century, I'm sure, and very fine."

"I'm sure the dealer will be particularly sorry to *lose* it," Laura said with a strange emphasis on the verb, "but Kenny hasn't been around all day."

Sherry glared at her and headed toward Joyce.

Joyce gave her the same quiet, "I need to be alone just now. Sorry."

Sherry gave her a curious look, then stalked over to our table and sat down next to me with an irritated flounce.

"You must not have heard what happened in the village today," I told her.

"I've been out of the village since ten, and just got back. Eileen's neighbor gave me a ride. She was visiting her sister, but if I'd known she was going to stay so long, I'd have caught a bus back. What happened?"

"There have been two deaths," Dorothy said in a hushed voice. I suspected this was the closest she'd ever come to tragedy.

"They weren't simply deaths," I pointed out. "They apparently were murders."

Sherry stared around at each of us in turn like she was waiting for somebody to burst out laughing and admit it was a joke. "Who? Why? Where is Kenny?" Her voice rose in fear.

She tensed to spring from her chair, but I caught her arm. "Neither victim was Kenny, but somebody killed Jim. Sometime this morning, apparently."

She looked around the table and her eyes narrowed in suspicion. "Well, Kenny didn't do it, no matter what you think!" She jumped up and ran from the room.

That took the baking powder out of our biscuits. We sat there chewing Eileen's delicious meal like it was sawdust and foam rubber. The phone rang in the back of the house, then Eileen came through. "It's for you," she told Joyce. "Mrs. MacGorrie's secretary." Joyce didn't return to finish her tea.

Sergeant Murray arrived before seven to talk to me. We sat in the dining room while I told him I'd remembered hearing Jim quarreling with Norwood Hardin the previous evening, up the brae. "But that's probably pointless now," I concluded. "If Mr. Hardin himself has turned up in the other coffin, it's unlikely he killed Jim."

"Hphmm." That's the closest I can get to what he said, but it indicated that the bobby was first cousin to a clam. I figured we were done and I'd wasted his time.

He settled back and fixed me with a thoughtful stare. "Tell me aboot the quarrel."

I described as best I could what they'd said and how Norwood Hardin knocked Jim down. "Butted him, I think. I didn't see it happen, but that's what Jim told the laird's wife he did."

The sound of a violin, low and mournful, filtered through the dining-room door. For a startled instant I thought Jim had returned to play his own lament, but then realized it must be Sherry, honoring him in the way she knew best.

"The laird's wife was there?" The bobby's voice had a peculiar inflection.

"Yes, she came about the time Norwood knocked Jim down." I described how she had intervened and as much as I could remember about what everybody had said afterwards.

The bobby turned his cap around and around in his hand, much like our sheriff back home does when he's thinking. "The laird mentioned that he and Mr. Gordon were discussing business, but his wife did not mention knowing Mr. Gordon before. Ye're sure she did?"

"Oh, yes. She mentioned it last evening, Jim's wife mentioned it at breakfast, and the laird himself told me later in the cemetery that his wife and Jim were friends back in Georgia."

"I will check on that, then." He made a note. "When the men quarreled, you think it was because Mr. Hardin felt he deserved more—ah—"

"Money. Yes. Apparently his part of the business deal was to 'persuade' the laird—that's what he told his sister, anyway. She claimed that he persuaded her and she persuaded her husband. Jim was going to pay Norwood for setting up the deal, but Norwood wanted to be a partner. That's what the quarrel was about, as I understood it."

He stood. "I'll speak to the laird and his wife aboot this again, but it's all very puzzling. From what you say, Mr. Gordon may have had a remote reason for killing Mr. Hardin, and Mr. Hardin may have had what he deemed a good reason for killing Mr. Gordon. The question is, who might have had reason to kill them both?"

"You think it was the same person?"

"We dinnae ken. It wasnae the same method, and the only prints on the coffins are Ian's and, oddly, Mr. Hardin's on the one he was found in. He seems to have opened the lid."

"Do you know if he was killed there or moved?"

"Oh, he was killed there, right enough. Stabbed as he bent over the coffin, then bundled inside." He settled his hat on his head and changed the subject. "Has Mrs. Gordon returned?"

"None of us have seen her since breakfast."

"We havenae located her yet, either. It would help if we had a picture. Her description would fit so many people."

"Not at all. Brandi is drop-dead gorgeous. But wait! I have a snapshot I developed in Inverness." I ran upstairs and fetched the picture of Jim and Brandi standing beside the bus in Glasgow. "So Norwood Hardin was stabbed?" I asked as I handed him the picture.

"Aye, with a short sword, the kind we call a *sgian dubh*. It doesn't belong to any of our local pipers, nor did it come from any of our local shops. We're checking to see where it could have come from."

I felt very cold. "Can you describe it?"

"Aye. It's about this long"—he held his hands apart— "and has a particularly fine cairngorm worked into the hilt. A bonnie piece."

My first impulse was to say nothing until I could speak to Kenny. But I had obeyed a similar hunch that morning, and look what happened. "One of our group is a piper and has a *sgian dubh* with a cairngorm in the hilt. But he hasn't been here all day, either. That's his wife playing the violin."

"Would you ask her to step across here, please?"

I found Sherry playing with no light but the lounge fire. "The police would like to speak with you," I told her.

She jumped and looked around like she was searching for another door than the one I was standing in. "Why?"

"He wants to ask you a couple of questions."

"I haven't done anything!"

"Then you've nothing to fear, have you?" I held the door for her. She set down her fiddle and stood with a swishing of her long skirt. The way she walked across the hall, head up and chin at a slight angle, reminded me of a film I'd seen of Mary, Queen of Scots going to be beheaded.

When I ushered her into the dining room, the sergeant handed me a piece of paper. "Just jot down your address in America, please. Then that will be all."

I lingered in the hall, reading some business cards in a basket on the hall table. In a very short time Sherry was back, heading up the stairs. "He wants to see Kenny's *sgian dubh*." She sounded worried. No wonder. She came back down with a blank expression. "It's not there. Nor is his kilt. He must be wearing them, wherever he is."

The business cards had given me an idea. After the bobby left, I went to the kitchen, where Eileen was finishing the dishes. "Could I use your computer for a few minutes?"

I sounded like one of those people who can't be away from e-mail for two weeks without going crazy, but she led me to her private room without a word and turned on the computer.

"I'll be fine," I assured her. "You go on back to what you were doing." As soon as the door closed behind her, I went online and searched for "Norwood Hardin."

By now I have done so much Internet research on folks whom I've suspected of various crimes that I subscribe to a number of news sources. Normally I am astonished at how much the Internet knows about us all. This time I was astonished at how little it knew. I found only two mentions of Norwood in the past five years. One was an article in

Georgia Trends, discussing the growth of Albany businesses during the past thirty years. It mentioned Jim's former company, among others, and showed a handsome
picture of Jim in golf gear about to tee off with a partner
identified as "Norwood Hardin, former CFO of Hardin and
Gray Investment Firm."

Norwood received more press in a feature article a
statewide paper had done one June on "Marriages She
Should Never Have Made." Along with two stories of wives
murdered by their husbands, it told of Marilyn Gray's marriage seventeen years before to her husband's partner, Norwood, six months after her husband died in jail for
investment fraud, and how Marilyn herself had slit her
wrists less than two years later. The article was careful to say
that Norwood himself was at a community-theater rehearsal
the evening she died, and foul play was not suspected, but it
clearly implied Marilyn had a good reason for what she did.
The article was accompanied by their wedding picture: a
smiling bride and groom accompanied by a sullen, unhappy
teenager with long blonde hair, identified as "her daughter,
Jocelyn Gray, maid of honor." Apparently Jocelyn didn't
consider it much of an honor.

Other than that, Norwood had not achieved Internet
fame.

I typed in "Gilroy's Highland Tours." I found a number
of tours through the Highlands, the fine shiny buses that had
come to the ceilidh and a shot of Ginger Beard helping a
stout woman aboard his bus. I saw pictures of Gilroy hotel
lobbies and Gilroy tearooms we had visited, advertising,
"Gilroy's package tours provide the finest accommodations,
the last word in comfort." I did not see Watty and his de-
crepit old bus. I did not find tours that offered discounts to
folks who enticed others to come. Prices for a few tours
were equivalent to what Laura and I had paid for our tour.
Most were higher. And all tours said they required a minimum of twenty-five persons or money would be refunded.

Before I shut down, on a whim I ran a search on Jim Gordon and printed out three articles where he, his plain little
wife, and their tall plain daughter, Wendy, were shown at social events with other shining lights of Albany society. In

one, taken when Wendy was about fifteen, she stood beside a lovely contemporary I didn't recognize until I read the caption: "with Jocelyn Gray. "

I was scrolling down to the next article when the phone rang. Eileen stuck her head in the door. "There's a call for you."

It was Sergeant Murray, and apparently great minds ran in the same direction. "I see on the Internet that you've had some experience in working with law-enforcement agencies on other crimes, Mrs. Yarbrough. We do not welcome interference with our cases. If you learn anything more, please pass it along immediately." I promised I would, left Eileen a pound for her paper and electricity, and headed upstairs. This was, I reminded myself, a vacation in every sense, including a vacation from what Joe Riddley called, inelegantly, "meddling in murder."

❧ 22 ❧

I went upstairs to find Laura standing in the dark by the window, looking out over the invisible hills. When I heard a repressed little sniff, it felt like a repeat of that night with Joyce.

"Do you want me to leave?" Whether she was grieving Jim, worried about Kenny, or just plumb worn out from all that hill walking, she deserved her privacy.

"No." She spoke in a chokey little voice. "I'm just feeling a little lonesome."

"For Ben?" I asked hopefully.

"For *anybody* to climb with and talk to. I know I ought to be able to enjoy all this on my own. I *am*," she added fiercely, like she was trying to convince herself, "but I kept seeing things this afternoon I wanted to point out to somebody, and twelve-year-old Girl Guides weren't enough." She gave a rueful laugh. "And just now, I was thinking that none of this awful stuff would seem quite so awful if I had—oh, it's dumb."

I went over and stood near enough for comfort, but not close enough to make her feel hemmed in. "It's not dumb, honey. Having somebody around to share the good stuff makes it even better, and talking with somebody about awful stuff like what has happened today can make it seem less awful. Sometimes just having them *there* is enough. That's what Ben did when your folks died, wasn't it?" Joe Riddley claims I'm real good at beating dead horses.

"I wasn't talking about Ben, necessarily." She moved a step away from me.

"No, but he's a good propper-upper. What was it we nicknamed him back then? A Boy Scout totem pole—a wooden face with a kind heart?"

She gave a quick snort of disapproval. "He's not so wooden when he gets to know you."

She didn't have to tell me that. Joe Riddley and I had made it a point to get to know Ben better these past few months, since we had seen him getting more and more interested in Laura. After all, we were the closest thing to parents she had left. "He'd be good to have along right now," I told her. "We could both use some propping up."

She wiped her nose, her tears gone. "Do you miss Joe Riddley and wish he'd come?"

Convinced we'll have to answer someday for lies we tell, I was forced to admit, "Well, I'm kind of glad he's not here right now. If he was, he'd be wanting a full explanation of how I managed to be in the chapel when Jim's body was found, and how I managed to be up on the hill when Jim quarreled with the laird's brother-in-law."

She turned in surprise. "You were *there* when they found Jim? You didn't mention that."

"Well, I was. Remember how I went down to the chapel with the priest after dinner? He and Roddy found Jim then, when they started to move the coffins over so Roddy could clean the narthex. They were supposed to be empty."

She fetched a tissue and blew her nose. "Where did the coffins come from, again?"

I had suspected she wasn't listening wholeheartedly that afternoon when I'd told the story. Not until I'd gotten to Jim's death had she really begun paying attention.

I bent and switched on the bedside lamp. "Sit down," I invited, taking a seat on my bed and patting the space next to me. When we were both comfortable, I said, "According to the joiner—the man who made and delivered the coffins—Jim ordered them sent to the chapel for the play. I saw the order myself."

"Jim? What did he have to do with the play?"

"Not a blessed thing, according to Joyce. Nor do coffins, for that matter. They weren't needed at all. So that order is one of life's little mysteries. Another is why Jim told them to take the coffins to 'the chapel' instead of to 'St. Catherine's Chapel.' You'd think whoever told him to order them—if somebody did—would have known the difference." I took time out to explain about the two churches and their common village appellations, finishing up, "The greatest mystery is how Jim wound up in one of them."

"Poor Jim." We were silent for a moment. Finally she asked, "But you had already seen him quarreling with the laird's brother-in-law? The one Sherry claims cheated her aunt Rose?"

"Yep, the same one who turned up dead after Jim did. And I did get the feeling he was the kind of man who could steal old ladies' retirement funds and never look back."

I filled her in on why Jim had come to town and what his argument with Norwood had been about. I didn't tell her that Norwood might have been killed with Kenny's *sgian dubh,* though. I still didn't trust her feelings for Kenny. Besides, Scarlett O'Hara was not the only Southern woman smart enough to know some things can be worried about tomorrow.

Laura's response to what I told her was different from mine. I was caught up in the question of who killed Jim. She, with an MBA, couldn't figure out why he had been planning to go into partnership with the laird. "I mean, why choose this village?"

"Because he knew Norwood—or at least Norwood's sister, the laird's wife."

"Nonsense, Mac. When you're starting up a business of that magnitude, you don't run through a list of people you know who might be interested in putting a hotel in their hometown. You look for the ideal location. Then you figure out what leverage and networks you have that could help. Besides, didn't you say the laird's wife was Jim's first wife's friend? That's a mighty strange partnership."

"I forgot to mention that she has the money." I explained about Kitty's former magnate.

"So Kitty and Jim were building the hotel?"

"No, when I spoke to the laird this morning, he was quite definite that he and Jim—"

"You spoke to the *laird*?"

That entailed a little detour to explain about my cemetery encounter with Godfrey and his master. "He clearly said he and Jim were planning to put up a first-class hotel to attract the skiing crowd, and that Jim was planning to add a golf course to attract visitors year-round."

"But why Auchnagar? The Guides were grumbling this afternoon that the skiing isn't reliable. Some winters they get very little snow. They were unanimous that you'd do better to go to Braemar or Aviemore to ski. And Auchnagar isn't near a major city. A good golf course needs other attractions nearby for nongolfing spouses."

"It's a lovely place." I felt compelled to defend my village of origin.

"It's pretty," she conceded, "but what is there to do besides hike?" She sat and thought a few minutes. "Choosing Auchnagar for a development of that type would mean developing on a smaller scale than Jim was capable of doing. He had to know that, so he must have had some really compelling incentive to come here."

"Like what? A tax write-off?"

"No, I don't mean he'd lose money on the project, just that he wouldn't make what he could elsewhere. It's like when Daddy opened a used car lot down in Douglas. It's never made as much as it could have if he had put it nearer I-75, but he put it there because his cousin Swanson wanted to live near his mother and take care of her. Daddy always referred to it as our 'family plot'—meaning not a cemetery plot, but a plot to help Aunt Gladys stay in her own hometown for the rest of her life. Otherwise, Swanson would have had to move her and the rest of his family somewhere he could find work. The lot has never made a lot of money, but Daddy said we'd never close it so long as it continues to provide a decent living for the folks who work there."

She stopped and gave me a questioning look, like it was now my turn, but I was still recovering from yet another example of the fine man Skye MacDonald had been, with one notable exception. Finally, when the silence grew long, I told her, "If you're expecting me to give you a readout of Jim Gordon's mental processes, honey, you'll be waiting a very long time."

"But you have to admit, it's odd."

"Watty put a hotel here—or bought one." I was still stung at what felt like a slur on my ancestors' birthplace. "It seems to be doing all right."

"Watty did what?"

That entailed an explanation of Watty's low-down deception.

Laura found that hilarious. "There we were, tipping double what his work was worth every time he hoisted an extra bag, and all the time that poor old bus driver on his last legs was raking in every penny we spent. Oh, I do like that man!"

"I want to pop him one, myself."

"But who'd have thought he could carry off the deception so long?" She grew serious again. "Speaking of deceptions, have you noticed that while this was billed as a genealogical tour, not one person except you is really exploring their roots? I mean, sure, Sherry toured Eilean Donan Castle, but it obviously wasn't her first time there, and she's already done all the research on her family."

"And Dorothy got out and looked around at Tain," I picked up in total agreement, "but she's more interested in figuring out whether she's an artist or a librarian than in her great-grandparents."

"And if Brandi has a single Scottish ancestor, I'd be surprised," Laura added.

I began to nibble one thumbnail. "I would, too. She admitted to me that Jim promised her if she'd come on this trip, he'd let her landscape their gardens when she got home, so my guess is that she was here to provide cover for his real reason for coming."

"But why did he need cover? Why sneak in, if what he was doing isn't illegal?"

"I've been asking myself that question for twenty-four hours, and still don't have an answer." I sighed. "But whatever it was, it seems to have caught up with him. Somebody must have found out his secret and wasn't real happy about it. At first, I thought that could be Norwood—until he got killed, too."

"Maybe the laird killed Norwood because he killed the goose with the golden egg."

That's how far we had gotten when somebody downstairs started screaming.

We both knew it was Sherry. We'd had ample opportunity to memorize those screams on the trip. As I rushed after Laura, I muttered, "If a play in Scotland ever needs a banshee, that woman ought to try out for the part."

We clattered down the stairs with Dorothy and Joyce right behind us and Roddy barreling down from the top floor as well.

Sherry stood in the small back hall dressed in a long black skirt, black socks, and a black turtleneck sweater, exercising her lungs to their fullest capacity.

Laura hurried to her and caught her arm. "What's the matter?"

Sherry opened her eyes long enough to see who it was, shook Laura off and began screaming, "It's all your fault! It's all your fault." She tossed her head in fury and her hair clip went flying. Long ropes of hair slung about her head and shoulders.

Meanwhile, Eileen's Lab was hurling himself against her bedroom door with loud hoarse promises to tear us all to shreds as soon as he got out. Roddy dashed from the kitchen and spoke firmly through his mother's door. "Hush, Chancellor! That'll be enough." Eileen and Marcia must have already gone to visit her aunt. The dog subsided to low growls.

Since Laura wasn't achieving much, I pushed her aside and shook Sherry hard. "Stop it! Stop that right now! Calm down and tell us what's the matter."

Sherry gasped, then called me several things that could have hurt my feelings if they had been the least bit applicable. Her saliva spattered my face like venom, and she raised her arms with her hands curved like talons, screaming again.

Roddy shoved me aside, made a circle of his arms, lifted them over her head, and brought them down, binding her own arms to her sides. While he held her, he spoke with a gentleness I'd never have expected from him. "Noo, noo, you dinnae want to go bonkers on us. Calm down, noo.

Shhh, calm down. Everything's gonna be all right. Calm down. Shhh."

"Let me go!" She twisted and jerked until I thought he would lose her, but Roddy kept murmuring and held on. At last she grew still. Silence fell like a sledgehammer.

She began to take deep, sobbing breaths. Rage left her face and she stood like an ice-witch with midnight hair damp and matted across her forehead. Runnels from tears streaked her cheeks.

"Let's go sit doon and rest a minute." Roddy steered her toward the lounge and called over his shoulder, "Could somebody fetch us a cuppa tea in the lounge?"

"I'll get it." I hadn't noticed Dorothy standing wide-eyed at the kitchen door until she spoke. She turned and hurried inside.

When Roddy had escorted Sherry safely into the lounge, Joyce spoke from the bottom of the stairs. "I guess I'd better go in with her." She was no longer the prim, anxious tour guide we'd met ten days before. She was a pale, bedraggled woman with a pink nose and wet lashes.

I held her back. "Let her catch her breath and get some tea inside her."

Dorothy carried a steaming mug to the door and peeped in. Roddy took the mug and kicked the door shut. It closed with a sharp *click*.

The Lab whined behind the other door.

"What was all that about?" Joyce asked, looking from one of us to the other. Her color was coming back and, with it some of her poise. "Does anybody have any idea?"

"The young policeman was here," Dorothy said in a tentative voice, like she wasn't sure she was supposed to be telling, but didn't like to carry the responsibility for withholding the information. "Roddy and I were in the kitchen playing cards, so I answered the door."

I figured Roddy would always let a woman answer the door.

"He asked to speak to her," Dorothy went on, "so I fetched her from the lounge. They spoke at the back door, and the next thing we knew she was screaming—eh?" She went to the back door and peered out. "I don't know what happened to the bobby."

"Skedaddled to save his skin," I suggested.

"Roddy was real good with her," Laura said in a surprised voice.

"Eileen says he's a way with animals," Dorothy told us. "She says the bigger and fiercer the better. She thinks he would be good working with a vet—eh? But he can't seem to make up his mind to get the training he'd need."

I was glad to hear that Roddy had one shining talent, should he choose to exercise it, but it sounded to me like Eileen, as well as Marcia, was trying to do a bit of matchmaking. And why not? Dorothy was pretty, sensible, and employable—just what most mothers of sons pray for.

In a moment or two, he eased halfway out the door. "Which one of ye is Laura?"

When she stepped forward, he motioned her in. "Mrs. Boyd would like to speak wi' ye."

As she got closer to the door, he muttered, "Go easy, noo. She's still not completely calm."

She certainly wasn't. As soon as Laura appeared, she started to yell again, "It's all your fault! You sent them after him, didn't you? You've landed him in jail, accused of murder, and I'll be there, too, as soon as he starts spilling his guts. And it's all your fault! I hope you're satisfied!"

I don't know about the others, but I was having trouble breathing. Kenny arrested for murder?

Her shouts, of course, set off the dog again. This time I went to the door of Eileen's room and talked him into a modicum of quiet. We could still hear his growls behind the door, though.

When things had been silent for a minute or so, Joyce started for the lounge. "I ought to be in there," she said again.

I held her back once more. "Roddy can handle her, but I think we should call the doctor. She'll make herself sick at this rate."

"I don't know about our insurance—" Joyce objected.

"They have the national health," Dorothy reminded her. "Shall I call?"

It was Joyce's decision, and she shook her head. "Not yet. Maybe the worst is over."

The worst over? With Sherry's husband arrested for murder?

As if she'd done all the deciding she could for a while, Joyce sank to the bottom step and sat there, her head in her hands.

We could hear Roddy, murmuring, but Laura still hadn't come out. The dog whined uneasily behind the door.

Trying to distract our attention from the lounge, I told Joyce, "I understand that the second dead man was the laird's brother-in-law, the one we were both looking for."

She nodded, and gave a not-funny little laugh. "I guess he had a good reason for missing rehearsal, huh?" She rubbed her palms on her thighs as if to warm them.

Laura stepped out of the lounge, a bit strained around the mouth and eyes, and came over to where I was standing. She looked down at me like she used to look up at me when she was little, had gotten herself into trouble, and wanted me to talk to her parents. "I told Sherry you're good at detecting. She wants to talk to you."

Joyce gave me a startled look, as if I'd just developed a second head. "Detecting?"

"Laura's exaggerating, honey," I assured her. I was about as eager to go into that lounge as I used to be to go into Mama's henhouse when I was six, knowing half the biddies were going to peck me when I robbed their nests and somewhere in the dimness lurked a ferocious rooster with spurs. "I don't have any legal standing in Scotland," I reminded Laura. "And the local police are perfectly capable."

"I told her you'd try to help." Laura sounded about six, too, and desperate. "They've arrested Kenny. His *sgian dubh* stabbed the laird's brother-in-law."

I should have warned Laura this could happen, prepared her. Too late now.

"Has he confessed?" Joyce was trembling. Poor dear, this was worse for her than for the rest of us. She'd put the trip together and been entrusted with getting us to Scotland and back. She already had a murder to deal with. And now she had a murderer? That was more than any tour guide signed on for. Maybe the rest of us ought to write her a testimonial. Not that she'd be likely to want to be a tour guide again, but she could show it when she applied for another job.

If you wonder why I was standing in that unheated hall thinking about writing testimonials for a trip none of us might survive, it was because my feet weren't making any tracks toward the lounge door. Laura gave me a shove. "Just go talk to her."

"I've been listening to her," I pointed out. "It has not been good for my eardrums."

"She won't scream at you like she did me," she promised.

"Can you guarantee that, honey?" However, I am a decent person, and a trained magistrate. If an American woman needed to talk because her husband was accused of murder, I knew I ought to listen—up to a point. "If she starts screaming, I'm out of there," I warned.

"Just go," Laura begged. That got me going. Laura MacDonald never begs. Never. I saw she was struggling to hold back tears, too, and Laura used to never cry. As soon as I turned toward the lounge, she dashed upstairs and I heard our door bang.

I sure hoped she wasn't breaking her heart over Kenny Boyd.

Sherry sat in the same chair she'd occupied earlier, her fiddle case at her feet. "Have you been playing down here all night?" I asked when I got inside the door and closed it behind me.

Roddy, beside her on the couch, looked surprised at my opening line, but Sherry nodded. "I was thinking of Jim. He was so talented. It's such a waste." Her voice was bleak and her eyes turned toward the fire as if those flames had consumed him. Had Kenny killed Jim out of jealousy?

"What did you want to talk to me about? And I warn you—if you start yelling at me, I am out of here so fast you won't see the dust from my shoes."

"I won't yell at you." She sounded so listless I wondered if Dorothy had put something in the tea, but then I saw the mug, virtually full, sitting on the tile curb that surrounded the hearth.

"So what did you want to talk to me about?"

"Laura said you're a judge, so I thought maybe you could tell me what to do. Kenny's in the Aberdeen jail."

I had opened my mouth to tell her I knew nothing about Scottish law and little enough about criminal law, since that's not what magistrates do, but she had already gone right on.

"The policeman think he killed Norwood Hardin because he was killed with Kenny's *sgian dubh* and they caught Kenny—caught him—" She began to gasp as if the oxygen had gone from the room.

"Breathe slowly and talk when you can." Roddy said quietly. "Shhh. Breathe. Breathe. That's right. Shhh."

Sherry took several deeper breaths, then bent to pick up her mug. She didn't drink, though, just cradled the mug in her hands, rolling it back and forth between her palms. "Kenny was at the Aberdeen airport, trying to get a plane."

"To where?"

She gave a short laugh. "Who knows where? He was running out on me, is what he was doing. Leaving me holding the whole bag. Bags and bags and bags and bags—"

She began to laugh, and her laugh was worse than her scream.

"Shhh," Roddy told her. "Calm doon. Shhh. It's going to be all right. Nobody is going to hurt you. I promise. Calm doon." Still the laughter continued. He threw me a pleading look.

I headed for the door. "She needs a sedative," I said firmly. "I'm going to tell Joyce to call the doctor."

❧ 23 ❧

Joyce and Roddy could greet the doctor. They didn't need the rest of us around, so I followed Laura up to our room.

"Okay," I said, closing the door behind me and not bothering to turn on a light. A soft glow filled the bay window from the rising moon, and I didn't feel like bright lights at the moment. "Tell me what Kenny and Sherry have been up to."

Maybe it was the darkness that made it easier to talk, maybe she felt she owed me a story for the ones I'd told her earlier, or maybe she was finally adequately worried. In any case, she took a seat on her bed and motioned me to sit on mine across from her.

"The restaurant is going under. They can't meet current expenses, much less their debt service. They took out a huge mortgage to buy the place, because Sherry's aunt Rose needed money to finance her retirement in Florida. And neither one of them is good at managing a restaurant. When he realized they faced bankruptcy, Kenny wanted to sell, but instead, Sherry went in cahoots with somebody she knows who makes bogus credit cards. She furnished him with names and card numbers from some of their customers, and in exchange, he made her ten cards they've been using on this trip to buy stuff to stock a Scottish gift shop on one of the English-speaking islands in the Caribbean. She was born there, and actually holds dual citizenship. So she flew down last month, rented a shop with an apartment upstairs, and got a business license. Their plan was to abandon the place in

Savannah and fly directly to the islands from Atlanta, before charges start showing up on people's credit ratings."

"But that's stealing, pure and simple," I protested.

Laura spoke impatiently. "Kenny knows that, but Sherry doesn't care, and she has him over a barrel. He persuaded her to cosign a big loan last year to expand the restaurant, so now she says it's his fault they're in all this trouble and he'd better do what she says or they'll lose everything and go to jail." Her eyes gleamed in the dimness, full of tears. "Kenny's been worried sick, but he doesn't know what to do."

What worried me was Laura getting so upset about a man like Kenny. Remembering his remark on the plane coming over, I suspected he was far less worried about the morality of the thing than he was about getting caught.

"So today he came up with an alternative plan." I had meant to hide the disgust I felt, to keep her talking, but it came out anyway. "Skip out and leave Sherry, as she so delicately put it, holding the bags and bags and bags."

Her head came up quickly, and she asked in disbelief, "Is that what she says he did?"

"Apparently it *is* what he did. They caught up with him at the Aberdeen airport and now have him in the Aberdeen jail."

"But she said they've discovered it was his *sgian dubh* that stabbed the laird's brother-in-law, so they arrested him."

I shrugged. "Maybe he killed Norwood Hardin and then ran."

She shook her head. "If he was running, it's my fault, Mac." Her voice was rough with pain.

"How in tarnation could it be your fault?"

"Last night he asked me for a loan, to get them through the crisis, but this morning I turned him down. I don't trust Sherry, and Kenny's not good at standing up to her, so I couldn't be sure the money would be used to pay their debts."

Whatever her sentimental feelings, Laura was, at base, a businesswoman. So am I.

"Absolutely not," I agreed. "You'd have been wasting your

money. And Kenny's a grown man, responsible for his own choices and actions, so don't go beating up on yourself. "

I didn't add that I wouldn't have trusted Kenny to use the money to pay debts, either. He obviously liked fine things and high living. But if I was going to upset Laura, I'd rather focus on what might have happened than on what hadn't. "You don't reckon Kenny asked Jim for a loan later, do you?"

"Then conked him on the head when he refused?" Laura has never been dumb, but I could tell she wasn't real happy with that scenario.

"Kenny's quick with his fists. It could have been an accident. Jim could have fallen back on something instead of being hit from behind."

"I don't think Kenny would have done that." But she spoke so weakly, I knew she was considering it. "He wouldn't stab anybody," she said desperately. "Sure he has a temper, but—"

I had no idea what I myself might be capable of, given the right provocation. I certainly couldn't speak for a man I'd only known ten days, a man with a most uncertain temper. He'd already had one reason for being hostile toward Jim: Sherry's obvious admiration of the way Jim played the fiddle. He certainly might have finally knocked Jim down and accidentally killed him. And if Norwood Hardin had been killed with Kenny's *sgian dubh,* Kenny was the most likely to have used it. Particularly if Kenny, like Sherry, felt that Norwood and his partner stole Aunt Rose's retirement fund and saw that as a primary root of their own current distress.

I had finally found what I'd been looking for all along: something or somebody to tie the two murders together. But there was so much we didn't know.

Downstairs, the grandfather clock started to boom. I automatically counted the chimes, but surely I'd missed one. Could it possibly be only nine? Tea had been at six, and that felt like hours and hours ago. Still, my chats with the bobby and with Laura hadn't taken long, and while Sherry's bizarre episode had been exhausting, it had also been relatively short.

I came to a decision. "There's nothing we can do for or about Kenny tonight, but there are other things we could be doing." I slid down off my bed. "Get your coat. I want to go down to the hotel bar, and I need you to come with me."

She gave me a skeptical look. "Planning to drown our sorrows in drink? It's not your style, Mac. And frankly, with Jim dead, I don't feel a bit like partying."

"I don't feel like partying, either, honey. This comes under the heading of asking a few important questions. And if you tell Joe Riddley, I'll string you up by your thumbs."

She put her hands over her head and chuckled. "You'll have to reach them first."

I went downstairs considerably relieved to think I might be getting the old Laura back.

By the time we got downstairs the doctor had already arrived and Dorothy, Joyce, and Roddy were standing around in the hall at loose ends. We invited them to come to the hotel with us. Dorothy and Roddy accepted.

We settled near the fireplace in the snug bar at the Gilroy Hotel, which was paneled in oak and had red leather wing chairs scattered in conversation centers around low tables and private booths lining the far wall. All the place needed was a dog dozing on the hearth rug.

Poor Morag, I knew she'd agree. I cast a look around for her mother. She must be the petite woman in a plaid skirt and green sweater over talking to the bartender. She had auburn hair that might have started out as fiery as Morag's and a sweet, serious face. Could she possibly be having a romance with Watty with her daughter's knowledge?

I mulled that over while Laura fetched our first round of drinks, and we chatted for a few minutes, but the whole time Roddy was searching the room with his eyes. Finally he pushed back his chair and announced with obvious relief, "Some of my mates just came in. Do you mind if we join them?" He pulled Dorothy up by one hand toward a couple who were heading for a booth in the far corner. I wondered if Laura also would have preferred joining people nearer her own age, but she was peering gloomily into her drink. "Do you think we ought to go to Aberdeen and try to bail Kenny out, Mac?"

"No, I think we ought to let him stew. I don't like Sherry, but a man who could fly out of the country and leave his wife holding—" I stopped.

Laura looked at me. I looked at her. In unison we chanted, "The bags and bags and bags—" Then we started laughing.

Once we started, we couldn't stop. I felt sick at my stomach and knew we were laughing because things were so dreadful, if we didn't laugh we might bawl, but each time I looked up I caught Laura's eye and we went off into gales again.

"I'm glad to see you're enjoyin' yourselves." Watty pulled out a chair and motioned for a drink. "Mind sharin' the cause for all this hilarity?"

It was a minute before I could speak. "Kenny's in jail—"

"—Because they think he killed the laird's brother-in-law—" Laura gasped.

"—And he was trying to skip the country, leaving Sherry—" We got the giggles again.

Watty sipped his drink and nodded judiciously. "Aye, I can see that would tickle some fancies. Nivver got amused by murder and wife desertion myself, mind—"

I contemplated his maroon cashmere sweater, starched white shirt, and knife-creased gray wool slacks, and finally was able to catch my breath and regain my sanity. "No, you old fraud. You get amused by pretending to be a bus driver when you own the whole blooming business."

"Och! And who's been talkin'? Eileen? Always did have a big mouth on her."

"Well, you've got a lot of nerve," Laura informed him. "Accepting our tips like you needed them—"

"An extra pound always comes in handy. But how about if I buy you another drink and even the ledger a bit?" He motioned to the barman and at the same time called to the manager, "Megan, come over and meet these twa ladies. They're on my tour, and they've caught me out."

"He's a dreadful wretch," she said, rubbing his hair

down where it was sticking up, "but we put up wi' him, bad as he is."

I was trying to figure out how to respond when a little voice called from the door of the bar, "Granda? I'm r-r-ready for bed. Come r-r-read my book, now." Morag stood there in a long pink nighty and scuffed bunny shoes, carrying a bear under one arm.

Watty rose. "I'm being paged. Be back in a wee whiley."

"You be sure to come back," I called after him. "We want to talk to you."

Megan slid into his chair. "Dad has more fun on these inspection trips of his than any other time of the year, but I keep telling him it's not fair to folks on the tour. He ought to tell you who he is."

"He's your *father*?" I voiced aloud what my brain was having trouble processing.

"Aye. I'm the youngest of five, and he's got us strewn out all over Scotland, learning the business from the ground up. My husband and I manage this hotel—he's down in London presently, on business. And I think you met my brother Jock, who drives one of the buses, over in Skye at the ceilidh—skinny chap with a ginger beard? Dad says we all have to understand the business before we can decide what to do with it when he's gone. Not that we expect him to go soon, mind. My da is still in fine fettle. But I quite like the work, myself."

I was relieved when trouble started at Roddy's booth. It kept Megan from seeing my flaming face and maybe guessing what I'd been suspecting.

⊰ 24 ⊱

The first sign of trouble was a loud voice. "Come on. It'll be fun." I peered around and saw that Roddy and his two friends were standing, while Dorothy still sat in their booth. Roddy was tugging at her arm.

"I'd rather stay here," Dorothy protested. "I haven't finished my drink."

"We'll get more drinks," Roddy promised. "And we're goin' to a far more lively place. There's music, and dancin'—"

"I'd rather stay here," Dorothy repeated, looking anxious.

"I'll walk her home later." I hadn't noticed Alex until he slid out of a nearby booth and went to join them. Dorothy threw him a grateful smile, but the stunning peroxide blonde he'd abandoned was looking daggers at his back.

Roddy looked daggers, as well. "Don't butt in, Alex. This is my date."

Alex ignored him and bent toward Dorothy. "Would you like to join us?"

She nodded and picked up her glass.

Roddy turned and aimed a fist at Alex's chin.

Megan jumped to her feet and hurried in his direction. The bartender watched with a wary eye. "Keep your brawling outside, Roddy Lamont," Megan told him crisply. "We'll have no fighting here."

Roddy breathed hard and glared down at Dorothy. "Come along, then."

She looked from Alex to Roddy, and I could tell she was

wavering—probably from a fear that she was causing all this trouble and ought to help dissolve it.

"What do you *want* to do?" Alex asked gently.

I waved, to catch her eye.

"I want to go back and sit with Laura and MacLaren." She slid from the booth and marched to our table with her color high. When she sat down, I could see her sweater vibrating from the thumping of her heart.

Roddy's pal draped one long arm around Roddy's shoulders. "Ye cannae win them all, mate. Come on. We'll find ye another skirt." The three of them trooped out.

Alex returned to his date, but she didn't look any happier than Roddy.

"That's her fast asleep," Watty announced in the tone of a man with a job well done as he came back to our table.

Megan was approaching from the front door, where she'd apparently gone to make sure Roddy and his companions left. "Thanks, Dad. Take my seat. I need to catch up with some paperwork."

As he lowered himself into the chair, he peered up at her with a thoughtful expression. "I think we need to rethink our policy on pets. A wee kitten could be kept in your quarters and wouldn't be much trouble."

She laughed. "It's easy to see who's been twisting her granda around her wee finger. Don't forget that a kitten grows into a cat, and you've always said—"

"Och, I know what I've always said." He waved one hand to show how unimportant that was. "But the lassie wants a kitten, and I think she ought to have one. She'll take care of it, it'll be nae bother—"

"We'll talk about this later," she said firmly, then turned to us. "It's been grand chatting with you ladies. I hope you'll come back to Auchnagar. We don't customarily have two murders in one day."

When she'd left, I turned to Watty. "Tell us about this trip we're on. Is it a Gilroy's tour, or an American tour that hired a Gilroy's bus and driver?" When he hesitated, I added, "It's not on your list of regular tours. I checked the Internet."

"And it's an odd tour," Laura said bluntly. "There aren't enough people to make it financially feasible—"

"—And some seem to have gotten discounts you don't generally offer," I finished.

He picked a smidgen of paper from the ashtray on the table, rolled it into a pill, and pushed it back and forth on the polished table with one forefinger. "I've been thinkin' myself there's something rum about the tour, so let me tell you how it came about. Last summer, Joyce called from America, wantin' a tour of Scotland that would end up in Auchnagar for three days and four nights. I told her that Auchnagar is nobody's idea of a tour destination, but she was quite firm. Said we must arrive here this weekend, because they were doing a play Saturday evening the group would enjoy. She also said they must go to Dornoch and Poolewe, because one member of the group particularly wanted to see the gardens. I informed her we have no hotel in Dornoch and the hotel here would be closed this week, but she said she would make other arrangements for those two places. She asked what was the smallest group I could take, and I told her twenty-five. She said, 'But you have a no-refund policy three weeks before a trip, right? So if twenty-five pay but fewer than that show up, do you go ahead with the tour for those that did come, since the others have paid?' I said, 'Och, aye, if I must, but I generally like to book thirty-five reservations to be sure we make our minimum.'"

He winked at me. "And to be sure the hotels and tearooms do a boomin' business. But then she says to me, 'If I can *guarantee* you twenty-five paid fares, even if some of them don't come, ye wouldnae keep the ithers from goin,' would ye?'"

"Is that the way she said it?" I asked. "I didn't know Joyce spoke Glaswegian."

"Cheeky, isn't she?" he asked Laura.

"Invariably," Laura agreed. "But you accepted Joyce's terms?"

"Eventually. I'll tell ye, that lass knows how to drive a hard bargain. I'd no more than given her a tour for a guaranteed twenty-five than she's askin' if there's any way I can shave a bit off the total, seein' she's guaranteein' from the start. I told her I could give her a discount price on the whole trip if she'd be willing to let the tour be part of my annual inspection. She said that would be fine, and I told her she could ask folks if there was anything special they wanted to see along the way, and I'd try to accommodate them. If it was too far off my route, however, we'd just say that place had to be cancelled." He chuckled. "I neglected to inform her, however, that we'd be travelin' in auld Jeannie. I could see that put her off her stroke a bit when you first arrived. But Jeannie's solid, even if she's no longer young and spry."

"She's named for his wife," I explained to Laura and Dorothy.

He nodded. "Aye. We were togither a long time."

"Did Joyce say how she planned to guarantee the twenty-five?" Laura asked.

"I asked her that. She said, 'That's our problem.' She sent me the deposit the very day we spoke, and the rest arrived four weeks before you did."

"Was there a travel agency name on the check?" Laura thought to ask.

"No. It was a wire transfer from Bank of America."

"The brochure just mentions Gilroy's Highland Tours," Dorothy pointed out.

Watty looked from one of us to the other. "What brochure?"

I happened to have mine in my pocketbook, so I fished it out and showed him. "It was on the Web site for us to download and print ourselves. And now that I think of it, I don't remember a travel agency name and address, either. We did everything by e-mail," I added for Watty's benefit. He was too busy admiring the brochure I had printed out to hear me.

"Will ye look at that?" he murmured, turning it over and over. "Looks like the real McCoy—or the real Gilroy, as may be—except ours are printed on glossy paper. We never printed these. It would be too dear for such a small run. You say you downloaded and printed them yourselves?"

I nodded and repeated, "We never got a thing about the tour that didn't come via e-mail or as an attachment."

"Is that right?" He tapped one finger on the table in admiration. "That could save enormous amounts in printing.

I'll have to speak wi' Joyce about how she did it. I'll admit, though, I was fair surprised to see how few of you actually showed up."

Laura's forehead creased in thought. "Do you reckon Joyce could have paid for the whole tour just to get her play produced?"

"I'd be more inclined to suspect that Jim underwrote the tour," I answered. "Joyce deferred to him several times. I thought it was because of all his money. But now—"

"Another part of his plot to sneak into Auchnagar?" Laura suggested. "Why don't you tell Watty about that. He may know something about the people on this end."

I related what I had heard between Norwood and Jim and between Kitty and Norwood, what Brandi had told me while we were walking through the gardens, and what the laird had said in the cemetery. Watty was scandalized. "They're plannin' on puttin' in a hotel?"

Megan, who had brought some supplies to the bartender again, came and stood behind Watty's chair to listen. I had forgotten I was describing competition for their own hotel.

"With a golf course," I added.

"But he dinnae say where?" Watty demanded.

I tried to remember. "No, just 'down the road' beyond the cemetery. Is that where the ski lift is? He said skiing was to be the main winter attraction."

"Aye, the lift's doon that way, and the laird owns most of the land between it and the village, but the ground is very steep, which is why he's reforested most of it and given the rest over to sheep." He turned and spoke to Megan rather than to us. "I cannae mind where they could put a golf course, can you? There's nae much land that's flat enough, would ye be thinking?"

She shook her head. "Just the Geddys farm. They'd run into a frontage problem, too. Barbara and Ian have all the land along the road, there. The laird's land lies behind."

Watty gave his daughter the same look he must have given her when she brought home good grades. "That's right enough. And I cannae see Barbara and Ian selling out, can you?"

Megan shook her head again. "Especially not to support

skiing and golf. Barbara's dead set against the skiing. Says it clutters up the village all winter when we need to catch our breath from the summer season. And you know Ian. He never parts with anything that's his."

"Maybe *you* could ask the laird," I suggested to Watty. "Approach him saying you heard there were possible plans for a hotel with Jim Gordon, and wondering if he'd be interested in discussing the same proposition with you. You don't have to build the dang thing," I added when I saw the flash in his eye.

"Och, I was just thinking how much we think alike, you and me."

"I never dress up and pretend to be somebody I'm not."

"Och, ye dress up like a harmless auld wifey when all the time ye're a judge and right handy in solving murders. Ye're not the only one uses the Internet, ye know. I had a most interesting wee read last night."

I was about to tell him what I thought about people who invaded my privacy on the Internet when a woman announced to the room as a whole, "Then you can stay here and rot! I'm not movin' to the back of beyond so you can sit around hoping to sell a picture or two. You used to be an artist. Now you're—you're a nothing!" The blonde at Alex Carmichael's table jumped up and snatched her purse from beside her.

Standing precariously on heels that looked like they'd been fashioned from toothpicks, she swung the purse to her shoulder and glared down at him. "You will never amount to a thing, Alex Carmichael. You're a worm, not a man!" She pivoted on one heel and stomped out. Alex threw some notes on the table and followed her. Dorothy watched him with concern written all over her face.

"Good riddance, if he has the sense to know it," Watty muttered to the rest of us. "He's a fine lad, Alex is. Deserves better than that one." He gave Dorothy a little wink, then turned to Laura. "So let's get clear on this, noo. Jim Gordon may have asked Joyce to get together a trip of people to come to Scotland and muddle about for a week or so, then come to Auchnagar and stay long enough so he and the laird could transact their business with nobody the wiser. And if she couldnae find twenty-five, she should get as many as she could, and he'd make up the rest?"

Laura nodded. "Which is why Auchnagar was so important to the itinerary."

"But why the secrecy?" he challenged her. "Except for me, who's likely to care if they build a new hotel near the village? Most folks would be standing on the roadside cheering."

"We don't know," I admitted. "That's the big question. Another big question is, what happens to our group now—and to Joyce? Are all the bills already paid?"

"Aye, you're covered back to Prestwick Airport, but I wonder about Joyce."

"Are you paying her?" Laura asked.

Watty tired of his little roll of paper and put it back in the ashtray. "We nivver pay guides from other countries. We'll provide a guide if the group wants one, but Joyce said that wasn't necessary. I expected her to come more prepared, mind—"

"—And instead, she's left it up to you," Laura finished for him.

He reverted back to his bus-driver persona. "Och, I chust told ye what I alriddy knew."

"Excuse me," Megan murmured. "I see the ten o'clock bus just pulled up outside. I'm expecting a parcel to come off it." She hurried to the front door.

She hadn't been gone a minute when we heard a familiar voice.

"Hey, you all! I am so glad to find you here." With her usual wide, friendly smile, Brandi Gordon strode into the bar and straight for our table.

I thought of Julia Roberts striding back into the hotel after her successful makeover in *Pretty Woman*. Brandi could have been a movie star paying us a surprise visit. Her suede boots exactly matched her short camel's-hair coat. The scarf at her neck brought out her eyes and reflected mahogany highlights in her hair. If possible, her hair looked bouncier and had more sheen than usual. Her skin looked fresh and moist—not like it had spent over a week touring the mountains. Even her makeup was fresh. And both her arms were full of parcels. Some of them looked pretty heavy.

She dumped them on the next table with a sigh of relief. "I've been trying to call Jimmy for hours to ask him to meet the bus, but his phone must not be on. I came in here to call our landlady, to ask if she'd send her son down to help me carry all this up the hill. The bus only comes this far. Could you all help me, instead? But first, I simply must have a drink." She turned toward the bar and called, "A long, tall gin and tonic, please, with lots of ice."

She dropped into our vacant chair and confided, "I have just had the most marvelous day. But I tell you the truth, I am almost dead."

None of the rest of us knew where to look. Watty excused himself. Laura and I took a silent vote and decided to let Brandi get a couple of swallows of drink inside her before we told her about Jim. "Where have you been?" I inquired.

"All the way to Aberdeen. I looked in the mirror this morning and saw that my roots needed a touch-up in the worst old way, so I thought I could pop into town to get them done and be back for lunch. It doesn't look far on the map, but the first part is all up and down. And nobody told me there wouldn't be cabs for hire in this place, or that after the six-thirty bus in the morning, there's none until eleven. By the time I arrived in town and got a hair appointment, I could only make the last bus back, which leaves at seven. But I had me a good old day in a real city. I got my hair done"—she paused to fluff it on her shoulders—"and my nails"—she held them out for our inspection—"and a terrific facial"—she brushed her cheek with her fingertips—"and still had time to shop a little." She held up several bags. "You all should have come. But I sure am bushed."

She wasn't going to be particularly energized by what we had to say.

I told her as gently as we knew how that as a trophy wife, she'd been put on the shelf. Actually, I just said that Jim had been killed that morning, and found in an empty coffin in the Catholic church.

Her response was to fling back her head with a peal of

laughter. "Jimmy wouldn't be caught dead in a Catholic church! And why would they have an extra coffin?"

"Jim ordered them for the play," I explained, "but he sent them to the wrong church."

"Jimmy didn't order anything for that play. He thinks it's going to be a dead bore, and we're already planning how we're going to skip out at the intermission and come up here." She took a long swallow of her drink and looked at us speculatively. "Did Jimmy put you up to this? Did he tell you all to come down here to wait for me and try to scare me to death because I ran off without telling him? If so, you should have come up with a better story. Coffins in a church? I ask you!" She laughed again.

We all assured her we had not been waiting for her, since nobody had any idea where she was or when she'd be back. (I didn't add that some of us had wondered *if* she'd be back.) Then I repeated that Jim had the world's best reason for not putting anybody up to anything.

She went from amused to belligerent in one second flat. "Now why would you make up something hateful like that? Neither Jimmy nor I either one ever did a thing to hurt you."

I was searching for words to convince her when Sergeant Murray loomed up behind me. I hadn't noticed him until he said, "Mrs. Gordon? I would like to ask you to come with me, please. I have some questions I want to ask you about your late husband."

As a convincer, that was a doozy.

Brandi's eyes widened and she pressed against the back of her chair. "You mean he really is dead? I thought they were joking. He was all right when I left this morning." She grabbed my hand and squeezed so hard, I wondered if we'd have to amputate. "Tell me this is a joke," she ordered.

I could see why some people respond well to torture. I'd have told her almost anything to get my circulation back. But the policeman was saying again, "I need you to come with me, please. It's not far—just a few steps down the road."

She flung down my hand and slapped her palms onto the tabletop. "I'm not going without my friends." Her nails were now such a deep red they looked almost black. Laura threw me a slight smile. Sounded like we'd bounced back into Brandi's friendship circle. "And I need to finish my drink before I go anywhere." Brandi held it aloft.

"I'll wait for you in the lobby, then." He bowed stiffly and departed.

Brandi dawdled, but it's hard to make one drink, even a tall one, last forever. As she sipped, she peppered us with questions: "How did Jimmy die?" "Was it an accident?" "Did he have a heart attack?" Her eyes were worried, and she kept drumming the table with her nails.

To every question I replied, as was proper and true, "You'll have to ask the police." Finally I said in exasperation, "You'll have to talk to the police about everything, Brandi. We really don't have any official information."

Her eyes widened. "Why are the police involved? They don't think he was murdered, do they?" When I didn't answer, she cried, "He *was* murdered! And they think I did it."

Several people were looking at us curiously. "I told you—" I began.

She slid back her chair and stood abruptly. "You haven't told me one blessed thing. I guess I'll have to go with the policeman, just to get some answers. But if those two cats think they can pin this on me, they have a another think coming." She strode away toward the lobby, leaving us to pay her bill and carry her parcels up the hill.

❧ 25 ❧

I woke Saturday hoping Friday had been a nightmare. Then I opened one eye and saw Laura looking at me with an expression that mirrored how I felt.

She muttered, "If we don't get up, will it all go away?"

"Darn. I hoped I was the only one who had that dream." I shoved back the covers, sat up, and fumbled for my slippers. "I guess it all happened, then."

She yawned. "More happened than you know. I went downstairs to read after you went to sleep, and Brandi came back and spent an hour telling me how all this is a plot by Joyce and the laird's wife to keep her from inheriting Jim's money."

"At least she didn't get arrested. That's something."

"Yeah, but the bobby told her not to leave the village."

"He told me not to leave the village." I found my robe tangled in the spread and pulled it on. "Why should Brandi think Joyce and Kitty are plotting against her? Surely she doesn't think they killed Jim just to pin it on her."

"She didn't mention a motive, just that those two want to frame her for Jim's death."

"Did she explain when and why Joyce and the laird's wife got together to conspire? The only connection I know of between them is the play." I stretched and felt my muscles complain a bit from all that walking up and down hills. Then I trudged over to the mirror and took stock of what I saw. Nothing I wanted inflicted on other people, so I got busy with cold cream and paint.

"She said they resent her because of Jim's first wife."

I looked at her through the mirror. "How would Joyce have known Jim's first wife?"

"Brandi said Joyce and Jim's daughter went to school together." Laura sat up and swung her legs off the bed. "I'm not going back to sleep, so I might as well get up, too. Has Joyce ever mentioned to you that she knew Jim and his daughter?"

"No. But she did say she'd need to call Jim's daughter—that Brandi wouldn't be likely to do it. And she said her parents came from central Georgia."

"That could have meant Albany." Laura frowned as she threw off her robe and started putting on warm clothes. "This trip is beginning to feel like something out of *The Twilight Zone*." She stood on her toes and stretched so high she nearly touched the ceiling. I watched her enviously and hoped that when I got to heaven, I'd be tall.

"So when did Brandi let you come to bed?" I asked.

"Oh, she came up around midnight. I stayed down trying to reach Ben." She added, in an offhand tone, "I thought he'd be finishing work about then."

Aha. If she'd sat up waiting to call after work, things might be looking up between them.

Or so I thought until she added, in a flat voice, "But he wasn't there."

"Didn't they say where he was?"

"No. Said he'd left early on Friday and told them he'd be back on Monday morning. I tried his place a couple of times after that, but he still hadn't come in by ten."

I did the math and figured she hadn't gotten much sleep. "If you keep up these hours, you are going to need a vacation to recover from your vacation. Try him now. He ought to be asleep."

Half dressed, she reached for her cell phone and pressed one number. She must have called Ben pretty often to have his apartment on international speed dial. I tried not to pay attention, but couldn't help hearing when she threw down the phone and said, "Dang it, he's still not there. Or sleeping too sound to hear the phone."

"Maybe he's on a fast plane to Scotland."

"Yeah, right. Since I don't think he's ever been out of the

state of Georgia, a passport is not likely to have been high on his agenda these past few years."

I was still trying to think what to say when we heard the breakfast gong.

I was surprised to find Roddy again sitting at the table in the bay window with Dorothy. They were the only people in the dining room. As we came in, Dorothy was saying, "I can't go. I have a painting I want to finish."

"Don't be a gloomy Gussie. You don't want to spend your life painting pictures. Come for a wee ride," he wheedled.

"I can't," she repeated. "Besides painting, I promised Alex I'd frame pictures. His assistant is home with a new baby, and he has fallen quite far behind."

Roddy stood with a petulant scowl. "Well, I'm off for a wonderful ride on my motorbike. Your loss." He stalked out.

Dorothy turned to us with anxious eyes. "Do you think I should have gone with him?"

"Honey," I told her, "what I think you should do is decide what *you* want to do. Then do exactly that. Don't let other folks always tell you what you ought to be doing."

She gave me a stricken look through those golden eyes. "But maybe he's right. Maybe I am a—whatever he said."

Laura leaned forward to whisper, in case Eileen should come through from the kitchen, "Or maybe you're more mature than Roddy and know what you like." She reached for a piece of cold toast from the rack and put it back. "I know what I like. Warm toast." She got up and went through the door to the kitchen.

"Take a lesson from Laura," I told Dorothy. "Asserting yourself takes practice, and she's been practicing for twenty-six years."

Dorothy looked silently from me to the door, which was swinging gently behind Laura. Then we both ate our eggs in silence. I wondered what she was thinking.

"Start by doing exactly what you want to today," I finally suggested, just as Laura came through with two pieces of what looked like hot toast.

"I guess." Dorothy got up and left with a dubious expression.

"If you're giving up Ben and Dorothy's not keen on Roddy," I said sadly, "it looks like there'll be no romantic ending to this trip."

Laura shrugged. "You can always fix up Marcia with Watty. So what's next?"

"I don't know. I thought I'd look in on Sherry to be sure she's all right, then mosey down the village. I still haven't done much research on the MacLarens. You want to come?"

"No, I'm going to follow your advice and do what I most want to: go back to bed."

I planned a fishing expedition, but I didn't exactly know what I was fishing for so I didn't know what to use for bait. I said a little prayer as I tapped at Sherry's door: "Don't let me do anything dumb."

I was surprised when Joyce opened the door. "Come on in." She wore that tight, bright smile she put on for difficult times. "Sherry's having breakfast in bed and I'm keeping her company." She herself was pale. Probably from worry and exhaustion.

Sherry lay in the exact center of the double bed with a tray on her legs, looking like the Queen of the Hill. Still, poor thing, she didn't look her best in that room. The pale lilac walls and dark purple spread made her skin look yellower, her hair dull and lifeless. Most of her breakfast still covered her plate, but she was sipping a cup of tea with a decent look on her face until she saw me. Then her usual scowl descended.

I perched on a chair upholstered in purple flowers and said, "I wanted to check on you and see if there's anything I could do."

"Like what?" She sounded like she suspected I was volunteering to arrange her hair for the firing squad.

"I don't know, maybe run an errand into the village?"

"You could run to Aberdeen and get Kenny out of jail." She said it with no emotion whatsoever. I wondered if the doctor still had her sedated. When she turned her black eyes on me, though, the pupils were so close to the color of her irises, I couldn't tell.

"Sorry. Don't think my running shoes would last that far.

But maybe we could put our heads together and come up with another suspect. You got any ideas, Joyce?"

"Me?" She sounded like I had suggested she'd committed one of the murders.

"I understand you went to school with Jim's daughter, and Jim seems to have known Mrs. MacGorrie and her brother back in Albany. Did you know them, too?"

"No, and Wendy, Jim's daughter, was in my kindergarten class." She gave me a strained smile. "That wasn't exactly yesterday."

Strike one. I turned back to Sherry. "You mentioned that first night in Atlanta that your restaurant has bought liquor from Jim's old company for years. Did you all know him back in his Albany days?"

"Not personally," she admitted.

"And you don't either one know anything from his past that might have gotten him killed?"

They both shook their heads, then Sherry added, "Unless his first wife got mad that Jim sold her daddy's business after he died and Jim became CEO."

I doubted that was the motive. I hadn't noticed any short female Southerners skulking around the hills, unless you counted me. But I could ask the sergeant if there were other Georgians in town besides our group.

The discouraging fact was, Norwood was still, far and away, the best suspect for Jim's murder, and I doubted that anybody could ever prove it. And who killed Norwood? Unless the police could prove Kenny did, it was probable that none of the rest of us would be allowed to go home for a while, because who else could have gotten hold of Kenny's *sgian dubh*?

"Still, I heard that Jim's wife took him for a pretty penny when he left her," Sherry added snidely, tracing the bedspread pattern with one finger.

"Have you kept up with Jim's daughter all these years?" I asked Joyce.

"I told you, Wendy and I went to kindergarten together. That's not usually an age for making lasting friendships."

"My husband and I met around then," I informed her.

"And I asked because I wondered if that was why Jim hired you to put together this tour."

She drew her eyebrows together in bewilderment. "What makes you think he did?"

"Laura and I were talking to Watty last night, and he said you guaranteed twenty-five places on the tour. We wondered who paid for the people who didn't come."

"People who didn't come," she said shortly. "That bad spring storm over here in March scared a lot of folks away, but they had already passed the date to get a refund."

"Oh." Strike two. That let a considerable amount of hot air out of my balloon, but I still hoped it might rise. "But did Jim suggest the trip? Was that why you planned it in the first place, to end up in Auchnagar? Or was it your play?"

"Neither." She stood and brushed lint off her tailored navy skirt. "My *company* put this tour together because they thought people would enjoy exploring their Scottish roots."

"But nobody has, except me," I pointed out.

"Sherry saw Eilean Donan, Laura visited MacDonald sites, Dorothy went to Tain"—she ticked them off on her fingers, her face flushed and her eyes glittering—"and you still have two more days to explore yours here in Auchnagar."

If you quit pestering me like this. She didn't say it, but it hung in the air.

At the risk of pestering her a little more . . .

"But if Sherry and Kenny got discounts for persuading Laura to come, Laura may get a discount for bringing me along, and Marcia got a two-for-one deal because her aunt owns this bed-and-breakfast, it sounds like the only people who paid full fare were me, Jim, and Brandi. How can you take a tour with only three full fares?"

She gave me her professional smile, having regained her poise. "You'll have to write to the e-mail address in your materials to ask that question. Somebody at the parent company may be willing to explain their finances to you. They don't explain them to me." Her voice sounded a little bitter. "I'm just the hired hand. And if you will excuse me, the hired hand has some things to do. I have to talk with Brandi about sending Jim's body home once the police release it, I have to talk to the police about Kenny for Sherry here, and I have to go down to the theater and pick up props that are no longer required."

She departed, leaving Sherry and me to understand that we might be able to slack off on this lovely Saturday, but some people had enormous amounts of work to do.

I knew Sherry expected me to leave, too, but I had another question for her. "Something has been bothering me. If Kenny didn't kill Mr. Hardin, how could anybody have gotten his *sgian dubh*? Didn't you all lock your door?"

"Kenny lost his key," she admitted. "Right after we got here. He swore he left it in the lock when we went down to the bar Thursday evening, but it wasn't here when we got back."

"Maybe Eileen saw it in the lock and took it back downstairs for safety."

Sherry shrugged. "Maybe, but I think Kenny probably dropped it somewhere. He's incredibly irresponsible about things like keys. I left the door open when I went out yesterday morning, because he'd said he'd be coming and going." Her mouth twisted at what that had meant, and for perhaps the first time in two weeks I actually felt compassion for her. Being married to Kenny couldn't be easy.

But before I could feel too sorry for her, Sherry snarled, "He must have come up as soon as I left, put on his kilt, packed a few clothes and his bagpipes, and split. I don't know why he didn't take his *sgian dubh,* he was so proud of it. It was a real bargain on eBay."

The venom in her voice rocked me so, I couldn't think of anything else to ask. I was half out the door when she screeched for the world to hear, "The rat took all our traveler's checks, too. And do you know his bus stopped in the next village and I saw it, but I never saw him on it?"

I figured Kenny had made sure of that.

❧ 26 ❧

The sun outside my window didn't fool me one bit into thinking the day was warm. I put on a cardigan under my coat, pulled on my gloves and my soft wooly hat, and closed the door quietly to keep from spoiling Laura's nap. As I stepped into the hall, Joyce was leaving her room, wearing a lightweight trench coat.

"You need a heavier coat," I admonished her as we headed down the stairs.

She gave me a wan smile. "I forgot my parka at the theater yesterday. I just hope the place is open so I can get it now. I want to get my books, too." We fell into step down the brae, she accommodating her longer stride to mine. As we passed the school, she said hesitantly, "MacLaren? I heard Sherry shouting as you were leaving her. I know you are trying to help, and that you may fancy yourself like that detective on television reruns, the woman from Maine? But please don't pry into other people's lives, and stop giving advice. I've heard you talking to several of the others, and I feel you are a bit too—"

"Nosy?" I was stung.

She gave me her prim little smile. "I was going to say motherly. I don't want to offend you, but please, stop asking so many questions. Let people tell you what they want you to know. And we are all grown-ups. We don't need advice."

That certainly crashed my computer. I wasn't offended, I was hurt, and couldn't think of a thing to say. I was actually glad to hear my name being called from the door of the police station. When I turned to see what the bobby wanted, Joyce continued on down the hill.

Sergeant Murray pulled his door shut behind him and came to join me. "You've a splendid weekend for your visit. The weather is chust grand!" He peered down at me. "I dinnae suppose ye've heard anything from your traveling companions that might assist in our inquiries?"

"I've just been warned off asking questions," I told him sourly. "Our tour guide didn't exactly call me nosy, but she came mighty close."

"Och, she's got a lot of responsibility," he said comfortably. "I'll need to ask her a few questions myself sometime today."

"Well, I have a couple for you. Are you positive Mr. Hardin was killed with Kenny's *sgian dubh*?"

"Aye. It was still in the wound when we found him, and Watty identified it."

Watty hadn't said he had talked to the police, but I did remember the young bobby saying they would talk to Watty if Jim was on a Gilroy's tour. That made more sense now.

"Do you have any motive for Kenny killing Norwood? As far as I can determine, they didn't even know one another. However—" I told him about Sherry's aunt Rose and her diminished retirement. I concluded, "And Kenny does have a temper, but even if he came across Norwood and learned who he was, I can't believe he would stab him to death in revenge."

The bobby surprised me. "Och, we know Mr. Boyd's innocent of *that* murder. Mrs. Gordon told me last night that she and Mr. Boyd both traveled in to Aberdeen on the eleven o'clock bus, and Mr. Hardin ate lunch at home at twelve-thirty, then was seen a wee bit later driving into town. We found his car behind St. Catherine's."

"Then why on earth did they arrest Kenny in the first place?"

"He acted suspiciously at the airport. He showed up asking where the next plane out was going. They told him it went across to Ostend, but was already full. He immediately asked where the next one was going. When they told him Israel, he said that was even better and he'd like a one-way ticket. They pegged him for a possible terrorist."

"Kenny?" It boggled the mind. "In a kilt?"

"Aye. After all, he's nae a Scot. They figured he might be planning to bomb any plane he could get on, so they alerted security, who held him. When they asked for his address in the British Isles, he gave Heather Glen, Auchnagar, so they called me. The call came in as I got back from learning that his *sgian dubh* was missing and sounded very like the one that killed Mr. Hardin, so I told them to hold him overnight. They're bringing him back this morning, and he'll get a full apology. That's your quota of questions, now. Tell me what you've got."

I filled him in on my conversations with Watty, Joyce, Laura, Brandi, and Sherry, and concluded, "Looks like nobody on our trip had a motive to kill Jim, and nobody even knew Norwood Hardin, so can we go now?"

I didn't mean it to come out sounding like a child who'd been at the mall too long, but that's how I was beginning to feel.

"You mentioned that Mrs. Boyd had a relative who felt betrayed by Mr. Hardin?" He arched one eyebrow like a question mark.

"Norwood's company apparently lost her aunt's retirement fund, and as a result, both Sherry and her aunt have had a hard time financially. But you've proved that Kenny was long gone from the village before Mr. Hardin was killed, and Sherry was in the next village all afternoon, shopping. Eileen's neighbor gave her a ride, and they didn't get back until we were at tea."

The bobby stopped and looked speculatively down at Gilroy's, where a bus was pulling to a stop. "There's a bus that goes through that village at one-thirty, gets here by two, turns around and leaves here at two-thirty bound for Aberdeen, and arrives back in the next village by three." He seemed to be talking as much to himself as to me. "I'll chust check with yon driver to see who was driving that route yesterday." He picked up his pace and I had to trot to keep up with him.

The police Land Rover headed our way. "Looks like

Constable Roy has managed to successfully fill the car with petrol." The way his eyes twinkled, I suspected Sergeant Murray was a pretty fair judge of Constable Roy's capabilities and shortcomings.

"Wait!" I called him back. He turned. "If Kenny caught the eleven o'clock bus, doesn't that mean he couldn't have killed Jim Gordon, either?"

He hesitated. "Unfortunately, no, it doesn't exclude him on that one."

Which was why they were bringing Kenny back instead of simply releasing him. He didn't say it, but the implication was clear.

I continued down toward the bridge, mulling over the murders.

One scenario I liked was that Norwood and Jim got into a fight, Norwood bopped Jim and killed him immediately *after* Jim stabbed Norwood with Kenny's *sgian dubh.* Jim and Brandi returned before Kenny and Sherry on Thursday night, so Jim could have taken Kelly's key from the door and stolen the dagger then. And hadn't I read a story in which somebody got stabbed and was able to walk about for quite some time before they collapsed? In which case, Norwood might have gone home to lunch—

With a sgian dubh *in his ribs?* asked a pesky voice that lives in my head and gets in the way of all my best ideas. *Don't you think the laird or his lady would have noticed? And why would Norwood and Jim fight in the Catholic church? Wouldn't even Roddy have heard a tremor? And surely you weren't about to suggest that when Norwood realized he was dying, he returned to the church at the exact time Roddy was fetching cigarettes and laid himself down in the other coffin, à la Romeo and Juliet?*

It wasn't my own good sense that kept me from admitting it. It was a blue Jaguar barreling onto the bridge at such a speed, I barely leaped out of the way before I got flattened.

I leaned across the parapet feeling downright sick, gasping for breath and imagining Morag's chiding voice in my ear: "Fit ye *deein'* in the middle of the r-r-road?"

I peered around to see where the Jag had gone and saw Kitty MacGorrie climb out next to the post office. It was past ten, but her brother's murder had probably messed up her schedule.

Grieving sister or not, my first impulse was to march into the post office, accost the woman, and demand "fit she thought she was deein'," driving like that in the middle of town. But I had no idea of the prerogatives of lairds and their ladies. For all I knew, she owned the road.

And while it would be comforting to think she'd developed her haughty airs in Scotland, it was more likely she'd learned them at her mother's knee. She made me want to carry a poster wherever I went in Auchnagar: "Georgians aren't all like her."

I'd been woman-handled all morning, between Joyce, Sherry, and Kitty. Fuming and furious, I stomped on along the way I'd been going. When I got to the main road, I turned toward the cemetery without thinking, my feet remembering the way. I did at least make sure to walk along the right of the road instead of the left, and was careful to stay well over on the verge.

I passed the cemetery and kept walking. Eventually the rhythm of my pace dredged up a little prayer I used to teach kindergartners in Sunday school: *Guide my thoughts and keep them pure. Guide my hands and make them yours. Guide my heart and keep it sweet. And please, dear Jesus, guide my feet.*

But my thoughts were still in turmoil, and the only place my feet were going was in a straight line. If I walked far enough, would I eventually get to either Edinburgh or London, where I could catch a plane home?

On my right was the burn, then the mountain which we saw from Heather Glen and which dominated the village. On my left, as Watty had pointed out, a wide strip of pasture lay between the road and the shoulder of the mountain as it began to rise. There wasn't as much flat land as you'd find in Middle Georgia, but few places are as ideally situated for golf as Augusta. Somebody could carve a pretty decent course out of these pastures, if they preferred a few people chasing balls to a lot of sheep eating grass.

Of course, a couple of centuries ago, somebody had preferred sheep eating grass to farmers feeding families. Perhaps this new rage to develop Scotland for tourism was just the Highland Clearances in a new manifestation. In America, it was big box stores rising in small towns like Hopemore, destroying smaller businesses like ours. I suddenly saw history as successive waves of grabbers rolling over the earth, taking what they wanted and little caring whom they shoved out of the way. Seen in that light, Alexander the Great and Genghis Khan were no more heroes than corporate CEOs and big housing developers. Maybe we ought to rewrite history books and call former heroes what they really are: Takers of the Earth.

I knew, though, that I was currently fuming at those people to keep from examining what truth there might be in what Joyce had said about me. Mama always said, "The truth about ourselves is a lot like chocolate-fudge cheesecake. We can't take but a little of it at a time."

"Miss? Oh, miss?" The voice broke into my thoughts, but I did not recognize it was calling me until I heard the familiar bawl, "Fit ye deein'?"

Morag stood beyond a low stone wall that enclosed a two-story stone house standing in a rough lawn. The house was large and unlovely in the highest degree, gray granite with gray trim at the windows and a gray front door. The only color was a break of evergreens that sheltered it from the worst of the wind and a scraggy broom with a few yellow blossoms at one corner. Flowers might eventually brighten patches of broken earth scattered about the rough lawn, but this early in the spring it was a stark old place, standing apart from the rest of the village.

"Isn't he a wee dear?" Morag crooned, running to meet me and holding a tiny calico kitten up to her chin. The mother cat followed close underfoot. Morag bent to give her a pat, then dropped the kitten into the mother's path. We watched as the mother picked it up by the scruff of the neck and carried it back to its siblings in a basket on the single step leading into the house.

"Aren't they dear wee things? Barbara would give me one, but Mum says no." Morag's lower lip jutted out in the universal symbol of children's disapproval of adult decrees. "Granda says I could keep him in our rooms, but Mum says he'd be sure to get out. He wouldn't, really he wouldn't. And I'd do all the work."

I couldn't tell if I was a practice audience for a later performance or being coached as a fellow supplicant on the kitten's behalf. "You and your mother will have to work that out," I told her. "Are you down feeding the animals today?"

"Och, no, just visitin'. Barbara's arthur-itis is bad." Morag made it sound like a disease that sat at a round table. "I rubbed her poor swollen wrists with ointment and made the tea, so she wouldnae have to lift the kettle."

"I'm sure she's glad to have you around."

"Would you like to come in and see her? I know she'd like some company. It's lonesome so far from the village."

Had Barbara gotten so lonesome she'd decided to sell their land and move closer into town? That was a possibility. "Maybe I'll just come in for a little while," I agreed.

As we got to the step I peered into the basket. "How many kittens are there?"

"Four—no, three." She peered up at me with an anxious expression. "Don't talk to Barbara about how many there are, okay?"

"Okay." I nodded, wondering what had happened to the fourth kitten to make Morag so reluctant to have it discussed.

Morag scooped up the calico kitten again, then led me into a chilly hall stretching from front to back of the house, with two closed doors on either side. But when she threw open a door on the left, the room inside was surprisingly warm and welcoming. A cheerful linoleum patterned in red, yellow, and brown lay on the floor while creamy walls rose above it to a border of scarlet poppies. A fat brown couch and two matching chairs sported bright quilts where dogs and cats could exercise their claws without damaging the suite, and a bright fire burned in the grate.

Barbara sat in the chair nearest the fire with a West Highland white terrier on her lap. "Here's somebody come to see you," Morag chirruped. The dog gave a slight *grrr,* but made no effort to jump down.

"I've been into the post office a couple of times," I reminded my startled hostess. "And just now I was passing by and Morag invited me in. My name is MacLaren Yarbrough, and I'm staying up at Heather Glen."

"Aye." By my second sentence she had already set down the dog, which curled nearer the fire, risen painfully to her feet, and hobbled toward the table, on which sat a metal teapot, two mugs picturing the Queen and Princess Anne, and a plate of store-bought cookies and two cold pancakes. "Will ye have a cup of tea and a biscuit?" she asked.

Oh, these Scots with their overflowing teapots and endless biscuits and pancakes. I would be round as a pancake myself by the time I got back to Georgia.

"Put the kitten back wi' his mum and come help me," Barbara instructed Morag, but with far less brusqueness than she used to address the rest of the world.

As Morag complied, Barbara peered out at me from under her bushy brows and muttered, "The less said about those kittens today, the better. Have a seat, will ye?"

I took a seat in one corner of the couch and put my hat and gloves beside me on a plump cushion as Morag came running back in and fetched a third mug—Prince Philip, this time. Barbara fixed all the cups alike: a dollop of milk, three small spoonfuls of sugar (the Scots routinely use what I think of as demitasse spoons in their sugar bowls), and a cupful of hot, strong tea. Morag passed them out, walking carefully and using both hands, then passed me the plate of cookies. When I took a chocolate one, she carried the plate back to the table.

"Fetch the serviettes." Barbara nodded toward a large kitchen dresser at the end of the room. Morag went with the uncertain look of somebody obeying a new order. She opened the drawer Barbara indicated by another nod, and brought out three small linen squares of tartan with a questioning look. "Aye, that's right," Barbara confirmed. "Pass them around, then."

Morag brought me one like a little priestess delivering a votive offering. The pattern looked familiar, but so many of the tartans are blue and green with only minor differences, I wondered if even Scots can tell them apart.

While Barbara and Morag chose their own delicacies from the plate, I took the time to consider the house more

closely, since it was the only Scottish home I was likely to
visit.

It was not unlike the big old farmhouse I'd grown up
in—two rooms on each side up and down, with a long hall
running from front to back between them and a single-story
kitchen at the back. I wondered what influence Scottish ar-
chitecture had in the design of what Southerners called
"plantation plain" houses in the nineteenth century.

This room stretched the entire depth of the house, its two
doors into the hall indicating that it had once been two
smaller rooms. Since Ian Geddys was a joiner, he presumably also knew how to un-join, if he desired. One unexpected touch was that the staircase went up at the back.
Perhaps Ian had moved it when they'd installed central heating. That morning, however, as far as I could tell, the only
heat came from the fire.

In past years, how cold would that house have been on
bitter mornings for whoever rose to make the fire? No wonder Barbara looked so old. I could not imagine a child of
nine managing to clean and cook for a father and two brothers under those conditions.

We chatted of this and that while we ate and drank.
Mostly they asked me what it was like where I lived. I told
them about my children and grandchildren and my dog and
Joe Riddley's scarlet macaw—Morag's chief interest. Gradually I brought the conversation around to the land we
owned and farmed.

"I understand that a good bit of the land around here is
yours," I mentioned to Barbara.

"Aye, but we've neither the inclination nor the equipment
to go in for farmin' on a grand scale. I put in a wee kitchen
garden each spring, but my brother is a joiner, and I've
worked at the post office nigh on forty years. I guess we
never took to the idea of farming."

"We don't farm our land either. We've put some of it into
pine trees and our older son grows corn—what you call
maize—and cotton on the rest. Just in the summer, though.
He's a schoolteacher in the wintertime, and his wife is a
nurse."

"Did ye used to work, as well?" Morag took a dainty bite

from her cookie, clearly enjoying her equal status in this grown-up tea party.

"I still work," I informed her. "I have two jobs. For one, I am a magistrate."

"Ye're a judge?" I could tell I'd risen a notch in both of their books.

"Yes, and my husband and I have a plant nursery that also sells seed and animal feed—not dog food, mind, but food for cows and horses."

"—And sheep," Morag completed my list.

"Actually, we don't raise sheep where I live."

"No sheep in America?" She and Barbara both were clearly scandalized.

Hoping to recover some national status, I assured them, "Oh, yes, some people raise sheep, but not where I live. We mostly raise cows, horses, and chickens."

"Probably too hot to need much wool," Barbara told Morag softly. Morag nodded, but I couldn't help feeling that they both pitied me a bit.

"The biggest problem we have right now is people buying up farmland to either put houses on it, or things like resorts and golf courses," I prattled on. "You wouldn't believe the amount of perfectly good farmland that is no longer growing food."

"And what will ye eat when the farms are all gone?" Morag demanded, a worried furrow on her brow beneath the fiery wisps of bangs. I'd wondered the very same thing.

"They've no shortage of land," Barbara echoed the developers. "It's a very big country."

"I hear you've got a lot of land, too," I said casually. "That must be unusual. The laird seems to own most of the land around the village."

"This was my granda's farm, and his granda's before him. But och, the laird's a good neighbor, and he rents our fields for pasture." She waved toward the window, and the sheep I could see grazing just beyond the drystone wall.

I hadn't found out a dadgum thing of any use, and it was getting to be time to leave, but I had a distressing problem. "Could I possibly use your toilet before I go back up the road?"

Barbara didn't seem the least bit embarrassed. "Och aye. Morag, show her where."

The toilet was exactly that—a throne with a very cold seat, placed in a tiny unheated closet just off the kitchen, with no bathtub or place to wash your hands. I wondered how Barbara and Ian bathed. Could they possibly still use a tub in front of the fire?

I returned to find Ian Geddys sitting sideways on a chair at the table, munching a cookie and swilling tea. He had not been given a dainty serviette.

"And fa's dat?" He jerked his head toward me, but spoke to Barbara.

I managed to translate that into "who's that?" while Barbara replied, "She's one of the Americans stayin' up at Heather Glen. She was oot for a wee walk and stopped in for a chat."

"She owns a store that sells animal feed and plants for houses," Morag furthered his education. "And she's a judge!"

His eyes narrowed. "Ye were up wi' the bobby yesterday, were ye no? After that mannie was found in the coffin he'd ordered?"

I nodded.

"And ye're a judge?"

I nodded again. "In America."

His features rearranged themselves into a ferocious frown. "Oot!" he ordered, pointing to the door. "Oot o' this house. We dinna need ye pokin' and pryin' around here. Gie oot, noo. Oot! And tak that brat of a bairn wi' ye!"

Morag didn't give me time to discuss the matter. She grabbed my hand and shrieked, "Run, or he'll kill us! Run!"

❦ 27 ❦

Spurred by Morag's terror, I pelted after her down the steps and along the walk to the road. She pulled me through the gate and along the drystone wall, both of us gasping for air. When we reached the place where the barbed wire began, I clutched a catch in my side and dragged her to a halt. "I'm too old to run like that," I said crossly. "We didn't have to run because he ordered me out of his house. It's his sister's house, too, and I didn't even tell her goodbye. And I left my cap and gloves."

Tears poured down her cheeks and she grabbed my hand again. "He disnae like Americans. He knocks them down so hard they cannae get up. And they die."

"You're having nightmares," I told her.

"No, I'm not. I saw him. I swear it. I saw him!" She was crying almost too hard for me to make out the words.

I looked at her sharply. "When?"

"Yesterday morning. I saw him! I did!"

I was about to say "pshaw" or its equivalent when I saw Ian run out the front door. He scanned the road in both directions, and, when he saw us, loped toward the truck that stood just beyond the wall.

Morag saw him, too. "He's comin' after us. Run!" She grabbed my hand and jerked.

"We can't outrun a truck. Quick, climb through to the pasture."

"He'll catch us. He'll catch us," Morag screamed. "He can run faster than us both."

Her fear was contagious. I looked around for a weapon—

I once attacked a wild man with a dead pine bough*—but there were no sticks or stones in that pasture large enough to hurt a grown man. "Dear God," I moaned, wishing the child and I were both safe at home.

Suddenly I heard a roar and saw the single headlight of a motorcycle coming up the road. "Help!" I called, stepping into its path and waving both arms.

It fishtailed to a stop. "Are ye daft?" Roddy Lamont screamed. "I coulda killt ye!"

"Take us to the police station," I commanded. "And hurry. Ian Geddys may be after us."

"He wants to kill us." Morag jumped up and down in panic.

Roddy turned and looked over his shoulder to where Ian was backing his truck. I don't know if it was our terror or the pure thrill of the chase, but he yelled, "Hop on, then, and hold tight. Here we go!"

I jumped up behind him and dragged Morag up between us. I wrapped my arms around Roddy's chest and pressed against the child. He kicked off, and we hurtled down the road.

I had never ridden a motorcycle before, even with a helmet. The noise was deafening. I regretted leaving my hat and gloves at Barbara's, for my hair would surely blow off my head and my fingers were growing numb with cold. My eyes would also probably be plastered to the back of my skull for life. I pressed my lips together, lest I swallow a bug, and after one look at the pavement hurtling past beneath our feet, couldn't bear to look down again. I settled for closing my eyes, resting my cheek on Morag's little head, and sending up wordless prayers.

And yet, there was something wonderful and elemental about the ride. Nothing between us and the air rushing past, the sense of leaning into each curve and dip. For one crazy moment, I wanted to ride on forever.

Then Roddy looked over his shoulder, shouted something I could not understand, and picked up his pace. Even without turning around, I felt Ian Geddys's truck looming

Who Let That Killer in the House?

behind us. Now all I wanted was to reach safety alive. And I had to open my eyes. I did not want to die unaware.

As we made the turn before the bridge, the bike leaned so far to the left that I expected us to slide into town on our shoulders. Instead, Roddy righted us and barreled past the post office as Ian's truck squealed on the turn. When we passed Gilroy's, I caught a glimpse of Watty's startled face at the door.

Beneath my chest, I felt Morag's tense little body. I clutched Roddy tighter, to make sure she stayed on, and felt her squirm. Down through the village we roared, and up the brae. As we slid to a stop in front of the station, I saw Sergeant Murray and Constable Roy standing in their doorway, gaping like fish.

"Are ye daft?" Sergeant Murray barked at Roddy as he straddled the bike and took off his helmet.

I myself was so attached to that bike, I feared it would take a hydraulic jack to separate us. My legs refused to move. Then I turned and saw Ian's truck so close it would surely hit us. In one galvanized leap I got myself and Morag both onto the sidewalk.

"Help!" I said weakly as my knees collapsed.

Ian screeched to a stop and slammed his truck door with enough force to shake the street. As he pounded toward the station, Sergeant Murray swept me up. "Get the child, Neil," he ordered, and carried me in. By the time Constable Roy arrived with Morag, I was already deposited in the chair behind the desk and the sergeant was standing between me and the door.

Morag crept to me and held me tight. I pulled her onto my lap and felt her trembling—or was that me? "Hush, hush," I said softly. "We're all right now."

Or were we?

Ian strode into the station yelling oaths. "Fit's the bairn tellin' ye? It's lies. All lies! Dinnae heed a word she says. She lies like a r-r-rug!"

"Hold on," Sergeant Murray said, lifting both his palms and pressing the air gently. "Nobody's told us anything. They've just arrived."

Ian peered past the bobby and spied Morag and me behind the desk. "Ye'll keep yer mouth shut, if ye know fit's good for ye," he yelled at Morag. "If ye tell lies aboot me, I'll see tae it that ye—"

"Hold on!" Sergeant Murray said again. This time his voice was stern. "I'll nae have ye threatenin' a bairn in my station or anywhere else. Do ye understand me?"

Ian reached out to shove past him. "I'll nae have her tellin' tales on me, the wee sneak!"

Next thing we knew, Roddy and Constable Roy had thrown themselves at him as one unit, had knocked him to the floor, and were sitting on him. "Scrum!" cried Roddy gleefully.

"Cuff him," the sergeant said. "Nae mair oot o' ye, Ian, until I hear what these two have to say. And Roddy?" he added as Constable Roy clicked cuffs on Ian's wrists.

Roddy gave him a bland smile. "Aye?"

"Dinnae make a habit of careening through town. Now sit on yon bench with Neil, and Ian, you sit between them while we all catch our breath." Ian protested and twisted, but the two younger men wrestled him onto the bench between them and locked their arms through his.

Sergeant Murray pulled up a chair to the front of his desk, sat down, and looked at me and Morag. "Now suppose ye tell me fit this is all aboot."

I stroked Morag's tangled hair. "It's her story. Honey, can you tell the bobby?"

Her voice trembled. "Ian will hurt me."

"And why should Ian hurt ye?" Watty demanded from the door. "It's me who'll skin ye—baith of ye—for ridin' hell-for-leather through the village streets. Ye coulda killed yourselves—or somebody else."

"Hush!" I told him tartly. "Let the child speak."

He considered me a moment, then nodded. "Och, aye. I'll just have a wee seat here by the door, then, and let my heart catch up wi' my body. Go on, Morag. Fit dee ye have to say?"

"Yesterday I saw—I saw— Ye'll skin me," she cried to her grandfather.

He looked at her sternly. "Were you skipping school again?"

She dropped her gaze and nodded. "Just a wee whiley. I was afraid for Barbara's kittens. Ian doesnae like them in the house, so he told Barbara to leave them in the front garden. But they are beginning to creep everywhere. They could get onto the r-r-road!"

"So you didn't go to school yesterday morning?" I tried to hurry her on a bit.

"Did, too!" Her face was nearly as red as her hair. "It was when we went out to play that I took a wee walk, like, to see how the kittens were gettin' on."

I remembered that the school was up near Heather Glen, so Morag's "wee walk" had been well over a mile each way.

"The basket was in the yard, but—" She stopped, and I had the feeling she was deciding to leave something out.

"Tell the whole story," I urged her.

Her eyes flashed. "I'm tellin' it. I looked for the kittens, but I didnae see all of them until I crept up to have a wee peep in the window." Her grin was like sunlight after a storm. "There were three o' them, sound asleep under the table." Clouds gathered on her forehead again. "But Ian was there, too, wi' another mannie, and they were arguin', like. Then Ian hit the mannie so hard he went staggerin' like a drunk and fell with his head on the hearth."

"And hoo do ye know how a drunk staggers?" her grandfather demanded.

"Och, I've watched Roddy leavin' the bar."

That got a spurt of laughter from Constable Roy. Encouraged, Morag added, "But Roddy disnae fall doon spurtin' blood all over the flair."

My breathing apparatus was malfunctioning again, and not from our wild ride. I met the sergeant's eyes and saw his held the same concern. But before he could speak, a harsh voice demanded at the door, "Fit's gan on? And fit's this aboot blood on the flair?"

Barbara stomped in, slightly winded, her hair disheveled. "The lot o' them took off from my place like bats out o' hell," she explained to the bobby. "I'd hae been here sooner, but I had to come on my bike." She turned back to Morag. "Fit's this ye're sayin', noo, aboot blood on the flair?"

Morag gulped and swallowed, but her eyes met Barbara's

bravely. "I saw Ian hit a mannie yesterday and knock him doon. His blood spattered all over your flair."

"Did not!" Ian said hoarsely.

"Och, that wasnae a mannie," Barbara said with relief. "I didnae like to tell ye, but Ian stepped on the wee black kitten yesterday when he came home for a flycup, and he killt it. He got its blood on the hearth and on the flair."

"No!" Morag shook her head. "'Twas a mannie. I saw him!"

Barbara looked at Ian. "Tell her, then. Tell her fit you did." Before he had a chance to speak, she turned back to the sergeant. "I came home for my dinner and found him scrubbing up the evidence. He's aye been careful wi' his hands but clumsy wi' his feet. But Morag has aye been one for makin' up fancy stories, too." She peered down sternly at the little girl.

The sergeant looked at Morag. Morag looked at Watty. "Tell them," Watty said.

"I took the wee black kitten," Morag said in a whisper. "I dinnae steal it, exactly. 'Twas crawlin' in the yard, and I caught it up to keep it from the road. But then I looked in the window and saw him"—she nodded toward Ian—"hit the mannie. I ran and took the kitten—without thinkin', Granda knows. He saw it, did ye not, Granda?" Watty nodded.

"Ian?" Barbara asked, her voice unsteady.

"It's all lies!" Ian leaped to his feet and lunged in her direction. As Roddy and Constable Roy wrestled him back to his seat, he shouted, "That lassie is lyin' like a rug, I tell ye! I was paperin' at the doctor's yesterday mornin'. Ask him. He'll tell ye. I was paperin' his spare room."

Morag cast an anxious look in his direction, but the sergeant told her, "Ye're in no danger. Roddy and Neil will hold him." But he waited to make sure Ian was calmer before saying to him in a mild voice, "I was thinkin' ye'd come home for a flycup, like, when you stepped on the wee kitten."

"It was a kitten," Ian roared. "I never saw any mannie and neither did she."

Barbara shifted uneasily from one foot to the other and never took her eyes off Ian.

"So tell me." The sergeant leaned toward Morag. "Fit did this mannie look like?"

"Old. Like Granda and her." She pointed to me. "But his hair was white and he was tall as Ian. They were rantin' and roarin' at one another something awful. And the wee kitten was trembling so hard!" She stopped and tears filled her eyes. "I chust took it because it was scared. Honest. I'll bring it back," she told Barbara. "But if ye tell Mum about me skippin' school and takin' him, I'll get in all sorts of trouble." She turned to Watty. "Are ye gonna tell her, Granda?" She began to blubber. "She'll never let me go down tae Barbara's again. An' I'll never, ever see the other wee kittens. Please don't tell. Please!"

The men looked helpless, but I have raised two sons and helped raise four grandchildren. I'm not susceptible to tears. "You are going to make yourself sick if you don't stop carrying on," I warned. "Have a drink of water."

Barbara went to pour her a glassful from a pitcher on a nearby table. Morag drank slowly, obviously postponing the rest of her story.

"Did the man ever get up?" I asked in a conversational tone. "The one you say Ian hit?"

She set down her glass and shook her head. "I dinnae ken. When Ian bent down to look him over, like, I was afraid he'd see me in the mirror over the dresser, so I crept to the back of the house and ran through the hen's gate to the pasture. I hid behind a boulder, waitin' for his truck to leave. He took a very long time. Finally I saw him come out and load two boxes in the truck."

"And fit did ye dee then?" asked her grandfather.

She looked as virtuous as an angel. "After he drove away, I came on down through the pasture to the road and went back to school."

"And fit did ye tell your teacher?" he demanded.

Morag looked down at a scab on her finger and started picking at it. "I said I'd felt sick and had to go home a wee whiley."

"And the kitten?" I asked quickly, before Watty could speak again.

Morag darted a quick look at Barbara, but Barbara was

still watching Ian, and it hurt me to see her face. She so obviously wanted to believe him, and so feared she should not.

Morag hung her head. "I kept him in my jacket and carried him to my room. Granda said he'd ask Mum if I could keep him." She threw her grandfather another anxious look, but he was examining his nails. I remembered him broaching the subject the night before when he'd finished tucking Morag up for the night.

The sergeant wasn't interested in kittens. "You don't know what happened to the mannie after that?" he repeated.

She shrugged. "I guess Ian dug a hole and buried him."

She said it so matter-of-factly that it was hard to believe she'd been in hysterics a few moments before. But she trembled again as Ian roared, "It's all lies! Dinna believe a word of it."

Watty roared back, "Quiet, or it's me ye'll be answerin' to."

The sergeant waved them both to silence as he leaned forward. "This could be very serious, Morag. Are you absolutely certain you saw this and are not making any of it up?"

"Aye."

"And did ye hear any of what they were arguing aboot?"

Her eyes slid to her grandfather. "Don't lie, now," he admonished her. "Tell the truth."

She heaved a huge sigh. "Well, I did, then. The mannie said the land was his, but I dinna ken what land. He said, 'I'll take care of you baith, but the land is mine. You've known that all along.' And Ian said—he said—" She came to a stricken halt.

"What did he say?" the sergeant urged.

She threw a frightened look at her grandfather, then whispered, "He said, 'I'll see ye in hell first.' I'm not supposed to say that word," she explained to me in a normal voice.

"You didn't," I reassured her. "You were just quoting what somebody else said."

She looked gravely at the bobby. "Will ye keep Ian here, so he cannae hurt me?"

"Aye, I'll keep him here until we get this sorted. You dinnae have to worry aboot him harmin' you."

Barbara spoke again, her voice harsh. "And fit mannie was this, Ian, talkin' aboot land and takin' care o' the twa of us?" Her eyes bored into his. "Fit mannie was it, then?"

A flush rose in his face with his temper. "'Twas Hamish, if you must know! Come back to claim his inheritance, he said. Wi' Dad's will in his pocket, leaving him the entire farm. Wi' the deed to the farm, as well. And wi' plans to go in wi' the laird to build a posh hotel with a golf course on our land! Said we had to know he'd return one day. Said we've had the livin' o' the land long enough. Said it was his and nothin' we could do aboot it!"

One gnarled hand crept up to Barbara's throat. "Hamish!" She spoke his name as one she had spoken in secret for many years. "He came back, and ye've killt him?"

"Dad left Hamish the farm, Babby. Nothin' a-tall for us."

She stood still for a long minute, then lifted both hands and waved them in front of her face as if dissipating a fog. "May God forgive the lot o' ye for all ye've done to me," she cried. Then she turned and stumbled blindly out the door. We heard the creak of her bike going down the brae, and nobody said a word for a full three minutes.

"Hamish retairned?" the sergeant finally asked, sounding stunned. "For sure?"

"Aye." The fire had gone out of Ian, leaving a sullen glare.

"And you killed him?"

"It was an accident," he said truculently. "Like she said." He nodded grudgingly at Morag. "I knocked him down, and he hit his head."

"Take him in the back," the sergeant told Constable Roy and Roddy.

He went struggling and swearing, as if he had expected that admission would secure his release. Morag looked up at me, puzzled. "Barbara is always sayin' we must make allowances for Ian, he's had a hard life, and he never had a mum, and his dad died when he was wee, and he's had to work hard always. But she had all those things, too, and she's not like that."

"It's a matter of choices," I told her, holding her close and feeling her tremble. "Barbara made good choices with the troubles she was handed, and she turned out good. Ian made choices that weren't so good, and so far—well, he's got time left to change. But remember, Morag. The choices we make shape who we become. That's why you need to choose to go to school." I figured I might as well get in a grand-motherly lick while I was at it.

"Och, school's a bloomin' waste o' time." She wriggled down off my lap. "Are we finished now? I'm supposed to be helping Mum count the sheets."

❧ 28 ❧

"Do you have anything to add to Morag's story?" the sergeant asked when Morag and Watty had gone.

I was thoroughly bewildered. "Jim Gordon was really Hamish Geddys?"

The bobby nodded. "Could be. He dinnae even change his name much, because the Geddyses are a sept of the Gordon clan, and Hamish is the Gaelic for James." He broke off and said, almost to himself, "Hamish Geddys, home after all these years, and struck down the day he arrives. What a waste."

"One of our group noticed his resemblance to Barbara as we came through the village."

"They were very like, now that you mention it."

"And Jim sat in the front of the bus the day we drove here, looking at the scenery like a man coming home," I remembered. "He'd never cared about scenery before. He told Watty that he'd seen the Five Sisters of Kintail in a geography book, too. It must have been a Scottish geography. They aren't in American geographies."

"They were in mine." He nodded again, as if that were all the effort he was capable of at the moment.

"And when I said I was looking forward to coming to Auchnagar—" I broke off. I didn't need to repeat what Jim had said I'd find there. He had sounded as if he had known, though.

"More important," I went on, "Alasdair Geddys is said to have made extremely good whisky in these hills, and

Eileen said some suspected Hamish worked with his father."

"Aye. I've heard that."

"Jim developed a recipe for an outstanding scotch in America, and used it to establish Scotsman Distillery in the north Georgia mountains."

That finally energized the sergeant. "I've had a bottle of Scotsman! An American policeman passing through boasted it was as good as any in Scotland. He sent me a wee bottle."

"Which cost him a wee penny," I said drily. "But would a father leave his whole farm to one son instead of dividing it among his children? And how could Barbara and Ian have lived here all these years without proving their father's will or showing anybody the deed?"

He thought that over. "There's no cause to show a deed so long as taxes are paid. Ye'd only need the deed if ye were sellin' your land. And while the Scots rule of intestacy would divide the land equally among the three children— which we've all presumed happened when Alasdair died— he could have written a will, right enough, leaving everything to Hamish. Alasdair had a bad sickness several years before he drooned, where they feared for his life. That maybe gave him a wee taste of mortality and frightened him enough to write a will."

Seeing my expression, he chuckled. "I'm too young to remember, mind, but Alasdair is a legend around these parts, both for his whisky and his music. My dad loved to tell how Alasdair caught a chill, developed pneumonia, and was put in hospital in Aberdeen. The doctor fair gave him up, but Alasdair sent young Hamish home for a bottle of his own whisky and his fiddle. After drinkin' one dram and playin' one tune, so the story goes, he got out of his bed and went home cured. If he wrote a will soon after that, he maybe left everything to Hamish because he was almost grown, while Ian was still young. Alasdair would never have left a thing to a daughter, although nearly half his land came to him from his wife. It was the MacLaren farm that adjoined his, and she was the last of the MacLarens after her sister, Margaret, died."

I felt like he'd poured ice water over me. "Ian and Barbara are half MacLarens?"

"Aye, their mother was a MacLaren."

"That was my mother's maiden name, and it's my given name, as well." I couldn't recall if I'd mentioned the name when I asked Barbara directions to the cemetery. She probably hadn't been listening when I introduced myself that morning.

He chuckled. "Maybe ye'll be puttin' in your own claim to the farm."

I shook my head. "No, but I came looking for relatives." I nodded my head toward the back room. "Seems like I may have found them." I sighed. So many things were clear now. The conversation Dorothy and I had overheard in the fog, when Jim had assured somebody (Norwood?) not to worry about his parcel, he had title to it. And the incentive Laura had been looking for—why he had been willing to invest in Auchnagar.

"The laird's wife can probably give you the name and address of Jim's first wife," I told the bobby. "They must have met not long after he got to America, for they have a daughter who's around thirty-five. She went to kindergarten with our tour-group leader."

He made a couple of notes.

"Do you reckon Ian killed Norwood, too, since he was in on the land deal?"

Sergeant Murray stood. "We'll look into that." His voice was courteous, but I was being dismissed. "Thank you for your assistance. You go on up the brae, noo, and maybe have a wee rest, after all the excitement."

I tried to stand, but my legs wouldn't support me. Sergeant Murray called through to the back, "Neil, come run Mrs. Yarbrough up to Heather Glen."

Roddy came to the door. "Shall I run ye up on my bike, then?" He grinned.

When I saw the Land Rover and how high I'd have to climb to get in, I almost requested the bike. What I really wanted was to be pulled up the hill in a little red wagon.

As the sergeant helped me into the Land Rover, he said in parting, "I'll ask Barbara to have a look around for that will and the deed to the land. Ian will not have destroyed them. He's too canny for that. But ask Mrs. Gordon to look through her husband's papers, too. It's possible he took copies to show Ian."

When Neil pulled up close to Eileen's back door, he asked solicitously, "Do ye want me to help you in?"

I assured him I could make it on my own, but as I staggered into the house and hauled myself up the stairs, I muttered, "If I make it to my room, I may never leave it again."

When I reached the upstairs hall, however, I remembered the sergeant's request. Feeling the way I did, I might not live long enough to talk to Brandi if I didn't do it right away, so I dragged myself over to her door and knocked.

She answered in a long turquoise fleece caftan that could have come from the *Vogue* lying on her bed, but her eyes were pink and her nose red and swollen. "Yes?" she asked in a voice clogged with tears. When she saw who it was, she got a strange expression in her eyes.

"I have a message for you from the police."

"Oh! Do they know who killed Jimmy?" Her voice lit with hope, but she was still staring at me with that odd look on her face.

"They haven't arrested anybody yet." I may be sworn to speak the truth in matters of law, but I don't have to tell all I know. "But the bobby asks you to look among Jim's papers for the will of Alasdair Geddys and the deed to his farm here in Auchnagar."

She drew her fine brows together. "The lawyers will deal with Jim's papers."

This woman was not as dumb as she pretended, so I answered with some testiness. "They think now that Jim may have been murdered because he either had or claimed to have those papers. It's possible he had them on him and the killer took them. But it's also possible he took copies with him and left the originals among his things." I slowed to what my sons refer to as "Mama's Summing-Up Voice." "If the originals *are* here, you could be in danger, too."

Her eyes widened and flickered. "Where would they be? And what are they, again?"

"A will," I repeated deliberately. "Written by Alasdair Geddys, leaving the property to his son, Hamish Geddys. And the deed to the Geddys farm in Auchnagar."

"I don't know Alasdair or Hamish Geddys."

"That doesn't matter. Look for the papers. And if you find them, take them to the police station at once."

"All right. But they'd probably be in here." She picked up Jim's briefcase. "It's locked."

"Force the locks," I said fiercely. "Jim is not going to care."

My urgency penetrated the clouds in which she so carefully concealed her brain. "I'll ask Eileen for a screwdriver." She gave me one more strange look, then clattered downstairs in frivolous turquoise mules.

I headed to my room reflecting that it ought to be as easy to buy beautiful clothes as sensible ones. Maybe I could remember that next time I went shopping.

Thank heavens, Laura was out. I didn't want to talk to another soul.

I did, however, want to lock myself in. Ian had shattered the myth that I was safe in Auchnagar. I could feel his fury sending long tentacles all the way up the brae. I wondered if Morag felt them, too.

My bed was calling my name loud and clear, so I staggered in that direction. But as I passed the dresser, I happened to glance toward the mirror. I saw a woman who looked like she'd been vacationing in a wind tunnel. My hair stood out all over my head, and I didn't have on a speck of makeup. No wonder Brandi kept staring like she'd never seen me before.

"This gives new meaning to 'the windswept look,'" I muttered, grabbing a brush to try and restore the style to anything I didn't mind wearing in public. If there was a salon in Auchnagar, I hadn't seen it. And Saturday was sure to be their busiest day.

I did not achieve notable success.

"Oh, well," I quoted Mama as I tottered toward my bed,

"not everybody can be beautiful, but anybody can be special."

Before my head hit the pillow, Eileen rang the gong for dinner.

❧ 29 ❧

I considered skipping the meal, but my stomach sent up such a protest that I revived and managed to get downstairs. The strong greasy smell of fish and chips wafted from the kitchen, and bowls of Scotch broth were already on the table when I entered the dining room. The first person I saw was Kenny, sitting with Sherry at the small table for two by the wall, already shoveling down his soup. He ignored my greeting.

I joined Laura, who sat with Joyce and Dorothy at the table by the bay window. Dorothy was shyly talking about the pictures she'd framed that morning and her plans for painting that afternoon. Neither of the other two seemed to be paying much attention.

From what I could hear from the Boyd table, Kenny was both truculent and boastful about having been inside a Scottish jail. Sherry treated him with a wary compassion that made me think she hadn't had a chance yet to ask privately what he had told the police. Laura she treated with icy contempt.

Kenny wasn't keen on Laura, either, turning around to glower at her from time to time to let her know the entire mess had been her fault.

Laura herself was distracted. It took her five minutes to even notice what I was wearing. Finally she asked, "What's with the head scarf, Mac? You find some gypsy cousins?"

"No, but I had to do something. I got kind of windblown this morning."

"I saw you riding Roddy's motorcycle." Dorothy's eyes were wide. "You were going really fast, eh? Weren't you terrified?"

That put me in the bull's-eye of the conversation.

"It had its moments," I admitted, then shrugged, like it hadn't been important. "Morag, Watty's granddaughter, wanted a ride, so I went along."

"On a *motorcycle*?" Now Laura was looking at me like I'd just escaped from an asylum.

Her expression didn't improve when Dorothy asked, "Why was that man chasing you to the police station?"

Before I could think up an answer to that one, Joyce added, "Yes, what were you doing with the police?" Her voice was sharp, and in her eyes I read a repeat of that morning's warning. "I saw you coming out as I was returning from the theater."

Laura narrowed her eyes. "Have you been detecting again, Mac? You know what Joe Riddley told you last time."

Kenny whirled around, and Sherry bored into me with eyes like black nails.

They were all going to find out eventually, so I might as well tell them. "No, I just went for a walk. But I sort of stumbled into the fact that Ian Geddys, the joiner, killed Jim."

Eileen—carrying in heaped plates of fish and chips—dropped mine with a clatter on the table before me. "Ian? He never!"

"He's confessed," I told her. "He didn't mean to kill Jim, but it turns out that Jim was actually Hamish Geddys—"

"Hamish Geddys!" Eileen and Joyce exclaimed in unison.

I nodded. "He was coming home to claim the family farm, which his father left him years ago. Ian got angry and knocked him down and Jim's head hit the curb of their hearth. Morag, from the hotel, saw it happen."

"Wee Morag?" That was all Eileen could take. She sank into a chair at an empty table, patting her heart like she was having palpitations. Marcia—who had brought in the rest of the plates—sat beside her with a worried frown.

I told the story as best I could. The whole time I kept one eye on Joyce, wondering if she'd finally admit that Jim had instigated our tour. She paid me the same intense attention the others did, but no more. I doubt that her play, though, if it had been performed, would have gotten a better reception than my tale. When I was done, the silence was so profound, I felt like standing to take a bow.

"I thought there was something fishy about Jim the first time I saw him." Kenny poured ketchup lavishly on his plate and speared up a forkful of chips that looked like they were dripping blood. I shuddered and looked away. "And about that German name he claimed to have? Ha. Anybody could tell he was a Scot. 'Hamish' is the same as 'Jim,' you know, and Geddys is a sept of the Gordon clan." How quickly he had forgotten his earlier complaint that Jim was messing up genealogists.

"But how dreadful!" Dorothy said indignantly. "To take the farm from his own sister and brother after they'd taken care of it all these years—how could he?"

"He played the violin beautifully," Sherry reminded her, as if that excused the rest.

"He must have gotten his music from his dad," Eileen murmured. "Oh, poor Barbara, to lose him twice. She's aye grieved over Hamish, you know. When she was young, she fair worshiped the ground he walked on." She turned to Marcia. "We'll go down to her right away. Roddy can put the dishes in to soak. I'll just bring in the pudding now, shall I?"

"Jim probably got his famous whisky recipe from his dad, too," Laura murmured to me when Eileen had bustled out. I knew what she was thinking. After today, a Scotsman whisky bottle would conjure up additional memories for both of us.

Joyce put down her napkin and her voice was brisk. "As sorry as I am about Jim, I am glad to have his death explained. I think we should leave first thing tomorrow, as originally planned, don't you? Does anybody mind?" Hearing no objections, she added, "But no more poking around, Mac. Leave that to the police."

I fixed her with what my boys used to call "Mama's

Killer Stare." "I have done all the 'poking around' I plan to,"
I assured her, "but if you've got something to hide—"

She rose and headed for the door. "I'll check with the police to see how soon we can go."

Sherry called after her, "What entertainment are you pro-
viding tonight, now that the play is cancelled? Will Watty
take us somewhere else on the bus—maybe into Aberdeen,
to catch a concert or something?"

Joyce gave her a look that would have sizzled Sherry's
gizzard, if she'd had one. "At this point, you are on your
own." She closed the door behind her with such a bang, I
could picture her hopping the next bus and washing her
hands of us forever.

Dorothy left soon afterwards, eager to start painting.
Kenny and Sherry announced they were going for a walk—
which I suspected would take them to a more private place
to yell at each other. Roddy brought more hot water for our
teapot, informing us, "Mum and Marcia are off to see Barbara Geddys. Do you need anything else?"

Laura gave him a considering look. "What's this I hear
about you taking Mac for a ride on your motorbike without
offering one to the rest of us?"

Roddy lit up. "Would you like a wee ride, then, to the
next village and back?"

"I'd love one." Seeing my surprise, she informed me,
"I've always wanted to ride a motorcycle, but you didn't
mention motorcycles in Daddy's house."

"Do your hair a favor and wear a helmet," I advised. "Not
to mention saving your head."

"Och, I require all riders to have helmets," Roddy informed me, then added with a snicker, "except when they hi-
jack me in the middle of the road, like." He headed back to
the kitchen, calling over one shoulder, "Knock on the door
when you're ready for your ride."

"I'll just wait until you get the dishes in hot soapy water,"
she informed him.

We lingered over our last cup of tea, then Laura pushed
back her chair. "Well, I'm off into the wild blue yonder.
What about you?"

"I'm heading straight for the Land of Nod."

* * *

Before I napped, I called Joe Riddley on the cell phone. He ought to be up by now, I figured. Sure enough, he was sitting in our john-boat down at our fish camp on the lake. "Didn't you get enough fishing on the Gulf?" I demanded.

"Can't ever get too many fish," he replied. "I've got enough to fill up the freezer."

"We can't fill up the freezer. Martha and Ridd's garden will be in in a few weeks, and we'll be freezing vegetables. Not to mention that pig he's feeding for us to butcher next fall."

"Little Bit, did you call me to discuss our winter menus? Because if you did, I see a fish jumpin' out there, and he's got my name written all over his back."

"Did you take any of the boys down with you?" I couldn't bear to hang up quite yet. Hearing his voice gave the illusion that he could be just down in the village.

"No, I brought Ben Bradshaw. Went by to get my oil changed yesterday, and he looked so doggone sad about Laura being gone, I figured he could use a little entertainment."

"Well, that's one mystery solved, at least," I said happily. "I'll tell Laura when she gets back from her motorcycle ride."

As soon as the words were out of my mouth, I regretted them. Why did I ever mention—

No, it wasn't the motorcycle word I feared. Sure enough, Joe Riddley zeroed in on the other *m* word. "What mystery is *not* solved?" he growled.

"Oh, nothing much. I'll tell you about it when I get home. I need to go now. You all have fun, and we'll see you Monday afternoon." When you've had as many years together as we've had, you learn when it's good to spend time conversing and when it's better not to.

I figured I'd fall right asleep, the house was so hushed and empty. But once I'd climbed into bed and pulled the covers up to my chin, I was wide awake. I lay there a while, replaying the morning over and over: Joyce's attempt to straighten me out, my unexpected visit with Barbara, the wild ride through the village, Morag's story, Ian's flaming admission that he'd killed Jim, and the unpalatable truth that I could be kin to both brothers. I hadn't mentioned that to the group when I told Jim's story. Now I kept hearing Barbara's final cry against the men in her family, "May God forgive the lot o' ye for all ye've done to me." What a prize bunch of cousins I'd uncovered!

Barbara might be a relative worth getting to know on another visit, but she'd have little use for me right now. Poor, poor Barbara.

I squeezed my eyes tighter shut, determined to sleep, but have you ever noticed that once you decide to go to sleep, you can't? Sleep is one of life's greatest unsolved mysteries. We do it almost every day, yet never learn how it is we either fall asleep or wake up.

Since I obviously wasn't going to sleep anytime soon, I climbed out of bed, opened the curtains, and swung Eileen's big chair around to face the bay window. Those hills had been there a lot longer than human beings, and would be there when I and all of my contemporaries were gone. I wanted to picture them lying peacefully beneath the sky in a world with no people to mess it up. Maybe that would calm me down so I could rest.

Instead, I noticed a man in the distance, beyond Eileen's fence, wearing overalls and a short-sleeved shirt, and remembered that it had been warming up when I left the police station. Why not sit in Eileen's garden for a while? It would be something to tell my grandson Cricket: "Me-Mama sat without a coat way up at the top of the world." So I grabbed my heaviest cardigan and a thick afghan Eileen had thoughtfully draped on our chair, and headed out the front door.

The sun was gentle, the breeze taking a rest. Daffodils nodded at my feet in the soft carpet of grass, and tulips were already several inches high. Shrubs were beginning to come to life after their winter hibernation, and birds were checking out various bushes and trees for future homes.

I chose a bench well down the lawn toward the stream, wrapped my legs tightly in the afghan, and sat enjoying that spectacular view. I murmured the one hundred and twenty-first Psalm: "I will lift up my eyes to the hills. Where does my help come from? My help comes from the Lord, who made heaven and earth." And I vowed that Joe Riddley and I would come back one day, and have ourselves a real vacation here. We'd follow deer tracks, shop in the village, eat Eileen's cooking until we were ready to burst, then come out and sit in her garden to doze.

Today, though, the hills didn't make me drowsy. They reminded me of the evening I had gone up the brae and heard Norwood Hardin knock Jim down. But who killed Norwood?

It didn't take much thought to discard Ian as a suspect. Like Norwood, Ian was quick-tempered, a hitter. Whoever killed Norwood had taken the time to lure him into the chapel while Roddy ran out for cigarettes, then stabbed him with a dagger procured in advance.

And managed to get into the chapel and out again without being seen.

Who could most easily walk about a chapel invisibly?

A priest.

Father Ewan had still been with the sergeant when I left the police station, but he could have left soon afterwards and run into Norwood. What was Norwood doing at the chapel? And why should Father Ewan kill him?

I know it's fashionable in the media to cast religious leaders as villains, but I've known a number of them and have known only one who committed a crime. So who else in Auchnagar might have had a motive to kill Norwood? Would I ever know? If I asked her, would Eileen send me the answer when the sergeant discovered it? I hate dangling ends in my life.

Kitty MacGorrie might have a real good motive, after living with Norwood for fifteen years. That probably went double for the laird. I've known a few nice murderers in my time.

At that point I hit a blank. I didn't know Norwood well enough to know who else might have reason to kill him—unless it was one of his former shareholders, like Sherry's aunt Rose.

I winged a little prayer. "If there's anything I know that could help uncover his killer, please let me remember it before we go home."

Armed for action, I considered Kenny and Sherry. Was there anything I knew about either of them that the Auchnagar police might not discover?

All that thinking did what the mountains had not. I laid my head back and dozed.

Behind me, I heard someone call, hesitantly, "MacLaren?"

I turned and saw Joyce coming down the garden path, again wearing her trench coat. I greeted her with a welcoming smile. "Hey. I'm just sitting here enjoying the sunshine."

She came nearer and stood with her hands behind her, pale and looking plumb worn out. "I saw you down here and came to apologize for what I said at noon. I've been real worried about this tour, but that was no reason to be rude to you."

"Nor for me to be rude to you," I agreed. "I'm sorry, too, and it's too nice a day to harbor grudges. Why don't you sit a spell, and tell me how things are going and what we're going to do next—if that doesn't sound too motherly?" I smiled to show that was a joke.

An answering smile flitted across her face for an instant. Then she shook her head. "That sounds nice, but not today." She took a step closer. "You know, don't you?"

As she looked down at me, she wore the same unhappy expression the camera had caught years before in the picture of Norwood Hardin's marriage. Again little things fell into place. None seemed important at the time. All were desperately important now.

"You're Jocelyn Gray," I said with a nod. "Jim kept calling you 'Josie,' and you called him 'Jim' before he came inside, although Brandi called him Jimmy. That migraine you had at breakfast yesterday gave you a chance to fetch Kenny's *sgian dubh,* didn't it? And I guess you did order the coffins and pay by mail, signing Jim's name to the order. Was one of them to provide a fitting, symbolic resting place for Norwood after you killed him?"

She didn't say a word.

"You sent them to the wrong place, though. Jim—Hamish—would have known the local distinction between the chapel and St. Catherine's. You didn't, and nearly fell down the stairs when I told you they had turned up in the Catholic church. You must have been on your way to kill Norwood that very minute, Kenny's weapon in your bag with the props."

She blinked, and I remembered what I couldn't after our nocturnal conversation. Her eyes were blue that night, until she went to wash her face. Then she must have put her brown contacts back in. This afternoon, in the soft Scottish sunlight, her mousy brown hair showed golden roots, and one look at her face confirmed my instincts from that evening: she was more wild woman of the mountains than mouse.

Slowly she brought her right hand from behind her. It held one of the swords from her play, and she looked like she planned to use it and knew how.

I gulped, my mouth dry. Why had I blabbered on so about what I knew? Heck, I hadn't even known most of it until I said it. Truth itself had come pouring out of depths I didn't know I had. But while the Bible says truth will set you free, it was about to see me freer than I'd hoped to be for a few years yet.

I couldn't hope to escape. I could not run with the afghan wrapped around me like a cocoon. Besides, this woman was thirty years younger and jogged almost every morning. Why hadn't I stayed in better shape? Learned karate?

The only weapon I had at the moment was my pesky tongue. I desperately hoped it would be mightier than her sword.

"Why did you do it?" I tried to sound more interested than judgmental while wondering wildly if anybody was in earshot if I yelled.

"He was a rat." Her voice was frighteningly calm. "An abuser and a rat. He let my daddy go to jail for his own crimes, then he married and beat my mother until she killed herself."

I prayed to say something calming and profound. Instead, I blurted, "So why'd you wait fifteen years?"

It caught her off guard enough for her to answer. "I didn't know where he went after Mother died. He just disappeared. Then last spring, like a miracle, he walked onto my flight from London to Zurich."

Miracles don't generally result in murder, but this wasn't the time to discuss the finer points of theology.

"Did you talk to him?" Talking was what I needed to do a lot of right then, until somebody came within hailing distance.

"No. I didn't want to be recognized."

She moved slightly, her arm slowly raising the sword while she went right on talking. I think she said she'd asked another flight attendant to chat with Norwood and get his address, but it's hard to listen while your ears are roaring and every pore in your body is focused on a sword aimed at your solar plexus.

"So you went to Jim and suggested you get together on this trip to Auchnagar?" Keep her talking. Let her think she has one safe person to whom she can spill all her beans.

"No, I told Jim I'd seen Norwood and he lived in Auchnagar. I was still trying to think how to get here when Jim called and asked if I'd get together a group. I didn't know why he wanted to come, but he said it was important that it be this weekend. He didn't mention Norwood, and neither did I."

"But you wrote a play for him to star in."

She nodded. "I knew it would hook him. The vanity of the man! The colossal vanity!" Her eyes narrowed. "You've got that, too, Mac. You think you're so smart—"

When she licked her lips and took a breath, I knew the end was near. My heart was thundering along in time to a silent prayer: *pleaseGodpleaseGodpleaseGod.*

I tried not to stare at the shining point winking in the sunlight as I slid my hands under the afghan and tensed.

The thrust was quick and sure, but I was ready. I grabbed the sword with both hands muffled in afghan and yelled as loud as I could. If I lost fingers, so be it. That was better than losing my life.

I clutched the blade through a double layer of thick crocheted wool and tried to wrest it from her hand. She jerked it back.

I felt it slice through the yarn and the meaty part of my left hand. The pain was like fire. But still I clung to that blade, forcing it back and forth and dodging while making such a racket that surely the police would arrive any minute.

If I could hold on that long.

Blood made the wool slick. I felt the blade slip in my hand.

When she tugged it again, I let go. She staggered back.

I rolled to one side, kicked free of the afghan and flung it over her. Then I pelted uphill in the garden, running for my life.

When I reached the gravel, though, I had to pause to breathe. A stitch in my side threatened to paralyze me. I snatched a quick peek behind me and saw she'd gotten free of the afghan and was more than halfway up the garden, holding the sword like she meant business.

"Dear God in heaven," I moaned. History was repeating itself. Jim had come over for his own version of the Highland Clearances. Now I was fixing to get my own private Culloden.

❧ 30 ❧

"Mac? What's up!"

Laura strode around the corner of the house like a happy goddess, swinging a helmet. "Man! I gotta get me—" She stopped and her eyes widened. "What have you done to your hand? You're bleeding all over the place!" She looked over my shoulder and called, "Joyce! Get us some towels or something. Quick! Mac's been hurt." She grabbed my arm and raised it above my head. As much as I hurt, I could see her, clear as day, in her Brownie uniform at seven, telling me seriously, "Me-Mac, I'm gonna cut off your blood, but it won't hurt one bit."

Now she gasped, "Hold that up a minute," while she whipped off her belt and made a tourniquet, then shouted over her shoulder, "Roddy, can you give Mac here a lift to the doctor? She's been cut."

I finally caught my breath enough to gasp, "Joyce— she—"

"She's gone for towels," Laura promised. "She'll be back in a minute. Until then, here." She jerked off her down parka and wrapped it around my bleeding hand.

Roddy scrunched around the gravel. "She'll have to wear a helmet. The sergeant'll have my license if I take her through the village twice without one."

Laura was already fastening the strap under my chin. "She's ready. Go, Mac!" She gave me the little pat she used to give her soccer mates before a big play. "I'll be right behind you." She raised her voice. "Don't bother with the towels, Joyce. Roddy's taking her to the doctor."

"Don't go in the house!" I cried. "She's got a sword!"

I could tell Laura thought I was raving from loss of blood. "She killed Norwood Hardin," I called urgently while Roddy pulled me by one elbow toward his bike. "Don't go in the house! Get the police!"

I don't remember much about my second motorcycle ride, but I now have a fuller understanding of the term "hanging on for dear life." Life had never seemed so dear.

I remember sliding to a stop, then I remember opening my eyes and seeing a magnificent red-gold mustache. "When did you grow a mustache?" I murmured to Roddy.

"Take it easy, noo," said a deep, musical voice I recognized as the doctor's. "Ye've just fainted, but you'll feel better soon." A firm hand steered me toward an open door at a turtle pace.

"I don't know if I'll ever feel better. My hand hurts." I held out the parka-swathed paw, stained with seeping blood.

That sped him up. Within seconds I was sitting beside a table and he was shooting my hand full of something to numb it so he could get busy with needle and thread.

While he worked, I tried not to look. But when I saw myself in the mirror over his desk—face white as chalk, hair like it had come out of a wind tunnel, I nearly fainted again.

"Careful, noo," the doctor warned, propping me up. "Ye've lost a lot of blood, so ye'll be weak. And if ye've not had a shot for tetanus—"

As much as Joe Riddley might prefer me with a locked jaw at times, I took the shot.

Laura arrived as I was tottering into the waiting room, and helped me out to the backseat of a little green Mini. "Watty borrowed his daughter's car for you to ride back in." Watty himself opened the front door with a flourish of his disreputable cap and intoned, "Where to, modom?"

"The police station," I said in a voice that wobbled. "How's Morag?"

"Frightened." He settled the cap on his head and went around to the other side. "Megan's letting her hang on to her coattails for the rest of the day." I wondered whether Megan would have let me hang on, too. Unfortunately, it was now too late to ask.

*   *   *

"So." The sergeant stood behind his desk and offered me the chair on the other side. Watty and Laura he waved to the bench along the wall. Then he sat down and asked, "What's this I hear about you accusing Ms. Underwood of murder?"

"Have you sent somebody up to Heather Glen?" I asked urgently. "She's got a sword."

"That's been taken care of." He looked down at a forefinger he was tapping on his desk. "What made you think she killed Mr. Hardin?"

"She thought I had figured it out, so she came looking for me, to kill me, too. And suddenly—oh, it was lots of things." I felt too listless at the moment to care.

Watty thrust a cup of inky tea into my hand. "Drink this. It's sweet and hot."

When I'd had a few sips, the sergeant picked up where he'd left off. "And did she give you any reason for Mr. Hardin's murder?"

"She is—or was—his stepdaughter, Jocelyn Gray. You can find her picture on the Internet if you search under either Norwood Hardin or James Gordon. She came here expressly to kill him, and wrote the play because she knew he couldn't resist amateur theatricals."

My voice trembled at the end, for I'd remembered Joyce's accusation of Norwood—and of me. Mama used to say we are most critical of people who share our faults. *Oh, dear God, don't let me be like Norwood Hardin.*

The sergeant gave me a long, level look. "I thought the trip was set up so Jim Gordon could come to Auchnagar to make a business deal with the laird."

"That's how it was financed, because Jim wanted to come incognito to claim his family's land. But Joyce was the one who told Jim that Norwood was here. And she agreed to lead the tour because she planned to kill him."

Watty grunted. "A match made in hell."

The room felt hot, and was beginning to get blurry around the edges. I waved my good hand and said sleepily, "I can't talk much more today, but it's all true. Are you sure you've sent somebody up to Heather Glen? If Eileen or

Marcia—if anybody goes in there—" That was all I could say for the moment.

Laura came and put a hand on my shoulder. "She's killed herself, Mac. Locked herself in the bathroom with a sword, and—" She cleared her throat. "I told the police, like you said. The sergeant went himself. He found her."

I'd already felt weak. Now I felt like the stuffing had been sucked out of me in one glob. Could I have done anything at all to prevent that?

When I flexed my sore hand, I knew the answer. Was that why Joyce ordered two coffins?

That night, the six of us who remained in the tour group sat in the lounge until the fire died. My hand was starting to throb, and I would soon need to take another pain pill and get to bed, but as I looked around the room—at sleek Brandi, foxy Sherry, truculent Kenny, dear Dorothy, and mournful Marcia—I discovered I had come to love them like family, warts and all. The knowledge that we, like all such groups, would separate the next day and never gather again made me incredibly sad. Could I have only known these people two weeks?

On the mantelpiece was propped Dorothy's unwitting contribution toward solving the puzzle we had known as Joyce Underwood. Dorothy had come home that evening oblivious of what had been going on in the village, bearing a small oil painting. "Careful," she had warned. "It's still wet. But I wanted you all to see, eh?" She held it up proudly. "I painted it yesterday and today."

It showed the side of the Roman Catholic church facing Alex's deck, a private courtyard framed with yews. Bright daffodils grew around the step where two figures were entering the side door. The man was short and stocky, with gray hair. The woman was taller, with brown hair. She wore a pale blue parka and carried a green bag.

Dorothy had warned me that when she was painting she never saw what she was painting. However, she also painted what she saw.

"So," Laura said lazily to Marcia, "you'll be staying on for another week?"

Marcia gave us all a luminous smile. "Yes, and then I'm going back to Calgary, pack up my things, and come back. I'll be helping Eileen with the guesthouse."

"What about you?" Laura asked Dorothy.

We could see Dorothy color up even in the firelight. "I'm going to apply for a visa to come back for a year. I'll work at the gallery in the morning and paint in the afternoon."

"Send us Christmas cards to keep us posted about what's going on in your lives," I commanded them. I didn't want to die without knowing whether Dorothy married Alex, Roddy, somebody else, or nobody—and whether she eventually became a full-time artist.

"I'm sorry I can't come home with you tomorrow." Brandi spoke with what sounded like real regret. "I have to wait until they release Jimmy's body. But I've got your card, Mac. I'll call you about landscaping my garden. I want it to be a memorial to him."

I wouldn't count on the job. It was one of those things people say at sentimental times. But I wouldn't mind seeing her again.

"What about you folks?" Dorothy asked Kenny and Sherry.

"We're going back to Savannah," Kenny replied as Sherry said, "Oh, we're about to start a new business." They sat there glaring at each another.

Laura got to her feet. "Well, I'd better get Mac here to bed. We've got an early start in the morning. I just hope I can keep better track of her between now and the time I'm supposed to deliver her back to her husband."

I knew I ought to be delighted to be heading home, but I felt downright miserable as Laura and I dragged ourselves up the stairs. It wasn't just the idea of leaving the folks down in the lounge, either.

"If Joyce had only talked to somebody," I mourned as Laura helped me get ready for bed. "She must have felt so incredibly alone." I took the glass she handed me, and downed my pill.

"It's about choices," Laura reminded me. "Isn't that what you always say? We are—or we become—the sum of the choices we make?"

"But some of us get more help than others in making better ones." I collapsed on the side of my bed, feeling a hundred and ten.

I knew that I'd be mourning Joyce, and Jim, and even Norwood and Ian, for a while yet.

She sidled over to the dresser and turned her back. Then she stood there and raised her hand, and I saw a flash of light. "What's that?" I demanded.

She came over and held out her left hand. On the third finger sat the prettiest solitaire I'd ever seen. She lifted it up to catch the lamp light and wiggled her finger to make it sparkle. "I've made a choice."

"What *is* it?" I thought for one wild second that the craziness of the past three days had caught up with levelheaded Laura, and she'd stolen one of Brandi's gems.

She chuckled. "Och, chust a wee bittie ring I thought I'd wear home." She added in her own lazy drawl, "I'm choosing to make you happy, Mac. I'm gonna marry Ben. Not because I have to, mind, but because I *want* to." Her voice grew husky. "I want to real bad."

"You bought your own ring?" Laura has always been independent, but this seemed to be carrying things too far.

"Oh, no." Her smile was smug. "He gave it to me before we left. But I told him I wouldn't wear it until I was sure it was right."

"So what persuaded you—my undying devotion to Joe Riddley?"

She grinned. "Nope. It was riding with Roddy this afternoon. I kept wishing it was Ben whose back I was hugging, and Ben I was coming home with. I headed out a woman looking for freedom, and came back a woman looking for a home. Finding you bleeding all over the parking lot distracted me a tad, or I'd have told you right then."

"Have you told Ben?"

She shook her head and sank onto her own bed with a frown. "No, I've tried to reach him ever since we got back from the village, but I still can't. You don't reckon he's off gallivanting with some hussy, do you?"

"Could be," I told her airily. Then I reached for my cell

phone. "But if you're real good, maybe I can help you track him down."

Once I got Joe Riddley on the phone and determined that he and Ben were still at the fish camp, I handed my phone to Laura and he went to fetch Ben—who might consider getting a cell phone of his own after that.

I put on my robe and went to take a long bath while they talked. As I soaked, I made a vow to myself and whoever might be listening: "Insofar as is humanly possible, I am never going to meddle in murder again. I do not ever want to endanger my life, feel so miserable about unmasking a killer, or risk feeling so in sympathy with somebody who has taken another person's life. Amen."

By then, tears were sliding down my cheeks, salting my bath water, and I was getting drowsy from my pill. I climbed out and toweled dry, taking care not to bump my sore hand. Then I headed back to our room feeling clean and virtuous. From now on, I would lead a calm and danger-free life.

Of course, at the time, I had no idea what was going on back home in Hopemore, or that it would land me up to my neck, literally, in another murder.

But that, as little Cricket would say, is a whole 'nother story . . .

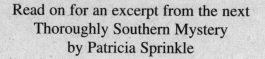

Read on for an excerpt from the next
Thoroughly Southern Mystery
by Patricia Sprinkle

coming in early 2007

I stood, alone and awkward, in the meeting room of the Hopemore Community Center after handing over my membership dues and first month's investment check to the Camellia Ladies' Investment Club. The room was full of big hair and big money, and I had neither.

What I did have was a cup of punch in one hand, a plate of brownies in the other, and no place to set either down. Given how often people attend stand-up social functions where food is involved, wouldn't you think evolution or the good Lord would have provided a third hand somewhere along the line? I hovered between two groups of women, trying to figure out how to eat my refreshments and which group to join.

A voice murmured at my shoulder, "I haven't met you yet, Judge Yarbrough."

Grover Henderson, the Augusta stockbroker who had given a very interesting talk on current trends in international markets, looked down at me with twinkling blue eyes and a smile that was just tentative enough to be charming. I found myself responding with twinkles of my own. Grover, like Joe Riddley, was one of those men who get better looking as they get older and who attract women of any age. He had a nice strong chin, broad shoulders, and graying hair that was receding except for a cute little tuft in front that he combed over to one side. His tan looked as though he'd gotten it on a golf course or tennis court rather than under a sun lamp, and he wore his navy blazer and loafers with a casual ease that implied he'd be equally at home in a tux or jeans.

"Do you already know all these women," he asked, "or shall I introduce you to them?"

"I know most of them. I've lived in Hopemore all my life. If it wouldn't give you a fair estimate of my age, I'd tell you I was a flower girl in Augusta Wainwright's wedding."

We laughed and looked over to where Augusta—self-styled queen of Hope County society and possessor of a bank balance most third-world countries would envy—held court. Her aristocratic old head wore an invisible tiara and her long, aristocratic neck was craned toward Rachel Ford, a small dark woman with an intense face, who stood nearby. Gusta sat on a throne set conveniently near the refreshments table, so she wouldn't have to juggle a plate and cup in her gnarled old hands. That would have been her granddaughter's doing. Meriwether Wainwright DuBose was both prettier and kinder than her grandmother. She was also possibly richer, now that Pooh DuBose had died, for Meriwether's husband was Pooh's heir.

Currently Meriwether was fetching Gusta a second cup of punch while Gusta told Rachel about Meriwether's new baby. Gusta invariably referred to the child as "my great-grandson," as if that defined him. I sincerely hoped it wouldn't.

Rachel was nodding in all the right places, but wore that glassy-eyed look single businesswomen tend to get when other people talk about babies.

"I don't know much about Rachel," I told Grover. "She's not from around here."

"No, she grew up in New York—or so I understand. She retired to Hopemore after a career in international law."

I lifted my punch cup and took a sip. "She must have been good at it, to retire so young. She can't be much more than forty." From the simple but expensive lines of her black dress and the emeralds that sparkled in her ears and on both her hands, I gathered that international law must pay well. Maybe it wore you out early, too, given that she was as skinny as an underfed pullet and had dark circles under her eyes.

"Forty-seven, actually." Grover's attention was across the room, where the Big Hair contingent was having a lively conversation. Nancy Jenkins (blonde), wife of the CEO of

Georgia Kaolin, was telling MayBelle Brandison (a lot redder than she used to be) about how stingy her husband was, while MayBelle, the sharpest real estate developer in three counties, was lamenting that she just couldn't make as much in Middle Georgia as she would if she moved up to Atlanta. I considered joining that conversation long enough to point out that some folks—including MayBelle's long-suffering ex-husband—kept reminding her there was nothing to keep her in Hope County since her divorce. But why bother? MayBelle was one of those women who would rather suffer and think up new ways of inflicting suffering than get on with life.

Speaking of divorce, the third member of that group was Sadie Lowe Hawkins—a brunette with the kind of curves that spell trouble. When she had divorced a New York magnate several years before, newspapers had claimed she'd won a seven-figure settlement, but I had still been surprised to hear that she had been invited to join the CLIC. She grew up in Hopemore and was thirty-seven, the same age as my son Walker. In their high school days, Sadie Lowe had been infamous for doing most of her socializing in backseats down near the water tank. I wondered who had suggested her for membership and how she had gotten voted in.

It was a safe bet that she had not been proposed by Wilma Kenan, who hovered around the refreshment table like a nervous bee. While I watched, she moved one tray an inch to the left and another an inch to the right, being the fussiest woman God ever made about things that don't matter. She called it being a perfectionist. I called it wanting things done her way. Because her family had been making money from cotton, both in the U.S. and abroad, for generations, she generally got her way.

Joe Riddley claimed that Wilma's attitude toward life had been shaped by the obstetrician who delivered her, who (Joe Riddley claimed) must have taken her little face between his two hands and pressed hard. That might explain why her eyes were too close together, her nose long and sharp, her lips little more than a bow, her chin long and pointed, and her mind so narrow you could measured it in millimeters. Nobody ever set a table, conducted a meeting,

ran a government, preached a sermon, fixed a car, or styled
her hair quite to suit Wilma.

Tonight she was in charge of refreshments and had
brought the punch in gallon jugs, claiming it was a secret
family recipe. She went back to the kitchen to fetch another
jug, poured it into the punch bowl, and stirred it a couple of
times with the silver ladle she had also brought from home.
But when she noticed I was talking to Grover, she dropped
that ladle and shot across the room to intervene.

Ignoring me, she peered up at my companion with an expression in her brown eyes that reminded me of a cairn terrier's when on the eager lookout for a rat. "Do you have
everything you need, Grover?" She had one of those voices
that are nasal and sharp even when the person intends to be
charming. She put a hand on his arm as if it had a right to be
there and gave him what looked like a smile she practiced in
front of mirrors. Wilma had never found the perfect man, but
she had never stopped looking. "Keeping myself ready for
Prince Charming," she often said, pursing her bright lips and
touching her stiff blond curls with polished nails that were
never chipped or broken.

"I'm fine," he said in an absent tone, still looking toward
Sadie Lowe, who stood with one hip stuck out as if she
knew he was looking.

Wilma gave Grover's elbow a gentle tug to bring his attention back to her. "I'll give you a call about next month's
program. I have a few ideas. As Granddaddy used to say—"

That's when I stopped listening. When Wilma got to talking about her granddaddy, she could go on forever.

I pitied Grover. Willma had just been elected president of
the club for the coming year, succeeding her first cousin,
Willena. Poor Grover would be in for a rocky year. On the
other hand, I had gotten the impression he was Wilma's broker, so maybe he was adept at handling her.

Speaking of Willena, I didn't see her with either the mon-
eyed crowd or the Big Hair contingent. She must still be in
the ladies' room washing mascara off her cheeks. After she
had passed the torch of the presidency to Wilma, Wilma had
presented Willena with a sterling silver bar set, complete
with a stainless steel corkscrew with a sterling silver handle

and a little silver shot glass. Willena was known to be fond of mimosas or chilled white wine at almost any time of day, and always cried at the drop of a hair bow. She had been so overcome by the present that her mascara had run down her cheeks like clown lines.

Wilma had commanded, "Go clean up your face. You look like a raccoon before breakfast."

Nobody seeing them together would ever have guessed the two women were first cousins, daughters of brothers. Whereas Wilma was thin and short, Willena was large and tall, with soft floury skin, fluffy brown hair, and eyes the exact same shade of brown. Wilma favored tailored dresses and pantsuits with dainty, prim jewelry. Willena wore dangling earrings, ruffled blouses, long strands of showy pearls, and full skirts in bright colors. What they shared was an absolute conviction that their granddaddy Will—for whom both were named—had been God's perfect gentleman and a firm determination to each find a husband just like him.

They also shared tight fists. As soon as Willena was out of earshot, Wilma had confided to the rest of us, "That set cost seven hundred dollars. I paid for it, but I move that I be reimbursed from the treasury."

If she was hoping for a second to her motion, she was disappointed. "We never gave a present before and didn't authorize one this year," Gusta informed her tartly, and that was that.

With Wilma claiming all of Grover's attention, I decided to make a run to the bathroom before the meeting resumed. After refreshments, we still had to reconvene to decide how to invest our money that month. I had no clue what the investment procedure would be, but given the way some of those women liked to discuss every penny they spent, I guessed it could take a while.

I trotted down the hall admiring the sheen our new custodian was getting on the beige tile floors of the community center and thinking about the shipment of summer bedding plants that we'd just received at the store. I hoped we hadn't ordered too many and that ours would be bigger and more unusual than those at the superstore. Maybe we ought to concentrate on selling in quantity to landscapers and not try to compete when the superstore could set prices below what we could afford to match.

That's as far as I had gotten when I pushed open the ladies' room door. It wouldn't budge.

I shoved again. "Willena?" She didn't answer.

I knocked. Still no answer.

"Willena?" I put my shoulder against the door and put all my weight behind it.

I felt something slide, then the door opened far enough for me to stick my head in.

Forever after, I would wish I hadn't.

Willena lay crumpled on the floor. One hand clutched her throat. The other was out as if she had been opening the door when she collapsed. And her ruffled white blouse and the taupe tiles around her were drenched in blood.

SIGNET   (0451)

TAMAR MYERS
PENNSYLVANIA DUTCH
MYSTERIES—WITH RECIPES!

"As sweet as a piece of brown-sugar pie."
—*Booklist*

"Rollicking suspense."
—*Washington Post*

Available wherever books are sold or at
penguin.com

S314

Kate Collins

The Flower Shop Mystery Series

Abby Knight is the proud owner of her hometown flower shop. She has a gift for arranging flowers—and for solving crimes.

Mum's the Word
0-451-21350-5

Slay It with Flowers
0-451-21455-2

Dearly Depotted
0-451-21585-0

"A spirited sleuth, quirky sidekicks,
and page-turning action."
—Nancy J. Cohen

Selma Eichler

"A highly entertaining series."
—Carolyn Hart

"Finally there's a private eye
we can embrace." —Joan Hess

MURDER CAN MESS UP YOUR MASCARA
0-451-21430-7

MURDER CAN BOTCH UP YOUR BIRTHDAY
0-451-21152-9

MURDER CAN RUIN YOUR LOOKS
0-451-18384-3

MURDER CAN SINGE YOUR OLD FLAME
0-451-19218-4

MURDER CAN RAIN ON YOUR SHOWER
0-451-20823-4

MURDER CAN COOL OFF YOUR AFFAIR
0-451-20518-9

MURDER CAN UPSET YOUR MOTHER
0-451-20251-1

MURDER CAN SPOIL YOUR APPETITE
0-451-19958-8

MURDER CAN SPOOK YOUR CAT
0-451-19217-6

Available wherever books are sold or at
penguin.com